these vicious reapers

F.M. ADEN

NORTHERN LIGHT PRESS
TORONTO

These Vicious Reapers is a work of fiction. Names, characters, places and incidents are the products of the author's imagination or are used factiously. Any resemblance to actual events, locales or persons, living or dead, is entirely coincidental.

Copyright 2026 by F.M. Aden

Cover copyright 2026 by Northern Light Press

All rights reserved.

No part of this publication may be reproduced, stored in a retrieval system or transmitted, in any form or by any means, without the prior permission in writing of the author, nor be otherwise circulated in any form of binding or cover other than that in which it is published and without a similar condition including this condition being imposed on the subsequent purchaser.

ISBN: 978-1-0692346-0-5 (e-book edition)
ISBN: 978-1-0692346-1-2 (trade paperback edition)

Northern Light Press
Toronto, Ontario

*For those who reach for the stars but grasp the night sky instead.
The dark welcomes you.*

Chapter 1

Nobody knew how the Corruption arrived. They only knew that one day the lands beyond the Silver Pass had breathed pine and blossom, and the next it had rotted.

Mud clung to Niah's boots as she made her way through the Witherwood, staining the pristine hem of her new robes. A flimsy black gauze veiled the bark and moss, the trees' leaves hanging limp and colorless from its arms.

Footsteps sounded. Within seconds, Niah summoned a blade forged of pure light.

"You're not permitted in these woods, cleric," Niah said in her sternest voice.

"Oh, please." Kesi rolled her eyes. "You were initiated into the Order last week, and already you've become overbearing."

Niah's mouth pulled into a pleased grin. She had come to the city of Caer-Sylisse as a war orphan from the province of Teren, hidden away on a narrow boat as they crossed the Ever Sea to escape the war. Back then, the king's Reapers had blocked the roads for just that purpose. It had been a cold, frost-touched morning as they moved between razored icebergs and sheets of glass so thin they seemed ready to shatter at the faintest touch of wind, scratching the hull like the claws of some maritime predator.

The holy war between King Stefan, who ruled the High North, and Queen Enid, who ruled the Low North, had been raging for over a century. The heretical mages had sown their rancor, their venom creeping outward, until a dark bloom had swallowed the land whole.

"It's dangerous, Kesi," Niah scolded. "You could die out here."

Kesi forged a blade no bigger than a kitchen knife. It illuminated her face, but that was it, whereas Niah's light had cast a pool of brightness around them in a wide arc.

Their magic frightened the diseased animals, who were prone to attack anyone who entered their home.

"That is not enough, Kesi," she said. "And you know it."

Kesi sighed, her blade fading. "That is all I can do. It's all any of us can do. We are powerless to stop them, to stop any of this."

Niah's mouth tightened. It was rare for Kesi to speak so solemnly. It reminded her just how dire their situation was. At any moment, the Reapers could arrive and slit their throats in their sleep. At any moment, one of them could be taken by the Sleeping Fever that had arrived with the Corruption and never awaken again.

Niah strengthened her blade, watching it morph into a staff. When she thumped it on the ground, the curling vines that reached for them with their decaying grasp recoiled. The rot retreated, slowly creating a path. Now the leaves were a lush green again, the black tips fading to ash. The sickly tint in the air faded, giving way to the scent of crisp moss and damp soil.

"That is rather impressive," Kesi said with a low whistle. "I see why Prioress Morgana thinks you're the next Lightbearer."

Rumors had been swirling around the monastery for days that Niah was the next Lightbearer, the one who would cleanse the lands of the pagans and their dark magic. Ever since the

Corruption, the people had needed something to believe in. Not to mention Niah's hair was entirely white, a symbol that only stoked the rumors claiming she was the Lightbearer.

There hadn't been a Lightbearer in five hundred years. It didn't surprise her that Morgana, the closest thing she had to a parent figure and the Prioress of their monastery, was singing her praises. The woman had a terrible habit of exaggerating, and this, Niah firmly believed, was simply another one of those moments.

"I am not the Lightbearer," she murmured.

Niah slept, breathed, and ate magic. From a young age, she had been enchanted by the thought of magic in their world. Her mother would often run a brush through her long hair, weaving tales of vengeful spirits that roamed graveyards, blood-thirsty corpses who fed on one's lifeblood and faeries who spun twisted bargains.

Teren, where she had been born, had sat between the warring continents. It had been filled with rolling, emerald hills with patches of farmland scattered across. Between the valleys was the River Penwyn that broke off into the Ever Sea. The air had smelled of fish, salt, and loamy soil.

Niah's mouth grew bitter with rage as she thought about all she had lost. Some days, grief clung to her like damp fog, seeping into her bones with a feverish cold.

Stray tendrils of her light lashed out into the opposite bough, burning a hole through its soft flesh, effectively destroying the old tree; the bark splintered as if it had been struck by lightning. Kesi gasped in alarm, and Niah's hand dropped. Dread coiled in her stomach; that was not the first time she'd lost control. Anytime her emotions grew mutinous, her magic turned destructive and dangerous.

Slowly, she took a deep breath, erasing her thoughts, and only when she had formed that blank canvas in her mind did she rebuild her blade of magic. At dawn, all the clerics of the monastery would meditate together, their breaths as soft as a prayer while they kneeled in silence in the oratory—a hushed, candlelit chamber with vaulted ceilings where the frankincense and withered myrrh smoke hung heavy.

"Sorry," she murmured.

"You don't have to apologize, Niah," Kesi said softly. "Nobody knows for certain if you are the Lightbearer. I think everyone just wants something to believe in."

Niah could understand that.

Because she wanted something to believe in, too.

The monastery was a stone edifice with wide shutters and twisting hallways lined with heavy damask carpets. It stood sentinel on the wind-bruised moors that lined the outskirts of Caer-Sylisse, rising from the heather like a lone flag fluttering in the breeze. The cliffs stretched in all directions like a flock of birds, silvered with mist and surrounded by bleached stone.

Caer-Sylisse was a city born of faith, a sanctuary built to shelter pilgrims and the devout on their sacred journeys. Narrow, winding streets led to small houses and unadorned chapels for the villagers to find solace. Miniature market stalls offered blessed relics from the time of the Saints, including handcrafted crystals, black pearl rosaries, and fragrant incense.

Niah and Kesi crossed the pathway towards the oaken doors. Lichen grew between the cracks that lined the statues of the old saints who stood upright in a dim puddle of milky light.

They stepped into the foyer, where the air was stale with the scent of parchment and candle smoke. Some corners were pristine, while others were covered in cobwebs that hung like decayed lace from the ceilings. The young clerics, sent by their parents and blessed with the light, milled around the corridors in their white robes. Only women were gifted with the light. The Prioress never told them why. There had been Saints who were men, but that was a long time ago. Morgana said they were given their magic to fight the Reapers.

The clerics' heads bowed in respect when Niah passed them, and she elbowed Kesi to behave. She was grinning at the attention, forgetting that humbleness was one of their sacred teachings.

The doors were marked with the animal tokens of the six saints. Niah remembered when she was a child, trailing her fingertips along the protruding wood as if their magic would bless her. Prioress Morgana would often tell her long-winded tale of their gifts. Her fables often dragged her down a sleepy river into a cave full of wonder.

"It wasn't just light that they commanded then," she said in her raspy voice. *"It was magic. Unlimited and divine."*

"But why do we only control the light?" she asked.

"Aubrith gives us what we need when we need it," she said. *"Nothing more. Nothing less."*

"Good evening, Lady Niah," the passing clerics chimed.

"Good evening," Niah said hesitantly.

It was always a strange transition going from a cleric to a full-fledged mage once initiated into the Order. The Order of the White Flame had been formed eight hundred years ago by the Queen of the Low North to ordain mages into the holy order as protectors of the realm. Some mages were sent to the borderlands to protect the lands from invasion, while others went on sanctioned excursions to the various woods in different provinces to aid the herbalists in their quest to find a cure for the Sleeping Fever. Different monasteries were led by the selected Prioress who acted as a representative of the Queen.

Outside, the wind sang a sombre tune, cold slithering between the gaps of the windows like a starving rat, as Niah made her way to the sanatorium.

"I'll see you at dinner," Kesi said, handing off her bag. While her friend had been kind enough to help her collect her plants, Kesi avoided the sanatorium. "You know how I feel about all those patients sickened by the Sleeping Fever. It is all so eerie, if you ask me."

Kesi was gone before she could say goodbye.

Niah traveled through the corridors and under the stone archway that led to the older wing of the monastery, which had now been converted into a sanatorium. Most people from the village brought their family members here to be taken care of until a cure was found. It was always difficult seeing the visitors' hopeless faces drooping like wilting flowers as they descended the cracked stairs and vanished down the path.

Niah never liked this part—the rows of wooden beds, patients with eyes sealed shut, paper-thin flesh, veins tainted in dark magic. The Sleeping Fever was no common illness brought on by stagnant, moldy water, or diseased animals. It was part of the Corruption.

"Niah, you are a godsend!" Sister Gwendolen said. "The Light Father smiles on us."

Her brown eyes crinkled as she grinned. Gwendolen was the oldest and most experienced herbalist who led the three young apprentices under her command in the convent.

"I couldn't find any poppy," Niah said. "I'm sorry."

"No, this is fine, darling," she said.

"Also, I can take the night shift," Niah said. "Siphon some of the dark magic from the patients."

It didn't awaken them, but she noticed their brows grew soft when she siphoned the dark magic, as if the nightmare that haunted them faded, giving room to sweeter dreams.

Gwendolen patted her cheek in a motherly gesture.

"What would we do without you?"

Niah smiled tightly, swallowing the guilt that coated her tongue. She had a meeting with Morgana tonight that she was avoiding. The Prioress had expectations of her that Niah knew she could never meet. Morgana needed a soldier, but Niah preferred the woods and the sanatorium to the training field.

Morgana had saved her, and she felt indebted to her, but she also didn't want to be a soldier. She didn't wish to kill and maim. Niah did not have the stomach for it.

"I can do tomorrow night, as well," Niah added.

Gwendolen smiled brightly, easing some of that terrible guilt. At least there was one person she wasn't disappointing.

Chapter 2

In the Grand Library, Niah's books lay scattered around her like a quilted blanket. Towering shelves hewn from black-cherry wood stretched towards the vaulted ceiling, each row crammed with tomes bound in cracked leather, gilt-spined volumes, and scrolls wrapped in midnight-blue silk. Stained-glass windows filtered moonlight, casting prismatic shadows along the marble floor.

The doors had long been sealed shut for the night, once she told the librarian she was more than happy to sleep on the floor. The old woman peered at her beneath chipped glasses and grunted her acceptance.

A few months ago, she would have been sent back to the monastery with her tail tucked between her legs for attempting to break the new curfew established during the height of the war. But ever since she had been handed her eggshell robes with the gold sash that signified her membership to the Order, she had received less strife for her odd requests. Now the people looked at her and saw a mage who served the queen and the realm, not a measly practicing cleric.

Niah recalled the ceremony that night—her candle flickering in the dark, bare feet gliding across the floors. The frescoes along the walls depicted Saints with star-bright eyes and swords tangled in vines, guiding her towards the bell tower.

Prioress Morgana's wraith-like voice beckoned her to speak the sacred oath.

"Do you promise to carry the light with righteousness and vanquish those who serve the dark?"

Once Niah had responded her fate had been sealed.

The letters in Old Virelle made her mind spin. They stampeded like wild boars past the pages, trailing thick tongues across the page until the words blurred. Niah was tired from all those night shifts at the sanatorium, and now she was hiding out in the library in the hopes that Morgana wouldn't find her.

"Not surprised to find you here," a smooth voice spoke.

Her eyes shot up to find Prioress Morgana standing above her. Her papery skin gleamed under the chandelier's soft light. Her white robe was impeccable. Niah tried to hide the tea stains on her cuffs, but from the knowing smile Morgana tossed her, she hadn't missed the effort. For all her strengths as a mage, Niah was often disorderly—dirt clinging to her hem like a wailing babe to its mother's hip, her sash dangerously askew, revealing her linens beneath.

"If you read in the dark like that, your eyes will grow as bad as mine," Morgana said.

"I think I have a few hundred years to go before that," Niah replied. "You are as ancient as these books."

Morgana tsked. "Your insults could use some work."

"If I wait any longer to practice, you might die on me," she said with a crooked grin. "Best to get my rough drafts in early."

Morgana was both her mentor and the closest thing she had to a mother. She had taken her under her wing after the attack in Teren, the small fishing village that lay like a curled horn in the middle of the warring territories. It was closest to the border that separated the continents and the site of the king's second victory. Teren hadn't been the start of the war, even if it felt that way to her.

The Reapers had come under the veil of night with their army of corpses. The king's pagan mages had drawn the villagers from their houses, forcing them to bend the knee.

Teren had been in conversation with the capital city Virelle for a few months, requesting aid from the queen. Queen Enid had granted their request, but Morgana and the other sister mages had arrived too late to save them. Her world had been reduced to ashes and choking screams by the time they arrived.

Morgana and the other Sisters had bundled up the orphaned children and rode through the forest to a small boat by the river. Morgana had said it was only nine days' travel, but to Niah it had felt like a lifetime. Soot covered her face, and a bandage wrapped her injured palm. Weeks later, when it healed, a small snow-white star remained in its place—a reminder of all she had lost: her mother and father, her kind, elderly neighbors, her life. Each ray of the star represented a different loss. Morgana had been fascinated by the unique symbol.

It wasn't perfect at all. It was tainted.

"I thought you were too old to hide from me," Morgana said. Her honey-brown eyes narrowed into slits. "You know my knees are too weak to chase after you."

Niah laughed, though the sound was forced. "I'm not hiding from you."

"Aren't you?" Morgana asked, fluttering a paper before her. "Your assignment was decided."

Her stomach rolled. From the way Morgana's eyes softened, she knew it wasn't the news Niah wanted to hear.

"The Order makes these decisions together, and I was outnumbered," she said.

Niah's face fell. The floor opened up beneath her, prepared to swallow her whole. Her greatest fear was war. One might think she had built a tolerance for bloodshed, considering her bleak childhood, but Niah cowered from it.

"I can't go up north, Morgana," she said in a choked voice. "This is my home. You and Kesi are here. I have nobody else."

"I know, Niah," Morgana said softly. "But the king's army is claiming new villages day by day. There will be a time when they come to Virelle and seize the entirety of the Low North. Nobody but a mage can fight a Reaper. No mortal man can defeat the heretics."

"I don't know if I'm ready. I lost control..."

"It does not matter to the Order that you are afraid. War makes desperate fools, they do not care if you are uncertain. If I try to dispute this, it will be brought before the queen, who will side with the Order," Morgana said. "You must believe in yourself, Niah, as the Order does, as I do. You are capable. You are strong. You are powerful."

It had taken her a long time to adjust to Caer-Sylisse—to eat their juniper-scented food, wear the heavy cloaks thickened with rabbit fur, and walk in boots made for the wet slush of snow. Teren hadn't been this cold, but down here it was like living in the belly of winter.

The thought of leaving brought back old fears and wounds from when she fled Teren, recalling the bite of beasts that haunted her mind and the terrible encounter before Morgana saved her.

She would never forget the boy who stood across from her in the black robes of the king's army who had marched from the capital of Raskovia. His breast was stitched with the scythe symbol of a Reaper, his face hidden by the carved bone mask worn by their kind.

Nobody knew about the boy or the mark he left on her.

The star-shaped scar burned like hot oil, and she bit back a hiss.

"I'll know if you're near me," he had whispered that night. *"I will always be able to find you."*

"It is late," Niah said, the lie flowing like poetry from her tongue. "And I am deeply tired."

"I'll walk you home," Morgana said.

"I'll pretend to be surprised tomorrow when the assignments are posted on the board," Niah replied.

There were already whispers that she was the Lightbearer, and her closeness with Morgana was clear as daylight. It would shock no one that she was being drafted into the war.

"I would appreciate that."

Niah walked ahead of her, lost in the turmoil of her thoughts. Her head was constantly stuffed with fears, shadows, and darkness. Some days, she worried the weight of it would drown her.

She wished to be known for more than her magic. She wasn't simply a girl touched by the Saints—she had a heart and a mind and dreams. But none of that seemed to matter in the midst of war.

They didn't need another girl whose eyes were painted with stars.

They needed a soldier.

"Niah," Morgana said. "I'm proud of you."

She could count on one hand the number of times Morgana had said those words. She was not an overly affectionate person, which suited Niah just fine, but still her chest warmed at the praise. She did not wish to disappoint her.

Niah would accept this destiny and her duties. She just hoped it didn't destroy her in the process.

On nights like this, when duty choked her with its grim fingers, Niah was often dragged into a nest of nightmares that pulled her under, forcing her to awaken with a ringing scream on her tongue. She could feel those starving, black tendrils sink into her skin. The scar tingled, and when she stared at her palm, for a moment the white scar looked dark, as though ink had spilled across her flesh.

She never told Morgana about their interaction—about the boy who had confronted her before she arrived. A boy with eyes as black as any abyss and skin as wan as moonlight. A boy who led an army of corpses. A boy who was a monster himself.

Niah shakily curled her fist. Something in her that night had broken when he touched her. Something that claimed her during the dark of night. A part of her was frightened of him. He had sworn that he would find her one day, and each time the wind blew, she feared that it was him.

It had been ten years since that night, and still she dreamed of him even now at eighteen. She felt his magic sliding along her scar like a sickness taking root, tainting her with his impiety, crawling into her mind like a spider weaving silky threads of darkness.

Slowly, Niah stretched her limbs, her linen nightgown grazing the stone floors, the fabric floating like a breath of fog. Her fingers coiled around the bronze handles, and she tugged open the door. A grinning face stared back, and a squeal of surprise escaped her.

It took her a moment to realize it was just Kesi.

"What are you doing up at this hour?" Niah whispered sharply.

"Heard your miserable screams." Kesi brushed past her, dark, curly hair braided neatly in two plaits. "Thought I could be of comfort."

Kesi folded her tall frame into the desk chair, curling her legs beneath her like a cat.

A war orphan from Teren just like her, Kesi's skin still carried the sun-kissed touch of farmland. They had never spoken in Teren, though they waved when passing. Kesi's family had managed the butcher shop, and Niah's mother had often sent her to fetch veal.

Now, Kesi was her only friend in the monastery, her last reminder of home, along with the vile scar on her palm.

Niah sighed, returning to her bed. She planned to sneak off later to the monastery's small library, with its chipped, mold-coated ceiling and stale air. With no librarian to maintain it, Niah had begun cataloguing old books of religion, magic, and myth. Much of the Low North's folklore was tied to the woods, to faeries, wood sprites, and mythical beasts. It made sense that the Corruption tainted the woods, a place so sacred to the Low North.

Her favorite was *The Three Branches of Brinwen*, a tale of a farmer who protected a Saint-touched tree and the many adventures with villagers who sought its enchanted branchlets. Niah liked to imagine it was her father who had been appointed the guardian of this sacred tree—his weathered hands clutching a silver sword.

Kesi warily eyed the column of books on her desk, as if it might leap off the surface and attack her.

"What if this falls on me and buries me in paper and ink?" she asked.

Niah's mouth quirked as she sat cross-legged on her thin bed. Relief slid through her at Kesi's silly jokes, at her ability to draw her mind from the dark.

"I can't think of a better way to die."

"I can," Kesi said. "Preferably between the legs of that strapping new scribe from Faen. He's only here for a day, but that's more than enough time."

Niah's cheeks burned. Kesi was blunt—a trait Niah both adored and feared. Whenever strangers came to the monastery for shelter, Kesi flirted with them and tempted them to misbehave.

"He's old," Niah said, wrinkling her nose.

"Ten years isn't so bad," Kesi replied.

"Why did he arrive?"

"The army torched his village," Kesi said softly. "Burned every mage stationed there, all the Sisters are gone."

The Order stationed mages in monasteries across the Low North. They were not only a religious faction, but also the Queen's secret weapon. The royal army was made of mortal men, but only light could slay the Reapers' bewitched corpses.

Before the war, the Sisters of the Order of the White Flame had attended court ceremonies and practiced their magic within monastery walls. Now they wore silver breastplates over their robes and marched like soldiers at the Queen's call.

Niah's throat grew dry. "Faen is not far from here."

Kesi nodded glumly. "Prioress Morgana is worried. They are creeping closer to the capital, to the heart of Virelle. They're sending the new batch of ordained mages to the frontlines. I'm glad I'm still a cleric."

Niah felt a glimmer of guilt for her reluctance to aid the war. The Order wouldn't have picked her if there had been another option.

"Do you think they'll send you?" Kesi asked.

Niah nodded. "Morgana warned me I wouldn't be part of the expedition team to study the Corruption. I thought if I proved myself by scavenging and volunteering in the sanatorium it might sway them, but it doesn't matter."

"Well, I don't want to be here if you leave," Kesi said. "I'll enlist myself."

Niah laughed, the sound dying when she realized Kesi wasn't joking. "You can't be serious."

"I refuse to let you take all the glory for saving the realm," Kesi teased. "Besides, it'll be fun. I'll have a sword."

"But you failed. You won't be assigned this year," Niah said.

Kesi had not passed the testing, and clerics who had not been inducted into the Order were not chosen to fight.

"I'll beg Morgana."

"She won't let you," Niah said. "This is serious, Kesi. People are dying out there. Women return with scars—some visible, some unseen. And some don't return at all."

Kesi's smile dropped.

"I know, Niah," she said. "But I refuse to stay here while you're out there risking your life."

Niah's anger softened. "It would soothe me if you stayed. Morgana will look after you."

"Morgana will do no such thing," she scoffed. "She only has a place in her heart for one orphan, and it isn't me."

"That's not true," Niah said.

But her words were futile, they had had this conversation before. It was impossible to change Kesi's mind once it was made. The Order was desperate, and they would not refuse her request. Morgana would accept it, because despite Kesi's words, she did like her.

"I wish things were different," Niah said softly.

"Me too," Kesi said. "But if you are the Lightbearer, Niah, it will change everything. You know that."

In the myths, the Lightbearer was born during times of turmoil and darkness to guide the people to a new path. Magic was rare these days, and with the Reapers strengthening their ranks and teaching their young to harness dark magic, it was easier to cling to these fables with desperate fingers than to accept that the world was falling to ashes.

"Then let us pray that I am not."

Smoke tickled her nose, and Niah sat upright. There was a fire burning, and shouts reached her ears, slow and sluggish as if wading through thick water. Something was terribly amiss.

Niah hastily drew on her robe. Hanging from her wardrobe was the armor she had received after being ordained into the Order: a heavy silver piece painted with the Burning Moth—it depicted a candle aglow, and before it, wings spread, a moth. The symbol of the Order. An ode to Saint Ylena, their patroness.

She strapped on her breastplate and drew open the heavy iron doors. Sisters ran like winter wolves, a blur of milky white. A torch had fallen, lighting the corridor with thick flames.

"The Reapers are coming!" a girl yelled.

Niah opened Kesi's bedroom, relief flooding her at the sight of her best friend.

"I need you to hide outside," Niah said. "The monastery is burning, and the Reapers are here."

"I'm coming with you," Kesi insisted.

"No," Niah said. "Promise me you won't do anything stupid!"

Kesi's mouth tightened, but she nodded.

"Find me after," Niah said. "And for Aubrith's sake, don't die."

"Same goes for you, Lightbearer," Kesi answered with a forced smile.

Niah hugged her so tightly it ached, then turned away without another glance. She raced down the stairs into the chaos spilling from the doors. There were about fifty Reapers—but they hadn't come alone. They brought their horde of undead, the Fallen. Corpses awakened from eternal slumber, forced to obey their every command.

Sweat slithered down her nape as flames licked up the monastery's sides, stirring memories she had suffocated. A hand touched her shoulder. Niah jumped—until she saw Morgana, a blade of light blazing in her hands as her lips pressed into a hard line.

"I have your back, Niah," she said. "We will see this to the end."

"To the end," Niah echoed.

The monastery would fall. It was only a matter of when. Soon it would be nothing but ash. Outnumbered and unprepared, the Sisters stood under a moonless sky, swords of light raised to vanquish the unholy.

Niah clutched her twin swords, weaving light until it rose in a towering arc. Her magic filled the air with a brightness so stark it made the soldiers wince.

She silenced her mind, reciting her mother's words:

You can be soft and strong, Niah. You need not pick one or the other. They will tell you to pick up a sword, and if you say no, they will tell you to pick up a shield. But you are not their puppet, and their words are not binding. You serve no master but your heart alone.

Be kind and brave and hungry and angry—but never docile.
This you must always remember.

Her anger, grief, and fear lifted, leaving only silence behind. She could hear every scrape of her breath, every harrowing thud of hooves echoing in tandem with her heart. The morning meditations had taught them that emotions had no place in magic. Magic was stable, and so its vessel must be the same.

There had been so many stories of the Reapers. Blood-caked horror tales that had flown through the monastery like a crow, spreading death and despair. There were whispers that they were seven feet tall–as great as the giants who once roamed the valleys of Teren–with hollow faces carved of bones. It was said that they were descended from the demons that filled Mirathe, the realm of the dead. That the Corruption followed their wake, plants and animals sickening with each path they crossed, like wildflowers pressed beneath their boots.

Staring at them felt like looking into the eyes of the Maiden of Death. Crystalline and void. They stood in their obsidian uniforms wearing cloaks of velvet trimmed with an expensive fur, likely ermine or fox. The neckline was thick and trimmed with dyed black fleece. Behind them stood dozens of rows of people who had once lived and breathed but now stood in empty silence. Farmers, fishermen, and traders who had died and whose burial site had been disturbed in a profane act of dark magic, and who now fought against those who protected their land.

The Reapers stood back as their army rushed forward, blindly attacking the women in white. The Sisters worked in unison, cutting them with their blades of light. Rotten blood spilled from their wounds, seeping like a thick broth.

Niah was a trained fighter, even if it was not her favored skill. She cut through the corpses, watching their insides boil under the light, and a painful wailing sound escaped them, reminding her that they had once been human. One of them looked no older than sixteen, and her heart cursed the Reapers as she sliced his head clean off.

Anger burned a flame in her gut, and she could feel herself losing control. Her mind, which had been clear of disturbance, began to grow chaotic. Her hands reached out, and thin arcs of light cut through the masses, severing the torsos of rows and rows of the corpses, giving the mages an uninterrupted path towards the Reapers. She had to seek mental clarity, but Niah's lungs choked with vengeance. The light climbed up her wrist, burning the edges of her sleeves. It did not hurt her flesh. The light and she were one. But if she did not wish to fight this battle naked, she needed to calm down.

Niah ran across the field, sticking close to Morgana. The Reapers were ripe for the taking. They didn't need so many Reapers when their corpses fought their battles. The more Reapers they killed, the more their Fallen would collapse once the weight of their magic was severed.

The Reapers were her true target.

Niah felt her blade clash against the closest Reaper's sword. He had leaped from his war horse in time to meet her attack. His blade was forged of Vykovian steel, the finest metal on the market. Its strength lay in its ability to withstand their light magic.

All around her, she could hear groans of pain and the thundering sound of the second wave of corpses flooding up the path, swarming them like ants.

How much longer could she fight before her magic gave out on her and she collapsed? How much longer until they breached their front line and overtook the monastery? What if she lost control again?

Sometimes, Niah feared that she would hurt those who fought on her side, that her magic would escape her and cause mass destruction.

Rounded pearls of sweat gathered on her skin as she made it past the Reaper's defenses, and slid her blade into his chest, leaving behind a gaping hole that tore through his organs. All of the Reapers wore a mask of white bone, except for the next one that charged at her. She had taken down five of them. It was her luck that not all of them had a blade of Vykovian steel because of its rarity; her light incinerated their weak metals, cutting their hands at the wrist.

Most of them had burned like wildfire under her magic, their organs swiftly melting under the force of her blade. But this next one would be a challenge; he appeared to be their leader. His mask was a lustrous wolf mask; the bone painted with a coal-black gloss. He was tall and lean, and his sword struck in a wide arc, sliding through her sword of light. Her scar burned, and she resisted the urge to scratch at it until it bled. Something tickled the back of her mind, a thought that vanished before she could grasp it.

Her blade collided with the Reaper's, the impact so intense her magic flickered, before reforming swiftly. His steps were lithe and graceful like a seasoned dancer, but Niah was small and quick. She evaded his brutal advances. Her foot slipped for a moment, leaving her neck bare, but the Reaper didn't sink his blade into her flesh. A flash of scalding anger spiked in her chest when she realized he was toying with her. He had a perfect opening to cut out her throat, but he spared her for his own cruel amusements.

She doubled her efforts and raised her hand to do the blade arc that would cut him in half when she felt a sword press against her throat. Another Reaper had slid behind her.

"Drop your hands before I sever them," the Reaper before her spoke. His voice was icy and controlled.

Niah debated killing him and letting his soldier kill her because she knew then that he was in charge. It wasn't simply the different mask. It was in his voice—confident, certain he'd be obeyed. The idea of disobeying him and dying out of spite was rather tempting. Especially, knowing that she had a chance to take him with her.

"Do not try me, cleric," he warned. "Your Order is losing. You have nothing to fight for."

"As if you will spare me," she spat. "I won't fall for your tricks."

"Do as I say, Lightbearer," he barked.

Niah stiffened. He knew what she was—or what people claimed she was. Were there spies among them?

"I am not afraid of death," she whispered. The lie slipped effortlessly from her lips.

"Niah!" Kesi's voice rang out.

Niah turned towards the cry. In that instant, the Reaper's leather-clad fingers clamped around her throat, squeezing until her vision blurred. Sparks floated before her like a sea of constellations. Then came the darkness, frigid and absolute, pulling her down into a deep, black abyss.

Chapter 3

Her head throbbed, and it took her several long minutes before her vision sharpened. The ground beneath her swayed unevenly, and she realized she was in a carriage—ornate, with a velvet bench and glossy wallpaper depicting a field of maroon dahlias. Between the flowers, yellow eyes watched lurking in the high grass like a wicked beast.

Niah turned from the wall, and a scream escaped her at the man sitting before her. His bone mask was sharp and frightful. His cloak lay draped beside him, the fabric bunched in a ball. He wore a black military coat with a pin attached to the breast pocket: a silver wolf with onyx stones for eyes. It was a regimental crest, though at what rank she could not say. The Order did not need frills. They fought on the ground, not behind shields of monsters, and they did not reward their victories with laurels.

The Reaper's thick, dark hair flowed around his mask, giving him an eerie grace amid the brutality of the bones.

It was said there was a time when the North was unsplit, cradled together like a babe in its bassinet. Before the war turned holy, it had been a rivalry between two princes, Nikolas and Casimir, who both hungered to be the one true King of the

North. The continent had cleaved—a region sliced for each brother like a celebratory cake.

Over the years, the war shifted to the gods, and strife rose like the turning pages of a short story—swift and thundering, often sealed by treaties that eventually crumbled.

Until King Stefan was crowned, and his feverish devotion drowned his citizens with its amoral touch. Anyone who turned from the faith was killed by his Reapers. They grew in power and might, multiplying like infection. They laughed behind their bone masks, calling others false-hearted as they burned huts, as if death were the truest gift.

Niah reached for her light to burn the Reaper to ashes, but nothing happened. She glanced down at her wrists—two thick iron bands encircled her flesh.

"Dampeners," the man said. "Pure Vykovian steel. Your flames cannot burn it. Your magic is silenced."

She'd never heard of Vykovian steel being used as dampeners. Their magic could not cut through the steel. It made sense to repurpose it to imprison the mages. The metal did not shatter or burn. It endured. It was impossible to find it anywhere, considering that the ore used to produce it took twelve years to mineralize, and the mines were based in Vykov, the King's territories.

Her stomach plummeted. Why would they need prisoners when they had no trouble killing them in masses?

They spared the untouched if they begged for mercy, but any Sister who served the Order was hanged. Worry knotted her gut, churning her insides like butter. Were Kesi and Morgana safe? Did the others survive? Who had won the battle?

"Where is everyone?" Niah asked. "What happened?"

He was silent. Not giving her the slightest indication of how the battle had fared. His cruelty choked her, tightening invisible fingers around her throat.

"What do you want from me?"

"I told you I would find you," he said. His voice clung to her like lichen on a tree.

Her heart galloped like a wild horse, and she jumped back, as if she had been struck. That cursed scar on her palm throbbed, and a small, strangled sound escaped her as he leaned forward. She felt the weight of his legs encircle hers.

"Get away from me," she said with as much strength as she possessed. "Don't touch me, you filthy heretic."

He laughed. The sound was harsh and cold.

"Heretic?" he said. "You are the heretic, Lightbearer."

"Where is everybody?" she asked. "Answer me."

"The untouched who surrendered down in the village were spared, and the mages who serve the Order were all killed," he said easily, as if they were discussing the weather.

Grief hooked its miserable fingers inside her, and it took everything in her to ease the sob that itched to climb out of her throat. To bury it deep inside her chest with all the other wretched memories that sought to destroy her. She would not crumble. She would not give him the air to gloat over her weakness.

Her Sisters were gone. The monastery had fallen.

"But if it is your loud-mouthed friend you speak of, she is in the carriage behind us," he said. "Think of her as an incentive to be on your best behavior."

"Kesi is well?" she asked hopefully.

"I am afraid so."

Niah let the relief wash over her. Morgana's fate still alluded her, but she prayed that she was safe and sound. Morgana was strong; she must have escaped. Niah refused to accept that she was another casualty of the war.

Kesi was here. That meant that Niah could not break. She had to be strong for them both. She had to survive whatever terrible ordeal awaited her.

"Show me your face, heretic," she said coldly.

He had leaned back in his seat, giving her the courage to be bold. She had no weapons or magic; all she had was her anger.

"Why don't you undress for me first, infidel?"

Her brows rose in horror.

"Impolite, isn't it, to make personal demands?" he asked.

"It is not the same," Niah shot back. "You simply enjoy being vulgar."

"I am not surprised you're a blushing virgin," he said. "Do you and your Sisters take vows of celibacy before serving Aubrith the False?"

"I will not discuss my private life with you," she said stiffly.

"It is kind of you not to put me to sleep," he replied.

The exchange distracted her from the full weight of her situation and the horrors that awaited her once the carriage came to a halt. Niah had to learn as much as she could about her and Kesi's new fate before they reached their destination.

"Is there a purpose to my imprisonment, or did you capture me to force me to speak with you because you have no friends?" Niah asked.

It wasn't wise to goad her captor, but something about his lazy posture and bored tone angered her. He sat as relaxed as a garden cat while she was powerless and frightened.

"How astute of you," the Reaper said. "I have brought you here to sing my praises."

Niah glared at him.

"Is this a joke to you?" she demanded. "Do you gain some perverse enjoyment from this?"

"I must say I do," he said. "You are easy to rile up."

"What did you mean when you said that you found me?" Niah asked, resisting the urge to shudder.

"Do not play dense," he said. "You know exactly who I am."

Niah could feel the memories she had burned deep inside her chest unfurl like a candle wick, illuminating the shadows that haunted her.

It had been raining that night like the sky was weeping. It always rained in Teren. There was a joke among the locals that there was a single season in Teren. Just Monsoon. The farmers had a complicated relationship with the ever-flowing water that both fed and drowned their crops.

Niah had been curled in her bed when the horses arrived, hooves thumping like a fist beating upon a goblet drum. By the time the villagers had gathered their farming shears and staves, it had been too late. They were outnumbered and their flimsy weapons stood no chance against the Reapers and their dark magic.

Under her mother's direction, Niah had curled under her bed. The sound of suffering wrapped around her in a blanket of despair, as her fingers trembled, nails digging into the wooden floorboards. It wasn't long after her mother vanished down the corridor that she heard the click of boots. The sour scent of decay filled her nostrils, making her gag. By then, she had known it was the King's Reapers. The corpses carried a vile odor.

"You can come out." A voice too deep to be boyish, but too wispy to be a man called. It was as if he had not yet broken into the sound.

Niah didn't move; not until their decaying fingers yanked her out from beneath the safety of the bed frame.

She clutched her father's blade outwards at the boy and the ring of corpses that circled her. The handle was made of the yellow tail of a sunfish her father had caught and skinned, and the tip was a polished silver blade.

The boy's eyes were a brown so dark it appeared black. As cold as the Ever Sea. Empty and plunging, his features were masked by his bone mask.

"I am Niah," she whispered under her breath. "I look upon darkness and I say I am not afraid."

"Reading your affirmations aloud does not exactly reek of confidence," the boy said. His hands were folded in his pockets, as if he were taking a midnight stroll and not coming to kill her.

"Go away, heretic," she said. "Leave me alone! In the name of the Light Father, I curse you and your kin."

"Ah, the same boring insults," he said, lowering down into the rocking chair her mother would sit in at night when she came to read her a story.

"Get off! My Mama won't like it if you sit there," Niah cried.

"How old are you?" he asked.

"I don't have to answer your questions."

His corpses came closer. Their rancid scent burned her nostrils. There were four of them under his command.

"Eight," she whispered.

He contemplated in silence. He could not have been much older than her, but his eyes were wise beyond his years. As if he had lived through many lifetimes.

"Do you surrender to the King of the High North, Stefan the I?" he asked. "Do you swear to serve him from this moment forth and forsake any oath of servitude unless it is to him and him alone? Do you vow to shun the followers of the Order of the White Flame and Aubrith the False?"

"No," she said between clenched teeth. "I belong to Teren, to the Low North, to Aubrith. I belong to the light."

"Tell me your name," he said. His Raskovian accent was thick and almost impossible to understand. The vowels contorted and sharpened the longer he spoke.

"Niah," she said bitterly. "Niah Yarrow."

"Niah," he repeated. Slow and measured as if he wanted to ensure that his accent wouldn't damage her name. Niah didn't even know why it mattered or why he cared. He was not her friend. He was her enemy. "Go back under your bed, Niah."

Her brows rose in surprise. The boy stood up, his corpses following him. His back was turned to her, and Niah knew this was her only chance to strike at him. To kill him. If she let him go, he would hurt her parents, and she could not stomach the thought.

Her blade sliced the fabric of his shoulder, and he moved swiftly, sword ripping from its harness. Her thin blade slipped from her fingertips with a single, brutal swipe. His blade retreated, slicing her palm in the process. A cry of pain escaped her, and the boy grabbed her wrist forcefully, inspecting her wound.

"I told you to listen to me," he said roughly.

Her hand tingled like someone had lit a torch to her fingers directly on the spot where his hand coiled around her flesh. She could feel something dark and pulsing twist inside her. The boy's eyes had grown monstrous, dark magic creeping into the whites and cloaking the entirety of his vision. His corpses distorted, evolving into long, hulking monsters twice the size of a regular man, as if they were bloated with dark magic. Niah watched in something akin to horror as they stepped forward.

It took her a moment to realize that she controlled them. She had willed them to protect her, and they now surrounded her in a shield.

The boy broke away from her, and when he did, the Fallen collapsed in a pile. As if the puppet strings that held them upright had been severed.

He looked at her with a mix of anger and awe.

Before Niah could say a word or even a prayer of protection, he grabbed her quickly and shoved her to the ground.

A whimper of pain escaped her as she fell to her knees. The pain dulled to surprise when she realized he was trying to push her under the bed. He was trying to hide her. Someone was coming upstairs. She could hear their footsteps against the flagstone.

"I will kill you one day," she whispered. Tucked deep under the wooden frame, all she could see were his black eyes staring back at her with interest. The darkness had fled as quickly as it had come on. "I swear on Aubrith, you will die for your sins."

"And I swear on the Dark Mother that I will find you if you run," he said. "Wait for me to return."

Niah didn't know how many hours passed while she remained tucked under that bed frame, as the world burned around her. She had no intention of sitting like a fox trapped in a snare, waiting for that horrid boy to come back and kill her. She didn't know why he had spared her, but she was certain that it was not for anything good.

Her prayers were answered because Morgana found her near an empty stable. And she had never spoken about the boy, the cursed magic, or the scar that remained from that cut ever again.

But she knew now with striking clarity that it was *him*.

Niah could see those black, morbid eyes staring at her with satisfaction. He could see the terror flooding her, and she imagined that behind the mask he smiled.

"I kept my promise," the Reaper said. "I found you."

Chapter 4

Snow drummed a soft cadence against the hickory shell of the carriage. Between the slip of the parted brocade curtain, she could catch a glimmer of the treetops. Wind rustled through their cocoon like the Breath of Aubrith, raising the messy strands of her once-plaited, powder-white hair.

Niah didn't muster a word as the carriage traveled to some unknown destination. Fear kept her mouth sealed shut as the Reaper's steely eyes watched her, awaiting a response that she refused to give him. His eyes glinted black as ink, depthless and devouring, as if he enjoyed this particular game. At a certain point, Niah fell asleep, her body drained from the magic she'd used. Her eyes had grown heavy, and before she knew it, she was lost in the dark.

A hand roughly roused her, the movement making her teeth click. Her eyes snapped open to stare at the Reaper.

"Come out," he said curtly.

The door to the carriage was cracked open, and it was dark outside. Stars glittered like stolen jewels in the night sky, surrounded by clouds that floated like spilled cream. A chill graced the air, and she folded her arms across her armor.

"Where are we?"

"Why don't you come find out?"

Niah shook her head. "I won't leave until—"

He grabbed her ankles, and she fell unceremoniously off the bench. He left her little time to catch her bearings before he caught her elbow and dragged her across the carriage floor and out the door. She stumbled to her feet, her fingers grasping the lapels of his coat for support, before she leaped away from him. Niah wiped her fingers on her robe, glaring at him.

"Unchivalrous bastard," she murmured.

"What was that?" he demanded.

"Do your ears not work?" Niah snapped. "Did you take one too many hits to the head?"

"Careful," he warned.

Niah looked up to find that they were at an inn that stood at the edge of the woods. Its crooked timbers were carpeted with ivy that ran like veins down the side, and smoke curled from the stout chimney. Worn cobblestones lay between a cluster of elder trees. Behind them were two dozen Reapers, waiting atop their horses. They had barely sustained any casualties, and her mouth flattened in dismay.

"They are itching to cut your throat out," her captor whispered. "It is my command alone that holds their blades."

He spoke the truth. Their eyes that peeked behind their masks burned with rage, and their fingers circled restlessly along their hilt.

"Where are we?" she asked.

He ignored her, walking ahead of her. It was strange to be trailing behind him in her lily-white robes like a ghost and her armor that glistened like frost under the morning light.

"Where is Kesi?" Niah asked. "Where is my friend?"

Her question was met with no response. Perhaps, he lied about Kesi, and if so, what else had he lied about? Suspicion bled through her, tainting every word he spoke in the last few hours. Not that he had said much, a few insults and some vague answers.

Why had he spared her? Why was she alive? Why had he looked for her? Those he had refused to answer.

Inside, the air smelled of old ash and spiced wine. The patrons sat upright at the sight of the Reapers. From their respectful stares, Niah knew they were no longer in the Low North, they were in the King's territories. She was trapped deep in enemy land, alone and weakened. The closest province that belonged to them--from what she recalled of the maps--was Burya. Several people raised their cups in salute and held a fist to their chest in recognition of the army.

The barkeep's eyes widened at the sight of her white robe and breastplate. A stark contrast to the Reaper's black. Her hair was a pearlescent white that fell to her back. Most of the Sisters had a single streak of white flowing through their locks, a mark from Aubrith that they were blessed. Except for Niah, whose hair was entirely white.

A nearby man made a gesture as if he were warding off evil, and Niah almost laughed. These pagans were afraid of her when the man beside her desecrated tombs and gravesites to replenish his undying army. How utterly foolish of them.

The Reaper grabbed the room key from the barkeep without uttering a single word of thanks. His ill manners were not just directed at her alone, it seemed.

He led her up the carpeted stairs, unlocking the bedroom. The walls were an uncanny shade of peacock blue, their edges peeling and curling away from the corners like the delicate rind of an orange. By the headboard rested a pillow faded and sickly, its once bright fabric now dulled with time and edged in frayed gold tassels. Draped across the foot of the bed was a heavy swath of bear fur, its coarse hair tangled and flattened like freshly cut stalks of spelt left out too long in the autumn sun.

The cloistered room grew smaller when he entered, ducking his head to walk under the short doorway. He was tall with a lean, muscular frame. Niah studied him, wondering how she could physically overpower him. Her magic was silenced, but the dampeners were not linked by a chain. They were designed to resemble bangles. She could still fight him in hand-to-hand combat.

"There will be guards outside your door and the windows are barred," he said. "I would not waste my time trying to escape."

Niah eyed his sword. It was now or never. She lunged at him, fingers reaching for the handle. The Reaper caught her wrist, twisting it behind her back. Niah didn't have a second to react before he had her pinned to the wall, his body holding her in place.

"Let go of me!"

"Did you really think that would work?" he snapped. "Or do you enjoy wasting my time?"

"Both."

His nostrils flared.

"Why are you keeping me alive?" Niah demanded.

"Because you are of worth to me alive," he said. "For now."

"How do I serve your purpose?" she asked, not liking the direction this conversation was going. Niah knew whatever he said next would shine a light on his dark agenda.

"Do you know what you are?" he asked. "Do you know what your gift is?"

"Of course, I do," she said in a voice that implied he was an idiot.

"You are not the Lightbearer," he said. "You aren't a Saint reborn."

Niah scoffed. "Right. Neither are you, Heretic."

"Just shut up while I explain," he said impatiently. "You are a conduit. Neither a Reaper nor a mage of the Order."

"And what exactly is a conduit?" Niah asked.

She would humor him. Listen to his lies and see how exactly he intended to weave this tale. This was what the Reapers did. They convinced people that they were the saviors brought to cleanse the realm of those who served the Order. In their story, they were the heroes.

He spun her around, staring into her brown eyes as if he

could read the secrets of her soul. Niah's fingers itched to pull off his mask, to bare him and stare at his wretched face, which no doubt matched his ruined soul. She hoped their time apart had been cruel to him.

"Conduits are vessels of great power," he said. "They have no ability of their own, but they can siphon magic to grant them power. It is why the Corruption spreads so swiftly, your kind have been drawing from the lands."

"You speak of the damage you are causing to the realm," she said. "The Corruption is a byproduct of your gifts, not mine."

How bold of him to cast the blame on the mages when the Reapers were the ones breaking the balance.

"You are the one who is drawing from the world around you," he said. The accusation was heavy in his voice. "You are all conduits pretending to be mages. You are ruining everything."

"Our gifts are from the Light Father. It is a blessing meant to protect us from the pagans who defy his laws," Niah hissed. "How dare you imply otherwise?"

He glared at her.

"You are so incredibly stupid," he said.

"And you are a despicable villain."

"Explain this then." He caught her hand. Long, graceful fingers swept over her palm like a film of snow.

Something dark and hungry spiked inside her. It reminded her of all those years ago when his touch had sent her into a spiral. She could sense those corpses outside, feel every single one of them as if their threads called to her, and if she tugged at it, they would respond. They would answer her call. It was a surreal feeling, as if she were in a vacuum with nothing but darkness surrounding her. It lured her like an enchanted flute to accept its will. Much like her nightmares, he was infecting her mind, poisoning her gifts.

To serve, to master, to control.

Niah yanked her hand back, shoving him as hard as she could, but he didn't budge. She brushed past him, her heart thundering in her chest, sweat gliding down her stiff nape and soaking her collar. If she had eaten so much as a morsel, she would be emptying her guts right now. Her scar throbbed as if it ached for his touch. Niah caught her hand, nails digging deep into her flesh.

"Don't ever do that again," she whispered.

"You are stronger than the others," he said. His voice rolled over her, dark and promising. "So much more powerful than the other conduits. You could become the strongest conduit who ever lived."

"I will not support your cause," she said, chin raised high. "I will die before I serve your ruthless King and his destructive Reapers."

"You will do as I command," he said. "It is only a question of whether you want the girl to live or not. Perhaps, your tune will change when I sever her tongue. Is an example needed to ensure your compliance?"

Her blood ran cold. Kesi. How could she forget? Her best friend was a captive just as much as she was, but where was he hiding her? He could just be bluffing to keep her in line.

"I want to speak to her," Niah said. "I need to know she is well."

He stepped out the door, and several moments later, a Reaper stepped inside with Kesi. Her hair was a mess, and blood coated her forehead, but beyond that, she was in one piece. Niah wrapped her arms around her, holding her tight.

"God, Niah, I thought you were dead," she said, her voice strangled. "This brute hasn't spoken a single word since I was captured. I don't even know if the others are well."

The Reaper was in the room—the one who had brought in Kesi. It was eerie that they could not see their faces, just their hollow eyes. This one had bright blue eyes.

"Things are bad, Kesi," she whispered, speaking in Virelle. It would be impossible for him to understand them. "He is weaving all kinds of lies."

"Who is? Commander Winterson?" she asked.

"No, the Reaper who—wait, why do you think he's the Commander?"

Niah had suspected him of being in charge, but it did not make sense. He was young, only a handful of years older than her, from what she recalled when he was a boy. Most likely twenty or so. Far too fresh-faced to be leading one of the greatest armies in the realm.

"That is what the idiot back there called him."

"That can't be," Niah whispered.

"I'm afraid so," Kesi said. "What did he say to you?"

"Lies and threats," Niah said, rubbing her wrist as if she could erase his touch.

"Why are they taking us captive?" Kesi asked. "They have never done that before."

"I don't know," she said. "But their intentions cannot be good."

"I think we should use our feminine wiles to get them to free us."

"What?" Niah asked.

Her brows furrowed at this ill-thought idea.

"I mean, we are young, beautiful women," Kesi said. "It is not an absurd idea. Will they wear those masks when they take us abed?"

"Kesi. Focus!" Niah said. "I can't tell if you are repulsed or intrigued by this deranged plan of yours. That is a concerning thought."

"Well, I'm nervous. How am I to react?" Kesi asked.

"Like you don't want to secretly bed these monsters," Niah hissed.

"At least I am pitching some ideas," she said. "You look like you are about to faint."

"Because that...that beast attacked me," Niah said. "And god knows what he intends to do to me when he returns. We need a serious plan that does not include seducing them."

Kesi's brows furrowed as she thought. Five seconds passed before she sighed.

"I have nothing."

"We have to figure out how to get these dampeners off," Niah said. "We need magic."

They had fashioned an identical pair for Kesi to keep her magic subdued.

Kesi nodded quickly. "Good plan."

"That is enough," a detached, familiar voice spoke.

Dread filled her when his shadow filled the doorway, arms folded neatly across his chest.

"Take her back," he ordered.

"Wait," Kesi called. "It is rather hot, do you mind if we remove our robes?"

His head cocked.

Niah glared at Kesi as she slowly began to unclasp the sheath that held her robe. She wore her linen nightgown underneath. They both did. There had been no time to dress properly during the attack. At least Niah had the added shield of her armor.

Niah stood stiffly beside her, watching her terrible attempt at seduction *after* she had warned her it was a bad idea. Kesi rarely listened to any form of good advice. She was as willful as a tempest.

"If you remove these dampeners, Niah will take off everything," Kesi said.

Niah shot her an incredulous look. There could be a blade to her throat, and she would not debase herself before these monsters. Kesi was not made for captivity, her eyes burned with desperation and her fingers shook. She was beautiful with a gazelle-like frame and raven hair that was always braided stylishly in the way that the women of Teren favored. Also, she tended to mask her fear with humor which was *exactly* what she was doing right now.

"Is that so?" the Reaper asked, folding his arms across his chest. "Prove it."

His dark eyes were locked on Niah.

"Never," Niah said between clenched teeth. "We won't bend to your will or reveal our flesh to your wandering eyes. You are a filthy animal."

"A shame," he said dryly. "Mikhail, take the girl to bed. And make sure she keeps all her clothes on."

Kesi's eyes widened, surprised that her attempt had failed.

"Yes, Commander," the man said.

His soldier took Kesi away, and the door clicked shut behind the Commander, who thankfully did not linger.

Niah sat on the stiff bed, resting her back against the headboard. Her stomach growled in hunger, and she clasped her hands on it as if she could silence the ache.

It seemed that everything she did was doomed to fail. She had lost her first battle, which did not bode well for the war.

Each year that passed, the King's domain stretched like an immortal rope. He ruled the High North, and now the Low North was within his ravenous grasp. His Reapers grew stronger, and their belief that they were the righteous ones heightened with each victory, as if their deity, Bersula, the Dark Mother, watched over them.

It sickened her to think of the fate that would befall the Order and all her Sisters, of what would happen to Kesi if Niah stepped out of line. It was clear to see that they were to be used as a pawn in their machinations.

Her fingers curled into a tight fist.

Be kind and brave and hungry and angry.

Niah chose then to be angry. Anger would keep her warm during the winter night, stoking her belly like a quiet flame. She would nurse it and let it grow into a wicked storm. Until it devoured everything in sight.

Chapter 5

That morning, a cloak awaited her—black as a raven's wing, with a thick fur collar. A shudder stole through her as her fingers sank into velvet, dark and fluid as a starless sky. Fleece shorn from cloud-white sheep and dyed to match their sinful souls lined the inside. How nice it was to be able to afford such fabric for soldiers. It was clear to see the King's coffers were not lacking. Niah turned her nose up at the offering and tossed it aside.

A silver tray rested on the table, bearing a bowl of deep crimson beetroot soup that glistened like spilled wine. Beside it sat warm, stuffed buns, their golden crusts split open to reveal a savory filling, slices of smoked meat, dark and glistening with fat, winked at her. A chilled glass of whisky completed the spread, beads of condensation trailing down its sides. Niah ate the food like a madwoman. Not a single drop remained when she finished.

Her heart stuttered when the door was unlocked.

It was him.

She could tell by his unnatural height and those eyes that cut as sharply as glass. His face remained hidden. It was a power tactic, she realized, a means of studying her while he remained a secret.

"Put on the cloak," he asked. "That sigil on your armor will bring you no goodwill around these parts."

"That is the cloak you Reapers wear," she said. "I will not dress like you."

"Fine, come along then," he said.

The sun shone dully that morning, as if it could sense her bleak mood. The markets were slowly rousing like a turning tide; stalls being set up with willful fingers. The villagers' curious, frightened eyes were locked on Niah. Their displeasure wafted off them like a foul odor, and Niah let the Reaper's frame conceal her from their scrutiny.

"I told you to wear the cloak," he said smugly.

A rock hit her ankles, and she looked into the eyes of an angry young boy.

"Bad mage," he called, pointing a finger at her.

Her mouth parted in surprise. These people had been manipulated so thoroughly that they looked at the Reapers like they were the heroes and glared at her as if she had committed a grave ill. A sour taste filled her mouth as she resisted the urge to lecture the young boy. It was his parents' beliefs that stoked the flame in his eyes. It was no opinion of his own. Yet she could not help that she was upset by his reaction.

The Reaper pushed her gracelessly into the carriage, slamming the door shut behind her. It seemed he was not interested in enjoying the pleasure of her company that morning. Her fingers brushed aside the curtain, and she felt relief fill her at the sight of Kesi entering the carriage behind her. Kesi had the good sense to wear the cloak they offered, unlike Niah, whose stubbornness would probably one day be the death of her.

"Where are we going?" Niah asked.

He had come to grace her with his bland presence halfway through the journey, and the sigh he released when she spoke was enough to make the strands of her hair flutter. From his reaction, one would think she had been hounding him for hours. But these were the first words she had spoken in the past twenty minutes, and she could not silence the questions that buzzed through her mind like a swarm of bees.

"The capital," he said.

Niah sucked in a sharp breath.

"We're going to Raskovia?" she asked. "To the King."

He chuckled, the sound low and mocking. "Don't be ridiculous. I wouldn't dare bring a weak mage such as yourself before the King. Not without proper training at least."

"Then where will you take me? To prison?" she asked bitterly. "The coal mines for a few years of hard labor?"

"Don't give me any ideas."

"Stop dancing around my questions."

"I don't dance," he said. "Not my style."

"Did someone tell you you're funny?" Niah demanded. "Because they lied."

"I reckon it was the same person who told you that curiosity is a good trait to possess," he said.

Niah glared at him.

"You said you wouldn't bring me to the King without proper training," Niah said, reading between the lines of his words. "Is that what you intend to do with me—to train me?"

He was silent, which was louder than any response he could have given her. Her stomach bloomed with worry. She was not clay for him to mold into his perfect soldier. She would never serve the Reapers. King Stefan was cruel and unjust, and to deny him was to have one's throat cut till there was nothing but bone and sinew. But she would rather tilt her neck for his blade than fall out of grace with her people.

Niah would have to be clever about how she navigated these

treacherous waters. Now that Kesi's fate was tangled with hers, she would have to bide her time to make her escape.

She would have to gain the Commander's trust before she carved out his worthless heart.

Eight days of sporadic inns and harsh commands passed them in a blur. On the third day, Niah had taken the cloak after the weather had taken a cutting turn, rain turning to snow, and the days shrinking like petals bending under a harsh wind. Her once-white robe had grown sticky with dirt and sweat and stale blood, and the armor made her shoulders ache miserably. Her words had been a shameful grumble when she'd asked the Commander for a clean cloak. His eyes had shone in victory as he handed her the dreaded ink-black fabric.

The dark charcoal building that stood before them was covered in moss that painted patchy murals across the frame while ivy clambered up the starving spires like a pair of stockings. Thick black grilles ran across the window in an ornery pattern, and mist cloaked the pointed tips like a frosty crown.

Slowly, the Reapers began to dismount their horses as the gates were rolled. They were not like the Sisters of the Order. There was no laughter or ruthless ribbing or gentle hair-tugs. Their steps were controlled, and they moved in unison like a blade cutting through flesh and bone. Something shifted when the Reapers walked onto the opposite side. Their shoulders relaxed, and slowly they began to peel off their masks, tucking them under their arm. Conversation loosened their tongues. And she watched in dark fascination as they transformed from morbid hunters to young men and women.

Niah was unnerved by their expressionless, pale faces—so bloodless they looked carved from alabaster. Stranger still was the silver metal that adorned their bodies: glinting cuffs looped through their ears, thin bars piercing their brows, delicate chains draped from lip to chin like ceremonial bindings. The metal caught the light like moonlight on water.

But what unsettled her most were the slivers of bone they carried, displayed like sacred relics. Some wore them woven into braids, the fragments coiled like ivory serpents among dark strands of hair. Others let them dangle from threads around their necks, tapping lightly against their chests with each step. She couldn't tell if the bones belonged to beasts... or something worse.

Her eyes warily turned to the Commander beside her, but his mask remained fastened.

"Where are we?" she whispered.

"Silverwood Hall," he said. "A religious war college for Reapers to study their gifts and to prepare for service."

Niah's mouth tightened. An arm coiled around hers, and she looked at Kesi's wary face as they stared out at the foreigners before them. They were far from Caer-Sylisse. How would they ever survive the journey back, surrounded by enemies and trapped in a foreign land? How would they survive this imprisonment with their souls intact?

Guilt coiled in her belly. She hadn't even told Kesi about the dark magic—how he had stained her with his touch all those years ago, and how he was now watering the rotten plant he had grown inside her soul until it flourished. She hadn't even told Kesi his lies about their gifts. There was so much she could not speak, in fear that it would give the words weight.

"Come along," the Commander said.

He led them towards the arched doorway carved with a sigil of a wolf tangled in ancient whorls. The door opened to an antechamber. Framed in the center was a stone sculpture of the Maiden of Death. Their people had a name for her—Bersula.

Iron chandeliers flickered over the statue, casting her in a pallid glow. Dark beams ran like ribs along the ceiling, coming to a crisscross at the center. A staircase with lacquered handrails ran along both sides of the floor, intersecting on the second floor like a pair of clasped palms.

"Demian," the Commander called. "Show them both to their chambers and explain their purpose."

A young, lanky boy came towards them with a loose smile and dark brown curls. He was waiting for them in the antechamber like a trained pet.

The Commander walked away without a parting glance.

"Pleasure to meet you both," he said. "You may call me—"

"We don't care," Niah said coldly. "We will call you Reaper or heretic."

"Agreed," Kesi said, folding her arms across her chest.

He cleared his throat awkwardly.

"Well, what shall I call you?"

"What would you call someone who would slit your throat in your sleep?" Niah asked.

His lips lifted, brown eyes glowing in amusement.

"A murderer?" he asked.

"Enemy," she corrected. "You may call me your enemy."

Demian chuckled like she had just told a splendid joke. Her eyes narrowed, and the sound drowned in his throat.

"I will show you around the fortress," he said. "Silverwood is a reformed estate that belonged to Lord Filip Silverwood. He donated it to the army ninety years ago."

Niah opened her mouth to say that she didn't care about the history of this place, but that was a lie. She did care, because knowledge was power, so she clamped her mouth shut as Demian barreled on to his heart's content.

"It has been expanded since then, and a separate quarter was furnished to act as the dormitories," he continued. "The adjoining gamekeeper's building was also enhanced to fit the Commander and his soldiers during their stay and resembles a small barracks."

How convenient that he had just told them where the Commander lay his miserable head.

They passed a wall lined with small, gilded portraits. Stern men and women, their long hair tied behind them with leather knots, stared at them frigidly. Most Northern men kept their hair at shoulder length or longer, one of those traditions Niah did not understand. Teren, on the other hand, picked up more southern traits, and the men kept their hair shorn close to their scalp. The docks were always filled with sailors from the Seven Marches and the Kingdom of Iyre, their sea-salt accent lapping at their vowels and their spices gracing their food.

Beneath their plaques was a platitude commending their military service, and for the deceased, a small prayer from the Death Codex:

May the river guide you to Bersula, the Dark Mother.
And may her hearth warm your soul like a flame on a winter's night.

"Are we your first captives?" Niah asked, the word *captive* making her stomach roil.

Demian hesitated, uneasy with the question.

"Yes," he said. "Think of it as a trial. If you perform well, perhaps the others can be spared."

Niah laughed bitterly. "So, if we behave properly, you will enslave the rest of our people. What a great incentive!"

"Unbelievable," Kesi said.

"It is more complicated than that," he said. "Your magic is—"

"Don't even start with that spiel," Niah warned. "We won't fall for your lies."

"What spiel?" Kesi whispered.

"I'll tell you later."

Demian led them through a walkway that connected to another building. The foyer felt unusually warm. A quilted blanket lay draped across the leather chairs, its faded patchwork sinking into the folds and creases. Several students lazily sat around, whispering among themselves. Books spilled across the floor in a careless cascade, ink pots glistening like the beaded eyes of a crow. Stray gazes flickered towards them, studying them, some with curiosity and others with thinly veiled anger. Niah felt like a strange creature from a children's storybook.

"The library closes at midnight," Demian said. "So, the students usually return to the Commons to study."

"Study?" Niah asked. "I thought you were training."

"The coursework is divided between theoretical studies and physical training," he explained. "To wield magic, one must understand it first. And we serve at the pleasure of the Dark Mother."

"The left wing is the girls' dormitories, and the right is the boys'," Demian said. "The Commons is for intermingling or quiet study, depending on the hour. Curfew is at a quarter past midnight."

"Will these dampeners be removed?" Kesi asked. "How are we to practice if we are shackled?"

"That is for Valek to decide," he said.

Niah's head snapped towards him. "Valek?"

"I should have said Commander Winterson," he said. "Excuse my informality. We are cousins."

"You are related to that beast?" Niah gasped.

"Most people are either amazed or reverent when I tell them that little fact," Demian said. "I've never had a horrified reaction before."

"He sickens me," Niah said. She looked at Kesi. "He sickens us both."

"I am sorry to hear that," Demian said.

It was worse that he sounded genuinely apologetic, as if he could control who he was related to. Niah was silent as he led her up the crooked stairs to the second floor. The room was modest. Two narrow beds stood on opposite sides, their linen sheets crisp and untouched, tucked with the kind of precision that hinted they were now in a military institution. Between the frames were two beechwood desks that faced the barred window, their surfaces bare save for an ink pot and a candle.

A small hearth squatted in the far corner, its stone dark with ash, though no fire had been lit. Icy air floated like silver mist across the room.

"This is your bedroom," Demian said. "I will remind you that there are guards stationed outside the dormitory, and you will have escorts assigned to take you to your classes tomorrow."

"Thank you," Niah said reluctantly. Demian looked to be a year or so younger than her and had these wide-set brown eyes that reminded her of a kicked dog anytime she said something cruel. It wasn't as enjoyable being dreadful to him as it was to the Commander.

His smile brightened. "You're welcome."

The door clicked shut behind him, and Kesi sighed, collapsing on her bed.

"What a mess," she muttered. "How did we find ourselves here?"

Niah sat on Kesi's bed, crossing her legs under her.

Niah's fingers absently stroked the frost-white strands of her hair, brushing it back as if she could hide it. As a young child, she had always been self-conscious about the strange coloring. It had felt like a mark, or rather an omen. In Teren, magic was shunned. To the people, it didn't matter if you wielded light or darkness. A witch was a witch. The first streak of white had sprung from her hair like a daffodil at the age of four, when her magic had first appeared. Her mother, who was far more generous than the villagers, liked to tell her she was a descendant of the First Queen who ruled back when the territories hadn't fractured like a broken bone and the Saints' magic covered the lands in its wispy veil.

"The First Queen had hair as white as frost," her mother would say. "Your hair is a symbol to be worn with pride. The magic of the lands flows in your veins, and soon you shall be sent to the monastery to serve the Order and the queen. One day, you will bring glory to the realm."

It didn't feel magical anymore. It felt like an augury. A beacon that lured her enemies to her.

"Do you remember when we met?"

"When you tried to cut off my hair in my sleep?" Niah asked with a pointed stare.

Kesi smiled sheepishly. "I was so envious of your hair. It was all anyone could talk about. They called you god-touched. Even before your magic impressed them, you were a wonder. It was odd to learn that beauty was such a valuable currency. And what made it worse was that you hated it, so I figured I would do something about it."

Niah dropped her hand. Her words made her feel ungrateful.

"I don't enjoy standing out." Niah sighed. "It makes me feel small."

"You are too hard on yourself."

Niah didn't like speaking about her insecurities, so she swiftly changed the topic.

"What are we going to do about this?" she asked, waving her wrists. "I'm surprised they didn't separate us."

"They don't seem too concerned that we'll escape," Kesi said.

"I find that odd," she said.

"Maybe they know we are two idiots," Kesi said. "I mean, the seduction attempt failed miserably."

"That was your idea!" Niah said, exasperated. "I told you it wouldn't work."

Kesi flung her pillow at her, and Niah snatched it before it whacked her in the face.

"Do you think of Teren?" Niah asked. "I don't remember what it smelled like anymore."

"Like animal musk and sun-warmed soil," Kesi said. "Salt, too. So much damned salt. It burned. Do you ever think we'll go back?"

"I want to see it again," Niah whispered. "Before I die."

I want to go home.

Chapter 6

A flaxen-haired girl with a sharp, hawkish nose and a gelid stare was sent as their escort that morning. She led them down the corridors in silence, keeping a brisk pace as if she didn't want to be too close to them. Behind her, three corpses followed her lead. They descended the stairs to the first floor and walked down the hallway, passing the oval windows. The tower across from them was a darker stone than the rest of the building, hinting that it was a new addition. It stood like a rook in the dark.

A piece of Niah's soul had withered that morning when she'd drawn on the neat black robes that had been left on their bedroom bench. It unnerved her that someone had entered their room while they had been asleep. Her mood further soured as she tied the black ribbon around her hair. It was blasphemous to wear their clothes, as if she were darkening her soul. So, different from the white robes she wore at the monastery.

"What crawled up her arse?" Kesi whispered.

"I heard that!" the girl said sharply.

"It wasn't meant to be a secret," Kesi said.

"Kesi," Niah chided her. It was too early to be making enemies. Not before she drank her customary cup of coffee. She hoped the girl was leading them to their first meal of the day.

That dream was crushed when they passed the refectory with its rows of benches and chairs. Students milled around in their dark robes, intermingling as they ate. The bitter waft of coffee made her stomach yearn for the strong drink.

"Where's Demian?" Niah asked.

"Lord Demian," the girl corrected. "The Wintersons are a highborn family and are related to the King, which makes Lord Demian fifth in line to the throne and Lord Valentin third in line. The Wintersons are also the Wardens of the Silver Pass and the territory beyond the Vales."

"Valentin, you speak of the Commander?" Niah asked.

Demian had called him Valek, but perhaps he was closer to the wretched beast, enough to call him by a pet name.

The girl gave her a dirty look. "Who else?"

Kesi opened her mouth, most likely to insult the girl, but Niah caught her hand, squeezing her in warning. She was gathering useful information.

"Are there other captives like us?" Niah asked.

"You are the first," the girl said, confirming what Demian had said. Niah was not thrilled by the idea that they were the first. "I do not know why the Commander thinks you can be trusted. It is obvious you are hunting for answers, and that you don't have the slightest inclination to learn more about us."

"We do not intend to serve your army," Kesi said. "We were taken against our will."

"You mages are causing the Corruption, suckling every last inch of magic from the lands," she said. "We are righting your wrongs, and you have the nerve to be ungrateful."

Kesi looked like she was mere moments away from punching the girl, and Niah came between them, nearly stepping on the girl's heel. A blistering silence followed them as she led them to an office where a woman with spectacles sat behind an oaken desk. The secretary swiftly stood up, wearing one of those fashionable blouses and tailored skirts worn by working women in the North.

She cracked open the door behind her before she nodded for them to enter.

The girl spun on her heels, disappearing as swiftly as she had arrived, as if a rabid dog were at her heels.

Niah took a deep breath before she entered the office. She had expected the Commander to be there, staring at her with those ink-black eyes and thick, dark lashes. His face, framed by that fearsome mask. But it wasn't the Commander who awaited them. A woman with a shaved head stared at them with rheumy blue eyes. Her mouth was long and thin, like a slash along parchment.

"Sit," she ordered.

Niah sat stiffly in the leather chairs, afraid that it would swallow her whole.

"Welcome to Silverwood. I am Headmistress Greymont," she said. "For the next few months, this will be your home. You will be trained among those chosen to ascend as Reapers."

Niah's mouth tightened. She could hear the creaking sound of Kesi's chair as she dug her nails into the armrest.

"Mages who are trained by the Order are unfortunately ill-advised about the source of their gifts," she continued. "Mages such as you and your Sisters are conduits, and the preservation of our lands requires us to correct these teachings. You are here out of the grace of Lord Valentin Winterson, our Commander, and with permission from the King. The Commander believes that mages such as yourself can be taught instead of slaughtered."

"And what if it is you who are causing the Corruption?" Kesi demanded. "What if you are the monsters?"

"We have followed the ways of Bersula before the name Aubrith graced the mouths of the peasants," she said. "Our magic is older than you can imagine. We draw our magic from the bones of our ancestors. Not the trees of life, not the light that seals the realm."

"How are we to learn your ways if we are to wear these cursed dampeners?" Niah asked.

"Those only weaken your light magic," she said. "You will be perfectly capable of learning our magic."

"What happens if we refuse?" Kesi asked.

The Headmistress blinked, unamused by the question.

"You will be executed like the rest of your Sisters," she said.

Kesi frowned, not particularly pleased by that answer.

"You will soon learn that we do not fear death," the Headmistress said in her stoic voice. "Death is our mother."

They were dismissed after that jarring introduction.

And those unearthly, devoted words ran through her mind like a sonnet.

Death is our mother.

The secretary handed them both a separate slip of paper that detailed their coursework and training schedule. Niah frowned when she realized they shared only one class. Kesi's mood further soured when that terrible girl came to escort her to her classes. Niah was sympathetic, wondering who would come to find her. The girl was rather unpleasant.

Niah stared at the short, yellow sheet and the courses listed:

> **Introduction to Necromancy**
> **Bone Talismans**
> **Battle Strategy**
> **Lunch**
> **Combat Lessons**
> **Spirit-Control and Divination**
> **Dinner**
> **Night Prayer**

Niah folded the sheet, tucking it into her satchel, feeling

slightly light-headed. Usually, she would be thrilled at the opportunity to learn. She had enjoyed her education at the monastery and the few courses she'd taken at the university to diversify her studies. But all she felt when she looked at the thin sheet was dread.

Several moments passed as she stood in the empty hallway until she saw Demian racing across the hall. His books spilled out of his unclasped satchel, hitting the ground in a sea of ink and paper. Niah fell to her knees, helping him sort out his belongings. He reminded her of the young clerics in the monastery, always running down the corridors like it was a race.

"Sorry," he said breathlessly. "I was halfway across the courtyard when I recalled I was assigned as your guide."

His hair was wet with snow, and he shook it like a ragged dog. Niah's mouth pursed when several droplets hit her face.

"Sorry," he sputtered again. "I am wretched at this."

"It's fine," Niah said. "In truth, your tardiness saves me from going to class."

"So, Headmistress Greymont." He nodded at the door. "Did she frighten you as much as she does me?"

"She was distant and curt, but I expected as much from a High Northerner. Your manners leave much to be desired," she said.

"We say that the Low North is full of religious fanatics and drunkards," he said. "It is said that you wouldn't know if your breeches were on fire."

"It is a false rumour that all we do is drink gin," Niah said, squinting at him. "You should know better than to believe everything you hear."

"I could say the same to you."

"Do you expect me to think kindly of your people when my wrists are chained, and I am being forced against my will to learn your magic?"

"Many think that the war is about land and territory, but it is not," Demian said. "It is about magic. *Everything* is about magic."

There was a time when the North was one single, beating heart pumping blood into all the territories, but now it is cleaved. The High North despises the Low North, and everything is muddied and foul."

"So, the answer is to destabilize one half to strengthen the other?"

"The answer is to learn each other's ways," he said gently. "We have learned yours. We know the Book of Light and the Six Saints and the Eight Mandates. We know your magic and faith, and folk tales. Perhaps, you should give us a chance to teach you ours."

Niah was silent. The only reason she wanted to learn about them was to share this intel with the Queen of the Low North and her Sisters once she escaped. Niah had no interest in empathizing with her enemies.

She would only learn as much as she needed to betray them.

And she prayed that she retained her soul in the process.

Her first lesson was being held in the crypt beneath the chapel.

Niah's stomach rolled as she stepped down the stairs with the rest of her classmates. Demian had left her side to attend his class, but said he would return to escort her to her next class. Niah shoved her beliefs and distaste to a shadowy corner in her mind. If she wanted to survive, she would have to learn their magic and teachings as a scholar. She had to erase her bias and open her mind to soak up as much knowledge on her enemies as she could.

The students chattered lightly as if conducting their lessons in a crypt was a perfectly normal thing. Once in a while, they would throw her a curious glance.

The hollowed archway opened up into a dim space with antique candelabras made of blackened iron placed sporadically around the space. Some rested on three-legged mahogany stools, casting wicked shadows along the ceiling that stretched like paint on canvas.

Hollowed into the walls like an empty eye socket were ceramic urns of ashes, and at the foot of the wall were tombs. The stone walls were marked with symbols, and Niah raptly studied the funerary art. Some of the carvings depicted the martyrdom of the Six Saints, also known here as the Sinners. There was Saint Aelgan the Martyr, the patron saint of secrets and wisdom, Saint Ylena the Flamekeeper, the patron saint of light and prophecy, Saint Mera the Drowned, the patron saint of sailors and sacrifice, Saint Helwen the Healer, the patron saint of healing and mercy, Saint Carywen, the patron of spring, rebirth, and midwives, and Saint Elirien the Lover, the patron saint of love and song.

One of the few beliefs shared across the North was the myths of the Six. Except in her faith, the Saints were miracle-workers who committed acts of goodness, while here in the High North, they were Sinners who were hanged for their bad deeds.

There were four wooden benches placed in the corner and a total of twenty students in the class. Niah slid into the second row, ignoring the eyes that followed her like a stain.

A tall woman in dark robes entered the crypt. Her eyes scanned the room, and her crooked smile wavered when it fell on Niah. Her gaze lingered for several long minutes, forcing Niah to shift around in discomfort.

"Would you like to share your name?"

Niah hesitated before she answered.

"Niah," she said.

"Please, welcome Niah," she said. It was said in an obligatory way as if she were reciting the lines of a play. "I am Mistress Sonia. Your instructor."

Niah hunkered down in her seat, detesting the stares she received. It was like the monastery all over again. She was too odd, too special, too much. It was as if every room she walked into was always just a little too small to fit her.

"Niah, what do you know about the origin of our magic?" Sonia asked, slowly pacing the front of the room.

"Nothing," she said, unable to mask the chill lacing her words.

It was a foolish question to ask someone from the Low North who believed all of them to be heretics and pagans.

"What about the *Tome of Miracles*?" she asked. "Have you read that particular text?"

It was one of the Low North's famed books.

"A little," she lied.

Sonia smiled tightly, as if she knew her words were false.

Of course, Niah had read it multiple times. It was one of her comfort reads, but she refused to confess that. It seemed Sonia was determined to find a common thread between them, but there was nothing to grasp. The Commander had revealed that they had studied their teachings. So, it was no surprise that Sonia mentioned this popular text, and attempted to strike conversation.

"Then you must recall the references to the Maiden of Death, Bersula."

"She was never mentioned by name," Niah said. "She was just called the Maiden of Death."

"What else do you know about us?"

Niah pursed her lips before she reluctantly answered.

"I know the Reapers serve the Church of Bersula," she said. "I know that Bersula is said to lead the spirits to the Lower World."

"A good start," Sonia said, not mentioning how utterly lacking her knowledge was. "Who can provide some more information to Niah about our faith?"

A girl raised her hand eagerly, and Sonia was quick to call on her.

"It is said that the First Reaper was revived by Riven, Bersula's son," the girl said dutifully. "During the War of Faiths, the clerics that served the church of Aubrith had burned all the churches of Bersula and hung any practising Reapers. For centuries, Reapers were executed for merely existing until King Stefan ascended the throne and claimed the Reapers as his chosen soldiers and protectors of the realm."

It was strange that Riven was so well-regarded in their myths. In the Low North, he was considered a high demon that lived in Mirathe. It was said that he had hungered for power and sought to combine the Lower World with their mortal realm. It was Saint Ylena who had subdued him, not with her blade of light, as it was foretold that no magic could truly destroy him. Instead, she had bound him beneath the chambers of the realm in an eternal slumber.

Niah felt nauseous at the girl's voice that reeked of devotion and admiration.

They truly believed that their magic was not built on the bones of the dead and the lies of their King.

"There are three principles that define our gifts. Can anybody explain the three principles and their orders?" Sonia asked.

The same girl raised her hand, and Sonia ignored her, calling on a reluctant boy who sat to Niah's left.

"The three principles are resurrection, communing, and soul-stitching," the boy said. "Death, spirit, and soul."

"Please elaborate."

"Everyone knows this," he mumbled.

"Not everyone," Sonia said. Her eyes fell on Niah.

"You mean the disgraced cleric," the boy spat. "Why is she even here? Why are we pretending like it is fine for her to sit here?"

Niah stiffened, fingers curling tight around her quill. She had been busy jotting down notes, but the words faded at his open hostility. She resisted the urge to trade insults with him.

"Would you like to share your opinions with Commander Winterson?" Mistress Sonia asked.

Silence descended in the room. The boy's fist clenched on his lap, but he didn't speak another word against her. The tension bled from Niah's shoulders. For a moment, she worried she might have to stab him with her quill.

"Answer the question, please, Viktor."

"The strongest Reapers control the threads of the Fallen," he said. "While Diviners can commune with spirits in the Lower World, and Stitchers can revive people with their souls intact, there are limits to this. Nobody outpowers a Reaper."

The Fallen was a rather apt name for their dead soldiers.

Niah's mind spun with this new information. They had known so little about their enemy. She hadn't even known other principles fell under their study. It explained why they had different colored collars—crimson, midnight blue, and raven-black.

The Commander's collar was as black as his soul. So, that must be the color of the Reapers.

"Close," Sonia said. "But not quite."

She called on another boy with spectacles and bright forest-green eyes.

"Controlling the Fallen is just one aspect of our magic. It is not the most important one," he said. "A Diviner who can speak with spirits can give valuable intel to their commanding officer. And a Stitcher is the only thing that stands between a Reaper and the Lower World."

"Excellent!" Sonia said. "It is important to understand that power does not mean you are invincible. Arrogance and posturing will get you killed out there."

Sonia demonstrated to them the act of raising the dead. On a bier lay a corpse Niah had not noticed, covered by a flimsy, white sheet. The sheet was peeled back to reveal an old man with hay-blond hair.

"To raise a Fallen, a Reaper must bind their soul to the corpse," she said. "If a Reaper dies, their Fallen dies."

That explained why, anytime they had killed a Reaper in battle, all their Fallen would collapse in a heap.

Niah watched in horror as Sonia's hands reached forward and

her fingers danced as if she were weaving a thread. There was nothing to reveal the physical nature of her magic. Unlike the Sisters, they acted their magic in secrecy. Their magic was summoned from an invisible world that she could not see. It was frightening when the dead man twitched. Niah flinched at the sight of his worn face. His moth-eaten clothes hung in tatters on his frame and his bones creaked as he shifted. The stench of rot filled the air.

And when he stared ahead at them with his blank gaze, Niah had the urge to flee. Her nails dug into the spine of her writing book. Her quill clutched so tightly in her grip she feared it would snap in half.

Sonia's eyes were black and shadowy. Like the Commander's all those years ago.

It was like she was trapped in her nightmares all over again, facing the unknown.

"We often don't raise Fallen that are this old," she said. "It is not ideal to have soldiers unfit for battle, but for the sake of teaching, you have been given access to this tomb. Tomorrow, you will all have a chance to practice."

Niah raised a hand.

"Yes, Niah."

"Why are your eyes like that?" she asked.

It was quite unnerving.

"It allows us to see the threads of their lifeline," she said.

Suddenly, the King's victories made sense; there were all these factions that they hadn't known about. Not only did he have the Reapers, but he also had other gifted necromancers that he used as his weapons of war.

It was why Commander Winterson had to die. He was their most powerful Reaper.

And Niah vowed that she would be the one to kill him.

Chapter 7

The library was a grand chamber, its sharp oak panels shimmering beneath the soft glow of sconces. Shelves stretched endlessly, sharpening into shadowed corners. The warm scent of aged parchment wrapped around Niah like a familiar embrace. It was almost as if she had stepped into the hallowed halls of the Grand Library in Caer-Sylisse.

Students clustered at worn, quill-scratched tables, chipped porcelain cups cradled in their hands, steam curling upward. Brows furrowed over thick leather tomes. There were guards situated all around the graystone walls in black uniforms. Their brass buttons were carved with the winter wolf—the sigil of the royal family—and they did not don the Reapers' robes. It was safe to assume they were the untouched who had been hired for the role.

Niah walked towards a petite elderly woman who stood behind a narrow desk. Her quill scrawled neatly in a catalogue, and the scraping sound was oddly soothing. Her head raised curiously when Niah stopped before her mahogany desk, resting her elbow on the polished surface. The glossy panels reflected Niah's sharp face.

"I was wondering if you had any books related to necromancy, that is, death magic?" Niah asked. "Also, anything related to the Sain—the Sinners and the War of Faiths."

The library was far too vast for her to navigate, and it would save her time if she could find the texts she sought as soon as possible.

"We most certainly do," she said. "Follow me."

The woman led Niah through a labyrinth of shelves and up a spiral staircase to the second floor. It was quieter up here. There were no tables or students. Just endless shelves and hidden nooks. Niah planned to hide away up here to read, tucked in one of the many sharp corners rather than downstairs where she would simply be a spectacle. She was a novelty to them.

"Are you the one they call the Lightbearer?" the Library Keeper asked.

"Yes, my name is Niah Yarrow," she said.

"Niah, lovely name," she said kindly. "I am the Library Keeper, Eliska. Have been for the last six years."

"You must have seen a lot," Niah said. "And read a lot."

Eliska wrinkled her nose. "Caught a few students with their pants down, hidden away in these shelves. Seen enough naked behinds to want to end my tenure."

Niah giggled. It was the first time in weeks that she had laughed. And the sound startled her.

"Are you a mage?" Niah asked. Much like the secretary, she wore a simple, ankle-length gray skirt that fell neatly over her leather boots and a simple, cornflower-blue blouse. Eliska snatched books from the shelves, and Niah offered to help her carry them.

"No," she said. "Besides the students and the instructors, everyone else here is untouched."

Niah nodded. That made sense.

"Ah, here is our final shelf, related to the Sinners," she said. "This section will have what you need. From their early childhood to the wars they manipulated and their ultimate demise. Ring the bell on that wall if you need any assistance."

"Thank you."

Niah waited until she left before she began perusing the shelves, piling any books of interest by her feet. Her classes had her thinking about how limited her knowledge was when it came to them. It was obvious the heretics had studied them with zeal, and Niah intended to do the same.

Niah plucked out a thick epic poem and sat down to read about the Sinners. Both faiths intercrossed like the lacings of a corset, one worshipping life and the other death.

But the stories were different, a slight variation, as if the translator had misunderstood the definition of a certain word. Different dialects were spoken in the north. Some were only distinctly different, while others felt entirely foreign.

Niah sat curled on the carpet. The rug was thick and embroidered with a pattern of swords and songbirds. Hours passed as she flipped through stiff pages, feeling the weight of the leather casing on her fingertips. A crick grew in her neck, but she refused to creep down and sit at the desks with the others.

She read until her eyes hurt, and she felt slightly dizzy.

"There you are!" Demian said. "We were worried about you."

"Speak for yourself," Kesi said, kicking her boot. "I told you she'd be here. The little ferret loves chewing on books."

"I didn't miss your insults," Niah said, yanking on her braid.

"Come on, I'm starving," Kesi said, grabbing her elbow and yanking her up. "I could eat a Reaper."

Demian's brow raised. "Good thing I am a Diviner."

Niah chuckled as they headed towards the possibility of a fresh meal.

The refectory had giant windows that faced the courtyard. Moonlight seeped in from the glass, shining a dewy light across the wooden tables. Glazed tiles were assorted beneath her feet in a flash of ruby and ivory. Niah recalled Demian telling them that this had once been an estate. She could feel the echoes of wealth in lingering things like the odd, oily blue ceramic cups the students drank their tea and coffee from, and the pastoral tapestry that hung in the library. The tinkling chandeliers above them cast an opalescent light across the room.

Demian gallantly drew out both their chairs, and Niah frowned.

"You're certain you are related to Commander Winterson?" Niah asked.

Demian chuckled. "I am."

"Anything you can tell us about him?" Kesi asked, leaning forward. "Does he have a fear of spiders? Does he wear his mask because he is a demon who escaped from Mirathe, and he looks as wretched as one? Is it true he hit his head too hard, and that is why he rarely speaks?"

"Do you ever shut up?" a deep voice drawled. "Or do you simply like the sound of your own voice?"

Niah's stomach stirred at the sound of *his* voice.

Chairs scraped as the students all stood in respect. Demian arose as was customary to do for a senior officer. Kesi slowly stood up, her mouth slack as she stared at the Commander behind her. Niah sat stubbornly, feeling strangely hot under the attention. She could feel his stare on her back and a feverish sensation spread across her neck.

"Do you need a lesson on military etiquette, Novice?" he asked coolly.

Niah ignored him. Maybe if she treated him like a ghost, he would simply vanish, but the shadow across her plate remained. And each second that she remained muted filled the room with an air of awkwardness.

Hands that felt like a winter chill fell on her shoulder, pulling her from her chair. She knew it was the Fallen who had yanked her upright. Their stench permeated her senses, sinking deep into her bones. They spun her around, forcing her to face her captor.

Her mouth parted slightly at the sight of his maskless face.

His face was arrogant and beautiful in equal measure. Pale and sharp like a whittled blade—an ornamental piece and not a tool made for destruction. His dark hair was lustrous and shiny, falling to his shoulders like rainwater along a glass window. His gaze was no less forgiving than the day they'd first met.

Niah felt a strange bitterness staring at him just then. Beauty did not belong to men, and she couldn't help but feel that it was simply another thing he had stolen. He was nothing but a thief.

"As underwhelming as I expected," she said.

Niah didn't know why he brought out this venomous side in her. Nobody had ever gotten this kind of reaction from her.

His mouth curled, a flash of meanness sparking in his eyes.

"Kneel, Novice."

"*That* is not military etiquette," she bit out.

"No, but it is an effective punishment for smart-mouthed novices who do not know their place," he said.

Niah didn't move, refusing to break under his willful stare. The room was painfully silent, like the walls of an abandoned chapel. The Commander's eyes grew dark in that way they did when the Reapers were weaving their magic. His Fallen shoved her down until she fell to her knees.

Niah tried to stand upright, but their grip grew taut under her struggles. The ribbon that held her hair came undone, the strands spooling across her face. She glared at him with a stare that could wilt the most well-tended flower in a garden.

"Was that so hard?"

Small snickers erupted from the students as they watched his cruel display. Her throat burned to spit at his feet and just when she opened her mouth to do it his fingers clasped her chin. A warning look crossed his face. Her eyes widened, surprised that he knew exactly what she intended to do.

"Don't make an enemy of me, Novice," he warned.

The blunt touch of his silver rings seeped into her flesh like an illness. His gaze was dark and roving. Slowly, he released her, vanishing out the door and taking his soldiers with him.

"Really? He just came to torment Niah?" Kesi demanded. "He didn't even eat!"

Demian sat down. A guilty look crossed his eyes. His head bowed in shame as he lifted his spoon of white rice to his mouth.

"What's his problem?" Kesi demanded, staring at Demian like he would have the answers to her questions.

He swallowed slowly, shoulders braced in unease.

"He is not used to being challenged," Demian said. "If you want my advice, do not provoke him."

"He came here and attacked me," Niah said.

"Were you really going to spit at him?" Demian asked.

"Maybe," she muttered.

He whistled under his breath.

"That's my girl," Kesi said. "Demian said it'd be worse if I attacked him. I was about to punch his smug face."

Niah smiled softly. "Of course you were."

"If you want my advice, don't goad Valek," Demian said. "He has more power than you think and more admirers than you want to know. He's a national hero in the High North."

"He's a villain where we are from," she said. "I won't appease a tyrant."

Demian was silent.

Niah sighed and reached for his hand.

"I don't blame you for his actions," she said. "In truth, you are the most bearable person here."

"Agreed," Kesi said. "You remind me of this pup that would come to the monastery looking for meat."

Demian wrinkled his nose. "Did you just compare me to a stray dog?"

"A sweet, precious stray dog," Kesi said.

"He was rather cute," Niah added.

"I'll take cute," Demian said.

His mouth pulled in a lovely smile, dimples piercing his cheek.

Niah glanced at the knife by her dinner plate and when no one was looking she slid it into her belt hook. The next time Valek came close to her she would make him regret his choices.

"What did you learn today?" Niah asked in the quiet of their bedroom.

The candlelight flickered on the windowsill, illuminating the small space and casting shadows across Kesi's face.

"That the Commander is beautiful? Who'd have thought?"

"Let me clarify. What did you learn that will assist our escape?"

"Oh." She gave a sheepish smile. "There are three gates. One at the entrance, another near the barracks, and the last behind the woods. They're patrolled daily on a strict rotation."

"How did you learn that?"

"I complimented that stick-in-the-arse girl," she said. "She's surprisingly easy to get information from. By the time I was done with her she was singing like a canary."

"Did you find their lessons odd?" Niah asked. "They think we are causing the Corruption. How absurd."

Kesi was silent. "We don't use talismans, and they do. Is that not strange? They're all covered in bones. It explains the masks."

"No," Niah said. "Their magic is unnatural, and they require aid. Ours is a gift from Aubrith. He gives us what we need—nothing more, nothing less."

Niah knew what doubt could do. It was a black hole, and if you missed your footing, you'd fall straight into the abyss.

Kesi's dark eyes drifted, glassy, her mind wandering like a buoy trapped in a wrathful sea.

Niah reached for her hand, squeezing it tight.

"Promise me you won't fall for their lies," she whispered, half afraid and half angry that they would dare to steal her best friend. "Promise me, Kesi."

"I won't, Niah," she said. "I promise."

The weight in her chest eased.

"Good."

Kesi smiled, revealing the small gap between her teeth. It did little to soothe the gnarled knot in Niah's chest.

Niah fell asleep, restless and burdened by their enemy's false words.

Niah felt an emptiness in the days that followed their arrival. Her magic was far from reach. For the first time in years, she didn't feel the warmth of its touch surrounding her fingertips, or that tingling sensation travelling up her sternum, spreading vine-like across her torso before slipping from her palms.

Now all she felt was a jarring absence—as if a limb had been hacked off. She often scratched at the dampeners on her wrists, as if sheer will might claw them off. She prayed, but the Light Father felt far away. In this wicked place, his soothing palm did not touch her frayed mind. He did not shatter her shackles or give her what she desired most—her magic.

That hollow pit in her gut widened during her class on the importance of talismans. The heretics wore bones intertwined around their frames: some coiled in their hair, others looped on necklaces of thread or silver. Silver, she realised, was a favored metal of theirs.

Some classes were faith-based and rooted deeply in theology and military study, as if the two practices were inseparable. Niah paid avid attention to the faith-based classes, not because she had any interest in their teachings, but because she wanted to learn as much as possible about their world and weaknesses.

It was said that many of the new followers of the faith believed more in Riven than Bersula, the Dark Mother. This led to the Cult of Riven, a sect mad with devotion. They were said to live in old tombs and chapels, awaiting his promised return. To speak with Riven, they offered him a soul. Innocents were slaughtered in his name—a depraved, outdated practice. A shudder ran through her at the thought.

An odd shift fell over the air as the students sat cross-legged in a circle on the ground. Nobody spoke or moved. It was like some unspoken rule. Each had a small casket before them, made of different materials—some in tortoiseshell, others gilded.

Niah peeked inside hers and saw a single finger bone.

A sharp snap of a cane struck her knuckles.

"You do not open the box without permission, Novice," a worn voice said.

Her eyes rose to an old man whose face was creased like a folded handkerchief.

"You should be careful with Master Laszlo," the boy beside her whispered once the instructor turned away. He had dark red hair and sparkling green eyes. "He's older than the Forgotten Monoliths and has just as much patience."

Niah frowned, wondering why he would risk Laszlo's wrath.

"Deaf in his right ear," the boy went on. "And a bit in his left too, so long as he doesn't see—"

Master Laszlo turned, and the boy straightened with a blinding smile.

"One more smile, boy, and I'll knock your teeth in," the old man warned. "Open your boxes. What do you see?"

Niah stared at the finger bone. This was an introduction to Divination—her second least favorite principle. From what she'd gathered, a Reaper controlled the dead, a Diviner communed with spirits, and a Stitcher tethered the living and the dead

Reapers raised the Fallen, while Stitchers could revive someone with their soul intact—necromancy in its purest form.

But there were limits. A Stitcher could only awaken a person once in their lifetime, and only within ten minutes of death before the soul was claimed by the Dark Mother. At least they couldn't raise ancient villains to fight beside them. The last thing the High North needed was another monster alongside their Commander.

"Bones are more sacred to Diviners than to any other," Laszlo said in his weathered voice. "They are our tether to the departed. A strong Diviner is accepted by the spirits and taken into their fold."

He paced the room, his cane sweeping the floor with each step, demanding obedience. But his tone was calm, thoughtful.

"Reapers believe they are the most powerful of Bersula's gifted, but a Diviner favoured by the spirits is unstoppable," he said. "Secrets can be gathered, ancestors communed with—"

Niah had gone from wary to riveted. Every word Laszlo spoke, she scribbled down furiously. She hadn't realised the lesson had ended until she looked up to find his milky eyes fixed on her shackled wrists.

Shame tightened her stomach. The shackles were a symbol of her powerlessness.

"Why must we learn these disciplines?" Niah asked bitterly. "We do not serve your deities. We do not believe in the Dark Mother or her Son."

"I've always been fascinated by how the two continents mirror each other," Laszlo said. "Aubrith, the Light Father. Bersula, the Dark Mother. And Riven, the Son. Almost as if they were once a family, before a terrible separation altered the fate of the realm."

"What do you mean?" Niah asked. His riddles grated on her.

"It is said that long ago in the Lower World, Aubrith sat beside Bersula. His hair flowed like a waterfall, his back sprouted ivory wings. They dwelled only among the dead. Aubrith grew tired of the realm. It was dark, miserable, hungry as an empty belly. He craved light and a world of love and hope. As his heart desired, the world cleaved, and the First World of mortals was born.

"It was neither pure nor wicked. Flesh could rip at the slightest prick, and blood dripped like tears. A mirror of Bersula's darkness and Aubrith's light. Then the holy war began. Bersula, enraged by his abandonment, claimed Aubrith's mortals as her own, gifting them death magic. In return, Aubrith blessed a rare few and named them his Saints."

"I have never heard that tale," Niah said, squinting at him.

"Nobody wants to accept that we were once one," he mused. "Your Saints are our Sinners. Our truth is your lie—and vice versa. It makes one wonder…"

"Wonder what?"

Laszlo smiled, yellowed teeth glinting like amber.

"Which story is true?"

Chapter 8

The stained-glass window spilled fractured streaks of silvery moonlight across the pages of Niah's book. She had discovered a small, intimate corner in the belly of the library. The desk was small and round, its weak third leg tipping the surface just enough to make each page a subtle challenge. A frustrated groan escaped her as her bottle of ink crashed to the floor, leaving behind a ruby-red stain that resembled a gash on a throat, reminding her of the carnage that day at the monastery. Niah ignored the mess, determined to deal with it after she finished reading her book on the evolution of death magic, the gilt-threaded spine bruising her fingertips.

It was almost midnight, and she had missed dinner to read the volumes before her. Something about what Kesi had said about the talisman had stuck with her. It was odd that the Saints used talismans as well. There was the radiant sword called the *Lightbearer* that Saint Ylena possessed, which had coined the namesake of their promised savior, the golden chalice that always had one's desires appear that belonged to Saint Carywen, the lyre that could strike love in the most disbelieving souls that Saint Elirien carried. Their miracles had always revolved around their sacred objects.

Niah's favorite stories had been the miracles of Saint Elirien.

As a young, wide-eyed girl, she had swooned when she heard that a pair of forbidden lovers had sought the Saint under a Hawthorn tree. The girl had been a nobleman's daughter, and the boy a wandering musician with nothing but his lacquered violin to his name.

They had knelt before the roots in desperation as the boy sang a prayer to Elirien, asking her to change his fortunes. The despairing lovers slept beneath the tree that night, and the next morning awoke to a pocketful of gleaming gold coins nestled in the wildflowers, as if the tree had wept riches instead of dry leaves. And it is said, even now, that if two hearts kneel beneath a hawthorn in bloom and speak not with words but with truth, Elirien may hear and answer.

Niah had a deep-seated need to learn the truth. She wanted to use their own resources to crumble the foundation of their logic. It brought a cold smile to her face, thinking about the horror and despair they would feel when she proved them to be the cursed ones.

A chair scraped along the wooden floorboards, rattling her senses. Her head shot up in time to see him sit in the chair across from her. Niah straightened, eyes narrowing, blood thinning to ice.

"You can't sit there," she said coldly.

His dark, luminous eyes stared at her with an equal measure of distaste. Niah studied him closer than she had the other night. His ears were lined with silver rings. It was Northern tradition to adorn oneself with silver, as it was for the South to drape themselves in gold. It was also a common trait for Northern men to look just as beautiful as their women, and Niah hated that he conformed to those conventional ideas.

"I said you can't sit there," she repeated. Her lips thinned into a slash.

"I heard you perfectly well the first time," he said, lacing his fingers together. "As did the entire library. That shrill voice of yours could raise the dead."

"My voice is not shrill," she said.

"You missed my class," the Commander said. "Were you itching for a punishment so soon? I would have thought that humiliating dinner ordeal would straighten you up."

"I didn't miss your class," Niah said. "I changed it."

Niah had spent her lunch break in the main office, pleading with the secretary to change her combat class. Kesi was in the morning group and said there weren't many students in that one. The students who came from important families were slotted into the class Commander Winterson taught. It was the only lesson he taught, from what she'd heard.

The secretary had been kind enough to have her transferred.

"May I see?" he asked calmly.

Niah smiled smugly as she passed him her schedule. Slowly, he perused the sheet before he cut the paper in half. The slash echoed in the chamber and her lips dropped into a frown.

"What are yo—"

"You don't get to transfer out of my class without my permission," he said.

He continued to slice the torn sheets to ribbons, letting them flutter on the desk like snowfall.

"I won't attend your class," she said, folding her arms across her chest. "My schedule was updated, and nothing you say or do will change that."

He leaned forward, an infuriating smirk tugging at his lips.

"Shall we see about that?"

His dark eyes were locked on hers, gleaming with challenge.

Niah began to stack her books, prepared to leave. She wouldn't indulge him in his silly games. The office would provide her with a new schedule identical to the one he tore. This changed nothing.

Valek Winterson had no power over her.

He arrogantly plucked the book from her fingers. His dark hair fell into his eyes, and the iron rings in his ears twinkled as he turned to see the title.

"A History of the Fall of the Saints," he read aloud.

He tossed the book aside, and she flinched as the spine cracked ominously against the wall. What kind of monster injured a book for no apparent reason? There was something utterly twisted about him. It took everything in her not to race after the book and check for damages.

"If you had questions, you could have come directly to me," he said. "Not drown yourself in this garbage written by the untouched. They don't understand us, and they never will."

"There is no us," Niah said, lips curled in disgust. "And there never will be. You Reapers are spreading rot and death everywhere you go. I am nothing like you."

"As much as it sickens me to say this, we are more alike than you think, little saint," he said. "As vastly different as our gifts may seem, once trained, you will see what I see."

"Don't call me that," she said between clenched teeth.

"What shall I call you then?"

"Nothing," she said. "Do not address me at all, and I will do the same."

"How about…" He rubbed his chin, as if he were thinking long and hard. "No."

Her fist curled beside her, and she resisted the urge to knock out his perfectly straight teeth. It was a shame that the war had left him so unblemished. He hadn't suffered yet for all the atrocities he had committed, and Niah promised herself that she would see his downfall one day.

"We have the same goal," he continued. And then his voice dropped an octave, slipping into a light whisper. "We want to save the world."

Her stomach churned at his words.

"You are a Raskovian lord," she snarled. "You are the King's whore."

His face tightened, and she realized—perhaps belatedly—that she should not have goaded someone who held her life in the palm of his hand. But it was easier to be angry than to be wise, so she did not mince her words when she next spoke.

"What would you know about fighting for your beliefs?" Niah demanded.

"You are rather quick to point fingers," Valek said. His mouth had thinned to a tight line. "It was you conduits who siphoned from the earth and destroyed the woods and creatures. Everything is diseased and spoiled because of you. You must be stopped."

"Do not make yourself seem so noble," she sneered. "This is not about the Corruption. It is what it has always been about. Power."

Men grew thick on the flesh of weaker men. It was how the world had always worked.

Valek's face was an impenetrable mask. Staring into his eyes was like looking into an abyss, harrowing and frightening. And with each second that passed, she fell deeper into a trance.

"Were your hours of research useful?" he asked, swiftly changing the subject. "What have you learned?"

"As if I will share my findings with you," she said.

She had found nothing of substance. Threads of folktales and myths had intertwined into a vine of lyrical nonsense. She could not, for the life of her, figure out what they claimed the conduits were and how this differed from the teachings of the Order and their death magic.

"A conduit is, as the name says," Valek said, slowly as if he were explaining a dense subject to a child. "They can siphon their magic from anywhere—the earth, a talisman, another mage. To a Reaper, a conduit is a valuable asset. There was a time when most Reapers had a conduit bound to them. The relationship was similar to one between a craftsman and their apprentice."

Niah shuddered at his words.

"What do you mean?"

"You felt it that day we first met," he said. "Unimaginable power when we touched."

His fingers floated above hers, and Niah drew her hands onto her lap.

"I am a mage who follows the path of the light," she hissed. "I shall not slip into the mouth of darkness and be consumed."

"What if it is all a lie?" he asked, tilting his head. Dark eyes stared at her curiously. "What if there is no light and darkness? What if there is simply magic?"

"Your magic," she said with a sniff of her nose. "Because mine is apparently wrong."

"Exactly," Valek said, ignoring her sarcasm. "Give me your hand."

"No."

Footsteps thudded, soft against the carpet. Her eyebrows rose at the sight of his Fallen; their skin had an unearthly sheen to it—blue and translucent like a gossamer veil. Uncanny eyes trailed over her with brute interest.

Niah thought about fighting him. She did not want to feel that tether between them, the flow of magic that was both dangerous and arresting. She did not want to accept this path before her, but she didn't know how to resist it. Not when he outpowered her. Not when his soldiers were poised to attack.

Valek's eyes were a shell of darkness. His voice sharpened. "Do as I say, Novice."

Niah stared at his pallid hand and long fingers. Strong and beckoning. His nails were painted black, the ends slightly chipped. He wore several iron rings, and one of his smallest fingers looked like a bone had coiled around his flesh to make a ring.

After what felt like a long enough pause that was toeing the line of disrespect, she caught his hand before his mouth opened to direct his soldiers.

Niah felt that familiar charge of magic, and her fingers tingled in awareness. A heady sensation fell over her, and she watched those black tendrils lock around their conjoined palms like rope. Valek's lips parted in surprise. It could not be real. It had to be a figment of their shared imagination. Because their death magic wasn't tangible. Yet those cords of darkness were visible. The air grew charged with their combined magic. It smelled like death.

Niah realized that she was close to him; she didn't know when she had stood up and come to stand before him like a maiden brought forth for a dark sacrifice to some corrupt deity. She could count every strand of his spidery lashes and the faint echo of stubble that graced his jaw.

Valek slowly released her, breaking her from the spell. The headiness that had filled her began to slowly trickle away. That twine of magic between them had been decadent. It was a sensation unlike any other she had ever experienced. And that frightened her.

"Feels good, doesn't it?" Valek asked, leaning back in his chair like a king.

She could sense the corpses waiting in the woods. All of the ones Valek had risen. It was like she was tethered to them. There had to have been hundreds just lying dormant in the woods. And she knew there were two of them just a few feet away. It was said that most Reapers could only control ten of the Fallen. That the Commander was an anomaly—a chosen of the Dark Mother. He could wield a hundred Fallen without breaking a sweat.

Students with permission from the headmistress could bring their corpses with them on the grounds, but only a maximum of two, while the soldiers were to leave them stationed in the woods. It was why they were expressly forbidden from entering the woods filled with the tall, black pine trees.

She felt connected to the Fallen in a way that disturbed her. There was far more in his hoard than the dozen that had travelled with them. She realized that he kept an army just waiting for his command. It would be difficult to escape knowing that information.

She wondered if she could turn them against Valek. Even if it went against everything she believed in, she wondered if she could use this malevolent gift to escape with Kesi.

"You can't use them against me," Valek said.

Her head snapped towards him, surprised that he had picked up on the direction of her thoughts. Niah had to do a better job of masking her face.

His mouth was slightly tilted as if he found her murderous attempt amusing, like a child playing with a wooden sword.

"They are mine," he said.

"How does this work?" she asked, pointing between them both. "I still do not understand."

"Conduits are special for many reasons," he said. "You are stronger than any talisman. We can draw on each other to strengthen our gifts tenfold. It is a beneficial relationship."

A shudder slid down her back. He stood up, staring down at her beneath his aristocratic nose.

"You have a future ahead of you," he said. "It would be wise to embrace it rather than to fight me at every turn. You don't want to make an enemy of me."

"Too late," Niah said.

His mouth raised in a cruel smile.

"I will enjoy breaking your spirit," he said.

"Likewise."

Valek's eyes gleamed like he was looking forward to it. He brushed past her, taking his dreadful creatures with him.

Niah collapsed in his abandoned chair while her heart galloped like a frightened horse. If Valek thought he could control her so easily he was mistaken.

Chapter 9

The refectory stretched with long, scarred wooden tables, crowded with the hunched backs of chattering students. In the far corner, a squat elm-wood table bore their meagre offerings, like trinkets gathered for the Saints: mounds of pallid rice, a choice of beef or chicken gone gray at the edges, and a jade-green tureen of soup whose steam carried the sharp scent of onion.

Niah could make out Kesi's charcoal-dark hair, knitted in delicate braids that fell across her spine like a hymn. Demian leaned forward, regaling her with a story, fingers flying as he described the scene. Between the both of them, Niah didn't have to do much talking and could sit back and listen. She'd never been the chatty sort. Kesi had always been the more charming one.

Sometimes the instructors dined with them. Rarely did they see Headmistress Greymont grace them with her presence, even though a dais was set up in case she decided to join them. Niah drew out her chair and sat with her friends.

"You don't think he'll retaliate?" Kesi asked her. "I mean, I love that you're in my training class now, but was it a good idea, Niah? Should you be goading our captor?"

"I'm not switching back," Niah said, folding her arms across her chest.

It did not matter to her that her schedule had been ripped to pieces. Niah had a good memory and would not risk having a new copy written up at the office in response to the Commander's request.

"I admire your stubbornness, but I don't think he will feel the same way."

Niah shrugged. "I am not afraid of him."

"Demian, why do they want conduits for this war?" Niah asked, staring at his brown eyes.

His brows widened in alarm.

"Um... I'm not—"

Kesi held her fork to his throat, using it to tilt his chin.

"Come on, Demian," she purred. "We're all friends."

Niah smiled widely, nodding. "Yes, we are."

"I can't tell if you are threatening me or flirting with me," Demian said.

"Both," Kesi said. "Now answer our question."

"I think the end goal is to have our highest Reapers bound to a conduit," he said. "I'm talking commanders and lieutenants, not mere foot soldiers. As you know, there are limits to how many Fallen a Reaper can control, but with a conduit, the army would be untouchable."

"What does it mean to be bound?"

"If you do a power exchange often with a Reaper, you can forge an unbreakable connection," Demian said. "A bond."

Niah stilled, thinking back to Valek's hand. They had done it three times now. Her stomach tightened in fear at the thought that she may have inadvertently solidified this bond. A cold sweat broke out on her neck at the implications of this dark gift.

"I have to go," Niah said.

She had to return to the library before it closed in a few hours. Niah had to learn more about this bonding process and if there was time to undo it. She could not risk tying her life to a Reaper—especially one as vile and cruel as Valek Winterson.

Demian's mouth grew tight with regret. He wouldn't divulge any more than he already had.

Just as Niah slid out of her seat, the doors were drawn open, revealing the Commander. His dark, windswept hair curled around the sides of his face and fell in unruly strands over his brow.

His eyes sliced towards her, icy and barren.

Niah knew what this was about. She had missed his class, intentionally. It was clear he wasn't pleased that she had disobeyed him again. But she wasn't thrilled either; he had been forcing her to do a power exchange to solidify some perverse bond with her—one she did not understand and one he intended to use to enhance his gifts and ruin innocent lives.

There was a boy to his left, one with warm brown skin and chestnut-brown eyes, and to his right was a girl with dark hair layered in bones that twined in her long locks. On her chest lay a necklace with a thin, gnarled bone that looked like a broken rib. She stood close to Valek, shoulders grazing his elbow. He towered over her as he did everyone.

The room grew eerily silent and the students visibly recoiled at his presence.

"This can't be good," Demian muttered.

Niah stood upright, prepared to leave. It was cowardly to sit back down. So, she slung her leather bag across her shoulder and began to walk to the doorway. A shadow crossed the carpet, darkening the fabric, and she bumped into him.

Niah glared at him for intercepting her path.

"What do you want?" she asked stiffly. "I tire of these games."

"You skipped my class today," he said. "After I expressly warned you not to."

"I told you I transferred."

Niah brushed past him. His hand coiled around her elbow.

"Easy, Novice," he breathed.

"Release me," she said through gritted teeth.

"She's feisty," the boy beside him said.

His accent was impossible to miss. He was from the Low North—she could tell by the way his mouth shaped the vowels. He had the Tereni dialect. His neck was also wrapped in tattoos that hinted at his lineage, a common Tereni tradition. Niah's eyes slipped to his wrist, but she didn't catch sight of dampeners, which meant he wasn't a prisoner. Disappointment slipped down her throat like scalding tea. He was not here against his will.

"You got something to say, Novice?" the boy asked darkly.

"She's a judgmental one, Laith," Valek said. "Looks down her little nose at all of us."

"Maybe we should teach her a lesson," the Tereni boy, Laith, said. Something sinister flickered in his eyes.

Niah's jaw tightened. She'd tucked one of the dinner knives in her belt hook for instances like this. Her fingers fluttered to her side, waiting for them to make a move before she gutted them. Valek's quick eyes saw her hand stray.

"What do you have there, Novice?" he purred.

Niah didn't find the need to hide it anymore; she brandished her knife at his throat. The tip dug into his skin, and gasps sounded behind her. Maybe she should not have attacked him in front of all these witnesses, but this entire ordeal was bound to turn ugly. Chairs scraped behind her as students arose in shock.

His friends had the same cruelty in their eyes as he did. Even the girl watched them with cold amusement.

Footsteps sounded, and she felt Kesi behind her, clasping her hand. Demian stopped beside her.

"Valek—" Demian began.

"Commander Winterson," Valek barked. "You will address me properly, Novice."

Demian didn't seem startled by his harsh tone.

"Commander Winterson, Niah meant no offence," he said.

"Taking in strays, Demian?" Valek said with a click of his

tongue. "I don't think your father would approve of your actions."

"And I'm sure yours would approve of yours," Demian said. His tone was bitter. Something passed between them—charged and frigid.

"It's fine, Demian," Niah said softly. "I can fight my own battles."

Niah felt an inkling of guilt for dragging Demian into her ordeal. It was not fair to him or Kesi. She was the one challenging the Commander. Her blade was still pointed at him. His throat pressed against the metal with each word he spoke.

He caught her wrist, and before she could react, spun her around and pressed her blade to her throat in the span of several seconds. Her cheeks burned at how quickly he had disarmed her.

"Let her go!" Kesi said, lunging at Valek.

Laith grabbed her with a harsh laugh and wrapped his hand around Kesi's mouth, smothering her screams.

"Bite my hand and I'll snap your throat," he warned her.

"Let us go," Niah said. Her entire body shook with rage. It was one thing to attack her, and an entirely different thing to hurt Kesi. She would not stand for it.

"Let us speak in private," Valek said. "Or would you prefer to hash out our problems in front of your peers?"

"Fine," Niah said tightly. "Lead the way."

Slowly, his hand dropped, and he tossed her blade on the closest table. Niah gave Kesi an assuring glance. Laith had released her mouth, but he kept a tight grip on her elbow. Demian stood by helplessly, offering her a smile that lacked confidence.

"Do you enjoy ruining my dinner every night?" Niah demanded the second the door slid shut behind them.

"I could ask you the exact same thing," Valek snapped.

They glared at each other for one long, blistering second.

"Your room will be reassigned," he said. "Say goodbye to your friend tonight."

Dread filled her at the threat. She would not survive the absence of Kesi.

"No!"

Valek stared at her pointedly.

"Fine," she said, between clenched teeth. "I'll join your class."

"Perfect," he said. "Was that so hard?"

"I hate you."

"I wouldn't have it any other way," Valek said.

He brushed past her.

"Oh, and if you're late, Novice, you will regret it," he called over his shoulder.

Niah glared at him, hoping the venom of her stare burned a hole in his back.

Niah was late.

Her previous class was in the west wing, and she refused to run to his class. If she arrived huffing and puffing, he would know that he frightened her and that she had taken his threat seriously. And she would not give him the satisfaction. She could almost picture his smug smile and the thought made her shudder.

Everyone sat in a wide circle, and standing in the middle was Valek with his arms folded across his chest. He didn't say a word as she found an empty spot and sat cross-legged beside the other novices. Everyone had hung their robes on the nearby trees, and belatedly, Niah realized she had not done the same.

It seemed like everyone was holding their breath as she removed her robe in her spot, revealing her trousers and tunic. Valek did not resume his speech. He just stood there, staring at her with his impenetrable gaze. Her cheeks burned at the unbearable silence and the students mocking gazes.

"I need a volunteer for a demonstration," Valek said. "Any takers?"

Everyone was silent. Some people seemed to be reciting a prayer and refusing to make eye contact.

"How about you, Novice?" Valek said, glancing directly at her.

Niah debated the merits of playing dumb. His left eye twitched, a silent promise that she would regret it if she didn't accept.

Niah stood up, dread creeping up her spine. The air caressed her skin with its glacial touch, and the man before her did nothing to soothe the chill. If anything, he made it worse.

"The round is simple—lay your opponent flat on their back," Valek said. "Fail to do so, and you'll be punished."

"Punished how?" Niah asked.

Everyone's eyes widened as they glanced at Valek as if he would erupt in violence at her simple question.

"Perhaps I'll have you stripped and hung from that tree for the wild animals to feast on tonight," Valek said.

"Why must my clothes be removed for that?" Niah asked. "Sounds like a personal preference."

"Are you implying that I desire to see you naked, Novice?" Valek snapped.

"You are the one who threatened to strip me."

"I said I would have you stripped, not that I would partake in the action."

"It is odd that you would mention it at all," Niah said. "I knew you were a perverse man from the moment we met."

A vein ticked in his jaw, and Niah couldn't properly enjoy angering him before he dismissed her.

"Take a seat, Novice."

"I thought—"

"I would prefer someone more capable," he said sharply. "Not a little child."

Snickers arose, and her cheeks burned as she returned to her spot.

Valek picked another boy, whom he had laid flat on his back in less than twenty seconds. He paired everyone up, and Niah found herself against a girl taller and stronger than her. The girl's eyes were filled with determination, and Valek had barely finished his signaling whistle before she lunged. Niah evaded her fists.

Her combat skills were subpar at best. It was unnatural to fight without her magic to fall back on. Her fingers itched to summon her light, but it remained far from her reach.

The girl attacked while Niah took a primarily defensive role. For every pivot forward, she took one back. She was inches away from tucking tail and running—except that would prove Valek's point that she was no better than a little child.

A punch landed on her torso, and she felt the breath knocked out of her lungs. Before she could recover, her knees were kicked out, and she fell forward, wet twigs scraping her palms. Pain shot up her legs, and she winced.

The girl had won.

They did three more rounds, rotating partners, and each time Niah was left eating dirt. Anger weighed heavy on her tongue, and it took everything in her not to lash out at Valek, who watched with sheer amusement each time she lost. It made her want to fight harder, to prove to him that she could not be broken.

"Only one novice managed to lose every single round," Valek said. "Any guesses as to who that may be?"

"The traitor," a boy spat.

A chorus of agreement rang out at his call.

"Yes, the traitor," Valek said in agreement. "It is a wonder the Low North's army is still standing with such soldiers leading their charge. And this one is their supposed Lightbearer. A Saint reborn. But do you know what I see when I look at her?"

He cut her off before she could insult him.

"I see a pathetic little girl," Valek said.

"Remove these shackles and I'll show you what it feels like to burn," Niah snarled.

"If only her footwork were half as strong as her tongue," Valek said. "We would have a half-decent soldier."

Everything Valek said made the novices laugh, and she hated that he made her the target of their ridicule.

"You are all dismissed."

Niah was the first to vanish from the training yard. Her fists stuck tight by her sides.

One day, *she* would be the one laughing at *his* misery.

Chapter 10

Niah was heading towards the chapel to attend the scheduled night prayer when she caught sight of two figures cast in shadows. Behind an ivy-laced pillar stood Demian, his dark hair flapping in the breeze like the wings of a bat. Across from him, decked in ceremonial robes that folded around him like a shroud, was the Commander. His lips were drawn in that familiar, brutish line, and his unyielding eyes were locked onto his cousin.

A frown crossed Niah's lips. She had been under the impression that they could not stand each other. Slowly, she headed in their direction, pressing herself to the rugged trunk of the closest birch tree, using the thick foliage to conceal her frame. If Demian was spying on them to report back to Valek, it was best to confirm it now rather than later.

Niah was close enough to hear their low voices. Her fingers dug into the soft bark; her rushed breath escaping in wisps of fog.

"You need to stay away from those girls, Demian," Valek said. "They cannot be trusted."

"Everyone is treating them like they don't belong here," Demian said. "It isn't fair."

"Because they don't belong here. They are war prisoners," Valek said. "You know what that is, right?"

"Why do you hate her so much?" Demian asked.

"I barely acknowledge her."

"Not Kesi—I mean Niah. It's like you purposely go out of your way to antagonize her," he said. "You never came to the dining hall before, but now you cannot resist gracing us with your presence."

"You are dismissed, Novice," Valek said.

"Stop that. You can't always pull the rank card when you want to evade my questions," Demian said.

"I think being the Commander of the King's army means that I can."

Demian sighed. "I miss the old Valek. The one before the war who drank like a sailor and who knew how to smile."

"It does you no good to dwell on the past, cousin," Valek said, before he spun on his polished boots and vanished under the archway.

Niah was relieved that Demian was not conspiring with Valek. It didn't seem like they were very close, which was understandable. Demian was kind, and Valek was a beast.

Niah found a seat at the back of the chapel, a sense of dread clinging to her the moment she entered the nave. Her feet dragged unwillingly across the flagstone. Attendance at prayers was, unfortunately, mandatory.

Kesi collapsed beside her minutes later.

"Damn these nightly prayers," she cursed. "Why must we attend when we don't even follow their faith?"

"Another tool in their arsenal to break us," Niah whispered.

There were two prayer halls: the Church of Bersula and the Chapel of Riven. Unlike the grandiose statue of Bersula constructed in the main building, the Chapel of Riven held only a grand icon hung on the wall by iron nails. Void-like midnight eyes and dark hair stared at her from the gold-trimmed frame, with a plaque beneath it that read: *Riven, the Son of Death.*

Niah had never seen his image before, but he bore an uncanny resemblance to Valek. On the dais sat a golden coffin covered in blood-red rubies that winked like the eyes of an owl. Gauzy light spilled from the ornate chandelier, its bulbs twinkling like stars.

It was sealed shut, and a shudder ran through her at the thought of what lay inside. Her mouth tightened at the pure blasphemy of it all.

Sitting in the first row were the headmistress, Valek, and two other instructors.

"I hate this," Niah whispered.

"It won't be long," Demian said, sliding in beside her.

"Why does your deity look like your cousin?" Niah asked. "Did the vain bastard put his own portrait up?"

"Ha!" Demian chortled. "I suppose Valek would do such a thing."

"He does look like him," Kesi said. "Pretty as a peach."

Niah elbowed her, and Kesi stuck her tongue out.

"Stop complimenting him," Niah hissed.

"Stop pretending like he's ugly," Kesi retorted. "His insides are rotten, but not his outside."

Niah shook her head, lips tilting in amusement. As disturbing as Kesi's words were, Niah could not picture any person better than her to be stuck with.

"You are hopeless."

"And you are stubborn!"

"Girls," Demian hissed. "People are looking."

True to his words, students had turned their heads. Their glares were so potent it was a wonder the three of them didn't burn to ashes. Niah ignored them; it didn't matter what they did. Ever since they arrived, they had been met with suspicion and spitefulness.

"Some people say he is Riven reincarnated," Demian whispered.

Niah followed his gaze to Valek, swallowing back the urge to scoff. Of course, they believed the heretic was divine. Even from the back, she could see how they stared at their war hero with admiration and even desire. Men and women alike gazed at him like he was the answer to their prayers.

The pastor stood at the lectern and began a long sermon about the importance of magic and the Reapers. It was strange to see them twine faith and war into a single strand, as if their assault on the innocent were spiritual.

"It is the decree of Riven that we follow, to cleanse the earth of those who spread the blight—as it was his mother's before him. Peace shall not reign so long as the impious live. They call their savior the Lightbearer. But our great Commander brought this false prophetess to us to teach her the truth. To open her blind eyes—"

Niah's teeth clenched. This sermon was about her. The students turned to face her, staring at her with poisonous eyes.

He spent the next twenty minutes disgracing her name and exalting Valek's. The bastard must have been so smug.

The moment they were dismissed, she quickly slipped out the doors, a sigh escaping her lips. Finally, that torture had concluded.

"Wait," Demian said before she and Kesi could head towards their quarters.

He bent his head down to whisper.

"Usually, during the first week back, there is a small gathering held in the Old Chapel in the woods," Demian said. "Meet me in the Commons and I'll take you there."

"I don't feel like spending my precious sleep hours socializing with the enemy," Kesi said, crossing her arms.

"We'll be there," Niah said.

Kesi shot her a surprised look. It would do them no good to keep to themselves. They needed to start familiarizing themselves with their captors, learning their ways and the intricacies of their schemes. It would be valuable intel to share once they escaped and returned home.

"Will we have trouble with the guards?" Niah asked.

They always had eyes on them. Even now, three guards paced not far away, keeping watch.

"I'll distract them," Demian said with a cheeky smile.

Niah's eyes narrowed, doubting his promise, but if it gave them the chance to learn about the enemy, then it was not one she could pass up.

"So, what is the plan?" Kesi asked, combing Niah's hair, removing the tangles until it fell in a limp line. "Charm them?"

Kesi styling her hair reminded her of their days at the monastery. Her chest warmed at the thought. Even in this foreign place, there was a small shard of home for her to carry around in the form of Kesi's friendship.

"Something like that," Niah mumbled.

"You don't even know how to flirt."

"I do!" Niah said.

Kesi gave her a pointed stare.

"Fine, I don't," she muttered. "That is why I will try to befriend the girls while you entertain the boys."

"I found out some information on Valek's little friends," she said.

"Did you?"

Kesi nodded. "One of the King's lieutenants adopted the Tereni boy, Laith Greymont, after the battle, and his mother happens to be the headmistress. He is a traitor who grew up at court and willingly serves King Stefan."

"That is unfortunate," Niah said. "He could have been a powerful ally."

"Tell me about it," she said.

"And the girl?" Niah asked.

"Her name is Daria, that's all I know," she said. "And she comes from one of their noble families."

Niah and Kesi donned their robes and crept down the stairs to the Commons. Demian's teeth shone in the dark as he led them outside. As promised, he had gotten rid of the guards. For a moment, she wondered if they should take their chances with Demian and make a run for it. They likely wouldn't make it past the gate, but Niah couldn't help but imagine their eventual escape. Each day she remained with the enemy was another day she danced with danger. There would come a time when they would make her draw on their dark magic and force her into submission. The longer they stayed, the more she risked strengthening this mysterious bond with Valek.

Demian led them through the woods. Thin icicles hung from the trees like dangling earrings. The Old Chapel was a small, ruined building. Its walls were battered like a broken nose, and its windows were missing, giving them a glimpse of the people who mingled inside. There were no more than twenty students. All of them looked older than they were and were likely in their final year. The training at Silverwood Hall lasted two years, usually. But Niah and Kesi were to only train for a few months before they were thrown into the war. It didn't matter to their captors if they were ill-prepared or died on the battlefield.

Their gazes shifted towards them, almost birdlike with scrutiny.

Demian guided them forward, shielding them from the hostility, as he led them to the altar, where a table held jugs of wine.

"Ignore them," Demian said.

"It is like nobody has ever seen a pair of beautiful girls before," Kesi said with a roll of her eyes.

Niah stiffened at the sight of Laith sitting on a waterlogged bench with Daria. Her mouth was straightened into a grim line, while pure hatred dripped from Laith's eyes. She hadn't expected to see them here. They weren't students—they were part of Valek's squadron.

"Do you want to find a corner to sit while I bring the drinks?" Demian asked.

"What are Valek's dogs doing here?" Kesi asked.

"Spying for him, I reckon," Niah said.

"It is not a crime to have fun," Demian said, before vanishing into the flood of bodies.

Niah had turned her back to them, but she could feel their ill will crawling along her skin like insects.

"Let's go around and make conversation with people."

"Good luck," Kesi said, before she marched over to a handsome boy with shorn hair and a wicked smile.

Niah went to a girl sitting alone by a broken window, but the moment she was close, the girl scurried off. Niah frowned and switched direction to a pair of girls whispering in the corner, but the second they locked eyes, they turned and fluttered away like leaves in the wind.

"Nobody wants to speak to you."

Niah knew that cold, sharp voice. Fortunately, it did not belong to Valek, but unfortunately, it belonged to Laith, whom she disliked almost as much. Slowly, she turned to face him.

"Then why are you here speaking to me?" Niah asked.

"To tell you to leave before I have you dragged out," Laith said.

"May I ask you something?"

"No," he snapped.

"When did you decide to bend over for the enemy, and does it feel good to—"

His hand wrapped around her throat, tight and snug across her flesh.

"Finish that sentence, I dare you."

"Laith," a smooth voice whispered. Daria had her hand on his shoulder. "Valek does not want her dead *yet*."

Her lips pulled upward in a menacing smile.

"Yet? How optimistic," Niah drawled.

"I don't think she needs her tongue to be useful," he spat.

"Instead of bodily harm, perhaps you can think of another creative way to teach her a lesson," Daria suggested.

She and Laith exchanged a look that made Niah uneasy. It reeked of malice. His hand dropped from her throat, and he took a step back. Niah reached for the dagger strapped to her hip, prepared to attack if needed. This one she had stolen from the indoor training hall. It was far better than those kitchen knives she had been carrying.

Laith smirked at her dagger as if she wielded a wooden sword rather than a sharp blade.

Niah was furious that she could not call on her magic. If she dug deep, she could feel that vile thread of power she'd grasped when Valek forced their bond, but she refused to turn to the dark.

Laith raised his hand, and something wispy and smoky shot from his fingers. Before she could react, her limbs seized. Her eyes widened in horror as her blade rose to her own throat.

She didn't know what he had done, but she could not control her body. A bead of sweat trickled down her forehead. She tried to call for help, but her mouth would not move. It was like a pair of icy fingers had wrapped around her mind. As if she were a puppet upheld by invisible strings.

From the window, she could see Kesi, lost in conversation, and Demian was gone. Fear gripped her tightly, and she tried not to show it, but from Laith and Daria's matching grins, they could sense it.

"A powerful Diviner does not just speak to spirits. They also control them," Laith said. "We can use them to possess our enemies. Force them to hurt themselves. Force them to enact our will. Reapers are masters of the dead, but we are the masters of the living."

How had they never received intel about this? All they had known was about the cursed Reapers. The question must have shown on her face, because Laith went on.

"We aren't used on the battlefield much," Laith said. "Our gift works on one person at a time and is not effective for large-scale war. But we are useful when it comes to torturing our war prisoners... like you."

Niah couldn't speak. Her tongue refused to move. Everyone was watching them with eager eyes. Some were laughing into their palms.

"You are spirit-bound to answer my questions," Laith said. "Let us start with an easy one. Why did you come here tonight?"

Niah tried to swallow the truth that burned her throat, but she couldn't. It was as if her mind was locked by shackles that she could not break.

"To spy."

Gasps rippled through the room. By tomorrow morning, she would be despised far more than she already was.

"How utterly predictable," Laith said. "Why out of all the conduits did they pick you to come here? Why were you not killed?"

Niah couldn't speak of her strange encounter with Valek all those years ago. So, she spoke another truth. His magic demanded her honesty, but Niah realized she could pick *which* truth to speak.

"I am the Lightbearer," she said. "The prophesied hero who will rid the world of you infidels."

Her last word was spoken with disgust. Laith seemed pleased. It dawned on her that this ordeal was not to humiliate her but to isolate her. To ensure she never showed her face again at their drunken affairs. To prove she could not be trusted.

The door opened, and she saw Demian and Kesi with Valek. He wasn't in uniform, his hair boyishly mussed. Had Demian awoken him? To save her? As if Valek would intervene on her behalf. He had probably come to witness her shame.

"Valek, perfect timing," Laith said with a grin. "We were just getting to know our newest novice."

"Is that so?" Valek asked. His voice was sleep-drenched, warm and honeyed.

"I just thought of an excellent question!" Laith said, his

mouth twisting in a smirk. "Who is the most beautiful man in the room?"

"Valek," Demian whispered. "Stop him."

Valek tilted his head, studying her.

"Beg me," he mouthed.

Niah's lips tightened. She refused to ask him to save her. From his devouring gaze, she knew that he desired her submission. He would enjoy nothing more than for her to humble herself before him. Somehow, she knew that he would put an end to it if she asked for it. But Niah could not bring herself to do so.

"I don't think she needs my help," Valek said, eyes darkening with disappointment.

"If you won't do anything, I will," Kesi said. She stepped forward, but one of Valek's Fallen gripped her arms. Niah hadn't even noticed the five of them standing behind him.

"Answer my question," Laith said.

Niah fought the invisible shackles. She bit her tongue, hard, to stop the words, but it did not work. Her eyes lifted to Valek, burning with shame.

"Him."

An unreadable expression crossed his eyes.

"How fascinating," Laith drawled. "What do you think, Valek?"

"I think she is pathetic," Daria said. She had drawn closer to Valek, looking at him with adoration and then back to Niah with even more resentment than before.

"Should we find out how badly she wants Commander Winterson?" Laith asked. "Would you kiss him if he weren't a big, bad Reaper?"

Shame burned her gut. None of this was real. None of this was her. Imagining Valek as anything less than a Reaper was ludicrous. He was not a man; he was a monster.

Valek took an abrupt step forward, prying her chin back. Her mouth was sealed so tight that she had cut her tongue, and blood trickled from her lips.

"Don't hurt yourself, Novice," he warned darkly.

"She is defensive, isn't she?" Laith asked. "Must like you more than she lets on."

"This is wrong," Demian said. "You need to stop this, Valek."

"She can fight her own battles," Valek said. "Isn't that right, Novice?"

Niah stayed silent. Laith's questions bound her, but Valek's taunts did not. Better to deal with Laith than to give Valek anything.

"Ask me to save you of your own free will and I will have you released," Valek continued. "It is a fair offer."

"No," she snapped. Let Laith torture her. It was better than conceding to Valek.

But his coal-dark eyes still waited for a different answer.

"Just take his offer, Niah," Demian said. "Valek will keep his word."

Niah shook her head. Pride was all she had left.

Valek looked both irritated and impressed. She had already suffered more than she cared to admit, she would not ask this beast for a rescue.

"I tire of this game," Valek said at last. "Release her."

Laith raised a hand, reclaiming the spirit. Niah stumbled forward with a sigh.

"Niah, are you okay?" Kesi asked.

Niah gave her a weak smile. Demian's face was twisted with guilt.

Valek grabbed her elbow and dragged her outside, his Fallen marching behind with Kesi in tow. Demian mouthed a pitiful *sorry*. She simply nodded. It wasn't his fault. He had gone to Valek to protect her. He was the only decent person in this country.

"Nice friends," she spat.

"You shouldn't have gone," Valek said. "Did you think they would accept you with open arms?"

Niah's mouth tightened. Of course she had thought it might

be that easy. She had hoped the drink would loosen their tongues. Instead, Laith had cornered her. Now they knew her intentions, and worse, she had stroked Valek's ego.

"I didn't see everyone in the room," she said defensively. "I'm sure there were better-looking boys than you."

"I don't care about your silly infatuation."

"I am not infatuated with you," Niah snapped.

"Is that why you nearly severed your tongue? Afraid to let them know you would kiss me if you had your way?"

Niah laughed, sharp and bitter. "I was tired of his stupid questions. It had nothing to do with you."

"Oh, then why don't we return to Laith and continue his game?" Valek asked, stopping. "I am eager to hear your answer to *that* question."

Niah tried to yank her arm free, but his grip was iron-clad. One of his Fallen held Kesi, making her dagger useless.

"I hate you," Niah snarled.

"Good," he said. "I much prefer that to foolish puppy love."

"God, you are so arrogant—it is disgusting," Niah said.

He resumed walking.

"You will have to answer to the headmistress tomorrow for breaking curfew."

"And what about everyone else?"

Valek did not respond.

"So only I am to be punished?" Niah asked.

"Yes."

A frustrated, feral sound escaped her.

His mouth tilted in amusement. "Did you just growl at me?"

Niah wanted to do more than growl at him. If it was up to her she would plunge her blade into his heart.

Chapter 11

As Valek had promised, Niah was summoned to the headmistress's office during her break. She had expected to see Kesi in the corner, but sitting comfortably across from Headmistress Greymont was Valek. His long legs were spread before him, fingers interlaced across his stomach.

"Please, sit down, Novice," the headmistress said.

"Is there a problem?"

"Commander Winterson says that you are having trouble following the rules. This arrangement is intended to work in both our favor. You are to accept our teachings and serve our army, and in return, you keep your life. If this does not work for you, then you may as well tilt your neck for Commander Winterson's blade."

"I've been attending my classes and keeping out of trouble," Niah said through clenched teeth. "Commander Winterson has it out for me."

"Is that why I caught you roaming the grounds after curfew?" he asked.

Niah glared. "Was I the only one?"

"I didn't see anyone else," Valek said.

Her fist clenched in her lap, and his eyes dropped as if he

expected her wrath. A ghost of a smile crossed his mouth, vanishing as swiftly as it appeared. He was doing all this to get a rise out of her. If she mentioned the Old Chapel and the students, Valek would tell everyone she had tattled, and they would hate her more than they already did. If she accepted his version, then she would be punished. Either way, she was doomed to suffer.

"Were there other students?" the headmistress asked.

"No," Niah muttered.

"We do not take rule-breaking lightly," she said sternly. Her gaze shifted to Valek, waiting for him to decide her fate.

"After your evening classes, you will report to the armory and polish the weapons to a shine for the next two months," Valek said. "Is that understood, Novice?"

"Yes," she said between clenched teeth.

There was a long pause.

"Yes, Commander Winterson," Niah amended. Her words dripped with sarcasm.

"You're dismissed," he said.

Niah stood and walked to the door, slamming it a bit too hard on her way out. Was it childish? Yes—but she couldn't resist.

She hoped it made that satisfied look in his eyes falter.

Niah stood in the training room bouncing from one foot to another. Practice was sometimes done outside, but with the shifting winter weather and the sleet that now covered the grounds, they would remain indoors today. This was their Battle Strategy class. Unlike Combat, this one focused on fighting a war using both intellect and magic.

The room was circular with mats laid on one side. At the back stood training equipment—hooks suspending sacks of straw like limp bodies, and a rack of weapons intended to carve flesh. Niah plucked a silver dagger from the rack. She needed a better one than the knife she carried now—especially after last night. She refused to give Laith the chance to use his magic on her ever again. She peeled back her robe and slid the dagger into her belt hook.

Everyone was anxious, and the mood was infectious. Kesi and Demian were in this class with her, which was a comfort.

"Niah, I'm sorry about last night," Demian whispered. "I had no idea Laith would do that. It is forbidden for Diviners to use their gifts on another on school grounds."

"It is not your fault," she said.

"I thought Valek would help. It's why I brought him," he said. "I suppose I was wrong."

"That bastard wouldn't help his own mother if she were choking," Kesi said.

Demian was silent, his mind elsewhere as he spun his twin blades around his fingers. The hilts were curved to resemble a wolf's tail. He almost always had them twirling on his clever hands.

"Don't cut yourself," Niah warned.

"I'll be fine, Mother," he said with a wry smile. "I don't know about the rest of the students. Last week, Master Kole broke Karp's arm in five places, and Anastasia carved a smile on her own throat. He made a Diviner set their spirits loose on her. She needed twelve stitches and almost bled to death."

Niah followed his gaze to the tall girl across from them, whose throat was covered in thick white gauze. Between the gaping fabric, Niah glimpsed the reddened skin and the thread sealing it. Her stomach churned at the brutality. This was not how they had been trained in the monastery.

"You'll be fine," Demian said, nudging her elbow. "So will you," he added to Kesi. "Just don't let him think you're weak."

"I hate this place," Kesi muttered.

Niah couldn't agree more.

The stone doors were drawn open by the guards stationed in the hallway. The old estate was heavily fortified and guarded to protect the children of the noble families. Valek wasn't the only noble—several others wore thick family rings and walked around with their noses in the air.

Master Kole arrived in a loose tunic and dark trousers, not bothering with the instructor's robe. His face was ashen and gaunt, hidden behind a bushy black beard. One eye was covered with a patch, the other a frigid blue, much like the Ever Sea.

His gaze immediately landed on her. Her shoulders straightened; of course she was his first target. Sometimes Niah wondered if it was her hair—snow-bright and wavy, slipping down her spine like a ghost—that made her the object of fascination. For the hundredth time, she wished she could cut it off.

"Name, novice!" he barked.

"Niah."

"You are three weeks late," he said. "Come to the mat."

Niah had not picked her enrollment date. She was a war prisoner—or had he forgotten?

She expected him to give Kesi the same treatment, but his gaze never wavered from her. Niah wondered if Valek had put in a bad word. He'd already dragged her before the headmistress; she wouldn't be surprised if he'd warned her instructors about her disobedience.

Master Kole snapped his finger at a fair-haired boy. "Have the sentries bring in a fresh corpse."

Dread crawled up her spine. They were going to bring in one of the Fallen. Did she have to fight it?

The boy returned carrying a dead woman in his arms. Her skin was mottled like a dry raisin, and a dull thud echoed when he dropped her on the ground.

"Go on then, Novice," Master Kole sneered. "Raise your Fallen."

Niah could feel the threads of Valek's power within reach, but she refused to touch the noxious well. It had been a little more than two weeks since she arrived, and besides the times Valek had touched her, she had not drawn upon his magic. It was there, persistently, waiting like a trained hound prepared to attack at the faintest whistle.

"I don't know how," she said.

It was a lie. She had been taught in Mistress Sonia's class, but had made excuses each time she was called forward.

"Unacceptable," Master Kole snapped. "What are your instructors teaching you if not to awaken and command the dead?"

"I am not a her—" She swallowed back the word at his sullen stare. "It is a mistake. I do not have that power."

"No?" Master Kole asked. "Then why are you here?"

"I am a prisoner."

Niah jumped back when the woman began to rouse. She hadn't even noticed Master Kole's eyes darken until the corpse stood before her.

Niah ducked just as the woman's fist swung at her. She yanked out her dagger, aiming for the ribs, but the Fallen was swift. Her feet swiped Niah's ankles out, and she fell on her back. A gasp escaped her at the impact, even though the mat softened it.

The woman leapt on her, fingers closing around her throat. Fear made Niah feel small, like that little girl again, hiding under the bed while the world burned.

"Another weak novice," Kole spat. "It gets worse every year."

Spots swam across her eyes, darkening her vision. Her dagger had flung away during the struggle.

"She's choking!" Kesi cried.

The Fallen released her and returned to Kole's side. Sweet air filled Niah's lungs.

"Commander Winterson sees something in you that I do not," Kole said in his harsh baritone. "If it were not for him, I would not spare you. I would kill you where you stand."

Niah stood, jaw clenched at his insult. It had been a test, and she had failed horribly. She went to pick up her discarded dagger, tucking it into her sheath.

He turned from her dismissively and called on them to form a circle.

He picked a boy with dark hair and a cocky smile and a tall girl with a shaved head to battle. Both were Diviners. The boy flung the girl backward with no touch at all, forcing the air from her lungs. Niah imagined it was much like that strange, numbing possession Laith had used on her—like being held underwater.

The boy's eyes were focused, his arrogance matched by skill. The girl got in a few swipes, but she was no match.

Master Kole paired students by principle. There were four training units: two groups of Diviners and two of Reapers. Stitchers didn't join combat classes. They usually served the military in non-fighting roles, healing and reviving commanders as needed.

Diviners joined the military based on performance. Their gifts worked on a smaller scale. They could easily overpower an opponent, but not multiple attackers. Usually, they worked in prisons, forcing captives to reveal secrets.

"Look around you at your unit," Kole said.

Niah glanced at the three Reapers beside her: a boy with fetid-water blue eyes, a girl with a permanent frown, and a burly blond with big, meaty fists. They were not welcoming. She wished Demian or Kesi were on her team.

From their blunt stares, she knew they considered themselves superior to her because she had failed Kole's test and not revealed her magic.

"These are not your friends, but they are your allies," Kole said. "Only one training unit will pass this course."

Shocked whispers rose. Niah's stomach turned.

"All who fail will have a mark on their record. Three marks, and you serve eight years in the Salt Mines of Nivarka before you are retested," Kole said. "Not everyone will serve the King's army."

Niah looked at her unit. Hostility lingered, though some had softened at the threat.

"There will be a series of tests," Kole continued. "You will know the day of. Always be prepared."

The dark-haired boy in their unit spoke. "We should go around and introduce ourselves. Share our strengths and weaknesses."

Niah frowned. As if she'd trust him with her weaknesses. He noticed her look and called on her first.

"Would you like to start, new girl?"

"Niah. Strengths: I am a fast learner. Weaknesses: undetermined."

"If you were a fast learner, you'd know there's no point resisting your magic," the girl said. Her pointed nose lifted high. "A conduit can draw on their bond with their master, present or not."

"I have no master," Niah snapped.

The girl's cheeks flushed with rage, but the short boy spoke.

"You'll weigh us down. I can't think who is worse—you or the other prisoner. At least that one follows the rules."

Niah slid out her dagger and pressed it to his throat. "Repeat that, Novice."

Fury consumed her. Anything bright in her had withered like a sun-dried flower the moment he insulted her friend.

He knocked her elbow away, but she flipped her blade to her left hand and slashed at his collar. Not deep enough for stitches, but enough to mark.

He lunged, but the other boy gripped him by the collar.

"We are working as a unit," he hissed. "Enough. Names, strengths, weaknesses."

The blond glared. "Milo."

Niah didn't listen to the rest. Lies, all of them. The self-declared leader was Casimir—named after the ancient prince of the North. The girl was Eveline.

"I don't care what your differences are," Casimir said. "I don't care if you don't like the arrogant new girl. I don't either. But we work as a team. Understood?"

"You should be grateful I am on your team and not against you," Niah said.

Milo scoffed, Eveline laughed. Niah gritted her teeth.

They could not have paired her with people worse than this lot.

"You are afraid to use your magic," Milo said. "You're not much help."

"I don't need your heretic magic to win," Niah said. "I am clever. A skill you seem to lack."

"They say you're the savior of the Low North," Milo sneered. "Is this the best they have? A loud-mouthed brat who has become the Commander's bitch?"

Niah stepped forward, but Casimir pulled her back.

"I said enough," he snapped. "We meet tomorrow morning in the library to strategize." He shot them a warning look before releasing her arm.

"This is not the first time Kole's class broke a novice. Let's see that we are the victors," Casimir said.

As much as she disliked him, Casimir understood the priority: to win.

At the very least, they could agree on that.

Niah stared at the ceiling. Her eyelids were heavy, but she needed to speak to Kesi before bed. Kesi entered their bedroom, her hair curly from her bath.

"I need to tell you something," Kesi said, sitting cross-legged on her bed.

"Go on," Niah said.

"Promise me, you won't lose your mind."

"I make no promises."

Kesi wrung her hands, before she blurted. "Laith cornered me."

Niah stilled. "What did he want?"

"He said conduits are meant for Reapers, but he is going to put in a request for me with his adoptive mother, the headmistress," she said with a shudder. "He wants me to be his, like you are Valek's."

"I am not Valek's!" Niah exclaimed, surprised that Kesi would say such a thing.

"You know what I mean," Kesi said. "A mage can only have one conduit, and I'm certain it works the other way around. Of course, they would give me to someone else since you are now claimed. I don't want that beast, Laith. He is a dirty traitor. At least Valek's royal bloodline ensures his loyalty. What is his excuse to serve the enemy?"

Niah rubbed her brows. "We can't be here any longer. I feel it, Kesi. I feel his magic, and it calls to me. I...I don't know how much longer I can resist it. And these instructors are forcing us to use their magic. I don't think they are above killing me if I refuse."

Anytime she was in danger or afraid, she instinctively reached for it and released it swiftly after, but each day that passed, their lessons grew more treacherous, and their enemies spread like rot. They were surrounded by faithless waters with no land in sight.

"We cannot win without magic," Kesi said slowly, revealing a nasty truth. "If their cursed magic is the only thing at our disposal, is it so bad to use it?"

Niah gasped at the thought of accepting their gifts. It was an idea that had flickered through her mind, one she had dismissed as being too dangerous, too wicked to consider.

Niah's stomach churned. "Are you saying we should turn our backs on the light?"

"Only a heretic can defeat another," she whispered.

The words rang with a finality that haunted her. A reminder that it was time to make a difficult decision. One that would cost her far more than she could imagine.

Chapter 12

In an hour, the bells would toll, signaling that dinner was to be served, and while most students rested during this spare time, Niah made her way to the armoury to begin her punishment. The smell of old wood and aged stone greeted her when she entered the vast room. There were, not so shockingly, five sentries on rotation. Their watchful eyes traced her every move, a reminder that she was being constantly observed. It made sense that she would not be left to her own devices. That was too bad. She had intended to steal some weapons for her and Kesi.

She had barely slept last night; Kesi's words had played in a loop in her mind.

Only a heretic can defeat another.

Was she making a mistake resisting the only magic at their disposal? These shackles would be impossible to break without the risk of severing her wrist, and Valek did not carry the key. She had studied him intently and doubted he was foolish enough to keep it in his pocket. Without magic and trapped in a fortress, their chances of escape were slim.

"Niah?" the sentry asked. "You're scheduled from seven to eight."

Niah nodded as he marked his sheet to confirm her attendance.

"Another student should be joining you, but he's always late," the sentry said with a roll of his eyes. "There is a catalogue on that desk that will let you know which weapons are new and don't require cleaning. Leave those crates in the corner alone; they are a new shipment and need to be sorted."

The walls had been built with hooks to hold rows of weapons. There were also shelves with small containers that held hand-held blades and daggers. Behind the shelves were three iron-cast cannons. Footsteps thumped loudly on the floor.

"You're late, Suren," the sentry said. "Again. At this rate, you'll be done with your punishment by the year's end."

Her head turned to find a boy standing in the doorway, leaning against the wall. He was handsome, with olive skin littered with sparse birthmarks and jade-green eyes. His dark hair was thick and luscious. He didn't look like a Northerner. There was a foreign quality about him.

"I'm here aren't I?" he said with a bit of snark.

He brushed past the sentry and snatched the catalogue sheet from the table—the one she had been walking towards. Niah followed him as he flipped open the page, picked up a box, and went to a stool. The door shut behind them.

"Hello," she said. "I'm Niah."

"And I didn't ask," Suren said. He reached for a bottle of vinegar and snatched a cloth from the shelf.

"We'll be working together for the next little while," she said. It was difficult to rein in her temper, to speak evenly and calmly and refrain from snapping at him for being so rude. "It'll help to be cordial."

"It'll help if you shut up," Suren said, raising his head to glare at her. "I understand this is a punishment, but it doesn't have to be torture too."

Niah gave him the nastiest look she could muster. So much for being polite. She grabbed the catalogue sheet from his hand

and began to follow his lead. They wiped down the blades with vinegar to clean off the blood and dirt. She tried not to think about whose blood she was cleaning off while she worked, this could very well be the blood of her people.

Once that was done, they scrubbed the silver with a pumice stone to remove rust and grime.

During it all, Suren remained as silent as a mouse.

"You're doing it wrong," he said, staring at her aghast.

Niah shrugged. Who cared if their blades were dull? It worked in her favor to do a poor job, and that was exactly what she was doing.

"Don't mix yours with mine," Suren grumbled when she tossed her blade into his pile. "They'll make you redo yours."

"So desperate to please, are you?" Niah asked.

Suren ignored her.

"What did you even do to be punished?" she continued.

"You first," he said, staring at her with curiosity. "Didn't you arrive, three days ago?"

"I arrived three weeks ago," she said. "And Valek Winterson told the headmistress that I broke curfew when there were twenty other people who did the same."

"Really?" Suren asked, almost as if he didn't believe her.

"Yes," she said. "He is the worst person I've ever met."

"He is no saint," Suren agreed.

"He is a monster who hides behind his mask," Niah said. "Your turn."

"My father is an envoy to the Queen of Masfen," he said. "He is at court currently seeking a truce with King Stefan, and he thought it would be beneficial for me to play politics with the young nobles."

Masfen was the jewel of the Southlands, small in breadth yet fierce in spirit. Its dusk-colored vessels would come to Teren to trade saffron threads and cardamom pods for bolts of soft cotton and baskets of sun-warmed fruit. At the heart of the marketplace, their traders would raise silk-striped pavilions, the fabric catching the light like shards of colored glass. From the flaps, she would often hear their voices, speaking the language of trade in their soft, lilting accents.

"You are going to join forces with these monsters?" Niah asked.

"The war in the North is unsettling," Suren said. "As the Queen sees it, it is better to stand with your enemy than against them."

Niah's fist tightened. They were getting stronger. Each day she remained here was another day where the scales of the war tipped in their enemies' favor. She was supposed to be on the frontlines, destroying their Reapers, not stuck in the armoury polishing the very blades they would use against them.

"For what it is worth, I do not agree with my father nor my Queen," he said. "I think the nobles from Raskovia are snakes that would chew their own tails if it brought them closer to power."

Niah looked away from him, unable to look into his bright green eyes. His words did not soothe her. Suren would never know what it felt like to watch your country fall. She had watched it happen as a child in Teren, and now she was watching as they seized the rest of the provinces. How much longer until they breached the walls of the Rose Palace and destroyed everything?

"You didn't tell me how you ended up here in this room," Niah said.

"I stole a bottle of wine from the kitchen," he said. "And then I ran across the courtyard drunk and naked."

A snort escaped her, and his mouth tilted slightly.

"What possessed you to do such a thing?"

"Never been good at drinking," Suren said.

His gaze dropped to her shackles. "What does it feel like?"

He had probably heard everything about her and Kesi's arrival. The two war criminals whom they intended to train into proper soldiers. The Lightbearer they had captured from the monastery. The Order's greatest weapon, seized by King Stefan's little pet.

"Like my soul is trapped and I don't know how to free it," she said. "I don't know who I am without my magic."

"You are a conduit; your magic can be drawn from anywhere you choose, which makes you more powerful than you can imagine," Suren said. He pointed at her shackles. "If they intend to shackle you, then why not consume the power they offer you? You cannot fight a war from the sidelines."

The door opened, and the sentry who had led her in popped his head inside.

"Time's up. You're free to go."

She had a decision to make: stick to her resolve and refuse to use Valek's dark magic or take a risk and possibly gain her freedom. A thought filtered through her mind. She saw herself standing on the frontlines, dark magic blooming from her fingertips, corpses marching to the beat of her heart.

The world had not paused when she vanished from the monastery.

The war continued to rage on, and if she didn't make a choice soon, she would return to ruins.

Now that Niah had met Suren, she was rather curious about him. He sat alone in the dining hall and seemed to be doing the exact opposite of what he claimed he had come to do. He wasn't drinking at the table with the nobles but was instead glowering at his soup as if it had committed some great sin.

"What do you know about him?" Niah asked Demian.

"Suren Ayari is the son of an envoy from Masfen and is under the protection of the King while he remains on Northern soil,"

Demian said. "His father is brokering a truce between his nation and the High North."

"Why is he all alone?" Kesi asked.

"He keeps to himself," Demian said. "Not one for socializing."

It seemed the students were aware of his sullen temper and didn't bother to glance his way. It must have been nice to be invisible. Niah would do anything to escape the punishing stare of her peers.

Kesi elbowed her. "Are you interested in him? He's easy on the eyes."

"No!" Niah said. "Not everything is about *that*."

Kesi snickered, and Demian shot her an amused look.

"I hate you both," she muttered, as they fell into laughter.

Suren didn't like the High Northerners and had expressed that he did not agree with the King; perhaps he could help them in some way. Niah could not stop thinking about his advice. Much like Kesi, he too believed that she should take advantage of the magic they were forcing on her. How else could she win against them?

She hoped that the Light Father would forgive her for her sins. Even if she picked up the torch that Valek offered to burn it all to ashes.

Chapter 13

"My least favorite class," Kesi whispered. "My unit hates me."

Niah tossed her robe to the ground and began to strap on her leather vest as all the other students did the same. They were preparing for their first test, and Niah couldn't help but feel the nerves creeping up on her. Master Kole didn't seem to like her, which wasn't a surprise, but she hoped he didn't target her unfairly. She already had enough people ready to stab her in the back without including her instructors on the list.

"Same here," Niah said. "Milo would kill me in my sleep if he had the chance."

He was glaring at her from across the field. They were outside today. It was so cold she was certain she'd catch a fever by the end of their lesson. She should have been standing with her unit, but she refused to spend her precious time trading insults with Milo, with Casimir playing peacekeeper on the side. Things had been tense when they'd met up to discuss the upcoming test. Milo would not be singing her praises anytime soon.

"Did you both ever think of using charm to gain admirers?" Demian asked.

They both glared at him, and he laughed loudly.

"See!" he said. "Point proven."

"I'm charming," Kesi said. "When I wish to bed someone."

Demian's cheeks grew pink, and Niah elbowed her.

"You scandalized him," she said.

"I am fine," Demian said. "I can handle Kesi's straightforwardness."

There was a ten-foot stone wall in front of them. Hanging from hooks were several spaced ropes. Demian followed her gaze.

"Looks like an obstacle course," he said.

"What's beyond the giant wall of doom?" Niah asked.

"Inevitable death," Demian said.

Kesi swallowed loudly. "I don't think I'm ready for this."

"You'll do great," Niah said, squeezing her shoulder.

In the distance, she could make out Master Kole approaching them, and beside him was Valek with sixteen Fallen behind him. Niah did a quick calculation of the students; there were four students in the four units, which meant he had brought along a soldier for each.

"Good luck," Niah said.

Niah walked off towards Casimir and her team.

"Will we have to fight those things?" Eveline asked.

"Most likely," Casimir said.

"There are sixteen of them and sixteen of us," Niah said. "One per student."

Casimir nodded. "Good observation."

"Anyone could have noticed that." Milo rolled his eyes. "It is simple math."

"I doubt you could," Niah muttered. "I doubt you can tie your own boots."

"What was that?" Milo barked.

"I said—"

"Enough," Casimir said sharply. "I am sick of you two."

Niah folded her arms across her chest. Milo always started it, and she just finished it.

"We are going to fail now that Winterson is here," Milo said, mouth curled in rage. "He hates her and will target us."

"I can't help that Valek Winterson is a cruel bastard like you," Niah said.

It was at that moment that the class had fallen silent. Her truthful words echoed in the winter air. Milo smirked, and Casimir's brows furrowed in concern. She knew what would await her when she turned. Slowly and reluctantly, Niah spun around to see Master Kole behind her. His brows shot up in surprise, and he stood beside Valek, who had an unreadable look on his face, though his mouth twitched slightly in cold amusement.

"Novice!" Master Kole snapped. "Apologize to the Commander at once. You do not speak so vilely about your superiors. Ever."

"But he—" She pointed at Milo.

"Just stop," Casimir whispered. "You'll get us all in trouble."

Niah's fist tightened. She looked off into the distance and mumbled "sorry" so softly it would be a miracle if Valek heard it.

"You were willing to shout your insults at the top of your lungs, but are as quiet as a mouse now," Master Kole said. "Louder, Novice. And look Commander Winterson in the eye when you speak."

Niah's eyes unwillingly met his black ones that shone like ink drops on paper. The charcoal liner that decorated his lids made his unresponsive gaze look like glittering coals trapped in a mantle.

"I am sorry," she said.

"Commander Winterson," Valek added.

He got a kick out of hearing her call him that. It soothed some wretched thing inside him.

Niah's eyes burned as she spat out his title, watching his lips twist in satisfaction.

"They get worse every year," Master Kole said for the umpteenth time. "Line up in a single file behind your unit leader."

Casimir stood dutifully at the front with Eveline behind him, Milo, and then Niah.

"Why am I last?" Niah asked.

"Because you refuse to use your magic and you are the weakest link," Casimir said.

"It could be worse," Eveline said. "I think her friend is weaker than her."

"Kesi is twice the person you are," Niah said.

This wasn't the first time they had implied that Kesi was inadequate.

"Not surprised you are defending the other weakling," Milo said. "Nobody else would dare to befriend Low North's scum."

"Shut up," Casimir barked. "Focus."

"Every novice will do a round on the circuit, and you will be timed," Master Kole said. "You will be hunted by the Fallen, and if you are caught, you will fight to survive, but the time will cost you. Once your teammate returns and touches your shoulder, the next novice goes. At the count of three, you will begin."

Niah's heart thundered as Casimir raced off into the distance and Valek's soldier gave chase. The Fallen were quick, eating up the distance like it was nothing. Casimir, unlike the others, wasn't looking behind him. He was focused on making it to the end. Niah added that to her mental note: *Don't look back.*

They did not know what occurred beyond the wall—only that a shrill scream came from the other side, which made her flinch. Her neck snapped to where Valek stood. His eyes had those black shells blanketing his vision as he controlled his flock. It was said that, beyond seeing the threads of their Fallen, the other reason a Reaper's eyes darkened was that they were seeing the world through the eyes of their Fallen. He would know what was happening on the other side and was likely enjoying himself. Tormenting other people probably aroused him.

It took twenty minutes before Casimir returned, covered in dirt, snow, and sweat. He slapped Eveline's shoulder, and she tore off into the distance. To her left, Demian returned, tapping his teammate's shoulder. He had been chosen first to go on his team and was most likely their leader. To her right, Kesi, much like her, had been placed last.

People respected Demian because of his surname. Things would have been a lot worse without his company. Niah knew the other novices would have done far worse than send them deathly glares. But, as it was, the only people who tormented them were Valek and his stupid friends, whom Demian could not defy.

Casimir went off to the sidelines with the others who had returned. He had beaten their opponent by thirty seconds, giving Eveline a head start. Niah hated the unknown. It was impossible to tell what awaited them beyond the wall, and the others stood off to the side, unable to warn them.

There was a boy who returned limping, his ankle turned at a terrible angle, but he ran as quickly as he could to his teammate. Just as he touched him, he fainted. Another girl returned with gouges down her cheek, the skin unraveling like the petals of a flower—bright red and vibrant. Niah felt sick just looking at her.

Time fell in a slow trickle, and it felt like ages before Eveline traded Milo. Eveline was the last to arrive, but Milo, despite her insults towards him, was a beast. Even though he was rather big, it gave him the arm strength to climb up the wall like a spider.

Milo returned shortly after, blood trickling from a wound on his forehead. He slapped Niah's shoulder harder than was necessary, but there was no time to return the gesture. She shot off in the distance, hearing the ominous stomp of Valek's soldier. Their footsteps beat in tandem with her heart. She caught the rope and climbed as fast as she could, hearing the thud of ascent behind her. Her arms ached under the pressure. They hadn't done much physical training in the monastery. They had just practiced their footwork—a technique that resembled dancing rather than fighting. Unlike the Reapers, they did not stand from a distance and mindlessly control their puppets. Yet it surprised her that they trained far more intensely than the Sisters did, with a brutality that fit the reputation of their army.

Niah climbed down the other side as quickly as she could, refusing to look back. There was a thinning river ahead of her and four small beams for each team to run across. It was covered in ice, and her heart thundered rapidly. A fall from this height into the river would be fatal. Niah lifted her feet and swiftly kicked off her shoes. She would not make it across with them on, and she had also noticed that Casimir had returned in just his socks. Niah moved as quickly as she could, refusing to look beneath her or behind her. The Fallen's boots rasped like a saw through bone as they swallowed up the distance between them.

Beside her, a boy screamed, and Niah turned just in time to see him plummet to his death. Fear struck her chest, but she did not stop. Another cry sounded, and she saw Kesi lose her footing.

"Kesi!" she screamed, coming to a halt.

It was just enough time for the Fallen to catch up to Niah. Its weight made the beam creak, and it coiled its meaty fist around her throat, prepared to fling her into the river. The river's base bristled with rocks, cruel and angled like a crown of stone. Niah didn't think about the price of her actions when she raised her hand and felt the dark pour of magic from her fingertips wrap around the Fallen who gripped her, dangling her from the edge. It ceased all movement, its opalescent eyes trained on her with eerie precision. Slowly, its hands dropped, obeying her silent command. The invisible threads of darkness that wrapped around its soul forced it to follow her will.

Niah trained her eyes on where Kesi stood, fingers digging into the worn bark. The Fallen that stood above her, foot lifted to break her grip, froze the moment Niah's hand reached out in its direction, tangling the tendrils of her dark spell around it. Her heart stuttered at the thought of losing her. She would not survive without Kesi. She was more than just her friend. She was everything to her.

Niah felt resistance.

Valek.

She felt his presence—sharp and intrusive, like a blade

pressing just beneath her flesh. He was there, repelling her moves, attempting to sever her hold on his monsters. His power brushed against hers with a deliberate intensity and a forcefulness that made her bones rattle, as if daring her to flinch, to run, to hide, as she always did when confronted with the darkness of his powers. But this time she did not flinch—she met it with equal force.

And a silent war waged in the space between their minds.

"You have to run," Niah said between gritted teeth. "I can't hold them off for long."

Valek was stronger than she had imagined. Blood trickled from her nose at the sheer strength it took to control his monsters. Once Kesi was safely back on her feet, Niah released them and began to quickly make her way across the beam. Relief flooded her when her foot touched the snow, and then she was off racing towards the next obstacle.

A narrow strip of solid ground circled the marsh pit, its soil dark and dense like a water-soaked gown. She kept to the edge, footsteps light and wary, careful not to slip and sink into the mire that waited below. They had marshes like this in Teren, and it would take an entire village to pull someone out if they got stuck in its roaring belly.

The Fallen had stopped chasing Kesi and the red-haired boy who competed with them. They turned and began to come at her with raw speed. She knew what this was. It was Valek's anger that chased her like wildfire through brittle grass. It seemed he did not like that she wrestled control from him—that she dared to defy him.

Her heart raced frantically as they all came at her from different angles. She had to make it out of this course, or they'd kill her. Valek was not holding back anymore. The Fallen were charging at her like raging bulls, and if they tackled her to the ground, she'd be done for. Niah raised her hand and attempted to control them. It was odd to feel him so viscerally, like he was one of the ribs that shielded her organs—as if they were the entangled filaments that made a garment and were sealed by sheer determination.

When they fought like this, it didn't feel like his magic or hers, but theirs. Something that belonged to them both. It felt like reaching out her hand, knowing that Valek would clasp it.

Niah redirected the two Fallen to charge after the red-haired boy in the lead. There was this drowning need to outpower Valek. To remind him that she did not need the light to bring him down. That she would use his own gifts against him, even at the cost of her soul.

"Be careful," Niah called to the boy to distract him. "They're behind you."

He gave her a mistrustful look and faltered at the sight of them all converging on him. His eyes widened in fright, and Niah felt an odd satisfaction when one of them leaped in the air, tackling him into the marsh, biting his neck with zeal. A scream of despair escaped the boy as he sank beneath the wet mud.

Kesi was behind her. Her heavy breathing and occasional curses gave her away.

Relief bloomed in her chest at the sight of the wall. They had run in a circle, returning to where they started. Everything in her ached as she climbed upward, finally relinquishing control of Valek's Fallen. Her eyes had to be clear when she came to the top and not black as midnight. She didn't want to reveal to the students that she had used Valek's magic. Since, they knew she did not possess any gifts of her own. She didn't want to disclose that she had accepted his power.

Niah slid down the opposite side. Casimir leaped in joy, and Eveline clapped in enthusiasm. She had arrived first, and Kesi was quick behind her.

Niah ran towards her unit, doing a flip in the air and landing effortlessly on her feet. Casimir picked her up with a single arm, and Eveline cheered while Milo simply glared at her. For once, she had proven herself. She had not failed or crumbled under the pressure or shied away from the darkness of their magic.

This was the price she had to pay to survive.

The war had not stopped when she'd been kidnapped. It continued to eat away at the limbs of her country like a parasite.

She would be the Lightbearer when she was freed. She would be whatever savior or saint that they asked of her. She would no longer hide from her obligations. But until then, she would be this—a conduit.

"It seems we have a winner," Master Kole said.

Niah cast a worried glance at Valek. His face was tight with anger, lips drawn into a thin slash.

He could rip this victory from her. He could reveal that she wrestled control from him and had an unfair advantage over her peers. But to her surprise, he only spun on his heels and disappeared into the trees.

Master Kole sent some students to recover the others so they could be taken to the infirmary.

"A boy fell in the river," Niah said to Master Kole. "I don't know if he lives."

"We'll have a search party look for him if his body wasn't swept downhill," Master Kole said, but from the sound of it, he didn't seem confident that he'd be recovered.

Their team was awarded five points, and Kesi's team got three points, and both the other teams failed the first test.

"Congrats," she said to Kesi when they'd been dismissed.

Her voice dropped an octave. "Thank you for saving me."

"It was nothing," she said. Unease crawled up her throat. She was prepared to hear Kesi's admonishments about using his magic. It was hard to shake off the guilt of this new path she was determined to walk upon. Niah was worried that one day she would look in the mirror and see a stranger. That her white robes would be stained by the weight of her sins, and the light would abandon her even when the shackles were pried from her weakened hands.

"I'm sorry," Kesi whispered. "I know how difficult it is for you to use their magic."

"It felt…"

Guilt gnawed at her stomach as she thought of the war with Valek and the grasping, hungry touch of their magic. It had felt raw and powerful, like controlling something uncontrollable. It was akin to grasping lightning in your palm and molding it as you pleased. It should have repulsed her, that cold, unnatural power coiling from her hands, licking across the space between them like ink spilled from a pot. But it didn't. And that worried her more than anything.

"Wrong," she finished.

The word tasted dirty in her mouth. She had never lied to Kesi before, but how could she tell her how good it felt to succumb to the itch, to feel magic again after being empty for so long? Her finger twitched at the thought of drawing it to herself again. It didn't warm her like the light, but it fed something inside her. Something dark and depraved. The scar on her palm beat like an insistent heartbeat.

"Do you think Valek is mad?" Kesi asked. "He must not like you using his magic against him."

Niah thought of his face when she showed up, the anger that marred his beautiful face. He would punish her for it. She didn't know how or when, but Valek would collect his dues.

"Yes," she said with certainty. "He will retaliate against me."

Niah had been waiting impatiently to speak with Suren. She had all these questions floating in her mind, and nobody to turn to for answers. Demian didn't seem to know much about conduits, and their instructors rarely focused on the topic, considering her and Kesi were the only conduits in Silverwood. They droned on about Reapers and Diviners and, once in a while, the role of a Stitcher, but never about what they were.

"You're early," Niah said, surprised to find Suren at work by the time she arrived.

He shrugged his shoulders.

"You don't speak much," Niah said.

"I don't have to when you're here," he said. "You speak enough for the both of us."

Niah's lips reluctantly turned up at his jab. He wasn't exactly lying; she did speak quite a bit around him, but only because she was curious about him, and he didn't seem afraid to answer her questions, unlike Demian.

"Can I ask you something?"

"Will you ask it even if I say no?"

"Yes."

"Then, go ahead."

Niah smiled again. She liked that he was blunt. It was refreshing.

"You're a Reaper, yes?"

He tapped his black collar, which signified he was a Reaper. Diviners wore blue and the Stitchers red.

"What use would one have for a conduit?" she asked. "How exactly does the relationship work?"

"It is a mutually beneficial relationship," Suren said. "A conduit strengthens their mage, and a mage strengthens their conduit. A conduit's magic reflects their mage, so if your mage is a Diviner, you will possess the gifts of a Diviner, and if they are a Reaper, you will present as a Reaper and so on."

"Could a conduit control the Fallen of their Reaper?"

"Yes," he said. "The connection between a mage and conduit is complex. It is a bond unlike any other, stronger than the ties between a mother and child and two lovers. They are one soul in two bodies."

Niah shivered at the thought.

"Can you be tied to more than one mage?" Niah asked.

"No," Suren said. "It is why conduits are so rare. They can only belong to one."

"What if I don't want to be tied to Valek Winterson?" Niah asked. "How do I stop it?"

"You are the strongest conduit," Suren said. "We heard the whispers of you even in Masfen. The savior of the Low North, they called you, the Lightbearer. For you to control that much light means you are a prime source to absorb vast amounts of magic without it burning you out. You could trade immeasurable amounts of magic with him. You could fuel an undying army unlike any other. Why would Valek ever let you go?"

"So, if I use my magic..." Niah shook her head. "His magic, then we will have this bond, is that correct? I will be his conduit alone?"

"Yes."

"And what if I find another mage?" Niah asked. "Say I draw magic from Demian. What then?"

"Depends on how strong your ties are to Valek," he said. "If it is early on, the bond will wither, and you will build one with this new mage. But either way, Valek will know the second you do so. Is it worth risking his wrath?"

Niah sighed. "I hate this. I feel so powerless."

"Don't beat yourself up about this," Suren said. "You were captured against your will and forced to serve the King. You did nothing wrong."

Niah bowed her head. "Then why does it feel like I keep failing, like nothing I do is right?"

Suren's eyes shone with sympathy, and she despised it. She hated feeling small and alone, as if the entire world was against her. Most days, it felt that way with Laith glaring at her any chance he had, Valek constantly spouting his threats, and Milo with his many digs. Even the people who didn't insult her directly either sneered at her or kept a wide berth, like she was infected.

It was the opposite of how she had been treated in the monastery. She had been respected and feared, even if she had never given them a reason to be frightened. The rumors that she was the Lightbearer forced their supplication. At the time, Niah had despised it, but now that she was abhorred and mistreated, she would do anything to cradle the respect of others like a stolen token. The same way Valek was worshipped by his people. His mere presence made them quake with exultation, and she envied him for it.

How could she continue to use Valek's magic when it meant growing closer to him? It was far too great a price to pay for power.

Suren's hand reached out to pat her head. A snort escaped her at the gesture.

"What are you doing?" she asked.

"Comforting you," he said.

"I am not a dog."

"No?" He raised a brow.

Niah laughed and felt the tension seep from her shoulders.

"Do you miss home?" Niah asked.

"More than anything," he said. "The cold here is unbearable. It makes it hard to think, and the people are as frigid as their lands. I do not know why my father sent me here to indulge these spoiled children."

"Do you think it is the right choice for Masfen to broker a truce?" Niah whispered. "They could fight with the Low North."

Suren smiled sadly. "The Low North is losing. Our Queen's advisors reckon that King Stefan's army will seize full control in the next six to eight months. If there was some chance of the scales tipping in your favor, I presume we would reconsider, but as it stands..."

Tears flooded her eyes. Six to eight months was barely enough time to change the trajectory of this war. How could she make a difference if she were stuck here? There would be no home to fight for if their predictions were correct. Nothing but ash and destruction. It would be like losing Teren all over again, except this time the entire continent would slip between her fingers.

Suren's hand lifted to pat her head again, and this time she couldn't bring herself to smile. The weight of the world was on her shoulders.

"You know not everyone likes King Stefan here," Suren said thoughtfully. "They have a bit of a rebel problem, I heard. Some of the villagers are exhausted by the ongoing war and their sons being called to service. They fear that the King will never be satisfied with his wins and will always hunger for more. There are also some of the common folk who are sickened by the use of corpses for battle. They consider it an act of desecration."

His words comforted her far more than he realized. It was enough to plant seeds in her mind.

Chapter 14

It was only a matter of time until the Commander confronted her about the affairs that occurred during her test.

After her conversation with Suren, Niah knew what to do now with striking clarity. She needed to embrace her role as a conduit, even at the risk of being tied to Valek. He was the strongest Reaper who lived, and no other mage compared to him. If she were to turn her back on her faith and morals, then she might as well do it with the most powerful Reaper in King Stefan's army.

That day, she had proven that she could wrest control from him, that she could turn his own monsters against him. Perhaps she could do that again. Perhaps Niah could one day destroy him.

The night prayer had just ended when Valek gripped her elbow.

"Stay behind."

Niah's teeth clenched as everyone passed them. Daria glanced at the spot where his fingers lay wrapped around her flesh, her mouth tightening in irritation. Laith was right behind her, and he didn't resist sneering in her direction. God, she hated them both. Kesi cast her a worried glance, but Niah nodded at her in a manner she hoped was reassuring. The last thing she wanted was for Valek to make his friends drag Kesi outside and torture her.

"Well?" Valek asked when the door sealed shut.

He folded his arms across his chest. Long, onyx-painted fingertips wrapped around his elbows. She counted six rings in total on his hands—four on his left and two on his right. One had to be a family heirloom; it was engraved with a wolf wearing a seven-pointed crown, the royal sigil of the Wintersons. It was said that each point of the crown represented one of their seven great lakes.

"Are you picturing my hands wrapped around your throat?" Valek asked, running his tongue along his bottom lip. "Because I wouldn't mind obliging your desires."

"I don't care to bicker with you," Niah said.

"No?" He raised a brow. "Have you matured since we last spoke?"

"I can't be bothered to waste my breath on you either."

"Then why don't you just shut your mouth and let me do the talking?"

Niah's mouth tightened, refusing to fall for his bait. It was clear he intended to rile her up before he got to his point. He gained a sick fascination from spoiling her mood. She could have sworn his eyes flickered with disappointment when she didn't react to his words.

"Such a good little girl," he taunted.

Niah remained silent, and his eyes narrowed as if he were certain she would jump at that one.

"What you did the other day was unacceptable," Valek said. "You do not control my Fallen. *Ever.*"

"So, only you are allowed to draw on my magic, but not the other way around?" Niah asked.

She knew he had begun drawing magic from her as well, ever since the day she controlled his Fallen. Sometimes she could feel a tingle in her chest that disappeared as quickly as it arrived, and that cutting breath of air that whispered across her scar. When they had first met, they had touched to transfer magic between themselves, but it seemed they could now do the same across distance. It worried her that their bond was growing stronger, but it was the price she was forced to pay for freedom.

"Yes," Valek said. "Not until I trust you."

"And when will you trust me?"

Valek took a step forward. His cool breath grazed her cheek. "When you stop fighting me at every corner. When you stop looking at me like I am a monster."

"You *are* a monster," she whispered.

"Is it not better to stand with a monster than to fall alone?" Valek asked. "We could change the world, you and I."

Niah didn't speak. She didn't care to highlight their differences, to remind him how much she hated him. He never seemed to listen.

"Do you not want the Corruption to end and to awaken your people from the Sleeping Fever? Do you not want to save them?" Valek asked. "We could speak to the Queen of the Low North, you and me. We could convince her to surrender. We could train the conduits and pair them with our gifted. The North could stand as one."

Was that what he believed? Did he think that he was the savior in this story?

Niah's mouth curled in disgust. "Abandon our faith and crown to serve your power-hungry King and join his group of pagans? I'll pass."

Niah had already accepted his gifts to protect Kesi, but it was another to offer her loyalty to their twisted cause.

Valek's jaw clenched.

Niah took a step closer until their chests touched.

"I would rather die a million times over than bend the knee to King Stefan," she snarled. "I would rather cut off my arm than kill an innocent person in his name."

Valek's fingers caught her chin before she could step away, holding her in place, drawing her the slightest bit closer to him.

"You shouldn't make promises you can't keep, little saint."

He released her and spun on his heels. It irritated her that he'd gotten the last words, but she had been more unsettled by his proximity. He had been so close she could have counted each lash that coated his dark eyes, lined by that thick charcoal.

A beautiful, wretched monster.

Now that he was gone, she could breathe again, and she drew in air until her lungs expanded, as if she could erase the taste of his scent on her tongue.

Master Kole had been watchful of her since she had passed her first test. A part of her wondered if Valek might have revealed the truth behind her victory. Niah had not missed that he called on her more than the other students. His intelligent gaze often studied her like she was an unknown creature. It seemed her brief display during their last test had made her a topic of conversation. Niah didn't mind the attention; it meant that everyone kept a wide berth from her.

The Reapers were separated from the Diviners, who had been dismissed earlier. Niah knew that she would have to reveal her magic today. It had been days since she felt those cold, dripping tendrils slip out of her fingers. Back then, it had only been her and Valek who witnessed her performance. Nerves tightened her stomach, and she was thankful that Kesi had gone with the Diviners since she wasn't tied to any Reaper. Whereas Niah was publicly known to belong to the Commander—a reminder that brought a bitter taste to her mouth.

It was time to awaken her Fallen. It was one thing to seize control from Valek and another to awaken them herself.

To raise a corpse, a Reaper had to tie their lifeline to it.

Master Kole was making his rounds, critiquing the other novices.

Slowly, she took a deep breath and reached for the magic. She felt the shift in reality before she saw it. The world that unfolded around her felt like death. Solemn and bleak, it spread around her like a map unfolding on a table. The ground was carpeted with black grass. Ash hung in the air, gliding in slow spirals from a sky choked with smoke and swollen gray clouds. A blood-red river cut through the distance, sluggish and thick, winding through jagged rock as though the land itself had bled out. Nothing lived here. Not truly. It was a barren mirage—the antithesis of life.

Fear struck her like a blade to the throat. Her limbs were locked, horror dawning on her at the place that she had been lured into, much like a child drawn to the haunted woods despite their parents' warning.

Niah wasn't alone.

He stood at the river's edge, his silhouette etched against the burning horizon. In this hollowed-out place where the veil between life and death felt thinnest, she recognized the shape of him. The weight of his presence. As familiar as the dark caress of his magic. His ebony robes flapped in the wind like the wings of a bird. Thick hair mussed and heavy.

"You," she snapped. "What are you doing here?"

Slowly, Valek turned around, revealing his face. He didn't move. Just watched her, the way he always did—with that unsettling calm that masked whatever war raged behind his eyes.

"You called me," he said. "Dragged me from my war council to the Lower World. Explain yourself, Novice."

Niah swallowed. "I don't know where I am. Or what this place is."

The wind scraped through the trees like claws, and she flinched. This place was not made for the living. It was wrong to be here.

"As I said, we are in the heart of the Dark Mother's realm—we are in the Lower World."

"I can't be here," Niah said, wringing her fingers. Her voice raised slightly, quivering in this dark, abominable place. "I must leave."

Valek crossed the space between them. His inquisitive eyes trailed down her face, studying her like she was a fascinating creature.

"Is that why you called me here?" Valek asked. "Because you are afraid?"

"I didn't call you anywhere," she snapped. "The bond must have summoned you here."

"Do I make you feel safe, little saint?" he asked in a silky tone.

"No."

"Then why call me at all?" he asked. "I think you are beginning to trust me."

His words dripped with confidence. Dark eyes daring her to deny his statement. He was hungry for a reaction, and Niah was too disturbed by this situation to pretend to be undaunted. She was in Mirathe—or as the High Northerners called it, the Lower World. The place where dead things crawled, and the Maiden of Death ruled, as mentioned in the *Book of Life*.

"If I had a blade right now, I'd plunge it into your heart," Niah said.

"Last time you fought me, you got hurt."

Her eyes narrowed, ready to spit something sharp and cruel, but he moved before she could react. His gloved hand wrapped around her wrist. Unsettlingly calm.

"What are you—" she started, but his gaze had dropped.

He turned her hand upward, exposing her palm, where a thin, faded scar curled like a whisper across the skin. A mark from that night they had met—the first chapter in this tortured book that haunted them. It felt like the nightmares that would taunt her in the monastery except this was real.

He traced it with his eyes, and the weight of his silence felt heavier than words. It brought her some measure of comfort that he did not touch the ruinous mark. But she was still troubled by his gaze, which remained heavy and constricting.

"You need not come to the Lower World," he explained. "The Fallen do not have a soul. Theirs has long since departed. It is our Stitchers who make frequent visits to the Lower World and grasp onto freshly departed souls to awaken them fully. And we are not Stitchers... we are Reapers."

Niah's eyes shot open with a gasp. It felt like an eternity had passed since she fell into the Lower World, but only mere seconds seemed to have slipped by. Master Kole was still speaking to the boy with the star-like freckles across from her.

Niah could still feel the lingering presence of Valek. Her wrist was icy from where he had touched her. Her mind reeled from the reality of her magic. It was one thing to control the abominations, but slipping into Mirathe was unnatural. She could still taste ash on her tongue, feel the rancid wind against her flesh.

Niah stared at her Fallen and attempted to follow Mistress Sonia's guidance. Several moments later, her Fallen shifted, staring at her with vacant eyes, awaiting her command. Her mind remained in a daze until Master Kole called her to the circle. She was to use her command of her Fallen to fight Master Kole's Fallen. He had excellent control of his, and their fighting skills reflected his expertise.

"Your hold is breaking, Novice," Kole said sharply.

He had his Fallen swiftly put hers down. They had blades stuck in their arms and legs, pinning them to the floor. It wouldn't kill them—their wounds would staunch the moment the blade was removed. Only a severed head would ensure they died their final death. Once a Fallen died they could not be revived again.

Her breath caught in her throat as his Fallen marched towards her.

"What?" Kole demanded. "You expect your enemy to stop coming at you when your soldiers have lost?"

Niah yanked out her dagger, but she was too late. The first

punch to her stomach knocked the wind from her, and the second to her head had her ears ringing. Niah got in a few good swipes and even cut the tendon in one's foot, watching it topple over like a great tree. An arm of the Fallen coiled around her throat as Master Kole circled her, assessing her form.

"The Headmistress and Commander Winterson see something in you, Novice," he said. "But it is clear to see their hopes are misplaced. You are weak."

Her throat burned, and she dug her nails into its forearm. Anger burned her gut; she was stronger than she appeared. Master Kole knew it. Everyone knew it. Their tones had changed since she'd won the last test, and while Milo still hated her guts, Eveline wasn't so quick to take his side anymore, and Casimir placed the blame on Milo's shoulders during their spats.

Master Kole had the Fallen release her, but not until her eyes stung from the lack of air and her face turned bloodless. She knew there would be a wicked bruise on her throat come tomorrow.

She gasped hungrily as she fell to her knees. It was a wonder she did not get used to the shame, but it sat in her stomach hard as a fist.

"Dismissed," he barked.

Niah packed her belongings.

"Not you, Novice," Kole said.

Even though he didn't say her name, Niah knew he spoke to her. Casimir gave her a sympathetic nod as he passed her, and Milo simply smirked.

"Yes, Master?" she asked when the last student had left.

He folded his arms across his chest, scrutinizing her.

"You performed poorly today," he said. "Worse than yesterday."

"I never slept well last night," Niah said.

The truth was that encounter with Valek in the Lower World still fractured her mind. She was unsettled by his words and the possessive gleam in his eyes. He truly believed that they were alike. It was an unfathomable thought. Valek was the very rot that spread the fingers of the Corruption. It was he and his fellow necromancers who ravaged the world and spread misery.

"Excuses," he spat. "Do you not tire of them?"

Niah was silent. She didn't think he expected an answer to that.

"Headmistress Greymont believes you may be a gift from Bersula," he said. "Powerful soldiers are hard to come by, and your victory during your test has piqued her interest. You will not prove her wrong, is that understood?"

"Yes, Master," she said.

"You will spend your lunch here after classes. We will continue battle play until I am satisfied with your performance," he said. "It isn't just the Low North that fights against the King. There are factions in the North that are causing trouble—rebels who need to be hunted and punished."

"Rebels?" she asked.

"Valek did not return here to whip you into shape alone. He is also investigating these attacks," he said. "Shipments were stolen from a cargo vessel last night. Weapons that could be used against us by our enemies."

Niah's eyes widened, surprised by this information and more so that he was sharing it with her. She had been wondering why the King would allow the Commander of the army to be pulled from the frontlines.

"We need strong, loyal soldiers," he said. "Now more than ever."

"I will do my best, Master," she said.

He blinked at her. "Where did you say you hailed from?"

Niah's heart thudded. "I'm from Teren, sir, but I was raised in Caer-Sylisse."

"And you were a Sister of the Order of the White Flame?"

"I was," she whispered.

I am.

Better that he believed her allegiance had shifted than for him to doubt her.

"You must resent the King for stealing you from your home," he said. "For his actions against your country."

Niah swallowed bitterly, making sure her face did not hint at her true feelings.

"Never, Master," she said. His gaze was intense. His icy blue eye, the one unconcealed by his patch, attempted to read her true intentions. "I understand now what my purpose is. If we can unite the North to a single cause, I would much rather aid in those efforts than fight a losing battle."

Her words were steady as the lies poured from her mouth. If the instructors wanted to make her stronger, then Niah was not opposed to the idea. Let them help her hone the very skills she intended to use against them.

"Do you know what happens to traitors, Novice?" he asked. "They meet the Commander's blade and are strung up on the gates as fodder for the crows."

"Understood, Master."

He waved a dismissive hand. "Leave."

"Thank you, Master."

She was gone before he could question her more, before her mask slipped and he read the truth in her eyes.

Chapter 15

That same morning, two guards ripped her out of her class like wild prey caught in a trap. Niah thrashed and clawed, but her efforts were futile. The men—one with bright orange hair and a spectrum of freckles, and the other, a short, stout man with wheat-blond hair—did not flinch when she spewed an assortment of threats. They dragged her to the barracks she had seen in passing.

The air was thick with the scent of sweat and damp wool. In the distance, she could hear the occasional sound of boots on the floorboards. Tucked in the back corner beyond the bedchambers was an office. There was no plaque to mark the doorway, but Niah had a sneaking suspicion she knew exactly who had torn her from class at his pleasure.

"We have arrived, my lord," the guard who led her said with a curt knock.

"Let her in," Valek's sharp voice called.

The walls were lined with dark mahogany shelves. Each row was filled with leather-bound ledgers, rolled-up maps, and yellowed scrolls. A large table dominated the room's center—a war desk scarred by years of use, layered with sporadic ink stains and the fleshy, white lines of old blade marks. Scattered across the top was a mess of maps pinned with brass weights, troop rosters, dispatches sealed with wax, and a single oil lamp casting a warm, flickering glow over it all.

The guards dragged her inside. Their thick fingers locked around her elbows like shackles, and they deposited her roughly on the armchair across from him. Niah lost her footing and winced at the jolting pain of landing on her knees.

Valek sat in a high-backed chair of blackened wood and cracked leather, its worn arms smooth from years of use. He had been gone for a few days. Niah did not know if he had left the fortress or remained hidden in his office, plotting war schemes from afar.

"Careful," he growled.

"Apologies, my lord," they murmured in unison, quickly backing out the door before Valek changed his mind and had their heads severed.

"Could you not summon me with a letter?" Niah asked bitterly.

He raised a perfectly arched brow. "Would you have responded?"

Niah didn't reply. They both knew she would have ignored it.

"As I thought."

Niah straightened her robe and stared at him rudely. He looked tired and hadn't made the effort to shave that morning. It made him look mature and frightening. It also, unfortunately, did not lessen his beauty. He was like a dagger covered in adornment and jewels, but still sharp enough to cut.

Valek studied her as well. She had a few fading bruises on her face from Master Kole's class that his gaze trailed with cold scrutiny.

"Did you give as good as you got?" he asked.

"Of course," she snapped. "I just pictured your face and suddenly my fist was flying."

His mouth twitched, and he leaned back, crossing his ankles.

"Thinking about me? It has not been long since we last spoke. I reckon you miss me."

"Like a dog misses its fleas," Niah said.

"I see that tongue of yours has not been tamed," Valek mused.

Niah folded her arms across her chest, refusing to speak to him. It was a mistake to say anything at all. He would only rile her up more, and she refused to give him the satisfaction. His eyes were bright with amusement, erasing his tired demeanor.

"Why are you upset at me today?" Valek asked.

Niah didn't answer. The question was silly. She was upset at him every day. Today was no exception.

"Instead of acting like a disgruntled wife, perhaps you should tell me what I did wrong?" Valek continued.

"You cannot be serious," Niah hissed. "Have you committed so many crimes you cannot keep track anymore?"

"I spared your life," he said. "I am prepared to spare more of the conduits whom you served alongside. But that cannot be done if you prove to be a mistake. You are the catalyst that can shift this war. Everything depends on you."

"Do you think you are our savior?"

"I am the one who will end the Corruption. Once all the conduits are paired, nobody will draw from the lands. The blight will recede, and all will be as it once was," he said. "The North shall stand strong and united."

Niah glowered at him and his foolish logic.

"As much as I am enjoying our banter, I summoned you for a reason," Valek said. "Lord Winterson will arrive in two weeks. You will be presented before him, and he shall report back to the King on our progress. During this meeting, you will be docile and polite. You will perform as needed, and you will not step out of line."

Niah gave a dry laugh. That was why she was dragged here. He thought she would perform like a trained dog before his father? So, he could impress him?

"You are mistaken if you think I will put on a show for your worthless father."

Valek's eyes darkened. "Do not test me, Novice."

"You do not test *me*," Niah said. "Cancel this meeting before you humiliate yourself. That is my advice to you."

Valek smiled. A cold, baneful smile that dragged shivers down her spine.

"We shall see about that," he said. "You are dismissed."

Niah stood quickly, casting a wary gaze behind her as she headed to the door. His head was bent as he unravelled a letter.

It was as if he were not concerned about her threat. Her stomach knotted at what he planned to do if she refused him.

Niah bumped into a broad shoulder when she closed the door shut. Laith glared at her, and a deep sigh escaped her.

"*You*," was all she spat. "Move."

"I see you and that friend of yours were raised with the same manners," Laith said, folding his arms across his chest. "I thought you grew up in a monastery. Are you not supposed to be pious and devout?"

"Not to our enemies," Niah said.

"Who says I am your enemy?" Laith raised a brow.

"Your loyalty is to the High North, to the Commander and the King," Niah said bitterly. "You possess no spine."

"You know nothing about me," he said darkly.

Laith brushed past her, opening Valek's office, before he disappeared inside.

Valek was gone the next week—a relief for Niah, who would not be subjected to his unbearable presence. He had taken his dreadful squadron with him, which included Daria and Laith. A gift from Aubrith himself. They could dine now without being accosted.

"It's been quiet without the demons," Kesi said, chewing her bread. "Any idea when they'll return?"

Demian shrugged. "Once they capture all the rebels."

Kesi glanced at Niah. She had told her about what Suren said —that there were rebels who opposed the ways of King Stefan. Rebels with whom they could perhaps work alongside to bring down their common enemy.

"How many do you reckon there are?" Kesi asked.

They had decided that Kesi would ask any questions to Demian. He was less suspicious of her. Even though he was their friend, he walked a careful line of not providing too many political secrets but still educating them about his world.

"Enough to cause concern," he said. "Lord Maxim Winterson is arriving at the end of the month to address the issue."

"Valek's father?" Niah asked. "He mentioned he was visiting."

"He is the Royal Chancellor."

"Of course he is," Niah murmured.

The Wintersons were nothing short of power-hungry, much like the king they served.

"I cannot say I am especially keen to see my uncle," Demian said, nervously stirring his soup, chunks of bread floating in the mixture like lily pads in a lake. "He is rather stern. I used to dread my summers at their estate."

"Explains why Valek is so severe," Kesi said.

"I don't think he is," Demian said. "He is different from what he presents to the world. In many ways, he was born to be a soldier. His father trained him for the role for years before he could properly hold a quill."

"It doesn't matter who he was," Niah said. "To us, he will always be a monster."

She couldn't bring herself to sympathize with a man who killed as if it were his divine purpose. But yet Demian's words echoed in her mind like a bitter aftertaste.

Chapter 16

Niah received a letter late at night. The edges were crisp as autumn leaves, and the ink still wet.

Meet me at the front gates at dawn tomorrow.
V. Winterson

Niah sighed, annoyed by this new summon. It had been a week since she last heard of him. At least he hadn't had his guards drag her out of bed. She was curious as to what he wanted. Maybe he wished to threaten her some more, but if so, why meet at the front gates? It didn't make sense.

"Do you think he wants to kill you?" Kesi asked when she showed her the letter. "Slaughter you where there are no witnesses."

"The guards will be doing rotations, and he doesn't need to do it in secret; nobody questions him."

"Hmm," Kesi said. "Maybe he wants to kiss you?"

Niah's head spun to find Kesi smiling cheekily. She was surprised that she would suggest such a thing.

"I jest," she said. "But it is concerning. Will you go?"

"I doubt I have a choice," Niah said. "He'll just get his guards to ambush me and bring me to him otherwise."

"Do you want me to come with?" Kesi asked.

Niah shook her head. "That will just make him angrier."

There were things Valek knew about her that she didn't dare to share with Kesi. Mainly this connection they shared as conduit and Reaper.

"Good luck," Kesi said.

It was dark outside when Niah made it to the front gates at dawn. The sky hung low, swollen in shades of violet and gray, like an old bruise left to fester.

Standing at the front gate, dressed in their robes, were Laith and Daria. Daria's robe had the crimson collar that signified her as a Stitcher, whereas Laith's was blue, signifying him as a Diviner. They both sat on warhorses with fluttering manes and glassy eyes.

Behind them, standing dutifully under the shadows, were fifty Fallen. From the threads that tangled around their souls, she knew they belonged to Valek. She could only ever see Valek's magic on his Fallen, nobody else's. Niah wondered if this was an ambush plotted by the two soldiers before her.

"I thought I was meeting Winterson," Niah said.

"Afraid?" Laith asked.

"Of you?" Niah said. "Hardly."

Just before he could respond, the sound of powerful hooves echoed in the air, and she looked up in time to see Valek. His mask covered his face, and she shuddered when his black eyes stared at her from behind the bone frame. It was like looking into the eyes of Death.

"Do you know why you are here, Novice?" Valek asked.

"Your letter wasn't very informative."

"You will be going on your first sanctioned mission," he said. "You can read the briefing report as we travel."

Niah's eyes widened, surprised that he trusted her enough to bring her along and to give her access to valuable information.

"Where's my horse?"

Valek scooted a bit behind and patted the space before him. Niah shook her head vehemently.

"No."

"Yes."

As much as she wanted to resist this offer, it was too good an opportunity to pass up. If the price for information was to be unbearably close to Valek Winterson, then so be it.

His horse was a big, black beast with a silky mane and soft brown eyes. Niah petted her neck for a second, admiring her, before she hoisted herself up.

The gates were drawn back, and they disappeared into the horizon.

Niah silently read the battle brief; the only sound was the occasional rustling of her papers.

The pages documented the rebel crises in detail. It was the same issue Master Kole and Demian had vaguely touched upon. There were suspected rebels in the mountains who acted against the rule of King Stefan and had to be rooted out immediately. The last shipment of weapons had been stolen from the merchants before they arrived at the fortress. They would be conducting a search weekly, visiting residents and questioning suspected individuals until the culprits were caught.

Funny, that Valek thought she had any inclination to hunt people who shared the same beliefs as her. If anything, this mission presented her with the opportunity to learn more about the rebels and how their interests aligned.

"You must be wondering why I brought you along," Valek said. His voice sliced through her thoughts like a dagger.

"I figured it was for my good humour and charming disposition."

A soft chuckle escaped him that surprised Niah. It carried a boyish lilt, one she could not reconcile with the hardened soldier behind her.

"If I ask you a question, will you answer me truthfully?" Valek asked.

"No."

"What if I offer to answer a question in return?"

Niah thought over his proposal. It wouldn't hurt to learn more about him.

"Fine," she said. "But I get to ask first."

"Go on."

"Did you always want to be a soldier?" Niah asked.

It annoyed Niah that she was even curious about his background.

"That is your question?" Valek asked, seemingly surprised. "My choice of trade?"

Niah shrugged. She didn't think he would tell her anything of importance, and she could always lie when he asked his question. There was no harm in this silly game.

"No," Valek said. "It may sound shocking, but blood used to make me queasy."

"You were scared of blood?" Niah asked incredulously.

"Not scared, more unsettled," he said. "I accidentally entered my mother's bedchamber when my sister was being born, and I wasn't the same after."

"You have a sister?"

"Yes," he said. His voice softened the slightest bit.

"What is her name?"

Valek was silent. Niah took the hint that he wasn't comfortable sharing that information, and she wasn't quite ready for the questions to be directed at her, so she changed course.

"What did you want to be instead of a soldier?"

"A painter."

Niah snickered, but when he didn't laugh, she craned her neck to look at him. He had removed his mask earlier, and his dark eyes were locked on her.

"You? A painter?" Niah asked.

Her words were cloaked in disbelief. It was hard to imagine him as anything less than what he was––which was a force to be reckoned with.

"My tutor said I was quite distinguished at it, and I could make a decent living if I were anyone but the son of the Royal Chancellor," Valek said a bit defensively. "Turns out patrons like artists with humble beginnings, not spoiled noble boys."

"I can't picture it," she said.

"My turn," Valek said.

Niah stiffened, uncertain what he could possibly ask her. This entire conversation had been odd, and she wasn't sure if she should engage, but he would hassle her the remainder of the trip if she did not keep her side of the bargain. So, she simply sighed, a sign for him to continue.

"Does a part of you like our magic?" Valek asked.

He said the word *our* like he spoke of something intimate— the way one might speak of their child, as if it belonged entirely to them, and they could not resist their fondness for it.

"No, it feels wrong and forbidden," Niah said. "It feels impious."

"Don't lie to me," Valek said. He had drawn closer, and she could feel the rough graze of his stubble on her cheek. "You said you would be honest."

Niah thought of the stinging touch of magic that flowed

between them like water down a riverbed. It had felt consuming and overpowering, and if she weren't careful, it would sweep her away.

Valek's gloved hand wrapped around hers, and she felt the glide of magic between them. She could feel the threads that tied them to the Fallen, and if she let that magic flow, they would strengthen and distort, growing into monsters that surpassed any mortal man in strength and speed. Only a conduit's power could alter the state of a Fallen. To make them large and frightening. To make them monstrous.

It was wrong for anyone to possess such gifts. It went against the balance of nature. It was the magic of heretics.

The sheer absence of light.

Niah yanked her hand away, struggling to suck in air.

"Stop doing that," she said.

"We don't need to touch to pass magic between us," Valek said. "There was a time when a Reaper and a conduit could not siphon from such a distance."

A glum thought crossed her mind—one she was scared to ask. So she focused on another that itched her brain.

"There is no Corruption here?" Niah asked.

The trees were tainted by the furry coat of winter and nothing else. Black sap did not drip from the bark, nor did dead locusts hang from the peeling flesh like a symbol of rotten devotion. There were no signs of the Corruption.

"We wear our talismans," Valek said. He dug beneath his cloak to showcase a silver chain with a worn finger bone dangling from the ends. "And this." He tapped his bone mask that hung by his hip.

It was a surprising revelation to learn that their magic was not innate. That it was guided by *something*.

"I thought you wore those to frighten maidens," she said.

"It has multiple purposes."

His explanation disturbed Niah. As they had been taught, the Corruption had arrived when the Reapers did. The womb that had birthed their evil also ate away at the purity of the world. In Verse 108 of the *Book of Light,* it was said that when the cursed servants who followed the Dark Mother arose, the earth would bleed.

True to its word, there had been areas of the Witherwood where the trees dripped ruby tears.

"I do not wear a talisman," she said. "Yet conduits are said to be safe by your laws."

"You have a talisman," Valek said. His words were thin and disquieting.

"Where is it then?" Niah scoffed.

"It's me," he said.

His eyes locked on hers, dark and unreadable. Even when he glanced away, Niah could feel the unnerving touch of his words.

The villagers were gathered around their homes, watching their party with a mixture of fear and reverence. Hanging on the door of the chapel nearby was a wreath of rowanberry and dry mugwort beneath the sill. A small line of devoted villagers carried odd baskets of votive offerings for Bersula, the Dark Mother. Their fingers were laced in a knot of wooden beads, whispers gracing their mouths and causing puffs of fog to escape their lips.

"Split up," Valek said. "You both know your areas."

Valek tied his horse to the closest tree, and Niah reluctantly followed him to the first house, as Laith and Daria disappeared down the street. A woman with a wrinkled face opened the door. Her lips trembled as she greeted them.

"How may we be of service, Lord?" she asked.

"Commander," he corrected.

"O...of course," she rushed. "Commander."

Her husband sat on a nearby chair and stood up on weak knees when he met Valek's eye.

"We will keep it brisk," Valek said. "Do you have anything to share that has occurred in these parts? Anything suspicious that you think might be of interest to the Crown?"

"There has been a…a goat thief," the woman said shakily. "He strikes at night, and several neighbours have said—"

"Unless that is a euphemism for a crime of a greater nature, you will spare me the details," Valek said curtly.

He walked around the room, wrists folded neatly behind his back as he appraised the space, studying the threaded carpet as if it contained the secrets of the world.

"Novice, pat down this woman to see if she possesses any contraband," Valek said.

This was ridiculous. The woman looked like she was about to faint at his mere presence—hardly the constitution of someone who committed crimes in her spare time. Niah opened her mouth to refuse, but Valek's glare outmatched the frigid wind that howled outside the window. His patience was running thin, and Niah made the conscious decision not to stoke the flames of his temper.

She sighed and walked towards the woman. Niah lightly touched her shoulders and then the pockets of her dress.

"Give me and my novice a moment alone," Valek barked. "Wait upstairs."

The couple looked relieved to be dismissed, even if it was momentary.

"What?" Niah asked, annoyed. "I followed your orders."

"That was the most half-arsed pat down I've seen in my life," Valek spat. He crossed the room until he was inches away from her, staring down at her from his high nose.

"If you're so good at it, why don't you do the honors?" Niah hissed. "I'm sure she's hiding an arsenal under her dress. How pleased the King will be when you bring him such a bounty!"

"I will leave the task of searching them in your incapable

hands," Valek said. "Now is as good a time as any to teach you the proper way to search suspected offenders. Turn around."

Valek didn't wait for her to obey. His big hands fell on her waist, spinning her so quickly the room tilted for a brief moment. Niah now faced the wooden shelf filled with preserves.

"Grab the shelf," Valek ordered.

"I'm not—"

"Now."

Niah clenched her jaw. She didn't know what game he was playing at, but she refused to cower before him. Slowly, she grabbed the shelf above her, curling her fingers along the dust-covered edge.

"Good," he purred. "See how easy it is to listen to me."

"Just get on with it," she snapped.

Valek's fingers ran along her throat. When had he removed his gloves? She tried to recall if he had done so when they entered, but her mind was distracted by his shockingly cold touch.

His palms lingered along her shoulders and slid under her arms, making a clean sweep to her fingers before threading his with her own. His touch grazed the scar on her palm.

"I don't understand the purpose of this," she said breathlessly. "I would see if they had something in their hand."

"No, you wouldn't," he said. "Sometimes what you see and feel are complete opposites of each other. Like a fork in the road with two paths drawing you in different directions."

"Great," she muttered. "Riddles."

His hand fell on her waist, squeezing her flesh.

"If I wanted a smart-arse comment, I'd ask for one," Valek said.

"If I wanted a fumbling fool to feel me up, I'd go to a brothel," Niah snapped.

Valek's palm slid down her stomach. "Is that what you think I'm doing, looking for an excuse to touch you?"

His fingers fluttered along her ribs just below her breasts, and her breath caught in her throat. She could feel the weight of his body behind her, see the shadow of his polished boots beneath her robes.

"You can't blame me for my suspicions when you seem to make it a habit to sleep with your subordinates," Niah said. "I know there is something between you and Daria."

"Is that jealousy I hear in your voice?" Valek asked. "Or curiosity? Are you wondering if I'll break those very rules with you?"

"Neither!"

Valek leaned down, lips grazing her ear. "Then why are you trembling under my touch?"

"I am no—"

Valek's hand dropped.

"I hope you've learned your lesson."

Once they called back the couple, Valek decided there was nothing left to see. After a swift search, he painted a black mark on their door with charcoal and moved on.

"So, we won't search them anymore?" she asked bitterly. "What was the point of that?"

"Novices do not question their commanding officer," Valek said. "Not unless they want to do forty laps in the cold."

Niah mimicked him, pleased to be rewarded with a glare.

"Nor do they mock their commanding officer," he continued. "Unless they're itching to do a hundred laps *and* sleep outside tonight."

At the fifth house, Valek gripped the son of a woman, holding a blade to the boy's throat. The boy couldn't have been older than thirteen. His lips trembled as his mother cried out.

"Please, don't hurt him," the woman said. "He is my only child."

"I am beginning to tire of these answers," Valek hissed. "Tell me if there is anyone who would be of interest to the King, or I won't be held responsible for what I do."

"Winterson," Niah said sternly. "Let him go."

"No," he said. "You'll be surprised how quickly tongues loosen, once bodies start dropping."

The blade sank, blood trickling down the boy's throat.

"If you want answers, speak to Lefty," the woman rushed. "He is always up to no good. Just please let Tomas go!"

"I don't like being lied to," Valek said. "A message will need to be sent."

Niah unsheathed her blade and pointed it at Valek. "Release the boy. We have our answers."

She could feel the two Fallen she had silently summoned darkening the doorway.

"Stand down, Novice."

"You first," Niah said.

"As you wish."

The boy's scream split the air as he collapsed, blood pouring from his neck. His mother fell to her knees, cradling him.

Niah's mouth popped open, eyes widening in horror. A scream escaped her, and Valek dragged her outside. His fingers sank into her shoulders.

"Calm down," he barked.

Guilt sunk its iron claws inside her flesh, hooking in like pincers. A part of her blamed herself for goading Valek, for forgetting the monster she dealt with.

"You killed him," she said hoarsely.

"I made a difficult decision," Valek said. "Fear is a powerful motivator."

"You are a monster."

"My reputation is all I have," he said with a grim expression. "Sometimes, extreme measures are warranted."

"That boy was a child!" Niah said.

"The mother will survive," he said. His face was devoid of emotion. "As we all must."

He walked away. "Don't make me chase you."

Niah trembled but followed him. She would have to ride with him. The smell of that young boy's blood would sicken her.

His hand caught her wrist, before she climbed up.

"I won't hurt you," Valek said softly. "You are safe."

There was a glimmer in his eyes, that *almost* made her believe him. An earnestness that could not be ignored.

"I'm never safe around you."

Valek didn't speak as he lifted her onto the horse, and they rode back in silence.

Chapter 17

The clearing skimmed out before them like the Palm of Aubrith. Moonlight spilled through the canopy in silver ribbons, and frost clung to the bark of the larch trees like tiny crystals stitched to the bodice of a gown. Mosquitoes circled above their heads, tormenting them with their foreign song, hovering by the flanks of the mares to dig their paper-thin pincers into their flesh. Niah had held her tongue the entire ride back. Each scathing insult that crawled up her throat, she swallowed back reluctantly. Valek was unstable and she didn't trust how he would react to her anger.

The dry bones of the rabbit they had skinned and cooked lay in a loose circle, blackened with soot.

Daria sat beside Valek, having a one-sided conversation while he stared blankly ahead. A raven strand of hair fell torturously into his dark eyes. She wondered if he felt any remorse for his actions, or if his heart had long since turned to ice.

Black, dirt-smeared boots landed before her, and her shoulders stiffened when Laith sat beside her.

"What did you do to spoil the mood?" Laith asked.

Niah glanced at him briefly, studying his brown eyes.

"How do you do it?" Niah asked, switching to Virelle. Valek

tilted his head in their direction, his eyes narrowed in suspicion. "How do you pretend like everything is okay?"

"I am older than you," Laith said. "I remember far more than you do."

"Then why do you sit here and act like they are not the enemy?"

"Do you even know anything about your enemy?" Laith asked. "Or do you simply run your mouth as you see fit?"

"If you have something to say, then say it."

"He can understand us," Laith said, jutting his chin at Valek. "He speaks Virelle."

Niah's eyes widened, surprised by this information.

"Maybe stop for one second and think to yourself if what you are doing is really working," Laith said in a clipped tone. "Do you have anything to bring your enemy down? Any knowledge or power or a hint of an idea on how you plan to escape? You've done nothing but prove to everyone that you can't be trusted."

"I won't pretend to care for them," she said. "I won't be like you."

"One of us can walk freely without obstruction and the other..." He glanced down at the shackles that wrapped around her wrists. "Well, I don't need to remind you what you are."

He moved to stand, and Niah placed her hand on his thigh, nails slightly digging.

"Help me," she pleaded. "Help us."

For the first time in weeks, Niah felt a spark of hope. Laith was in a position of power. He had his freedom and remained unshackled by the enemy.

"Do you remember that day when I made you tell me your secrets?" Laith asked.

Niah glared at him. "How could I forget?"

"Another Diviner can dig through that silly head of yours, and the last thing I need is for them to find me tangled in your mess," he said. "Do you want a piece of advice?"

Niah looked at him a bit differently than before. The anger

that often marked his eyes was gone, and he seemed mildly bored by their conversation. Not to mention, it was nice to hear her home tongue on someone other than Kesi.

She had never considered for a moment that Laith might be playing his own game. That perhaps he was mistreating them to trick the enemy. He had just confessed that he wouldn't help her because he could not afford to be caught. It made her want to hatch her own scheme. Niah knew then *exactly* what she had to do. Tomorrow, Valek was going to question this supposed rebel, and if the intel was correct, he would kill him. Niah would not let him get the chance. She would warn the man and hopefully forge ties with his allies.

"If you think Valek is a monster, you should pray to whatever deity listens that you never meet Maxim Winterson."

Chills seeped down her back. Niah could not imagine what the man who sired her worst enemy could be like.

Niah was sharing a tent with Valek. Not so shockingly, she would not be left to her own devices. Daria was outside keeping watch, and Laith would take the second shift while she and the Commander both rested. Her bedroll was small but warm, nestled in the corner of the tent. The space was barely wide enough to sit upright, the sloped walls rustling faintly with each lick of the wind. A creaking whistle sailed through the air, making her draw her furs closer. The air smelled faintly of pine needles and woodsmoke.

A flickering lantern cast gold shadows across the fabric, drawing blotchy figures across the dirt floor.

"What were you speaking to Laith about?" Valek asked.

She didn't want to converse with him, but Niah also didn't want to cast any suspicion on Laith.

"Trading insults," she said.

"Why did you touch his leg?"

Did he ever miss anything? He had been in conversation with Daria, and she hadn't thought he'd noticed when she'd stopped Laith from walking away.

"Surprised you noticed with Daria practically straddling you," Niah said.

She couldn't care less about him and Daria, but she wanted to change the subject.

"Does that bother you?"

"No."

"Then why constantly bring her up?" Valek asked. His dark eyes searched her face as if he could find the answers if he looked closely.

He peeled off his leather gloves. Next came his robe and then his armor.

Niah glanced away, disturbed by the casual way he undressed before her. She could hear the click of his belt buckle and the rustle of fabric as he changed into clean clothes. Her cheeks burned as she stared at the opposite wall, at the ripples in the tent cloth.

"I just want to sleep, Winterson," she said. "It has been a long, miserable day."

"You may call me Valek in private," he offered.

Niah did not know why the gesture felt like a peace offering, as if he were feeling guilty about killing the boy.

"No, I will not," Niah said. "Now, if you don't mind, I'm going to try to sleep and pray that I do not have nightmares of the little boy you killed."

"You shouldn't trust Laith," he said.

He was crouched before her, midnight eyes tracing her face with open fascination. His fingers reached out to tuck a strand of her hair behind her ear. She wondered what he saw when he looked at the swan-white strands. Did he see the markings of the Lightbearer? Or did he simply see a girl who did not belong?

"And I should trust you?"

"No," he said. A simple word. His eyes studied her hair with the rapt attention of a scholar. "This is lovely."

Her eyes narrowed in suspicion. She could not tell if he was teasing her or not.

"You mean the mark of the Lightbearer?" she asked. "How can you admire a symbol that repels all you believe in?"

"I've never claimed to be faithful," he said. "Am I not a heretic?"

"You are," she said.

"Even a heretic needs something to believe in," Valek whispered.

His eyes were locked on hers with wicked zeal and her stomach clenched. Valek's hand dropped, letting her hair flow around them like stardust.

His touch was gone, and his eyes, filled with witchery, faded from her sight.

And that was all that mattered.

Valek had miraculously fallen asleep.

Niah stared at him for a moment. His lashes were long and thin like spider legs, casting shadows on his milky skin. The stark blue veins behind his eyelids fluttered for a moment before they stilled. He almost looked innocent when his guard was down. He had a beauty that could drown empires. It was a shame that he had dedicated his life to serving as a Reaper.

Niah slowly parted the flap and glanced outside. There was a tent across from them. Either Laith or Daria was outside patrolling. Niah didn't see anyone, so she slowly crept out of the partition and went to Valek's horse.

Niah followed the same path they had taken to the woman

whose son Valek had killed. She hoped that she would give her some more information about Lefty once she knew that she was not with the King's army.

The door was still ajar. The wooden panels creaked under her boots. In the corner, curled into a ball, was the woman; she didn't turn at the sound of her footsteps. It wasn't that she didn't hear her, but rather that she didn't care. Death would be a small mercy compared to the burden of grief. Niah just stood there for several minutes, lost for words as she watched her shoulders shake with anguish.

In that moment, Niah hated Valek more than she had ever thought possible.

The woman turned her head, eyes rimmed with despair. Niah crouched down, staring at her with sympathy.

"I am so sorry," she whispered.

The woman's eyes were wary. Her gaze locked on her collar, which signified her as a Reaper.

"I am not with the army," she said. She bent her elbows, so the sleeves of her robe fell to reveal her cuffs. "These silence my magic. I am from the Low North and am a part of the Order of the White Flame."

The woman sniffled. Her eyes were uncertain.

"I don't intend to hurt you," Niah promised. "I just want to know about the rebels. I want to help them. You said Lefty was a part of it? Is there a way for me to get word to him before the Commander seeks him?"

"Lefty is not the man he hunts," she said, her voice raw from crying. "He is a degenerate, but he wouldn't know the first thing about rebelling against the King. It would mean he had something to fight for."

"I understand," Niah said. "You wanted to mislead him. It will occupy him for a day or so, but he is a bloodhound. He won't stop until he gets what he wants, and the longer he hunts, the more dangerous he will become."

"If the rebels have any sense, they would be long gone by now," she said.

Niah placed a hesitant hand on her shoulder.

"What's your name?" Niah asked.

"Ani."

"He did the same to me years ago, Ani," Niah whispered. "Came to my home and left nothing but blood and destruction in his wake."

Niah needed to know where the rebels were so she could keep them safe from Valek. She could not stand on the sidelines while innocents who fought back were slain by the Reapers, and that was exactly what Valek Winterson was: an animal with iron teeth and infinite claws. A beast born from the Corruption.

"I can help keep them safe from him," Niah promised. "If you let me, that is."

"And if I don't?" she asked hesitantly.

"Then I shall leave you to mourn."

Niah stood up. Perhaps it was too soon to demand the loyalty of the woman whom she had just watched suffer a great tragedy. It wasn't right to ask this of her, and when no words came from her mouth, Niah turned around to return to camp.

Her fingers grasped the doorknob.

"Polina works at the apothecary; she may have some answers for you," Ani said. "The people are afraid. Our choices are to either fall to ruin or bend to their will. The King who sits in the heart of the capital is not our friend. We are alone and surrounded by his soldiers. Our taxes have risen. The ports down in the valley are receiving weapons but no produce. War is expensive, and our sons are used as shields for the Reapers, and when they fall, their corpses are desecrated and used as their shields."

Niah had underestimated how many people were unhappy with the King's war. It filled her with relief to know that they had potential allies. For weeks, she had felt unbearably alone in this foreign land, surrounded by enemies, but for once, she felt like she could breathe, like the world wasn't tilting beneath her feet.

"I want to help," Niah said.

Ani gave her directions to Polina's shop. It wasn't far from here. Every so often she would glance behind her, afraid that she would hear the beating hooves of Valek's horse.

Once she reached the described street, Niah tied her horse to a nearby tree. A young girl slid a key in the lock, prepared to close for the night. Her neck turned at the sound of her footfalls. The girl's eyes widened with fear, and Niah came to a slow halt, arms raised in surrender.

"I mean no harm," Niah said.

"You are a Reaper," the girl whispered.

"Are you Polina?" she asked. "I just want to talk."

"That is not my name," she said. It was obvious that she was lying. "I cannot help you."

"You may speak to me or Commander Winterson in the morning," Niah said evenly.

She did not have time to comfort her. Not when Valek could wake up at any moment and find her missing. Niah would never get another chance like this to speak with the rebels and build ties with them.

"I have little time to spare," Polina said. "My father will be expecting me."

"I won't be long," Niah promised.

Polina led her inside and slid the door shut. There were shelves of marked ointments and a small workshop in the back with jars of herbs and dried plants. There was a chair in the corner with indigo padding and little silver stars embroidered on the fabric. Niah sank into the seat while Polina paced in front of her. She didn't see how this trembling girl had anything to do with the rebellion. Her thin arms were coiled around her waifish form as if she could protect herself by sheer will.

"Ani sent me here," Niah said. "Her son was killed by Commander Winterson."

Polina's thin face grew faint. For a moment, Niah worried that the girl would cry.

"Ani misled him to a man named Lefty, whom I presume he will kill tomorrow," she said. "Commander Winterson will not stop until he gets his answers. I can help keep you safe if you tell me the truth."

"You are one of them," she said bitterly. "Why should I trust you?"

"I am a captive from the Low North," she said, letting her sleeves fall back to reveal her shackles. "I am a member of the Order. My loyalty is to the Queen."

"You are part of the Order?" Polina asked.

"Yes."

Polina seemed surprised by this admission. Slowly, she leaned forward as if the wind would steal her secrets if she spoke too loudly.

"They are here," she whispered.

"Who?"

"Your Sisters," she replied.

Niah stilled, surprised by her words. Her breath caught in her throat.

They had found her. They had come for her.

Her heart soared, and she wondered if Morgana was among them. Niah drew her hood away from her head, leaning forward to speak with her some more, when she heard Polina's sharp gasp.

"They are looking for a girl who fits your description," Polina said. "Hair as white as snowfall."

"Where are they?"

"I do not know," she said. "They come to me. They may return tomorrow night."

"I will come tomorrow then," Niah said.

She needed to speak to her Sisters. They would help her concoct an escape for her and Kesi. They would free them, and she would unleash the blinding force of her power on her enemies.

Niah returned to camp, feeling lighter than she had in weeks. She was tying Valek's horse to the birch tree when a gruff voice spoke.

"Where did you go?"

Her heart thudded when she turned to face Laith.

"A midnight stroll," she whispered.

His eyes narrowed. The air between them was tangled with unspoken words. Fear struck her at the thought of Valek learning about her escape. He would kill Ani and Polina and discover the truth that the Order was here, hiding in plain sight.

"Don't tell him," Niah said. "Please."

Laith didn't say a word.

Niah walked past him back to her tent, hoping that he kept his mouth shut. Her eyes sent him one last pleading look before she let the flaps drop.

Valek was still sound asleep when she crawled back into her bedroll, and she fell into a warm slumber.

Chapter 18

The next morning, they set off to a small bar across the village where their offender was said to frequent. The sun poured over them behind its shield of milky, colorless clouds. Niah's skin flared hotly as she kept her back as straight as possible. She was half-seated on the edge of the saddle in an attempt to escape the muscled chest of Valek. The ridges dug into her skin but she did not reward herself with comfort—not if it meant plastering herself to him.

He had drawn on his mask for their journey.

He made no effort to speak to her, and Niah was relieved. She didn't have the energy to argue with him today. She had only gotten a few hours of sleep last night. The sun had barely risen when Valek roused her from her slumber. Niah hoped that Laith kept his mouth shut. A part of her worried that he'd told Valek, and that was why he was giving her the cold shoulder.

The thought of facing her Sisters made her tremble. She was not the same girl who had been stolen from the monastery. She was tainted by death magic. She had been molded into a weapon and made to serve the Commander.

The scent of bitter ale and old smoke hung heavy in the air, clinging to the warped wooden beams like cobwebs. A few patrons were scattered among the battered tables, many of them slumped figures in stained tunics and dust-covered boots, nursing their drinks with desperate fingers as if they clutched the Codex. It was far too early to be drinking, yet their tankards were half-empty. Their dark hair and ashen faces lifted at the sound of their footsteps. Everyone stiffened when Valek appeared in his bone mask and heavy boots.

Their eyes were bruised and shadowy with lack of sleep, and their mouths dropped in gaping horror.

"I'm looking for a man called Lefty," Valek announced.

Everyone turned to look at a man in the corner. His skin was pockmarked, and his glare sharp enough to cut. Niah couldn't tell if he was playing at being brave or if he was fueled by drunken courage.

"Aye, it's me," he said boldly.

He stood up on bad knees as they approached.

"Shall we go somewhere less public?" Valek asked. "I have a few questions for you."

"Here is all right," Lefty said. "I got nothing to hide."

"Very we—"

Valek barely got his question out before Lefty dove to her right in an attempt to flee. Niah tried to grab him, but she missed the rusty blade in his hand. Pain flashed down her side, and she winced. The vagrant had sliced her. Niah applied pressure to her ribs, feeling the warm flow of blood down her side. She gritted her teeth, sliding down into the abandoned chair. Her vision flickered, and she could feel her fingers grow wetter the longer she compressed the wound.

Lefty had barely made it a step when Valek caught him by the collar of his shirt and flung him so hard he crashed into a table. Glass shards spilled on the floor, and everyone, including the barkeeper, ran out the door.

"Where is your rebel camp?" Valek demanded.

"I am no rebel," Lefty rushed. His eyes widened with fear. "I swear it!"

"Even if you are no rebel, you attacked my novice," Valek snarled.

Valek was on Lefty before he could react, fist crushing into his face so hard a tooth fell beside him, blood splattering her boots.

"How dare you lay your filthy hands on my novice?" he growled.

His fist continued to batter his face. Blood poured down Lefty's broken cheekbones and crooked nose.

"You do not *look* at, let alone *touch* her," Valek snarled.

It felt like hours passed by the time he finally got off him.

"Shite," Valek cursed. "He's dead."

He seemed mildly annoyed that he had killed their only lead.

Niah blinked slowly, feeling suddenly weak. She blinked rapidly, struggling to clear her cloudy vision. It was just her luck that she would be sliced by that man's filthy blade who knows where that weapon had been! It would be a miracle if she did not die from the contamination.

Valek came to her, crouching on his knees.

"How do you feel, Novice?" he asked.

"Like it should have been you who got stabbed," Niah muttered. "You're the one who came in here making all the demands. God, it hurts."

"Show me," he said, in that demanding tone.

"No."

Valek glared at her. "Now."

A ripple of pain cut down her side, making her breath stutter. She had to get it checked out by a healer. Maybe if Valek saw how serious it was, he would take her to one. Niah slipped her robe off with her good arm and lifted the hem of her tunic. A sharp line ran down her side, deep and ugly. Blood trickled down her ribs, and she reckoned she'd need a couple of stitches.

"You'll need stitches," Valek said, confirming her thoughts. "Come along."

Niah moved to stand, but he surprised her when he slid his arms under her knees and lifted her off the chair.

"Put me down!" Niah cried.

"Shut up."

"You shut up, you brute."

Valek carried her to a nearby house and knocked on the door so harshly it was a wonder the wood did not splinter under his touch. A startled young girl opened it, and he brushed past her.

"I need a thread and needle and a bottle of wine," Valek barked. "Now."

He walked to the nearest table and swept off the items with a swing of his arm. Glass shattered on the floor, and Niah had half a mind to scold him for ruining the villagers' belongings, but the pain kept her tongue still. Valek placed her down gently and began to lift her tunic. Niah didn't have the sense to be ashamed of his critical gaze, as the cool air licked the underside of her breast.

"Leave," he said gruffly.

It took her a moment to realize that he had spoken to the girl who had returned with his requested objects. It was silent again.

"Maybe she should patch me up," Niah said. "Have you ever done this before?"

"Some of the villagers don't like us," he said. "It is why the rebels hide out here; they know they have the support of the villagers. Do you want someone who could stab you with this needle, or me?"

Niah was silent. He had a point. Even if she didn't support the Reapers, she was dressed like one, and they didn't know any better.

"Drink this," Valek said, pressing the bottle of wine to her lips. He lifted her head, and she reluctantly took several good gulps. The wine was cheap and watered down. It wouldn't numb the pain as much as he thought it would.

"Take a deep breath," he said.

Valek ripped the bottle from her fingers and doused it generously over the wound. A hiss escaped her at the pain.

It was cowardly of her to flinch from this, but the pain was unbearable; she couldn't imagine what it would feel like when the thread and needle punctured her broken flesh. The wine alone had felt like acid on her skin.

"Wait," she said shakily. "I'm not ready."

"You are losing too much blood; it is now or never," Valek said. "What is your favorite color?"

"What?" Niah asked, confused.

"A color you prefer to the others," he explained slowly. "What is it?"

"The color of your blood when I cut out your throa—"

The needle sank into her skin, and a sharp gasp escaped her.

"What is a memory that makes you happy?" Valek continued.

Niah knew what he was doing. He was attempting to distract her while he worked.

"I reckon the day I finally get to kill you," she said.

Valek's mouth twitched. "Are all your favorite things related to me? If I didn't know any better, I'd say you were obsessed with me."

"Don't be ridiculous," she said.

Another ripple of pain tore down her side, and she squeezed her eyes shut. Her hand unwillingly reached for his thigh, and her nails dug in, feeling his hard muscles twitch under her touch.

"You're doing good," Valek said.

"I don't need your praise."

"Why is everything a challenge with you?" Valek sighed. "I tire of your flirting style."

"Flirting?!?" she asked.

It irritated her that he didn't take her threats seriously. That his infuriating mouth curled up to the side, as if she were being playful when she was being entirely honest.

"You told Laith that I am the most beautiful man you've ever seen. Why can we not return to the compliments?" Valek asked with a small smirk. "I would not be opposed to you showering me with flattery again."

"I was under his magic," Niah said bitterly. "And will you ever let it go?"

"No, I will cherish it," he said. "Since you will never compliment me again unless you are spirit-bound."

His voice was teasing, and she didn't like that he was finding amusement in her discomfort.

"Almost done," Valek said.

He tied the last stitch and cut the thread. He wrapped it with a cloth, and she frowned when he began to slip off his cloak and tunic. His arms rippled as he tore the fabric over his head, mussing his hair. There was a large tattoo on his left side of a roaring wolf that took up the entirety of that side of his torso. Niah stared at it with fascination. She knew the wolf was the national animal of the High North.

"Here," he said. "It's clean."

Niah was unsettled by his behaviour. He had stitched her wound and was now offering her the clothes off his back. He had been so focused and gentle while he worked, distracting her with his silly questions. It didn't sit well with her that he was acting this way. This wasn't the same man who had just bludgeoned Lefty to death with his fists and mercilessly slain a child yesterday. Her shoulders stiffened as she recalled the grieving mother's screams and the empty stare of the dead boy who had done nothing to deserve his end.

"You're doing it again," Valek said.

"Doing what?"

"Acting like I didn't save your life. Again."

"Nothing you do is selfless, Winterson," Niah said. "I would be a fool to forget that."

Valek sent a Fallen to summon Daria back to camp and then vanished into the trees after he switched into a new tunic. Niah still wore his cloak. It hung heavily on her shoulders and smelled like midnight and crushed violets.

"What happened?" Daria demanded.

Her eyes were locked on the oversized cloak. It swept the ground like a broom, covering Niah's boots. The clasp was different than hers. It had two wolves whose open jaws were interlocked to snap it shut.

"I got stabbed," she said. "Guess the Commander didn't want me slowing him down while he terrorizes the villagers."

"You got stabbed," Daria repeated.

Niah nodded, sitting on the log. She winced as pain shot up her side. Daria sat across from her, her gaze suspicious.

"It isn't what you think," Niah said slowly.

"And how would you know what I think?" she asked sharply. "You hardly know me."

Daria stared at Valek like he put the stars in the night sky. Niah had never loved a man, so she could not assume to know what she felt. Her entire life had been filled with war. Sometimes, Niah felt like she was still there on that boat, wind licking her hair and the ferocious waves dragging her towards the unknown. Other times, she was in her small childhood bedroom, her mother sitting on the rocking chair, reading her old fables.

Perhaps that was the curse of being a child of war: you never truly grew up.

"My father is working on a marriage arrangement for me and Valek," Daria said abruptly. "By spring next year, we will be wed."

Niah wasn't sure why she was sharing this information with her or how she was expected to react. It was as though she intended to strike envy in her, but why would Niah care about Valek?

"Congratulations?" Niah said.

"He didn't tell you?" Daria asked.

"We don't speak about our personal lives," she said. "And I'd like to keep it that way."

Daria stood up and walked to her tent. Even though Valek had sent for Daria to keep an eye on her, she left her on her own. It wasn't like she would escape without Kesi. All the extra eyes on her were useless. Besides, she still felt fairly weak from the attack. Her muscles were tight and every move ached. It would be difficult sneaking out tonight to see Polina, but it was a risk Niah had to take.

"Let me see your stitches," Valek said.

It was dark in their tent, and she was pretending to be asleep, so he felt comfortable sleeping early, and she could leave. But it also felt nice to not exert herself after the injury.

"You walked in here five minutes ago, Novice," he said dryly. "I very much doubt you are asleep. Also, you snore like a wild boar."

"I don't snore—"

Her words caught in her throat when she realized he had tricked her. His eyes gleamed in satisfaction.

"You were saying?" He raised a brow.

"You're not a healer. Leave me alone," she grumbled, pulling her furs over her head. "Also, the stitches you did are ugly."

"I said show me your stitches," he snapped. "Not describe them to me."

"Make me."

His eyes darkened, and he bent down on her bedroll. His fingers reached for his tunic. Niah hadn't packed any spare clothes, and she didn't think Daria would be kind enough to share, so she grudgingly wore Valek's clothes still.

Niah held the hem down, refusing to give in to his

demands. For one foolish second, she thought he would concede and fall back. After all, he was behaving rather brutishly.

"I will rip this off your back if you don't show me," he warned, fingers latched on the cloth.

"So desperate to see me naked, are you?" Niah sneered. "It's not the first time you threatened to undress me!"

"I am your commanding officer, Novice," he said darkly. "I forbid you from flirting with me."

"I am not flirting with you!" Niah exclaimed. "And you said a few hours ago that you liked my flirting."

"So, you were flirting?" Valek said. "I was right."

"No, you were wr—"

"Commander Winterson," Daria called.

She poked her head between the tent flaps, and Niah stilled. Daria's blue eyes were wide in shock, her mouth slightly parted. Niah could see how the scene before her could be misread. Valek was kneeling beside her, big thighs folded beneath him with both of their hands tangled in her tunic as if he were about to undress her, and she was aiding him.

"He's checking my wound, it is no—" Niah began, but Daria had vanished before she could finish.

Her hand went slack, and she couldn't even bother to fight Valek when he lifted the fabric and undid her bandage to check her wound. He grunted in approval.

He brought out a fresh bandage to replace the old one, working in silence. This was even more unbearable than when he had been stitching the cut. At least then she had been distracted by the pain; now she had his face leaning inches from her own, focused diligently on his task.

Facial hair darkened his jaw, and his eyes twinkled like burning cinders. The charcoal that lined his lids was smeared and coated his skin like a bruise. Her gaze traced the slope of his high nose to the full outline of his lips, bright as rubies and flushed from the chill. His mouth moved, but she could not fathom the words he spoke. A rushing roar ran through her ears like she was standing underwater.

His fingers touched beneath the cut where her flesh was bruised. A shiver glossed down her spine.

"Did you hear me?" Valek asked.

"No," she said hoarsely.

"I asked you if this hurt?" Valek asked.

Goosebumps crawled along her flesh like spiders.

"A bit," she breathed.

His finger circled the cut, landing at the top, just beneath the underside of her breast.

"And here?" he asked.

"No," she said quickly, in the hopes that if she answered fast, he would drop his cursed hands.

"I think your ribs are fine," he said. "Just some bruising."

"I could have told you that myself," Niah said. "You didn't need to play healer for that."

"I like playing healer," Valek said, drawing down her tunic. "Just as I like to see you wearing my clothes."

"Shut up," she said, shoving his chest. "Your arrogance knows no end."

A warm chuckle slipped from his mouth.

"Relax, Novice," he said. "I tease."

"I do not find your humor the least bit amusing," Niah said.

"Keep the cut dry," Valek said. "I'll remove the stiches in a week."

"I think I will go to the infirmary for that," she said. "Marta doesn't stroke my flesh like a wanton beast."

Valek lay down on his bedroll, stretching his long legs before him. He rested an arm behind his head, the ends of his tunic slipping out of his trousers. A flash of pale skin and faint hair revealed itself. Niah quickly looked away, her cheeks growing flushed. She didn't know what was wrong with her tonight. Perhaps the wound was infected, and she was coming down with a fever. Her body felt hot and taut.

"Sounds like the disgruntled words of someone who *wants* me to stroke them like a wanton beast."

"I doubt you know anything about pleasing a woman," Niah said.

"Are you offering to teach me?" Valek asked.

"No."

"Doubt a boring, monastery-born cleric like you has any tricks up her sleeve," Valek said, stifling his yawn.

He draped his arm over his eyes, shielding his vision. Annoyance flared inside her at his confident tone and dismissive gesture. He had ended the conversation without even giving her a chance to prove him wrong.

"That is not true," Niah said, between gritted teeth. "I have had many lovers whom I think on rather fondly from time to time!"

Her words had lifted to a shout. She hated when he was right. Niah had not so much as kissed a boy. It had always been Kesi who snuck between corridors and escaped to the village during the spring fête that celebrated Saint Carywen to kiss boys in barn sheds. Niah had remained behind pitifully alone, drowning under the weight of her responsibilities.

"Is that so?" Valek asked. His hand dropped so he could glare at her. "What are their names?"

"I said I recall their performance, not their life story," Niah snapped. "I am not a fool to be hung up on an old lover."

"Lover?" Valek asked. "Nobody calls a quick fuck a lover unless they are eighty years old or a lying virgin."

"I do not like vulgar words," Niah said.

"No, I reckon you only prefer vulgar acts to words," he said snidely. "Drop the ruse, Novice. I am not buying it."

Niah felt a sick sense of satisfaction that she had dug under his skin. His fists were clenched by his sides, and it was a wonder the tent did not combust with the heat wafting off his tense body. It should have alarmed her that he reacted so viciously to the mention of her with other men, but for some unfathomable reason, it comforted her.

"You should go speak to her," Niah said.

"Who?" he barked.

"Daria."

Valek did not respond.

"She likely got the wrong impression of us," Niah continued. "And I don't want her to glare at me more than she already does."

"She is not my wife," Valek said. "I do not owe her an explanation."

"Yet," Niah mumbled.

His head turned to stare at her. "What did you say?"

"I know about the spring wedding," Niah said. "I'd congratulate you if I didn't plan on killing you before you speak your vows."

"There is no wedding arrangement," Valek said gruffly. "And you can stop with the threats; I do not plan to wed the girl."

Niah bristled; she was not warning him off because she was jealous of his stupid nuptials. He was a ruthless villain who had ruined her life.

"You should still speak to her," Niah said. "It's the right thing to do."

"Not happening," he said, turning to the opposite side.

His words were spoken with a chill.

A clear hint that he was done with the conversation.

Two hours passed before Niah felt confident that Valek had fallen asleep. Slowly, she crawled out of their tent and made her way to Polina's apothecary. The bells dinged lightly when she opened the front door. Polina was wiping down the front desk with a cloth. Relief filled her face at the sight of Niah.

"I was afraid you wouldn't get the chance to return," she said.

"Me neither," Niah said.

Niah had thought for sure that Laith would tell Valek about the other night. She was grateful but uneasy that he had kept it to himself. She still did not fully understand whose side he played on. He was just as big a mystery as when they met. But she knew that he wasn't the Teren refugee who stood by the High North. There was more to him than met the eye.

"Hello, Niah."

Niah's eyes widened at the familiar voice. The woman who came from behind the shelves was a person she thought she would never see again. It was Prioress Morgana. She didn't wear her familiar white robes. It was strange to see her in trousers and a tunic, but she could understand the need for stealth. They were on enemy lands, and it was best to dress accordingly. Even the white streak that ran down the center of her hair had been concealed with dye.

"Morgana," she whispered.

Niah rushed towards her, falling into her warm embrace. She smelled of wildflowers and ink, familiar and comforting. A strangled sob escaped her as Morgana patted her head the way she did when she was a child. Niah had missed her and the other women. She missed her home so badly it ached.

"It is so good to see you, my dear girl."

Niah felt shame lick her belly when Morgana pulled back to look at her. She wondered if she could see just how blackened her soul had grown. The rot inside her was festering; each day, she grew farther from the light. It wasn't just the robes that marked her as altered. It was so much more. And she feared that Morgana's keen eyes would pick up on this change and that she would shun her for her choices. Without her Sisters, she would not be able to fight this war, but without Morgana, she would be lost.

"We heard rumors that they'd brought you here," she said. "We had to come find you."

It had been so long since someone had held her broken pieces together. Her eyes grew wet at the thought of fleeing this wicked land, of returning to her roots and the place she felt safest.

"They forced these shackles onto me," Niah said, revealing her wrists. And then softer, quieter, she added, "It isn't the only thing they forced upon me."

Nobody could see the dark tendrils of death magic that she could weave around the corpses. But if she reached out to the Fallen, she could show them a glimpse of it. They would see her eyes darken into shallow pools of nothing.

"I am so sorry to hear that," Morgana said gently. Her hands stroked her hair comfortingly, and Niah swallowed the urge to cry. "You were a prisoner. You cannot blame yourself for anything you did to survive."

"Kesi is with me," she said. "They captured us together."

"They wanted our Lightbearer to weaken us," Morgana said. "But we are stronger than ever. You are Saint-touched, Niah. You will save us all."

Niah swallowed, feeling the burden of this weight. It seemed even across all this distance, she could not escape her destiny.

"May I tell you a story?" Morgana asked, sitting across from her.

Niah had always adored Morgana's tales. Her raspy voice had often put her to sleep when she was a young girl with tales of Saints and silver-haired warrior women and the Light Father. Niah had cradled those stories like a flame in the palm of her hands, protecting it from the harsh wind.

"Once upon a time, Saint Ylena faced death made flesh, the one the heretics call Riven. A demon of untold power who sought to upset the balance and overtake our world. He wished to unlock the gates that seal the Lower World and destroy us. So, Saint Ylena blessed a chosen one, the Lightbearer, to protect us not just from the heretics who serve the demon and his mother, but to ensure that Riven is *never* awakened."

Chills slithered down her back. She knew the rumors of those who were part of the Cult of Riven, and she could not imagine how wicked Riven had been if his followers were so wretched. They killed innocents in his name, an offering to seek his blessings.

"It is said that when the earth begins to rot, then the spell that holds him has weakened," Morgana said. She spoke of the Corruption. "During these times, we will need the power of Saint Ylena to ensure that the prophecy does not unfold."

"The prophecy?" Niah whispered.

"Do not fret about it," Morgana said. Once more, shielding her from the truth. "The light is on our side. We will not fail."

"I want to come home," Niah said, tears in her eyes. "I cannot be here any longer. I cannot be tainted with their magic."

"Soon," Morgana promised. "This is the closest we have come to destroying them. We have Sister Catrin acting as a servant in the kitchens of their fortress. She says you are close to their Commander?"

Niah flinched, wondering what Catrin had seen. She had paid no mind to the servants, and she'd never heard of a Catrin before. Did she report on all the wickedness she had been forced to partake in?

"He is the one who kidnapped me," Niah said slowly. "He keeps me by his side always."

Morgana lifted her palm and placed a blade in her hand. It was silver, and there was the face of Saint Ylena's moth carved into the mother-of-pearl hilt. The moth was also the emblem of the capital of Virelle, the Queen's sigil.

"This belongs to you," she said. "It was Saint Ylena's, and it should be in the possession of the Lightbearer."

"You want us to remain there in that place?" Niah asked.

A part of her hoped that Morgana would say otherwise. That she would tell her the escape plan that would be used to aid their rescue, and Niah would never have to remember the torment of the past two months ever again.

But the war could not be fought from a distance.

"May I ask you something, Morgana?" Niah asked.

"Yes, my girl."

"Why is the Corruption only tainting our woods and not theirs?" Niah asked. "If we are the righteous and they the infidels, then why does Aubrith punish us?"

"It is not for us to think on the mysterious ways of the Light Father," she said. Her voice grew as sharp as a flying arrow. "Do not be fooled by their lies. They are nothing more than violent monsters who worship a demoness and her cursed son."

Guilt trickled down her throat like spoiled wine, burning her flesh in the process. How foolish of her to doubt. Morgana had fed her tales in her youth about the Reapers. Woven into the fabric of her wretched nightmares were the men she described who wore masks fashioned of the bones of their enemies, who marched to a song heard by none but them. It was said they had claws and fangs and fed on the blood of their dead. That was why they massacred the lands: to feed their depraved souls.

Had Valek not proven her words true? Had he not slain an innocent boy for his own pleasure? Had he not acted as the very beast they accused him of being?

Morgana's eyes softened.

"I do not mean to chide you, Niah," she said. "Only to guide you."

"I understand," Niah said.

"Is there any way you can learn about any upcoming military rotations? Gather some intel for your Sisters and me to plan our attack?" Morgana asked, not lingering thankfully on her silly question.

"I can try," Niah said. "But how will I reach out to you? I don't know when we'll come back to finish these rebel hunts."

"You may send your messages to Catrin to pass along to us," Morgana said. "We will not leave this land until they are all dead."

Niah stared at her reflection on the silver blade. Her slim-boned face and high cheekbones looked back at her with ghostly precision. Her eyes appeared wide and doll-like in the reflection.

She wondered if anyone else could tell that she was afraid or if she did a better job of hiding it.

"I will not fail you," Niah whispered.

"My precious girl," she said, drifting a finger through her hair. "I know you will not."

Niah was peeling off her boots when Valek awoke with a jolt. A blade was in his hand, and before she knew it, he had her flat on her back, the silver edge raised in warning. His other hand was coiled around her throat.

"Winterson," she gasped. "It's me."

"What are you doing awake?" Valek demanded.

His hair was ruffled from sleep. His brows furrowed in confusion.

"I...I needed to relieve myself," she said.

"You could have woken me up," he said, peeved. "I would have escorted you."

"And then what?" Niah snapped. "You'd wipe me clean?"

"Maybe if you asked nicely," Valek said.

"You're a filthy beast."

A frown marked his mouth. Niah assumed he was offended by her insult, but his thumb traced a tear that clung to her jaw. Niah could not contain the surge of her emotions. It had fallen on her like a battering ram when she left Morgana at the shop. The future frightened her with its grimness.

"You were crying," he whispered.

"No," Niah said, but the word lacked conviction.

Valek wiped the stray tear. His thumb lingered on her skin.

"Do you want to talk about it?" Valek asked, hesitantly, as if he were approaching a wild boar.

"It is quite foolish to unburden your soul to your jailer, do you not think?" she asked coldly.

Something that could have been mistaken for guilt crossed his eyes.

"Despite how it may seem, I do not enjoy seeing you upset, little saint," he said. He glanced at her tear-stained face. "It unsettles me."

"You are the one who torments me," she said.

"I don't know how to be anything less than what I was made to be," Valek said. "You may take me for what I am—ruined, wrathful, doomed—but do not ask me to change. I am incapable of it."

"Then why do you touch me like that?" Niah asked.

Like he was afraid she would crumble like powder if he pressed too hard. His palm lay flat on her cheek.

"I suppose even blood-stained hands can caress, once in a while," Valek said.

Niah closed her eyes. For a split second, they remained as such, locked in a painting, captured mid-brushstroke.

His hand dropped, and Niah curled down on her bedroll, attempting to forget his strangled, hopeless words. It would serve her no good to see the glimmers of humanity in a monster. The Reapers were not people; mortal blood did not traverse through their veins. Suffering and pain were the vowels of their language. Blood was the fuel that drove their famished souls.

And no amount of wishful thinking would ever change that.

Chapter 19

Niah had noticed that winter in the High North was far more ferocious than in the Low North. The thought of *home* brought a strange pang to her chest, tightening like a cord around her heart.

In the High North, the wind didn't arrive under guise, but with a grand flourish, forcing animals into hiding. Morning hoarfrost covered the grass in a delicate sheen while wolves had shed their coats for a pearlescent camouflage, and bears had hunkered down in their caves to fall into their slumber. The ravines had dried and whittled to empty caverns, and the birds' songs were absent as they headed back to the fortress. Sleets of ice covered the ground, slowing down their ascent up the crooked hill.

Niah did not risk sneaking out again, not since that night Valek had caught her slipping back in. If he learned that the Sisters were here, planning an ambush, he would destroy them. A shudder trailed down her back as she imagined his wrathful sword falling on their necks.

"It's so good to be back," Laith said, cracking his neck. "I've missed my bed."

"My body is littered with wasp bites," Daria grumbled, scratching her neck.

"Bunch of weaklings," Valek murmured.

"Says the one who spends half an hour shaving his face every morning and fixing his hair, so it falls dreamily into his eyes," Laith said. "I reckon you put a tint on your lips and cheeks too."

"You think my hair is dreamy, Laith?" Valek asked dryly. "I'm afraid you're not my type."

"How will I ever sleep at night?" Laith asked, flattening a hand on his chest.

"Do you both like each other?" Niah asked.

Her question was rewarded with a glare from Laith that delighted her. She rode with Valek so she couldn't see his face, but she hoped that he was annoyed by her question.

"Oh, they would certainly bed if they could decide which one is on top," Daria said.

Niah's brows raised, intrigued by the thought.

"I heard that," Laith said. He pointed a finger at Niah. "Get your head out of the gutter."

"It's obvious that I would be on top," Valek added, before he spurred his horse on, sprinting away from the rest of them.

"You paint a tempting picture," Daria said.

"Fuck you!" Laith called behind them.

Niah laughed, the sound strange and the sensation foreign. She couldn't recall the last time she had felt the tension in her shoulders loosen, and her teeth unclench.

Now that she knew Morgana was safe and alive, her amusement didn't feel like betrayal. For weeks, she had been cloaked in darkness and forced to practice their death magic, but now there was a chance she could blindside them *and* return home.

They entered the stables, and Valek placed his hands on her waist, gently lowering her down.

"We need to go to the infirmary to have your stitches removed," he said. A twinge slid down her ribs, reminding her that she had in fact been stabbed.

"It's fine," she said.

"I insist," Valek said.

"No, you don't insist you command."

"Don't pretend as if you don't like me playing the doting wife," Valek said.

"Do not *ever* refer to yourself as a doting wife." Niah wrinkled her nose. "You are a wicked infidel."

"And you need to think of better insults," he said. "You bore me with this current repertoire."

Niah glared at him. He reached forward and flicked her nose.

"Did you just do *that*?"

"Maybe."

Niah reached up to flick his nose back, but he caught her fingers and mussed her hair, ruffling up the strands like she was a child.

"You're going to regret that!" Niah warned.

She reached up with her free hand to grab a fistful of his hair, but the smug bastard only leaned back, catching her wrist with infuriating ease. Now, both her hands were trapped in his grip, and he pinned them against the stable wall.

His body pressed into hers, solid and unyielding, and heat bled through the thin layers between them. Stray locks of his raven hair fell across his eyes, wandering slowly over her face.

"I will kill you," Niah promised.

"I like it when you threaten me," Valek said. "It makes me feel special."

"You won't *feel* anything when I slit your throat."

Valek's eyes darkened. Her words were intended to repel him, but he simply seemed more intrigued.

Her voice was oddly breathy when she spoke, the words escaping her in a strangled gasp.

"Release me," Niah said.

Valek's throat bobbed slightly before he let his hands drop and took a step back.

"Come along," he said. "I haven't forgotten about the infirmary trip."

Niah groaned, but she followed him to the infirmary. She

would do *anything* to make him stop looking at her like a wild animal that would pounce at her at any moment.

"We missed you so much!" Kesi said.

"Indeed," Demian said. "Our days were cast in shadow and despair without our bright light."

Niah was tangled in Kesi's arms. She reached over to fondly pat Demian's cheek, chuckling at his words. She knew he was being his usual teasing, dramatic self, but she had missed them both greatly.

They sat tucked into a small alcove. Feather-light flurries of snow wafted down lazily to the ground. Muted light bled across the courtyard, gilding the stone walls.

"Did I miss anything exciting?" she asked.

"Only that Master Kole held off on the next test for your return," Kesi said.

"Wonderful," Niah said dryly. "Another opportunity for him to ensure my team fails."

"How was your mission with my cousin?" Demian asked.

Niah thought of the stables, of the weight of his fingertips on her wrists, stroking her pulse, of the heat that spread along her body like a wildfire.

"Are you blushing?" Kesi gasped.

"No!"

"You're full of shite," Demian said. "What happened? Tell me or else!"

Niah raised a brow. "Or else what?"

"Hmm, I have an idea!"

Niah didn't have a chance to run before he grabbed her in a headlock and began to tickle her. It was one of Demian's many skills. His ability to torture one into a confession. He didn't even need to summon his spirits like Laith. He just had to find that spot between her ribs, which was a challenge since he was attempting to avoid her injured side. His finger found the crook under her arms, and she jolted.

"Stop. I am recovering from an injury," she said. Niah planned to make some fake sounds of pain, but nothing but giggles escaped her instead. "This is not fair!"

Demian did not buy her lies, and he attacked her relentlessly.

"Kesi, help!" Niah said.

Kesi grabbed his elbow, drawing him away from her.

"Do you want to be tortured too?" he asked her.

Kesi's hand dropped quickly, and she took a step back.

"Never mind," she mumbled.

"Traitor," Niah said. Tears streaming down her face, she was laughing so much she worried she'd piss her pants.

"You win," she conceded. "I'll tell you the truth."

Demian stopped, his arm around her neck loosening. Niah slid out and raced across the courtyard. A dull thud hit her head, and it took her a moment to realize he had hit her with a handful of snow. Niah gasped as the shock of cold rattled her. She turned around slowly, war in her eyes.

"Oh shite," Demian said.

Valek was scrolling across the courtyard, and Demian dashed in front of his cousin, using him as a shield. Niah had already launched her own mass of snow at his head. The ball of snow crashed into Valek's back. He stilled, slowly turning to face her.

"Did you just hit me with snow, Novice?" Valek asked. His eyes were growing murderously dark.

"It was meant for—"

Snow crashed into her face, slipping into her parted lips. It had taken Valek less than a second to grab it and fling it her way, clearly not interested in hearing her defense.

"I'm going to kill you!" Niah yelled.

She bent over to grab two handfuls of snow and felt another ball of snow crash into her arse. A yelp of surprise escaped her. Niah glanced around to make sure that no students were lingering in the courtyard while Valek dusted off the speckles of snow from his leather gloves with a pleased look in his eyes.

She volleyed one at Valek, putting as much strength as she could into the throw. He moved swiftly, and she laughed when it hit Demian's chin and throat. He wasn't her current target, but he deserved it just as much as Valek did.

"Ow," Demian exclaimed. "We need to work together, Niah. Attack him, not me!"

Valek tossed a ball of snow at Demian's cheek.

"Shut up," Valek said.

And then another was lobbed in quick succession towards her. Niah jumped out of the way, watching it splatter against a rock. Kesi watched their fight, amused and unwilling to get her braids wet, she had run to the arched walkway to hide.

"Fine, we're on the same team!" Demian said to Valek, switching course. "Get Niah."

"I'm not a team player," Valek said, rewarding him with another hit of snow to the face.

Niah took advantage of their distraction and crept up behind Valek, her hands filled with snow. She launched onto his back, pressing her ice-covered palms to his cheeks. His hands slid backwards to hold her thigh. For a moment, she thought he would fling her off, but his hands remained firm on her flesh, fingers digging in the slightest bit. Her stomach lurched as he held her in place.

"You are going to regret that, Novice," he growled.

Niah was about to jump off and seek shelter, but Valek had other ideas. His hand shifted to her waist, pulling her around so she was in front of him, which was an altogether awkward and intimate position. Her fingers were wrapped around his broad shoulders, thighs clamped to his hips.

His dark hair fluttered into his eyes. His cheekbones tinted with an angry flush that made him look rather boyish. Valek bent down with an arm coiled around her, gathering snow with his left hand.

"Put me down, you brute!" she said, pounding on his chest.

"Not until you have suffered."

Niah's hands shifted upwards to claw at his throat.

"Leaving marks on me so people know who I belong to?" Valek taunted. "Clever, little girl."

Niah stilled.

"That is not what I am doing," she said defensively.

Demian laughed so hard he began to wheeze.

"Oh fuck, you both like each other," Demian said. "Looks like Kesi has a week's worth of my assignments to look forward to."

"You both bet on me!" Niah shrieked.

Kesi looked away nervously while Demian smiled sheepishly.

"Also, Demian will be doing your assignments," Niah said. "His assumptions are wrong."

"See!" Kesi said with a gleeful smile. "Pure hatred at its finest. I know my best friend."

"Your words lack a certain credibility since you're practically straddling my cousin in broad daylight," Demian told Niah.

"Put me down, Winterson," she snarled. "You're ruining my reputation!"

"What reputation?" he asked. "Everyone already thinks you are in love with me."

Valek leaned down. His mouth was startlingly warm when it scraped the tip of her ear.

"I didn't make you call me beautiful," he whispered. "Last I recall that was all you."

He was bringing up that damn night again when she'd been under Laith's influence. Would he ever let that go?

Valek released her abruptly. Her feet had just touched the ground when she was welcomed to a face full of snow, courtesy of the Commander. By the time she'd cleared her eyes and prepared to retaliate, Valek was long gone.

"You bastard!" she yelled after his retreating form. "I will hunt you down like prey. Sleep with one eye open, because I am coming for you and all you hold dear!"

Valek turned his head. A devilish smile danced on his handsome face.

"Niah, relax." Demian chuckled. "It was just a good old-fashioned snow toss. No need to get worked up."

"Besides, he had to trick you to win," Kesi said. "Didn't he, Demian?"

"The wicked cheat used his strength to overwhelm her," Demian said with a shake of his head.

Niah folded her arms across her chest. "Don't think I forgot about that bet."

"You know I just realized I'm late for my class," Demian said.

"Me too!" Kesi blurted.

"See you at dinner," Demian said, quickly walking away with Kesi hot on his heels.

"Cowards!" she called.

The only response she got was Demian's echoing laugh.

It was midnight, and Kesi hadn't come to bed. Niah frowned at the clock. It was past curfew, and she should have been here by now. Her fingers tightened around her blanket in unease.

Niah hadn't gotten the chance to debrief her on the recent mission and her meeting with Morgana. They hadn't had a moment alone since she returned.

Niah drew on her robe and silently walked down the corridor, searching every place she could think of. Kesi wasn't in the main hall or courtyard, or the library. There were no candles lit anywhere, and her stomach lurched.

"Looking for something?"

Valek was leaning against the building. His heel pressed to the wall. He had a bottle of wine in his hand, and his cheeks were flushed. He didn't have his robe, and his fitted jacket was unbuttoned at the throat. Niah frowned, surprised to see him so informal.

"Did you see Kesi?" Niah asked. "She didn't come to bed."

"I did," he said.

"Where is she?"

"Safe," he said. "For now."

Her heart thudded rapidly. Had Laith told him about the night she had escaped?

"What does that mean?" Niah asked, her voice small and nervous.

"Lord Winterson arrives tomorrow," Valek said. "Your behavior during his stay will be a deciding factor on what happens to your friend."

Even though he was drunk, his eyes shone with clarity and his words rang with force.

"What does that mean?" she repeated.

Valek pushed off from the wall, sealing the space between them. He was so close she could count every thick lash on his eyelids.

"It means that if he thinks for one second that you are anything but my obedient conduit, then I will slit your friend's throat and bring you her head," Valek said. "Is that understood?"

"Where is she?" Niah asked.

"Safe," he repeated.

"When can I see her?"

"When Lord Winterson leaves."

"Why do you care so much about impressing him?" Niah demanded. "It is pathetic. *You* are pathetic."

"I don't," he said defensively.

"Then why are you acting like a frightened little boy?" she taunted. "Is that why you are drinking so heavily, scared of Papa?"

The taunt was intended to upset him and she felt a flicker of satisfaction when a vein ticked in his jaw.

"Good night, Novice."

"Wait," she called. "I'll...I'll behave, just let Kesi come to bed. *Please*."

"I don't trust you," Valek said.

He walked away, his bottle clutched so tight in his fingers it was a wonder it didn't shatter under his grip.

A frustrated sound escaped her. If she had known he would use Kesi as a leash to control her, she wouldn't have defied him that day in his office when he asked her to perform for his father. It was her fault that Valek had targeted her friend.

How could she pretend to be loyal to Valek? To be his obedient conduit, as he put it, if she were anything but. It was exhausting, pretending to be his puppet.

It would have to be the performance of a lifetime.

Chapter 20

The impending introduction with the Royal Chancellor wrapped around her throat like a deadly garland. It was no secret that Niah had a bit of a temper, *especially* when it came to arrogant, high-handed men. For Kesi's sake, she would bite her tongue.

Her room was barren that morning, absent of Kesi's chipper voice. Nerves wracked her gut at the thought of any harm befalling her friend.

A reception was planned for the Royal Chancellor in the main hall, and all the staff and students had assembled in the foyer. Light spilled through the high stained-glass windows, tinting the polished floors in hues of wine-red. Fresh pansies and violas had been arranged in the ceramic vases.

Niah kept to the back with Demian, glaring at the heavy oaken doors. She felt like an idiot standing there, waiting to greet the Chancellor.

"Where's Kesi?" Demian asked.

"Valek took her," she said, fists clenched by her side. "He won't return her until I perform like a puppet before his father."

Demian hesitated. "There is something I must tell you. It will explain why this is important to Valek."

Demian grabbed her elbow and pulled her to a secluded corner.

"I'm listening," she said.

"Nobody knows this except the King's high council. Even the army doesn't know, because well, the news might cripple the war efforts," Demian said. "King Stefan has been gravely ill for years, and his deterioration has grown worse as the months pass."

"That doesn't explain why Valek has been more unbearable than usual," Niah said.

"Lord Winterson has been essentially ruling in his stead and was granted the power of authority to make decisions on behalf of the crown."

"What does this mean for the country?" Niah whispered.

"Everyone despises King Stefan, but it is Lord Winterson who is invested in the war, and now funds it," Demian said. "He was the Commander before he switched to politics and became the Royal Chancellor. If Valek is telling you to behave, it is because his father *is* the Crown. Anything he says is a royal decree, and if he decides to execute you, there is nothing anyone can do to stop it."

Niah swallowed, stunned. To her, King Stefan was the source of all their pain and suffering. This war had never been a holy war. It was not light versus dark or heretics versus saints. It wasn't even about the Corruption or any number of things that could justify the slaughter and bloodshed. It was about power. It was about land and men and hunger. And now she found out that everything was a lie. King Stefan was knocking on death's door and was nothing more than a puppet.

Shivers trailed down her back. It did not surprise her that the man who raised Valek Winterson was a monster.

"He is second in line," she whispered.

"What?" Demian asked.

Niah looked at his eyes. "Valek's father is second in line, so if anything happens then…"

Demian nodded solemnly.

"Thank you," she whispered. "For telling me this."

She hated Valek for not confiding in her. If he had told her she was essentially meeting the king, then she would have resisted the urge to taunt someone who could have her hanged with a flick of his fingers. Then Valek wouldn't have to steal Kesi and hide her god-knows-where to keep Niah in check.

"You are not a prisoner to me, Niah," Demian said. "You and Kesi are my friends. I don't want anything bad to happen to you."

Niah's face softened, and she reached over to squeeze his hand, ignoring the thick metal cuff that signified that they were anything but equals. Demian had always had her back, and his confiding in her was proof that he did.

Valek stood near Headmistress Greymont. His dark robes were pressed and regal. It was different from his usual one. This one shone in the light, and the flaps were threaded with silver vines.

The double doors were opened, and a tall, dark-haired man entered. His beard was threaded with flecks of white, and his void-black eyes crinkled as he assessed the room. He looked like Valek but older, his features harsher than Valek's soft beauty. Behind him was a retinue of soldiers wearing the King's livery.

"Lord Winterson, we are pleased to invite you to Silverwood," the Headmistress said. "It is our honor to host you during your stay."

Lord Winterson nodded, eyes sharp and scrutinizing. Finally, after what felt like ages, his gaze fell on Valek.

"Commander Winterson," he said, by way of greeting.

"Royal Chancellor," Valek replied.

That was as far as their greeting went.

Niah was surprised by their impersonal words. She hadn't expected Valek's father to embrace him, but he hadn't even inquired about his health or how he fared. For some odd reason, it brought a stab of sympathy to her chest.

Headmistress Greymont ushered Lord Winterson into the dining hall and towards the dais. They usually didn't dine together for breakfast. Most of the novices grabbed their fare and ate it on their way to class.

"Are you going to say hello to your uncle?" Niah asked.

"Maybe later," Demian said.

From his reluctant stare, she could tell he had no intention of speaking with his uncle.

The only mercy was that Valek didn't bring her to the dais. She knew he intended to introduce her to his father, but it wouldn't occur that morning, and that much was a blessing.

"Congrats," Suren said.

As much as she despised wasting her time in the armory, oiling and sharpening the hundreds of blades that were to be used in battle, it had become a quiet part of her routine. Suren didn't talk much, and Niah had learned to grow an appreciation for the silence. It reminded her of when she'd be scavenging in the forest, looking for herbs, with no one but the finches and rabbits as her companions.

Niah smiled, pleased. "I'm getting better at this."

She lifted the polished end of her blade to the light.

"I don't mean your ability to clean a blade," Suren said. "I am talking about your restraint in not flinging your meat knife at Valek."

"Wasn't it?" she agreed.

Suren was not too keen on Valek, which was a refreshing change, considering just how much everyone else loved him. Her favorite habit was collecting her insults during the day to share with him.

"You are a saint," Suren said, flashing her a rare smile.

He rolled the ends of his sleeves, too focused on his task to notice her smile had dropped. He didn't understand the weight of his words. The reminder that she was supposed to be Saint-touched.

"I don't want to be a Reaper," she whispered.

"Not even if it serves you?" Suren asked. "Not even if it grants you an army of the Fallen?"

A thought crossed her mind. Perhaps Suren would know how to escape. If Morgana's plan failed, it would help to have a backup plan in case they were killed for their treachery.

"Do you know of any way to escape this fortress?"

Suren rubbed his jaw. "You could kill every guard outside."

Niah whacked his arm when a smile crept up his lips.

"I'm serious," she said.

"If I helped you escape, I would be acting against the interests of my country," he said slowly. "Not only would I be considered a traitor for ruining a potential treaty, but I would also be executed for my crimes."

Niah glanced away. She knew Suren was in a precarious position and could not save her, but it still hurt.

Suren's fingers lifted her chin.

"The gates on the south wall are the least guarded. If you plan it right, you might find an opening," Suren said.

Niah smiled softly. "Thank you."

"Will you say goodbye to me before you leave?"

"I thought you hated being bothered," she said. "You compared me to a gnat last time."

"A mosquito," he corrected.

A throat cleared, and Niah's head snapped up. Valek was standing in the doorway, glaring at Suren. Suren's fingers dropped from her chin, and Niah straightened. They hadn't been doing anything wrong, but from the distasteful look on Valek's face, you would think they had been about to undress each other.

"I see you two are busy at work," Valek said in a clipped tone.

Niah sighed. "Is taking a break a crime now?"

"Yes," Valek said sharply. "Come along, Novice."

Niah waved at Suren before she followed Valek out the door. She had to jog to keep up.

"What do you want?"

"Congratulations," he said. "Your punishment is done. No more cleaning weaponry."

Niah frowned. "But I have a few more weeks left."

"Are you complaining?"

Niah kind of liked being away from the students who silently judged her. She had begun to look forward to her evenings with Suren. He was calm and reassuring, and never failed to make her feel like she was not alone in this. A small childish part of her had begun to think of him as a knight from a fairytale who had come to save her.

Valek spun around, forcing her to bump into his chest. His fingers caught her chin. Unlike Suren's touch that had been hesitant and light, Valek's was firm and commanding.

"He doesn't know you," Valek said. "He doesn't see the darkness inside you."

Niah swallowed, unnerved by his piercing stare.

"There is no darkness inside me," she said.

Their magic crackled between them. It always did when they were like this close, touching. It was why he always wore gloves when he touched her, even though that did not always contain this flow of magic, but this time his hand was bare, slim-boned fingers gripping her like she belonged to him. Her skin tingled at the cold rush of power that flooded her.

A few of his Fallen that marched behind them began to grow and distort into the monsters they were, shadowing them with their pure blasphemy. A shudder ran down her back. Somehow, their unholy magic settled her. It calmed the storm of doubt, fear, and wrongness that often drowned her.

"You feel that," Valek breathed. "You feel *us*."

Niah couldn't grasp the right words, her mind scrambled by his touch, by their magic. His hand dropped, and clarity trickled in slowly.

"We are dining with my father in private."

"Great," she said dryly. "He is no doubt as charming as you are."

"You should watch that smart tongue around him," Valek said. "I would hate to have to cut it out if he asks for it."

"I'm unsurprised you were made by a monster *and* that you serve him."

Valek ignored her, stopping before a pair of double doors.

"Remember, the fate of your friend depends on your performance tonight," he warned.

He pushed the doors open, not waiting for her response and led her into a small dining chamber adjoining a bedroom. The table had six chairs, and his father already sat at the head of the teakwood table. Valek led her by the elbow to the chairs to his father's right. He sat down and indicated for her to sit by him.

"So, this is your conduit," Lord Winterson said. His dark eyes studied her with undisguised interest. "The one who will change the tide of the war."

"Her name is Niah," Valek said. "She's a war prisoner from Caer-Sylisse."

"How do you know she can be trusted?" Lord Winterson asked.

"She has been properly broken in," he said. "And once our bond strengthens, there will be no secrets between us."

Niah shifted in unease. How would there be no secrets between them?

"Is that true?" Lord Winterson asked. His question was directed at her.

"Yes, my lord," she said. "I serve at the pleasure of the Kingdom of Raskovia and the High North."

"Why do I not believe you?" he mused.

His hand rose, and Niah realized belatedly that Maxim Winterson was a Diviner like Laith. She felt that strange magic wrap around her like a chain. Her eyes widened in panic as she glanced at Valek. He should have warned her about this. Not that there was anything she could do to protect her mind. She was at the mercy of Lord Winterson.

"Shall we try this again?" he asked. "How do you really feel about serving?"

"*Don't tell him*," a voice whispered in her mind. One that sounded exactly like Valek. Curt and devoid of emotion.

She felt his hand beneath the table, gripping her palm so tightly it hurt.

"*Just focus on me.*"

Niah's tongue held in her mouth. And the words remained trapped inside her. Lord Winterson stared at her patiently, awaiting her response. It was difficult to form any words—both truth and lie. His hold on her felt stronger than Laith's, resisting it hurt so badly. A dull thud echoed inside her skull, rattling her every thought. Her mind felt like it was being fractured. Pain bloomed, spreading behind her eyes like splintering stars. Blood trickled down her nose, and the ropes that secured her mind faded away, and a sigh escaped her.

"Interesting," Lord Winterson said, handing her the cream handkerchief from his breast pocket.

He didn't wear any robes. Just a pressed dinner coat and trousers.

"You're a Diviner," she said.

Lord Winterson's mouth tilted in a cold smile.

"And your bond is stronger than you admitted," he said. "I could feel Valek's presence in your mind, shielding you with his touch."

Niah shot Valek a wary look. How could he slip inside her mind like that? Could he hear her thoughts?

Dread curled through her, tightening its claws around her spine. There was so much that she did not know.

"She is not as loyal as you claim if you feel the need to hide her words," he said.

"She is a work in progress," Valek said. "But I know she will be worth it, she will serve our cause loyally."

"She is in one piece, as pretty as a picture," his father said. "You've never shied away from some light torture to ensure loyalty to our family before."

Niah stiffened, fear locking her limbs.

"What would you have me do?" Valek asked calmly.

His father placed a dagger on the table.

"An eye or a finger," he said. "Shall we give her the choice?"

"I don't want to look at an ugly face for the duration of this war," Valek said. "I'll pass."

"Finger, then?" His father asked. His eyes gleamed with cruelty. If she had thought Valek was bloodthirsty, it was nothing compared to his father. "You remember what I taught you. Power begets power."

Her eyes darted to the door. Perhaps she could make a run for it. It didn't matter if she was caught or punished. They were talking about cutting her up during dinner as if they spoke of the weather. She could not be blamed for escaping.

"*Calm down*," Valek said, his words slipping through her mind. He squeezed her hand so hard it hurt, but she couldn't stop shaking.

There were two of them. Two terrible Wintersons staring at her like wolves in the woods.

"She is good with her hands," Valek replied lazily.

His father laughed, sliding his dagger back into his holster. It seemed she was not a true threat if she spread her legs so easily for the enemy. Bitterness coated her tongue like poison, but she did not dare speak a word.

"How is the king?" Valek asked, swiftly switching the topic.

Now that the imminent threat of being carved like a tree was gone, Niah felt her shoulders drop. For some reason, Valek's hand was still wrapped snugly in hers, and Niah was afraid to let go, to remind him that he hated her. Because right now, he was the only shield protecting her from his depraved father.

"As he always is," Maxim said. Demian was right, the king was ill, and everyone was keeping it a secret.

"And Natalia?"

"Excellent, I've secured a betrothal for her. She asked you to be invited to the celebrations in two months."

Valek frowned. "What betrothal? I was not made aware of this."

"Lord Kasper has expressed interest," Maxim said. "His family has that successful mining company in Karsnek. Natalia will enjoy the countryside."

"Lord Kasper is a hundred years old, and Karsnek only has one season and that is winter," Valek growled. "I forbid it."

"Don't be dramatic, he is forty-five. Besides, you are not her father; I am," he said. "And the ink is dry and the date set. There is nothing to be done but to congratulate and support your sister. It will devastate her to know you do not care for her happiness."

Valek's fist landed so hard on the table, the plates rattled. Somehow, she could *feel* his anger, it swept over her like a shock of cold water.

"She is ten years old!" Valek snapped. "She is a child."

"You do not have a say in it," Lord Winterson said icily. "And I do not have the patience for your temper tantrums today, so I would hold my tongue if I were you."

Niah expected Valek to react, to unleash his anger. She could feel it wrapped around him like a glass armor, shattering with every passing moment. Valek continued to hold her hand, to grip it like she was the only thing holding him back from destruction.

Niah didn't know why she squeezed his hand. A part of her was afraid of what would happen if the men went head-to-head. Maxim Winterson was a different breed of evil. Even though she despised him, Niah was aware that Valek was the only thing that stood between her and Maxim. It worked in her favor to protect him. So, she stroked her thumb along his knuckles, soothing him.

Maxim turned back to his plate, and the only sound in the room was their cutlery scraping. It was awkward, eating with one hand. She could have let go of Valek, but from his firm grip, she reckoned he didn't *want* to let her go.

His eyes were murderous as he chewed. She wondered what his sister was like. They must have been close for Valek to be so upset by this news. Niah did not blame him for his reaction. Her heart ached for his poor sister, who was being saddled with an older man, all so that her father could benefit from their union. It was the burden women had carried for centuries—to be steered like beasts by lesser men. To be told their worth was in silence and servitude.

"Speaking of betrothals, have you given any thought to Daria?" Maxim asked.

"I am busy with the war effort to make time for a new bride," Valek said.

"And when the war ends?"

"I will consider it," he said.

Maxim grunted in reluctant acceptance.

"You will see the conduit perform tomorrow morning as requested," Valek said. Another switch of the topic. He was no doubt put off by the excess marriage talk.

Maxim's eyes lit with interest. Niah did not know what she was to do tomorrow, but the thought weighed heavily on her.

Maxim dismissed them with a loose wave of his hand. Valek released her palm and was out the door without a second glance. Niah followed him, struggling to keep up with his breakneck pace.

There was a decorative table with a glass case that held antique daggers. One moment it was upright and proper, and the next, Valek had swiped his forearms through it, destroying the fine glass with a loud crack. Shards showered them, and Niah's mouth pursed at the sight. Even though she could sense the storm that was his anger, she didn't feel threatened. It didn't surprise her when he ripped portraits from the walls, yanking out the indigo blue wallpaper with a sharp tear.

"Winterson," she said slowly.

His back was facing the damaged wall, and he tensed when her hand fell on his elbow.

"You're bleeding," she said.

Blood trickled down his bruised knuckles, sliding between his fingers to form a gruesome, scarlet ring.

"Your father is a nasty piece of work," Niah added.

Valek laughed, a dry, unamused sound. "If you thought that last half hour was unbearable, you can imagine what it was like growing up in his household."

Niah frowned, staring at the carpet, as if it would untangle the knotted mess that was her emotions. It felt wrong to sympathize, to understand at last why Valek Winterson acted and behaved the way he did. It explained why he had demanded her fake obedience before his father. He had done so to protect her. Niah knew that if she had mouthed off tonight to Maxim Winterson, she would not be leaving that room with all her limbs intact. If Valek hadn't protected her mind, Maxim would have discovered just how deep her treachery ran.

"Has he always been like that?" Niah asked softly.

The silence stretched for so long that she wondered if he had any intention of answering. Niah was surprised to discover that she was disappointed by his lack of response, that a part of her *wanted* to know exactly who Valek Winterson was.

"No," Valek said, after an eternity had passed. "I suppose that makes it worse that I have the misfortune of remembering a time when he was better. He never recovered after my mother passed away in childbirth, not long after Natalia was born. A part of him blames my sister for it, it's why he is throwing her to the sharks, to punish her."

"That's horrible," she said. "I'm sorry."

Valek turned around to face her, and her hand dropped back to her side.

"Are you?" Valek asked dryly. "You should be rejoicing in my misery."

"That would make me no different than you," Niah said.

He looked away from her, as if he could not bear the sight of her.

"How did you speak to me?" Niah asked. "In my head?"

"Our bond ties us together," he said. "If you didn't ignore it, you could speak back to me as well."

"Can you read my thoughts?" Niah asked nervously.

"No."

"I can...I feel your anger," she said. "Do you feel my emotions?"

"Not all, only when they're heightened," Valek said. His eyes rose back to her face. "Mainly, I feel how much you hate me."

Niah's mouth tightened. She hoped he hadn't felt her hatred flicker at his confession. She prayed that he never discovered that for one small moment, Niah had felt something more akin to pity than disgust.

"You behaved well tonight," he whispered.

Niah swallowed, confused by the shift in his eyes from blind anger to molten heat.

"I had no choice," she said.

"You always have a choice," Valek said. "You just chose correctly for once."

He was so close to her, leaning his tall frame slightly to speak with her.

"I want to reward you," Valek said.

Niah sucked in a sharp breath, alarmed and curious by the sudden shift in his energy. His eyes dropped, lingering by her mouth, his fists clenched at his sides, as though touching her would shatter whatever fragile restraint he still possessed.

"Where's Kesi?" Niah blurted. "That is *all* I want."

Valek's gaze rose. For one small second, she had thought she caught a flicker of disappointment.

"I'll take you to her," he said.

Chapter 21

They slipped down the dimly lit corridor of the boys' dormitory. It smelled faintly of antique books and sweat. The arched ceiling was lined with beams that intercrossed like a hollow ribcage. Lacy fingers of cobwebs lined the structure like milky veins.

"What if he killed her?" Niah asked, alarmed. "I wouldn't put it past him."

Between the cracked doors, she caught glimpses of bedframes wrought from blackened iron and the damask curtains, their once-rich scarlet coloring now faded to a bruised plum.

"Laith is harmless," Valek said. "The most he'll have done is play his mind games on her."

"And you think that is okay?"

Valek sighed as he led her up the stairs. Niah had the urge to shove him forward and watch him stumble, but she kept her hands to herself.

"I can feel your anger again," he tsked. "So murderous and deranged, like a vengeful little saint."

"If you don't stop, I *will* bite you," Niah growled.

"I think I'd like that very much," he said, throwing her a dark look over his shoulder.

Niah glared at him. "Deviant."

"Seductress," Valek snapped back.

"I am not seducing you!"

"Then don't threaten to bite me."

"I hate you," she said.

Valek knocked lightly before opening the door.

"We could hear you both ten miles away," Laith said.

Niah's cheeks burned. She looked around the space to find Kesi holding a book upside down, pretending to read. It seemed she did not want to converse with Laith any more than he did with her. Kesi flung the book away at the sight of her.

"Oh, Niah, thank god," she said. "I've been losing my mind, stuck in this damned room all day. I wasn't even allowed to go to those stupid classes they're forcing us to take."

"She drove me up a wall," Laith said.

"Can't say I am surprised," Valek said. "These girls are cut from the same cloth."

"Stop talking about us like we're not in the room," Niah said, wrapping her arms around Kesi. She was glad Kesi was safe and sound.

"He just sat there like a statue and glared at me the entire time," Kesi whispered. "He's weird."

"I can hear you, Novice," Laith barked. "You're on kitchen duty for the next month."

"What, you can't do that!" Kesi said.

"It's approved," Valek said. "Report for duty tomorrow."

Niah frowned. "You don't get to dictate what we can and cannot say."

"Laith outranks you, and I am the Commander of the King's army," Valek said. "We will change our stance if you both apologize with sincerity."

"I'm sorry," Kesi blurted.

Kesi hated doing chores, even back in the monastery. Niah wasn't surprised she folded so quickly. Niah, on the other hand, could not be bothered to posture for them nor to stroke their overgrown egos.

"*Both* of you are to apologize," Valek said. His gaze locked on her. She knew he couldn't care less about Kesi's apology, he *only* ever cared about her. Her gut burned with resentment. This was another one of his power games.

Something wild and consuming fluttered over her, and it took her a moment to realize it was *him*. His emotions were reaching out to her as they had earlier. He was hungry? Desperate? No, that couldn't be it. He was feeling something else, something raw and demanding. He needed her to submit, to fall to her knees.

Kesi elbowed her.

"Niah, I really don't want to be in the kitchen," she whispered. "It's hot, and I hate the smell of onions."

"We'll be together," Niah said. "It'll be fun."

"No, it won't," she whined.

"Did I mention that you will be on the early morning shift?" Valek said. His eyes sparkled at their exchange. "When do the kitchens open, Laith?"

"I believe at five," Laith said.

Kesi gasped.

"No, I think it's four," Valek said, enjoying this little game. "Definitely four."

Just when she felt a sliver of sympathy for the bastard, he reminded her *exactly* who he was. If she refused to apologize, Kesi would be upset at her, and if she accepted, Valek would win their silly game.

"Niah, do it for me, please," Kesi said.

Niah's eyes were locked on Valek. His mouth was tilted in a playful smile. It wasn't a battle of wills for him like it was for her. To him, this was their thing. They argued and bickered and fought for dominance at every turn.

"I'm sorry," she said, between gritted teeth.

"Are you really?" Valek asked.

"Yes," she said.

"Do you believe her?" Valek asked Laith.

"Not a single bit," Laith replied.

Valek raised a brow.

"I'm *very* sorry," Niah said with a forced smile.

"Good enough," Valek said.

"Didn't expect any better," Laith added.

"At least she gave us that pretty smile," Valek said.

"More like a grimace," Laith said.

Kesi grabbed her arm, pulling her away from her staring match with Valek.

"They're both bastards," Kesi said. "We'll get back at them one day. We'll crush their smug faces under our boots."

Niah smiled at her indignation.

"*Night, little saint,*" Valek whispered in her mind.

Niah stiffened. How had she forgotten about the rot spreading inside her that was their bond? It was one thing to feel emotions, and another to speak through their minds. How much longer until he could scour her thoughts like a thief in the night? How much longer until her secrets were lying bare for him to swallow?

"*Don't be afraid,*" he said. "*Your mind is far from my touch. Your secrets are safe. For now.*"

He could feel how anxious she'd gotten.

Niah waited until they were in their bedroom before she grabbed Kesi's wrist and pulled her to her bed.

"I have a million things to tell you," Niah said.

"Me too," Kesi said. "You go first."

Niah started with the rebel mission and her meeting with Morgana, and then finished with the dinner with Valek's father. She couldn't bring herself to tell her friend about the strengthening bond.

"Morgana is here?" Kesi's eyes widened. "Has she come to save us?"

"Not yet," Niah said. "She wants us to act as spies until they can plan an attack. Catrin is somewhere here pretending to be a servant. She will pass along any information I find to Morgana."

"How will you find information for her?"

"Valek's office is in the barracks. Anything important will be there," Niah said. "Do you think you can keep an eye on him tomorrow night while I rummage through his drawers?"

"Are you sure it shouldn't be me?" Kesi asked. "I reckon you'd have better luck distracting Valek than me."

"What does *that* mean?" Niah asked.

"Look, Demian knows that monster better than anyone, and he thinks for some reason that Winterson is keen on you," Kesi said. "Should we not use that to our advantage?"

"That is ridiculous," Niah said. "Besides, how would I live with myself if I played into it?"

"Men have fought wars for women," Kesi said. "Perhaps, you could make him end this war for you."

Niah could barely flirt, let alone seduce a man as powerful as Valek Winterson. It was outrageous for Kesi to even suggest such a thing.

"I can't do that, Kesi, and you read too much poetry," Niah said. "I've already sacrificed my faith and soul. I won't add my morals to it."

Kesi sighed. "Fine, whatever you say."

"Tomorrow night," Niah said. "Prepare yourself."

The quicker they got Morgana this intel, the better prepared she'd be to attack.

"We could go home," Kesi asked hopefully.

Niah resisted the urge to smile.

"We could really go home," she echoed.

The arena thrummed with bodies, students and staff alike packed the stone benches. Master Kole had set up another spectacle for their second test, except this one was for the benefit of the Royal Chancellor, who sat in the stands, staring at them with his crow-black eyes.

"We are going to be tested individually, but our final points will be tallied as a team," Casimir said.

Niah's mind was lost in the number of eyes that watched them with vicious interest. It was why Casimir was rambling, a thing he did when he was nervous. He didn't know that this spectacle was for Lord Winterson to judge her—Valek's new pet.

"Why is there an arena here?" she asked.

"Commander Winterson uses it as a mock battlefield to train his Fallen," Eveline said.

Headmistress Greymont sat in a private box with Laith and the Chancellor. Valek was surprisingly not with them. At the lowest level sat the other students. Casimir led them over to the corner to discuss their strategy, but the only words of wisdom Casimir had shared were *don't lose* followed by Milo's warning glare at her, as if she were their greatest chance of failure.

"Today, we will test each novice individually before their peers," Master Kole said. "One by one, you will rise when called and fight against me."

Niah wore black combat trousers and a black leather vest over her tunic. Strapped to her sides were her blades, but even with them, she felt ill-prepared for whatever torture Master Kole had designed to test them. Unlike Valek's lessons, Master Kole did not focus on combat, but rather on their ability to survive in battle by using every weapon at their disposal, both physical and magical.

A cart of corpses was drawn in, and three dead bodies were dumped at his feet.

First were the Diviners, who were forced to fight the Fallen that Master Kole raised. He wielded them against each student as they attempted to fight them with their spirits. Shouts arose from the stands when the students were injured. Whenever the crack of bones sounded, bloodthirsty chants would begin.

Niah felt sick. She dug her nails into her knee when Kesi was called forward. Unlike her, Kesi did not have a necromancer assigned to her to draw magic from, so she would have to use her wit and combat skills.

They charged at Kesi at once, and her eyes widened as she attempted to evade the first one. Her skills were rusty, and after a few minutes of being knocked to her back, she tapped out when one of them coiled their fingers around her neck, choking her. Nobody else had tapped out since it would disqualify the entire team. Even those who didn't do well just let themselves be beaten to a bloody pulp until Master Kole had mercy on them.

Niah gave Kesi a weak smile as she limped back to her team, who were glowering at her like she had murdered someone.

Niah was the last to go, and she stood up with a shaky breath.

"Commander Winterson has requested to challenge you," Master Kole said.

Niah hadn't even noticed Valek standing off to Kole's shoulder. He wore his dark regalia, and his face was concealed by his bone mask. Six of his Fallen stood behind him, staring ahead with blank eyes. Twice the numbers Master Kole had used to test the other students.

Her heart plummeted to her stomach. She had convinced herself that she would survive whatever Kole threw her way, but Valek? Valek was a different breed.

This was all for his father. To prove his point that she was a weapon to be feared.

Kole moved to the stands, and then it was only the two of them.

"Prepare yourself, Novice," Valek said.

He whispered in her mind. "*Impress me.*"

Without any word of warning, the Fallen lunged at her while Valek stood back from the chaos, mastering them effortlessly. One of his Fallen leaped high in the air and came barreling down on her, fighting with a speed and strength that was twice a mortal's. It was her magic that he used to strengthen them. Niah had just enough time to pull out her sword and drive it into the gut of the Fallen.

Niah had made him stronger, and now he would use her gifts to destroy her.

Her blade made a squelching sound when she pulled it from its gut. Black, putrid blood trickled down her wrist and slipped down her fingers.

Niah couldn't fight them all, and she refused to be cowed. She focused on three of his Fallen and forced them to turn on him. Valek wasn't surprised when they spun on their heels and charged towards him. His sword was unsheathed, and he swiftly cut their throats without so much as breaking a sweat. His arm moved in a fluid arc, a blur of motion as it took the head off the last opponent. He didn't even bother to use both his arms. Even though the sword was heavy — Vykovian steel always was —Valek wielded it like it was as light as a feather.

In his distraction, Niah used the remaining three soldiers to attack him as well. She let her magic curl around them, bloating them with power. Their bodies lengthened and stretched.

Valek's sword swung in a circle as he severed their heads. His hair brushed his mask like a menacing finger. Once they were destroyed, he walked towards her with his long sword, dragging it dangerously on the ground.

A spike of fear shot through her stomach.

This was the Valek Winterson who won the High North so many victories. The one whose enemies quaked at the mere mention of his name.

Niah held her sword at the ready as Valek made the first strike. His blow was hard enough to rattle her bones. His sword had a hilt made of black glass and a sharp, gleaming end. It was longer and had better reach than hers, which, paired with his long arms, meant he could easily bypass her defenses. Even though he was a few years older than her, it was obvious that he had years of training on her.

"Come on, little saint," he whispered tauntingly. "Show me what you've got."

Niah lunged for him, their swords scraping like nails along a wall. Each move she made, he counterattacked. She remained on the offense while he handled defense. At some point, he grew bored with their back-and-forth, and his leg kicked out her ankles, forcing her to her knees. His hand tangled in her long braid, and he used it to drag her head back, so she was forced to look up at him as he rested his sword on her throat.

"You look good on your knees," Valek crooned.

"Shut up," she said.

"Make me."

Niah slowly pulled out the dagger tucked in her boot and dug it into his thigh. She smiled when he grunted.

"That's more like it," Valek said, yanking out her bloody dagger and tossing it to the side. Even with his thigh bleeding, it didn't make him any less frightening. If she didn't know better, she would say the sick bastard was *thrilled* that she had wounded him.

Valek sparred with her, attempting to tire her out, undaunted by his gushing wound.

"You can surrender to me," he said softly. Not that anyone could hear him under the rising cheers of the crowd. His hand was in her hair again, yanking her head back to rest against his throat. She could feel his mouth moving along her hairline. "And me alone."

"Stop pulling my hair!" Niah hissed.

Her nails dug into his wrist to break his grip.

"Pull mine back," he said evenly.

Her back straightened, overwhelmed by the intensity of his gaze.

"You would like that, wouldn't you, you degenerate," she snarled.

"I would," Valek said, amusement threading his voice. "Very much."

Niah poured as much power as she could into her hands. She let her magic shoot out from her fingers. Shadowy, black tendrils of darkness wrapped around the Fallen as they awakened once more.

Valek's brows rose in surprise.

Once a Fallen was slain, they could not be raised a second time. This applied to both Reapers and Stitchers.

Niah watched as they grew, morphing before her into creatures that were more monster than man. Their nails elongated into curled black talons.

The crowd grew silent, and Valek's blade, that had found its way to her throat, slowly lowered.

"Stop it," he said warily. "Now, Novice."

Niah refused to cease her attack. She was no longer "little saint" because he was done flirting; now she was "Novice", but Niah was just getting started.

They were marching towards them. She could kill Valek. He stood behind her with nothing but his sword. It would be so easy to make them snap his neck, to watch him crumble.

Niah let the Fallen surround him, to intimidate him, to show him that she was stronger than he was, and that she was not afraid.

"Enough," Master Kole called. "Stand down, Novice."

For a moment, she was tempted to rebel, to launch her attack, but she had awakened only three Fallen and was surrounded by her enemies. The moment Valek was killed, a ring of Stitchers would rush to revive him.

Niah's hand dropped, and the Fallen crumbled to the ground, their limbs interlocking like vines.

Niah was drained, and she knew that the final show of power had depleted her. Silence came from the seating area, and for a moment, she wondered if anyone would react at all, if they would simply watch her with their horror-filled eyes until she was dragged away to be punished. There would be consequences to her actions, that much she knew. It was rather obvious she had been contemplating murdering him at the end.

"Great job, Niah!" Kesi bellowed. And with her cry of encouragement, the crowd broke into applause and whistles as they stared at her in awe.

She had bested Valek Winterson. The greatest Reaper of their generation. Pride stung in her chest.

"Well done, Novice," Valek said. "I'm surprised you didn't kill me. You have shown great restraint."

"I thought about it, but figured you'd be awakened not long after," Niah said. She stepped forward to whisper in his ear. "When I do kill you, know that there will be nobody there to awaken you. You will *truly* die by my hand."

Her threat would have been a lot more frightening if her vision hadn't blurred. She stumbled forward, falling into his arms.

And the last thing she saw before she lost consciousness was Valek Winterson's dark, impenetrable eyes, laced with concern.

Candlelight flickered in the dark, and whispers floated towards her. Niah blinked slowly, staring at the shadows that converged in the corner of the room. It was Headmistress Greymont, Master Kole and Valek. Niah swiftly sealed her eyes shut, softening her breathing to listen in on their conversation.

"Did you know she was that powerful, Lord Winterson?" Lady Greymont asked curiously. "Does the King know how powerful your conduit is?"

"She is untrained and untrustworthy. I do not think the King cares to know about a *potential* asset," Valek said. "The Royal Chancellor will pass the information along if needed."

"She is more powerful than you," Greymont said. "How is that possible?"

"She is not," Valek said, with a huff of annoyance. "Perhaps an equal, but she does not surpass me in strength. It will be years before she learns to fully wield her power. Her ability to revive the Fallen once deceased is a strong skill that will need time to grow. It is clear that she is a favored of the Dark Mother."

"She tried to kill you," Greymont continued. Voice rising in alarm. "She turned on you."

"That is how she flirts with me," he said. "I would be offended if she didn't at least *try* to kill me."

Niah mentally rolled her eyes at his observation. She had *not* been flirting with him.

"This is not a laughing matter, Commander," the headmistress scolded. "Your father would hang us all if any harm befell you."

"Oh, I am being serious," he said. "To Niah, that little display of rage was akin to a kiss upon the cheek."

"She is a temperamental one," Kole agreed. "You should have heard the words she had for Commander Winterson a few weeks ago. She never minds her tongue."

"The Chancellor may not like someone so unpredictable wielding that much power," Greymont said.

Niah could tell she was suspicious of her, which was not good. If she passed this along to the Chancellor, he might think she was too great a risk to take a chance on.

Her heart thudded rapidly. She should have restrained herself. She should not have let Valek's taunts get to her. She should not have sought to kill him in a public arena.

"She is gifted, I won't deny it," Valek said. "But she is still not fit to present to the King, she requires a great deal of training to reach her full potential."

"I will do my best to hone the girl's skills," Kole said. "Valek is right, she needs a firm hand."

"That is good," Greymont said. "I want you, Commander Valek, to have a one-on-one lesson with her every week on her magic control. Please see to it that it is added to her new schedule."

Niah didn't need to open her eyes to know Valek was scowling. The click of shoes sounded, and the door shut.

"You can stop pretending, Novice," Valek said darkly.

He was bluffing. He couldn't have known she was eavesdropping. But when Niah felt the cold grip of his fingers wrap around her throat. It took sheer strength to keep her breathing even and to not react.

"I can feel your pulse racing beneath my thumb," Valek said. She felt the light stroke of his finger along her skin. After a long pause, his hand dropped. "Perhaps I was wrong."

His footsteps retreated, and the door clicked shut behind him. Niah released a sigh of relief and opened her eyes to find Valek leaning against the door, smirking.

Niah cursed under her breath.

"You are so predictable," he said, walking slowly towards her. "It is almost painful to witness."

"I'd rather be predictable than heartless," she said. "You sold me out to Headmistress Greymont without batting an eyelash. I don't want to be presented before the King. Performing for the Chancellor was unbearable."

Niah sat upright, so he could feel the full force of her stare. "What is your grand plan for me? Do you truly think I will serve your army?"

Valek turned around, but Niah was not having this. He had kept her in the dark for far too long. If his schemes involved her, she wanted to know what role she played in it.

Niah caught his sleeve. He spun around and grabbed her throat once more, fingers flexing on her skin.

"You are nothing but a pawn. *My* pawn," Valek spoke

roughly. "And pawns do not demand answers. They do as they are bid."

    Her nails clawed at his hand. "Let go of me."

    He released her, throwing her a warning glance.

    And then he was gone, the flutter of his black cloak rippling in the air like a shadow.

Chapter 22

A feather-light touch roused her from her slumber. Niah blinked slowly, erasing the lingering haze of her dreams. She expected to find Kesi hovering above her, but it wasn't her best friend who peered at her behind a pair of cloudy, blue eyes. The girl before her was a stranger with long, wispy, corn-blond hair and a firm chin.

"Hello, Lightbearer," she whispered.

"Do I know you?" Niah asked.

"Morgana says she told you about me," she said. "My name is Catrin."

This was the girl Morgana had mentioned. She wore the dull, gray skirts the servants did with a matching blouse.

"It is lovely to meet you," Niah said, wrapping her arms around her.

Even though she did not remember her face from the monastery, Niah was pleased to be around one of her Sisters. It brought comfort to her unlike any other.

"Morgana wanted you to fetch something the heretics stole from us. A token to aid you in the coming battle," Catrin said. "Come along."

Niah dressed quickly, careful not to awaken Kesi. She would

insist on coming along, and if they were caught, they would both be punished.

Catrin reached for her hand, leading her out the door.

The corridor yawned before her like the gullet of a sleeping beast. Along the length of the passage, heavy tapestries sagged against the masonry, their scenes faded and fraying. Surprisingly, it did not depict the Reapers, but ancient knights who lived before the rise of magic.

The knights stood in verdant grass, clutching silver-bright swords and splintered shields raised high against the immortal creatures.

They stepped outside, and Niah braced herself against the chill of the air. Mist coiled over the ground, winding between the blades of grass like ghostly fingers, cloaking everything in its heavy veil. It was a blessing, as it was the only thing shielding them from the eyes of the guards, but it came at a cost. Niah could not see anything before her. It was like wading through thick water.

"Have you ever been to the Bone Hall?" Catrin whispered.

"No," Niah said. "It is only permitted to Diviners."

A place that belonged to their sect alone.

"They keep ancient bones in there. It is said the bones of the Saints are kept there as a reminder of their end, of when they betrayed Riven, the Son," she whispered. Her voice floated like a lullaby. "Morgana wishes for us to find the one that belongs to Saint Ylena."

The patron saint of the Order of the White Flame was the Saint of Light.

"Why?" Niah asked.

"Do you know about the prophecy of the Lightbearer?"

Niah shook her head. She rarely listened anytime the Prioress lectured them on the Lightbearer. It made her uncomfortable when the other cleric's eyes would settle on her.

Niah still didn't fully believe she was the chosen one. The one prophesied to end the war, but if the Order needed someone to believe in, then Niah would be that person. There was nothing stronger than faith, and they needed to believe that they could win now more than ever.

"It is said that when the Lightbearer is given the bone fragment of Saint Ylena, she will be granted great power," Catrin said. "It will strengthen you, give you an edge against our enemies."

"Like a talisman?" Niah asked

"No," Catrin said. "The heretics use talismans. You are Saint-touched. You are chosen to wield this power."

Her eyes shone with conviction, and still Niah doubted her words. Why were they resorting to the tricks of the necromancers? Why were they playing with the bones of the dead? It unsettled her that Morgana wanted her to do this. It felt wrong, and she was certain that Kesi would agree with her. This was blasphemy.

Catrin frowned at the alarm on her face. Her fingers tightened around her flesh, nails slightly pinching.

"Do not let uncertainty taint your faith," she said harshly. "Follow the direction of Morgana, and she will lead you to the truth."

Niah finally nodded.

A small sigh escaped her when her fingers loosened.

The Bone Hall was a room in the Great Church of Bersula. Besides the mandatory nightly sermons, Niah avoided the hall as best she could. The building stood tall with its towering spires piercing the sky and casting bleak shadows across the ground.

Speckles of snow dotted the structure. During the day, the church was maintained by the untouched. They roamed the dimly lit halls and crooked corridors, dusting the pews and offering sacrificial blood to the stone base of the Dark Mother's statue. But at night, it was eerily silent.

Demian had told her once that only Diviners were granted access to the Bone Hall. He said the whispers of the spirits would drive any other person to madness.

Footsteps sounded, and Catrin and Niah quickly tucked themselves behind the long curtain that covered the high windows, as the whisper of robes and the soft chatter of a pair of acolytes echoed in the grand space.

Niah waited several minutes before they stepped out. There were several doors with different plaques. She paused to read the first one.

The Archives

The next double doors had another plaque.

The Bone Hall

Entry is forbidden to all except those blessed by Bersula.

Niah's breath increased. What if she were driven to madness?

"Is this safe?" Niah asked.

"For you, yes," Catrin said. "But I must stay here."

"How do you know I won't go mad?" Niah asked. "I heard it will make anyone who is not a Diviner lose their mind."

"You are the Lightbearer," she said. "The Saints will protect you."

Niah hesitated. If she survived this, it would prove that they had been right, that she truly was the Lightbearer, a fate she'd ignored until now, until she was desperate enough to believe in something, anything, *even* herself.

"Do not fret," Catrin said. "You will be safe. I will be waiting here for you to return."

Niah took a deep breath and opened the door, sealing it shut behind her.

The Hall was unlike anything she had ever seen before, grotesque, reverent, and oddly beautiful. The walls were constructed with a multitude of bones—thousands upon thousands of human remains meticulously arranged in a macabre display.

From the ceiling hung a grand chandelier wrought entirely of human ribs, their curved arches splayed outward like skeletal wings. The walls flickered with a dozen beeswax candles. The light caught on the polished skulls, making them gleam like ivory relics.

Every inch of the chamber was carved with eerie devotion. Vertebrae spiraled into rosette patterns, scapulae formed floral motifs in the corners, and knuckles were fitted like cobblestones beneath her feet. Not a single bone was out of place; each had been chosen and placed with gentle care, as though the hall itself were a shrine to death.

The Sisters would have found it disturbing, but Niah found the terrible splendor magnificent. She could not tear her eyes away. It was art. In its highest form.

Slowly, she began to hear whispers. It trickled in like water through a ravine. Hundreds of chiming sounds flooded her head, drowning out her thoughts. Pain blurred her vision as a dawning headache split her from the inside out. A cry escaped her as she fell to her knees and squeezed her eyes shut tight.

"Stop," she said. "Please. I... I mean no harm."

"*You were not invited here, child,*" a woman's voice floated by her ear.

"I need your help," Niah said. "I seek the bones of Saint Ylena. Our patron saint."

"*There is a balance to power,*" the woman said. "*You must not defy the natural order.*"

"I am not one of them," Niah said.

It was her robes that had her mistaken. Hastily, she slipped her hood off, revealing her hair. Her white hair––her marker that she belonged to the side of light, that she was pure, and blessed. "You do not understand."

"*I understand more than you could ever imagine, child,*" she said. "*I am Zorya, the First Scribe, and I lived during the time of the Saints, and their magic nearly burned the world. We do not need another Saint.*"

The noise grew to a frenzy. Niah tried to leave, but her legs would not move. Panic flared in her chest.

"No, please," Niah said. "I don't want to die."

There was so much she hadn't done. The war had not ended. Her friends and the Order needed her. Perhaps, she had made a mistake searching for that which did not wish to be found.

"*Forgive me, child,*" Zorya said softly. "*But I must protect the future as I failed to protect the past.*"

"But I am good," Niah said.

Was that not all that mattered in the end? One's goodness. Their will to serve selflessly.

"*Goodness is neither light nor death,*" she said.

The noise vanished, and Niah opened her eyes. She was no longer in the Bone Hall. It was an abyss of darkness. The antithesis of life. Was this what Death was like, an eternal abode of nothingness?

"*You don't have long,*" a voice said.

Niah's head snapped up, reaching for her blade that was missing from her hip. Another sign that she was not in her body, she would never traverse the grounds with no protection. Not when her enemies grew by the day.

A woman stared at her with long white hair. It fell onto the ground in a thick carpet. She looked to be a decade older than her. Her brown skin glowed, and her eyes were bright and luminous.

Her fingers wiped the blood that stained Niah's cheek. She hadn't even realized she was crying, nor that her tears were crimson.

The whispering vanished, replaced with silence.

"Who are you?" Niah asked.

"Ylena," she said.

"You are the Saint of Light?" Niah asked in disbelief.

It seemed too good to be true that she simply stumbled upon her.

Her lips curved. "I am here to help you."

Ylena placed a whittled bone in her palm. When Niah curled her fingers around it, it burned with the light. It felt good to feel the caress of warmth after all this time. Even if it wasn't her magic, it soothed her.

"This will be your talisman," she said. "During your time of need, reach for it, and I will aid you."

"Can you give me my magic?" Niah asked. "Can you break these shackles?"

"It is hard to reach your mind. It is tainted with darkness. There is another who has gained hold of your soul," she said. "And I do not have a physical form. I cannot free you."

She spoke of Valek. Even now, far from him, he shrouded her in his shadows.

"How do I end this bond with him? He is cursed."

"All Reapers are abominations," Ylena said. Her eyes burned for one long second. "I can help you rid them of the world. You must accept me, and when the time comes, you must call on me."

"I shall," Niah said.

She reached for her hand and for a moment, Niah stared at her own reflection, and then she awoke with a gasp. Words echoed in her mind that sounded like Zorya's voice just before she scrambled up and ran out the door.

"Do not trust the Saint."

Chapter 23

Tonight, she would slip through the cracks of the Commander's office like mist to steal the secrets he guarded like glistening gold. Valek seemed to spend most of his days in his study—the closest thing he had to a sanctuary.

Catrin had threaded the bone of Saint Ylena around a piece of yarn and tied it around her neck. Now it lay hidden between her breasts, as warm as firelight. It frightened her rather than comforted her. For so long, she had run from the title of *Lightbearer*, but this small token meant that she had accepted the role. Like a king wearing his crown.

Niah slipped between the birches and ran to the outbuilding, careful to avoid any of the guards. The barracks were filled with the family-appointed guards of the nobles, along with those who manned the fortress. Many of them were the untouched, but some of them were Reapers who served Valek's squadron.

Her heart thudded as she moved along the stone walls. Snow sifted from the sky, blanketing the ground in a thick coverlet.

She made her way down the hallway, hearing the shouts and laughter from the dining hall. She hoped nobody saw her. It would be impossible to explain what she was doing here.

Niah made it across the corridor to Valek's office door. Unsurprisingly, it was locked, but she had prepared for this. She had filed down a piece of iron to act as a makeshift key. Niah rotated the pick, pushing it in slowly. She waited until the end met resistance and switched the angle to try another path. Footsteps sounded, and her palms grew slippery with nerves. If she were caught, she and Kesi would *both* be punished.

Just as she was about to abandon her attempt, she heard a satisfying click.

Niah rushed inside and sealed the door shut behind her.

His office was empty and neat. He'd cleaned up and organized since she'd last been in here. Niah went to his table and sat in his leather armchair. He was drafting the beginning of a letter, and she picked up the parchment, careful not to smudge the ink.

> *Dearest Natalia,*
>
> *It has been some weeks since we last corresponded, and I apologize for my delay in getting back to you. It delights me to hear you've made a new friend with the gardener's daughter. Father visited recently, and he spoke of a betrothal he orchestrated between you and Lord Kasper. You must be frightened, but you needn't fear — you will NOT wed that old geezer so long as I live and breathe.*
>
> *I have made a new friend as well. She pretends that she dislikes me, but I reckon she is rather fond of me. Maybe one day,* ~~*when she likes me a little better or even spares me a smile,*~~ *you two may meet.*
>
> *I eagerly await your next letter.*
>
> *Love,*
> *V. Winterson*

Niah slowly put the letter down, surprised by his gentleness and protectiveness towards his sister. She had never thought that Valek Winterson was capable of love, but this was proof of it. Something niggled at her heartstrings, at his last few words. It was rather obvious that he spoke of her. Niah didn't know why it secretly delighted her that he had mentioned her in passing. He'd scribbled over a line that she *hoped* was not an insult he had reconsidered. Perhaps it was a small mercy that he had erased it.

Niah searched his drawers and found some old letters from various field generals. Anything dated before this week was irrelevant, and she didn't bother looking into it. The most recent one was three days old.

We have fallen back in Wryn. The light mages have retained control of the village and the greater countryside. They have burned through our Fallen. Several of our finest Reapers are injured, and they launched a sneak attack on our cattle and water barrels. We had to relocate further than was planned to get close to a riverbed and heal our wounded. We await your direction, Lord Commander.

It felt good to read about a victory won by the Low North. Nobody here spoke of such news for fear that it would spoil the morale of the army. It seemed Valek's absence on the field boded well for them.

Niah found a map with stars lined across. It took her a moment to realize this was an outline of his stationed troops across the land. Niah found a blank sheet and began to copy the map onto it. This was valuable information. Some of these units were covert, and it made her nervous to think of how close they were to certain regions and their proximity to the capital.

Morgana would appreciate this intel.

Niah also came across a new brief on addressing the rebel situation. Valek was going to do another hunt in two weeks.

Niah reached for the bottom drawer, but it did not give under her pull. It took her a second to realize that it was locked.

Niah bent down, drawing out her pick and got to work.

Whatever was in there must be valuable indeed if Valek chose to hide it.

A soft click sounded before the wood gave way. Reaching inside, she found sheets of paper. Among them was a sketch of a young girl, small and frail. It took a moment to realize that those haunted eyes belonged to *her*. A small gasp escaped her. This had been the night he'd met her all those years ago. A moment that had sealed her fate. It shocked her to stare at her own face, to see the innocence and fear reflected in her gaze. She had thought she'd been so brave that night facing Valek, but that wasn't how he saw her. The truth lay bare for him to pick like a dog with a bone. He saw behind her shield. He always had. Long before their bond tied them.

Her throat tightened, and she dropped the sketch, letting it flutter down like a moth's wing. The next page was another sketch. It was her again, only slightly older. It had to have been drawn from his memory because she hadn't seen him again until many years later. He hadn't drawn her eyes, as if he couldn't remember them anymore.

The next page was another sketch and another. Each one depicted a missing year when they were apart, and in each, he hadn't bothered to draw her eyes. The last one was recent, and he had drawn her eyes. Her brows were slanted and angry, and her mouth pursed. Niah could feel the indents where his charcoal had dug too deeply into the sheet, as if he were angry. She swallowed, feeling the weight of the thin paper suddenly heavy in her hands. Why had he drawn this? Why had he drawn *her*?

There was nothing else in the drawer, and Niah tucked it inside, not sure how to lock it again.

What she gathered would have to be enough to aid their cause. And the rest, she would erase from her memory.

Especially those rough, piercing sketches.

Niah had the map she copied tucked safely in her pocket. Somehow, she had pulled off breaking into Valek's office without a hitch.

Kesi and Niah celebrated that night, jumping on their beds.

"I was so nervous when he asked about you," Kesi said. "He thought you'd reported for your punishment in the armory against his permission."

"He asked about me?" Niah asked. Her mind drifted to those sketches, and she shook her head to erase them. Whatever rabid thoughts ran through Valek's head when he'd been drawing those, Niah had no intention of finding out what they meant or *why* he kept it locked away like it was a dirty secret.

Kesi nodded. "Of course, he did. He scanned the room for you the second he walked in."

"And you told him what we agreed upon."

"Yes." Kesi grinned. "I described in detail that your bleeding womb had you in excruciating pain, and unless he planned to fluff your pillow and feed you grapes, his assistance was unwanted."

Niah's cheeks burned. "You did not say that."

Kesi was to tell him it was her time of the month. In those words, precisely—not goad him with impolite suggestions. How she even came up with such things was a wonder. Her mind was an intricate maze that Niah could scarcely understand.

"To his credit, he was not horrified by the suggestion." Kesi giggled. "I think he was willing to be of service to you in any way that he could!"

Niah couldn't help but laugh along. Perhaps it was a *little* funny that she had picked on Valek.

It felt good to gain a small victory after so many losses. For once, it felt like things were looking up.

Niah sat on the ground while the students sparred around her. Valek hadn't paired her with anyone, and she couldn't help but wonder if he was planning some grand humiliation. Maybe he wanted to spar with her to prove how weak she was. A punishment for besting him that day. It was dreadful, sitting there and waiting for him to concoct his unique brand of torture.

Valek stepped away from where he stood with folded arms and approached her. He crouched down to speak with her, hair falling into his dark eyes.

"Why so uneasy, Novice?" Valek asked.

Niah ignored the fact that he knew that by their connection.

"Why am I not in there?" she asked with narrowed eyes. "What are you planning?"

"Your mouthy friend said you weren't feeling well last night," he said. "Figured you could sit this one out."

Niah had almost forgotten about their lie. It surprised her that he remembered and was making an exception for her. It made her uncomfortable. A few eyes settled on them, probably wondering why they weren't going at each other's throats.

"Oh," she mumbled. "It's not a big deal. I can fight."

"I'd rather you did not exert yourself today," Valek said patiently.

Niah was silent, uncertain of what to do with this direction. Valek giving her a reprieve felt unnatural. Almost as disturbing as the fact that he had those sketches of her over the years in his drawer.

"The Chancellor left," he said.

Niah let out a slow breath. That was one less problem she had to worry about.

"He is impressed by your strength and looks forward to seeing you take your place on the field," Valek said. "By my side."

Dread filled her at the thought of standing on the wrong side of this war. Niah folded her arms across her knees. There was nothing to say to that. It didn't matter if she protested or refused or snapped.

The Winterson men did not care for her, and she would be a fool to forget that.

Valek returned to the group, and Niah could breathe again.

Chapter 24

The candlelight shone on her book. Niah had a map of the fortress sprawled before her.

It struck her that evening that she could find the ground plan for the fortress in the library, and sure enough, she had found the thick architectural scrolls on the second floor.

Niah intended to steal the scroll, so she didn't hesitate to mark it with what she learned from spending her lunch hour studying the guard rotations. Morgana would find this useful when she planned her attack.

Someone whistled.

"Smart girl."

Niah jolted, only to find Suren standing over her looking impressed. He pulled out the chair beside her and slid easily into it. Niah folded the scroll quickly and slid it into her bag.

"You scared me," she said.

"Maybe you shouldn't be plotting your escape in the *very* public library," Suren said teasingly. "And here I was thinking you were smart."

Niah grinned. "Good point."

"The armory was quiet without you," he said.

"Valek said I was done with my punishment," she said.

"Couldn't stand you having fun, could he?"

"Probably not."

"Speaking of fun, I'm having a small gathering in my bedroom tonight. A few friends and a stolen bottle of wine," he said. "I'd like for you to come."

"You have friends?" Niah teased.

Suren let out a gruff laugh. "Fine. They are my acquaintances who happen to have a stolen bottle of wine that I'd *very* much like to drink."

"I'm not trying to get in trouble again," Niah said. "I'd rather use my spare time on other matters, not cleaning stupid blades or scrubbing pots."

"You won't get caught," he said. "And you can bring your friends."

He lightly kicked her ankles. "Come on, it'll be our last time sharing a drink."

"You don't even like me."

"Well, you've grown on me like mold."

Niah laughed. It was hard to resist his offer after *that* charming compliment.

"Fine," Niah said. "We'll come."

Suren's lips lifted in a pleased smile.

He left, and Niah packed up her belongings. She had to find Catrin and pass her the information she found.

The heat in the kitchens pressed down on her. The air was thick with the scent of roasting meats and simmering stews. A woman's sharp voice rang through the haze, cracking like a whip as she barked orders to the flustered staff. Steam curled from every surface, blurring the edges of the room. Niah remained crouched behind a row of towering copper pots, the clatter of ladles masking her shallow breaths. Just beyond the gap of hanging metal pots, she spotted movement—a girl darting across the far end of the kitchen, her skirts trailing her like smoke as she disappeared into the shadows.

Niah grabbed her elbow. Catrin's lemony hair, gave her away from the other servant girls.

"What are y—"

"It's me," Niah said.

"Oh," she said. "You frightened me."

"Sorry," she whispered. "I have Morgana's message."

Niah passed her the sheet, and she tucked it in her palm, fleeing back up the stairs before they got caught.

Now all she had to do was wait to hear back from Morgana.

Kesi and Demian's arms were laced between her own as they trekked to Suren's dormitory under the blinding snowstorm. They ducked their faces low and had their hoods drawn, the ice hitting their faces like a slap.

"I didn't know you were close to Suren," Demian said.

Niah shrugged. "He's another outcast. It makes sense."

"A gathering with people who don't hate us should be a refreshing change," Kesi said.

"Is it fine that I'm coming?" Demian asked. "I don't think Suren likes my cousin."

"*Nobody* likes your cousin," Niah said. "And all you share is a surname and nothing else."

"That's true," Kesi said, resting her head on his shoulder. "We're going to miss you when we leave."

"Leave where?" Demian asked.

Niah stiffened. Why had Kesi spoken so freely? Demian was their friend, but he was not their ally. He did not serve their cause and could not be trusted with their plots. Ever since learning Morgana was here, the possibility that they would make it out of this place had become stronger.

"For battle, of course," Kesi said in an attempt to hide their secrets. "I reckon they'll put us conduits in the frontlines like their own personal shields."

"No, conduits are too valuable," Demian said. "You will be well protected."

Kesi switched the topic, and Niah's shoulders loosened. For one night, she would shut her mind off and attempt to have a bit of fun. It had been so long since she had taken a break from fighting. There was always a calamity on the horizon, a looming darkness, a burgeoning battle, but for one night, Niah wanted to imagine that there were clear skies ahead. She would pretend that she was just a girl, not a symbol or a spoken prayer made flesh, or a savior.

Suren's bedroom was decently sized. There were only four people besides them. It was a small gathering, which was a relief. Niah didn't recognize any of the faces. Demian went off to greet a short boy with fox-red hair, and Kesi followed. Everyone was tucked in the small seating area except for Suren, who was sprawled on his bed like a king. He gestured for her to come over, and she sat down beside him, resting her back on the headboard.

"You came," he said. "I didn't think you'd take a break from all your scheming."

He poured her a cup of wine and handed it to her.

"Even the wicked need to rest," Niah said.

"A toast," he said with his glass raised. "To the wicked."

"To the wicked," Niah echoed.

Niah's gaze drifted to where Kesi was twirling a finger around her hair and grinning at Demian's friend.

"I reckon he doesn't stand a chance against her," Suren said, following her gaze.

Niah chuckled. "Not one bit."

"You both are very different," Suren said, studying her with interest. "I cannot imagine you flirting."

"No?" Niah raised a brow. "I'll have you know I am an accomplished flirt."

Suren snorted so loud that a few of the students glanced their way. Niah elbowed him, *hard,* and he raised his hands in surrender.

"Sorry," he said cheekily.

"You are not forgiven," she said.

"Try it then," Suren said, sitting upright. "Flirt with me."

The wine was sweet on her tongue, and she glanced up to see Suren staring at her under his lashes.

"Very well," she said. "You have...eyes, and they are nice."

Suren bit his lip to control his laughter. "I'm flattered."

Niah raised her hand to shove him off the bed, but he grabbed her wrist. His eyes locked on her lips.

"What?" Niah asked. "Do I have something on my mouth?"

"Yes."

Suren caught her chin, and she was surprised when he leaned forward, pressing his warm mouth to hers. His lips were soft, and her heart lurched in nerves. She hadn't expected him to kiss her, but now that he did, she could admit that it was rather nice. Her finger tentatively touched his jaw, and his tongue trailed her bottom lip, sliding into her mouth. A low simmering sensation trembled in her belly.

"What the fuck are you doing?"

Niah leaped away from Suren.

"What's wrong?" he asked, alarmed. "Did I do something wrong?"

"No...I thought I heard something."

"Answer me."

He was in her head. Niah didn't even know if she could respond to him; she hadn't tried it that night when they'd dined with his father. But did she really want to have a conversation with him inside her head? She could barely stand him on a day-to-day basis. How could she allow him in her sacred space?

"What do you want?" Niah asked.

For a moment, she thought he wouldn't be able to hear her and she didn't know if she could survive a one-sided conversation with Valek. He was far too stubborn, and would seek her out if she didn't respond.

"*I asked you a question, and that doesn't sound like an answer.*"

"*I was sleeping before you woke me up with this dumb interrogation.*"

"*Then why do you feel desire?*" Valek asked. "*Are you with a boy or were you just dreaming about me?*"

"Niah," Suren said. "I'm sorry, I didn't mean to frighten you."

"You didn't," she said softly. "It was nice."

Suren smiled, a sweet, lopsided turn of his lips.

"*Fine, I'll come get my answers in person.*"

"Shite," Niah cursed.

"What?"

"Valek is coming," she said.

"Here?" Suren straightened.

"No, but he's going to check my bedroom."

"How do you know?"

"Stupid bond," she grumbled.

Suren frowned. "How did it get so strong so fast?"

"I don't know, but he's going to punish Kesi and me if we don't get back in bed right now," Niah said, scrambling up.

Suren sighed. "We didn't even finish the bottle of wine."

"I'll see you tomorrow for breakfast?"

He nodded. "I would walk you back, but I reckon that won't go over well with the Lord Commander."

"No, it won't."

Niah grabbed Kesi's wrist.

"We have to beat Winterson to our chambers," Niah said. "He's looking for me."

"I'm sick of that damned Commander ruining our fun all the time," Kesi whined. "Why is he so obsessed with us?"

They waved at Demian, who gave them a puzzled look, but there was no time to explain. Hopefully, Suren would tell him what happened.

They stuck to the trees and ran to their dormitory, fingers interlaced, boots thudding on the wet snow. Wind slapped their cheeks, and their hair floated behind them like the sails of a boat. Kesi cackled as if they were on a merry adventure. Niah felt her shoulders loosen when she noticed nobody lurking in front of their bedroom. He hadn't sought her out. Niah had been so certain he would come to catch her in the act.

Kesi opened the door.

"So, that kiss…" she began.

"What kiss?" a dark voice demanded.

Kesi yelped, jumping behind Niah. Valek sat in the desk chair, rotating his blade in the familiar way Demian always did. Niah wondered for a second if he had taught Demian that particular trick of flipping a dagger without slicing off one's finger. Maybe she'd ask Demian to teach her one of these days.

"What are you doing in our room?" Niah asked in a shaky voice.

"What kiss?" Valek repeated.

"We were kissing under the tree," Kesi lied. "Niah confessed her love to me an hour ago, and we plan to have the ceremony officiated by one of your pastors in the chapel tomorrow morning. You are invited to join."

"If I didn't find you so unbearably annoying, I might have laughed at that one," Valek said.

Kesi looked pissed that he called her "annoying". Niah knew the next words that would come out of her mouth would doom them rather than save them.

"Well, if you must know, the boy Niah was kissing is taller than you and his shoulders are far wider, and I'm sure if he dropped his pants, his co—"

Niah clasped her hand on her mouth, reeling her friend in like a wild horse.

"Kesi," she whispered harshly. "Why would you say anything?"

"Give me a name and we'll see if you are telling the truth for once," Valek said. His eyes shone like dark gems. "Let her speak."

"This is ridiculous," Niah said, letting Kesi go. "Why are we the only ones who get punished for having fun? Other students break curfew too."

"The other students are not *my* conduit," Valek snarled. "I expect better from you."

"I didn't ask to be your conduit or for you to force this stupid bond on me!" Niah said. "All you use it for is to spy on me."

"I saved you," Valek said. A vein ticked in his jaw.

"You ruined me," Niah yelled. "Infected me. You don't belong in my head, in my flesh, in my soul."

"If not you, then who else do I torment?" Valek demanded.

His hair was mussed as if he had run his fingers through it in frustration, and his eyes were wild and untamed.

"Who else am I to claim?" Valek asked.

Somehow, he had crossed the space between them, and everything in the room blurred, including her best friend, who was no doubt watching this exchange with horror. Niah couldn't move if she wanted to. Valek's presence was too overpowering. Strange how someone so corrupt could wield his power like it was divine.

"Anybody," she whispered. "Anybody else."

"It is too late for that," Valek said. His cold fingers traced her cheekbone. "Want is a strange, fickle beast that answers to no man. It consumes and devours, but it never submits."

"I don't understand," Niah said.

The words were foreign and thick in her mouth. She had only taken a few sips of her wine, but it felt like everything was all muddled, and if she turned her head, nothing but clouds would slip from her ears. All of his words made sense separately, but together, it was a thing she could not understand, like a pattern with variegated stitching.

"It's him, isn't it?" Valek said, ignoring her response. "The envoy's son."

Niah swallowed. "No."

"I can sense your lies," he said. "If it wouldn't cause a political mess, I would cut his tongue from his body and pin it to his forehead."

"Why his forehead?" Kesi asked, sitting on her bed and kicking her legs like they were a fascinating theatre performance.

"Why *not* his forehead?" Valek asked.

His gaze was still locked on Niah, but his hands had thankfully returned to his side. As if he had just realized they were not alone.

"Good point," Kesi agreed.

"Kesi!"

"Bad point," she corrected. "Very bad point."

Valek's mouth twitched.

"If you hurt him, Valek, I will never speak to you again," Niah said. "I swear it."

"Give me something in return, and I will leave him untouched," Valek said. "Also, make your friend leave the room, she is making me uncomfortable."

"What? No! I won't speak, but I want to watch," Kesi cried.

"Give us a second, Kesi," she said.

Kesi sighed, hanging her head like a chastised child. She closed the door behind her, but Niah knew she probably had her ear perched to the wood.

"What do you want?"

"Surprise me."

His eyes glided down her face, lingering for one long, painful second on her mouth.

Niah felt a shock of desire so hot it nearly brought her to her knees. It took her a second to realize that the feeling did not belong to her. It belonged to *him*. It was unfathomable to think that Valek Winterson wanted her, but she could feel his devastating need even though he didn't show it. His face was as unreadable as it always was, if they were not tied this way, she would have never known.

"I can't give you what you need," Niah whispered.

For a million reasons, but mainly because he was the villain of her story. And the hero didn't kiss the villain.

"Give me *anything* and I'll take it," Valek said.

Niah hesitated before she reached out and grabbed his hand, as they had done that day at the dinner table. It was the safest thing to do, the only thing that didn't compromise her heart and soul. His long fingers twined with hers, magic flowing between them in a steady thrum. A slight quiver ran along his limbs, warming her insides.

"A man stripped of his soul will hunger for even the smallest scraps," Valek said softly.

His thumb traced her knuckles, once, twice, and then he let her go and turned his back, leaving the door ajar behind him.

It disappointed her that he left without explaining that strange remark, and the worst part was that she felt ridiculous for holding his hand. Of course, that wasn't what he wanted. He wasn't a child who'd lost his mother.

Maybe he didn't want to kiss her either. Maybe he thought of another girl he liked who had drawn that dark well of desire forward. A girl who didn't fight with him all the time and didn't offer his secrets to his enemies.

Niah rubbed her eyes so hard it hurt.

"What happened?" Kesi asked.

"He threatened me, as usual," she mumbled.

"I'm here for you, Niah," she said gently. "No judgments if you want to tell me anything."

"Nothing happened," she rushed. "I swear it."

Kesi nodded. "I believe you, but even if it did, I wouldn't blame you for anything. You've been through more in the past few months than people have in years, and you have to give yourself some grace."

Guilt flickered through her. She had been so busy fighting Valek and her enemies, Niah hadn't once asked Kesi how she was handling all of this.

"How have you been doing?" Niah asked.

Kesi glanced out the window. "Sometimes...sometimes I feel at home here. Not always, but when you, Demian, and I are dining together, it feels right. It is easier to pretend that everything is perfect and that we are untouched by the war. I suppose that is quite silly of me to say."

"No," Niah said softly. "It makes perfect sense."

"He cares about you," Kesi said. "He'll be devastated when you leave."

"I love Demian, but he cannot come with us," Niah said with a shake of her head. "He is not loyal to us."

Kesi lay down, drawing her blankets over her shoulder.

"I do not speak of Demian," she whispered.

Kesi closed her eyes, sensing that Niah would resist this observation and the direction of this conversation. Niah didn't know how she could live with herself if anything ever happened with the Commander of the High North. Even if a small, tormented piece of her was intrigued by him.

By the man who imprisoned her and her best friend.

Her ruthless enemy.

Chapter 25

Finding Suren the next morning, had begun to feel like wading through a hedge-maze at midnight with nothing but the sulking moon to guide her path. It was near impossible. For a moment, she worried that Valek had done something to him. Niah waited until nightfall to see if he had shown up to the armory to clean the weapons. A sigh of relief escaped her at the sight of him scrubbing the metal with a rag.

"Suren, you're alive!"

"Barely," he said.

Niah wondered if she should bring up the kiss. It had been foolish to think that she could escape the burden of her duties for one night. She had put Suren in danger by being so reckless. It was a mistake she would not repeat.

"I didn't see you in the morning," Niah said.

"Kitchen duty," he said. "His Greatness, Lord Winterson, felt that my evening duties were not punishment enough and had me scrubbing pots before the sun even rose."

Suren yawned. His eyes were tired and bloodshot.

"I'm so sorry," she said softly. "He guessed I was with you. I don't have many friends, so he didn't have to try hard."

"I don't get why he cares. Everyone breaks curfew. The abandoned chapel turns into a brothel on Friday nights."

"He hates me," she blurted. "It is his life mission to make me as miserable as possible."

"At least he is gone for now," Suren said.

"Is he?" Niah asked.

Suren nodded. "Saw him ride out this morning."

That was good to know. Niah wasn't ready to face him yet. Not after everything that happened last night. She still didn't know what to make of it all, so she tucked it into a dark corner in her mind where she kept all the things she was too afraid to acknowledge.

"What's your punishment?" Suren asked.

Niah shrugged. "He'll probably tell me when he comes back."

Suren placed down his blade and turned to face her.

"How strong is your bond?" Suren said. "Did he speak to you last night when we kissed?"

Her cheeks warmed; she had been wondering when he'd bring *that* intrusion up and now was as good a time as any to address it.

"He did," Niah said.

"Has he done that before?"

Niah nodded, and he frowned.

"They say the bond between a conduit and a mage is like two souls interwoven. You are tied by forces greater than you both," Suren said. "It takes years to be able to communicate with each other. It should not have happened this quickly."

Unease slithered up her spine.

"Do you think if I leave, he'll be able to find me?" Niah asked.

"Do you sense him now?" Suren asked.

"No."

"You still have time to leave before it gets stronger," Suren said. "Distance weakens it, which is a sign that you are not fully bonded to him."

Niah stood up, and Suren caught her hand.

"I think I might miss you when you leave," he confessed.

"You think?" Niah teased.

"No, I know."

He stared at her with his emerald green eyes like he wanted to kiss her again, and a small part of her wanted him to kiss her, to make her forget about all the bad things, but they both knew it was hopeless.

Niah would never see him again.

Until the war ended, she would have no time for boys and stolen kisses and dreams. A part of her mourned the loss of his touch when his hand dropped. War had eaten away at her youth like a moth gnawing on silk, leaving her a hollow victim in its wake. Every time she closed her eyes, she saw the flames burning Teren and then again, the battle at the monastery. Blood soaking the crystal-white robes of her Sisters.

Niah left, closing the door behind her with a finality that rang.

It was their third test in Master Kole's class. It was scheduled weeks later when the Commander returned. It was obvious Valek had a keen interest in this course.

Niah always dreaded Master Kole's lessons and their unconcealed brutality. Her stomach churned as she saw what was coming towards them. Four prisoners whose heads were covered with bags were brought to the arena. The ends of their white robes were covered in grime. Niah knew who they were. She didn't need to have the gift of foresight to know who those women were. Her limbs locked in fear, and she chewed her lip, blood sliding into her mouth where she cut the flesh.

Was it Morgana and the Sisters? Had Valek found them at last? Had they been rotting in his prison all this time?

The stands were empty today except for Valek and the Headmistress. They sat with stony faces as they stared ahead.

Niah stood with her team, but her gaze flickered to Kesi, who gave her a nervous look.

"The test is simple," he said. "Each team will pick their weakest member to execute one of the traitors before us who were brought in from a monastery in Wryn."

The guard ripped off the brown bags that covered them. Niah did not recognize them, but she knew those ivory streaks that ran along their hair marked them as mages of the Order.

It was obvious this test was designed to test her loyalty. What other Reaper would falter at the chance of slaying their enemy? It explained why the Headmistress stood in the distance, doubt tightening her face, and beside her was Valek with an air of indifference, but she could feel something brewing beneath his chest: anxiousness.

"Pick your executioner," he called.

"The obvious answer is you," Milo said. His eyes were bright, and he licked his lips. "This should be fun. Do you know them?"

Casimir stared at her face, picking up on her distress. Niah didn't even have the energy to rise to Milo's taunts. The women standing before them ranged from seventeen to forty-five. They hid their fear well and did not falter. They were warriors, and they did not fear death.

"Maybe I should do it?" Casimir said. "I don't think she can handle it, and we can't afford to fail."

Niah drowned out their words, staring at the women. Their gazes were on her; they could tell by her hair that she was one of them. Relief crossed the eyes of the youngest, as if Niah could save her. Niah shook her head sadly. She let the ends of her sleeves fall so they could see the chains that bound her, the exact ones that stifled their gifts. Nothing she did today would change their fate. Not when they were deep in enemy territory.

Every person had picked their slayer. Niah was relieved when Casimir stood forward, giving her a small nod. It was good to see that Kesi's team spared her the gruesome task. It would be unbearable to watch it, but Niah would never survive being the one to wield the sword. It would destroy her.

Master Kole made his way down the choices. When he stopped at them, he clicked his tongue, unimpressed by the selection.

"Switch places with the girl, Novice," Master Kole said.

"Who? Eveline?" Casimir asked, playing dumb.

Niah felt a wisp of gratitude that Casimir was facing Master Kole's wrath to protect her. But it was not Eveline whose loyalty was in question, it was hers.

"Do not play daft," he snapped. "Come here, girl."

Niah's feet were frozen. She didn't even feel when Milo grabbed her elbow with punishing fingers and dragged her forward.

"Wish I could be the one to kill her—to kill all of them," he breathed in her ear. "I would take my time and *really* make it hurt."

Something snapped in her, and she shoved her fist in his face, hearing the satisfying crack of his nose.

Milo howled in pain, and Niah smiled.

"Enough!" Master Kole barked. "Return to your position, Novice."

Milo walked back to the others, gripping his bleeding nose.

Niah's breath escaped her in strangled gasps. Panic made her vision waver.

"*Don't make me,*" she whispered into his mind. "*Please, Winterson.*"

"*The Chancellor wanted your loyalty tested. This was his idea,*" he said. "*The Headmistress will act as witness and report back to him.*"

He paused.

"*He didn't trust me to tell him the truth. He knows that you are important to m—to the war. And that I wouldn't want you harmed.*"

"*Did you capture them?*" Niah asked.

Silence.

He had been gone for three weeks. He must have gone to Wryn. He had left after the missive that was sent. The one that spoke of their losses.

"*Anytime I think you are half-bearable, you go off and disappoint me,*" she said bitterly. "*You are the spitting image of your father.*"

Niah spoke the only words she knew would hurt him. Last time, she had mentioned his similarities to his father, he had flinched as if she had slapped him, and from the piercing quiet, she knew it had worked.

"Now, Novices," Master Kole said.

The other student ran with their hilts raised. The women were weaponless. They did not flinch from the onslaught. Together, they clasped hands and tilted their faces to the sky—like the Seven Maidens sacrificed to calm Penmaer's storms. Saint Mera the Drowned had plucked them from the sea and gifted them a song that lured mortals to their deaths..

A gruesome line cut through their flesh, leaving behind red ribbons that smiled in the light. All of them, but one. Niah's target.

"I gave you a command, Novice," Master Kole growled in her ear. "You serve the King's army. You wear the sacred cloth of Bersula. You are the Hand of Death."

"Please, Mas—"

He drew out his dagger and held it to Niah's neck.

"If you are not loyal to us, you serve no purpose," he said.

From the corner of her eye, Valek stood up.

"I need more time," she said. "Give me a few weeks I will be ready then. I swe—"

"Whom do you swear to? Aubrith?" he demanded. "You swear to the light?"

"No!" Niah said quickly. "I don't."

"You cannot play both sides, child," he said harshly. "I told the Chancellor I would keep an eye on you. He gave me his permission to cut your throat at the slightest sign of disloyalty."

Kole's eyes lifted to lock with Valek's gaze.

"I am under the protection of the Chancellor and the King of the High North," he said. His words were meant for Valek alone. Valek was granted the highest level of authority in Silverwood. It surpassed the Headmistress. As far as titles went after the Chancellor, he was the most powerful man in the realm. But Kole had his father's blessing and that was its own shield.

He could kill her.

"So, what will it be?" Master Kole asked. "Whom do you serve?"

Her words were trapped in her throat. The blade in her hand weighed her entire body down. It was a miracle she kept her head up. This ruse was crumbling like ashes. There were no more lies to craft, no more tricks. This was how she protected her soul. This was how her story ended.

Niah feared death and the unknown. The Book of Light rarely spoke of it. There was mention of a Maiden of Death, but beyond that, it was veiled in secrecy.

"*Do it, little saint,*" Valek pressed. His words were thick with concern, with fear. "*My father protects him. I cannot save you.*"

"Do me a favor," Niah said. "*Protect Kesi. She is a spitfire, but inside, she is softer than spun sugar.*"

"Nonsense," Valek said. "*If you don't kill the prisoner, I'll kill your friend.*"

"*You are lying,*" she said.

"*Try me,*" he snarled. "*The second he slits your throat, your friend will suffer the same fate as you. Make your choice: the prisoner or the girl.*"

Master Kole's blade had cut deep enough to draw blood.

"*You are no martyr,*" Valek snapped. "*You are* mine.*"

"Niah!" Kesi called. "You're hurting her. Stop."

Valek crossed the arena and stood by Kesi. His eyes locked on Niah in warning. His fingers drifted along his hilt. The message was clear: kill the innocent girl before her, or watch her best friend die.

Niah silently cursed him and all the depraved necromancers who served the king.

"I'll do it," she said hoarsely. "Release me."

Master Kole's blade dropped.

"Do not disappoint me, Novice," Kole warned.

For a moment, she imagined her blade slicing his head off, followed by Valek's. The image satisfied her, but she could not hide in her head anymore. The creatures under the bed from her childhood were real and alive. They surrounded her, staring at Niah with eyes devoid of feeling.

Niah whispered a prayer.

May the light guide my blade and the cut strike true.
May the darkness wither and hope shine through.

"Forgive me," Niah said.

The girl's eyes stared above. Her lip trembled before it curled.

"You are a disgrace," she spat. "Death is more honorable than servitude."

"I have no choice," Niah said. "May the light guide you."

Niah slashed at her throat with full strength. Her head fell with one quick swipe.

Disgust coiled through her belly, feeding on her from the inside like rot. She swallowed back the urge to vomit.

"Excellently done, Novice," Master Kole said.

Her ears rang, and a fist squeezed her chest. Footsteps sounded as everyone left, and she fell to the ground. Soft arms caught her before she crashed to her knees.

"Niah, it's okay, I'm here," Kesi said. "You had no choice."

"But I did," Niah whimpered. "There is always a choice."

Kesi shook her head sadly. "Not this time."

"You should have seen the way she looked at me," Niah whispered. "She hated me."

"No, she hated them," Kesi said. "Not you."

"Is he gone?" Niah asked.

"Master Kole? Yes," she said.

"Not him."

Niah could not bring herself to raise her head and look around. She didn't think she could wrangle her anger and tuck it away like the other times. If she saw him, she would kill him.

"He left," Kesi said. "I'm glad Morgana wasn't among the captured."

"Me too," she said softly.

"We can pray for them tonight," Kesi offered.

Niah let out a dry laugh. "Do you even know any prayers?"

"No," she said. "But I know how to close my eyes and look remorseful."

A reluctant smile crossed her lips as Kesi held her tightly, stitching the broken pieces of her soul together. Kesi brushed her lips against Niah's forehead. Tears fell from her eyes, burning her skin like poison.

"I have your back, Niah. Always," she said. "We are the only ones who understand the difficulties of our situation. We are persisting in the hope that someday we can overpower them. It is not betrayal, it is survival."

"I don't know what I would do without you," Niah said, resting her head on her shoulder. "I would be lost."

Kesi held her while she wept. The only person in this place who understood the burden thrust upon her, and Kesi didn't even know why Niah had changed course. She didn't know that Niah had killed the prisoner to save her friend's life, that Valek had given her no choice.

Chapter 26

Niah sat at her cluttered desk, ink-stained fingers stiffening as she worked on her map that laid out the guard rotations and their timing. The soft scratch of her quill echoed in her quiet room. Outside, the moon hung heavy, veiled behind a shifting curtain of clouds, leaving flecks of light across her parchment.

A soft knock interrupted her concentration.

"Come in," Niah called.

The door creaked open just a crack, and a slender figure slipped inside.

"Apologies, Lightbearer," Catrin said, voice low and urgent. "I had to find you to deliver a message. Morgana says that when you hear the whistle tomorrow, you must hide."

Niah sat upright.

"The next rebel hunt," she said. "They will be making a stand. Some of the villagers are supporting them. It won't just be the Sisters."

Niah stared at the summons on her desk.

Laith had requested she prepare tomorrow morning for another mission, the same one she had warned Morgana about.

Her Sisters were going to strike while Valek was away and take advantage of his absence.

It soothed her that he was gone. She could not bear to see him after that test.

She was surprised Valek even allowed her to leave the fortress without him sticking to her side.

"Okay," Niah said nervously.

Catrin left, shutting the door behind her with a soft click. Niah wondered what it was that Morgana was about to do.

All she knew was that tomorrow Morgana intended to send a message.

The air was tense that morning. Daria gave her an annoyed glance, and Laith's hard face was lined with a scowl. There were two boys with them who looked like brothers, both of them Reapers.

"Boris and Viktor, take the rear," Laith said. His brown eyes locked on her. "I don't have to warn you about what happens if you step out of line, do I?"

"No," Niah said. "Message received."

Laith cast her one last warning look before he clicked his tongue and his horse marched forward, the gates rolling upwards. Niah had her own mare today, a small, willful beast with a gray hide and silky white hair.

They didn't go to the village today but traversed the nearby fields. There were empty houses broken down by old storms.

"We've got word that the rebels are hiding out in these parts," Laith said. "We're going to split up an—"

A whistle sounded, and the next thing she saw was an arrow flying into the eye of the boy beside her, Boris—or was it Viktor? They looked so alike it was hard to tell. Niah leaped off her mare and fell to the ground, using the foliage to cover herself. Laith yelled out some demands, but the arrows were flying like shooting stars. Niah crawled through the mud to reach one of the abandoned houses.

She slammed the door behind her, heart racing, fingers sticky with sweat. It had begun. Morgana had made her move.

"Hands up!" A voice growled.

Niah didn't have time to react before an arrow buried itself in her shoulder. Pain blinded her, and she fell to her knee, sucking in a sharp breath.

"You idiot," a girl said. "Morgana said to leave the white-haired girl alone!"

"Oh shite," the boy said. "Her hood covered her hair."

He had a point. It was only when she bent down in pain that it had slipped from her head.

The girl and boy before her were a few years older than Niah. Their clothes were simple and dull, their bows and arrows made of fine wood. They were the common folk, the ones who churned butter and skinned animals. But they were here fighting against their own people in the name of peace. They were brave, and Niah admired them even if she was rather annoyed that they had shot at her.

"Come," the girl said, sliding an arm under her shoulder. "You can hide out in this bedroom till it ends. Morgana wants to speak to you. Dimitri is going to go get her."

She laid Niah down in an old, dirt-stained bed.

"I can't remove it," the girl said sympathetically. "You'll bleed out without a healer."

"It's fine," Niah said, between gritted teeth. Sweat dripped down her forehead. The pain was unbearable. "What's your name?"

"Bethan," she said. "And yours?"

"Niah."

"That's a lovely name," she said, sitting on the edge of the bed. "Has anyone told you, you look like a doll?"

"No," Niah said. "Soldiers don't sit around flattering each other."

"No, I suppose not," she said.

Bethan stood up and walked over to the window, peeling back the tattered curtain.

"It'll be over soon."

"Why did you become a rebel?" Niah asked.

"My brother joined the army. He wasn't a Reaper, just a regular man who was forced to fight a holy war. All of the people who support our cause are not mages, just common folk, and the Low North women. We bow in fear of the King's Reapers and all the other dark servants. We are interrogated every few months, our minds picked apart by their Diviners to ensure our loyalty. We have no freedom, no peace, just an endless, fruitless war."

Her bitter words touched Niah's heart. She opened her mouth to express her own fears when the door burst open. It wasn't Morgana who stood in the room, but Laith, his forehead bleeding. Bethan let one of her arrows loose on him, but he ducked and rushed at her, tackling her to the ground.

"Stop," Niah said.

Laith wasn't listening to her, he outweighed her in both muscle and training, and he slammed her head against the floorboard. Once, twice, by the fourth time her skull split and blood poured from her head like an overturned chalice. Her stomach revolted at the sight of her corpse.

Niah's pleas were left unanswered, and she watched numbly as Laith picked her up from the bed.

"We need to leave," he said.

"The others?"

Laith stared at her, his words dark and empty. "*Dead.*"

He climbed out the window and ran through the high grass. The sun was beginning to set, and their horses had scattered during the attack. Her body was racked with shivers.

"Don't die, Novice," Laith snapped. "Or the Commander

will kill us both. Wait at least till we're at the fortress and amongst the Stitchers."

"He can't kill me if I'm dead," Niah said.

Her words were an empty slur as he raced them back to the fortress. The will to fight faded, and she resigned herself. How many more people would she watch die? How much more heartache could she survive before it destroyed her?

"I do not wish to be awakened if I die. Promise me?"

Laith said something, but darkness cloaked her vision, and then there was nothing but blissful silence.

Chapter 27

The infirmary was silent. The cots beside her were clean and vacant. Marta, the healer, forbade visitors, so she wasn't surprised that she was alone. It was dark except for the moonlight pouring in from the window like spilled milk. Niah felt small and alone, lying there by herself.

Her trousers were on, but her shirt was gone, and the rough woollen blanket scraped her skin. As inconvenient as it was that an arrow had struck her, it would help hide the fact that she was aiding the rebels. At the very least, nobody would think she had anything to do with the attack since she had been injured.

The door opened, and she looked up expecting Marta's scowling face, but it wasn't her. Valek was back. His dark hair shone when the iridescent light hit it. His mouth was covered in a day's worth of stubble. Niah was too tired to fight or bicker with him tonight. Her shoulder throbbed, and the pain rippled down her arm any time she so much as took a deep breath.

Niah closed her eyes, pretending to sleep even though they had gazed at each other less than five seconds ago. She felt his hand on her cheek, his thumb caressing her cheekbone as if she were a delicate creature.

"I'm sorry I wasn't there, my little saint," he said.

Niah would think he was lying, but she could *feel* his remorse tangled with his anger through their bond. It seemed the more they interacted and remained close to each other, the stronger their connection grew. Even with the proof of his words, Niah couldn't hide her disbelief.

"I am going to kill every last one of those rebels," he promised. "I will cut out their worthless hearts and bring them to you."

Niah's eyes shot open, unable to pretend anymore.

"It is not the rebels that I fear," she whispered.

"Does my touch hurt?" Valek asked. His fingers fluttered down her cheek to linger above the column of her throat.

"It is your actions that hurt and your cruel threats," Niah said. "You do not need to raise your hand to make someone cower."

His fingers loosened and dropped to his side. A shadow passed over his face, veiling whatever raw emotion lurked behind his eyes.

"You used my friend to manipulate me," she said, between gritted teeth. "You used Kesi as a pawn in your game. *Again.*"

"I couldn't lose you," he said. "You were determined to die. I could *feel* it. I could sense your resignation."

He said it like *she* was the one who had betrayed him.

"So?" Niah snapped. "You could find another conduit. You could find another prisoner. What is so special about me?"

"Everything," Valek said, sharply, quietly. "Do you understand me?"

His words were laced with something deeper, something destructive.

"Where were you?" Niah asked, switching the topic. She was secretly frightened of where he intended to lead this conversation. Because for some reason, it didn't sound like he was simply speaking about her *gifts*.

"I had other matters to take care of," Valek said. "Do you want to see something?"

Before she could respond, Valek dug his hand into his pocket and brought out a handkerchief. He slowly unraveled the cloth, revealing an eyeball. Niah sucked in a sharp breath.

"Whose is that?" she asked, her stomach revolting at the sight of the icy blue iris.

"A souvenir from my trip," Valek said. He had a small, vengeful smile on his face. "You were the first person I wanted to show."

"What impression did I give you to think that I would like to see *that*?"

"Do you want to keep it?"

Bile crawled up her throat. "No!"

Valek let out a soft chuckle and tucked the eye back into his pocket. It was silent for a small moment before he spoke.

"Lord Kasper was attacked a few days ago by some thieves," he said. "He was robbed and killed. It was a tragedy."

Niah wondered why he was telling her this until it clicked. His sister's betrothed. In the letter, she read Valek had said he'd take care of it, and so he had. He had left to protect his sister. The realization made her mouth turn in a tiny, unwilling smile. It soothed her to know that the young girl would not be forced to marry an old noble. As much as she disliked Valek and his father, Niah cared about little children, even ones whose surnames were Winterson.

"Did the thieves also happen to take his eye?" Niah asked.

"According to the reports," Valek said.

This conversation reminded her of the last time she was injured when he'd confessed that he wanted to be a painter. It seemed the mask he permanently donned only fell when she was hurt. As if her vulnerability made him want to be honest.

"I wanted to be a healer," Niah blurted.

Valek's brow furrowed.

"I wanted to solve the Corruption," she explained, "to find a cure for the Sleeping Fever, to fix things with my mind and skill."

Valek sat down on the bed, one knee hiked up, and the other leg lying flat on the ground for support. He stared at her with unhidden interest.

"A healer and a painter," Valek mused. "Between the two of us, we wouldn't have a single coin to spend on food."

"We'd be happy," Niah said softly. "Isn't that all that matters?"

"And in this fairytale, would you still hate me?" Valek asked. His dark eyes were inquisitive and consuming.

"I wouldn't have a reason to."

Valek stared at her, grasping onto her words as if *I wouldn't have a reason to,* was the closest thing to mercy he'd ever been offered.

In some unnamed world where they were just two strangers without a war shadowing their every step, Niah might find it in herself to appreciate all the facets of his personality.

"And if I am just Commander Winterson, is that not enough?" Valek asked.

It hurt to remain silent, but it would ache more to say it aloud.

It had always been so easy to say, 'I hate you,' but not tonight when she could feel this odd yearning drifting from him to her. It reminded her that Valek was not the unfeeling, cold creature he presented to the world, that some small, part of him cared for her in his own twisted way. And Niah, to her utter dismay, found this side of him to be quite likable. It was for that very reason that she refused to answer his question, because her response frightened her.

Niah turned onto her uninjured shoulder.

It wasn't until several minutes later that she heard his footsteps retreating and the door clicked shut with a finality that made her chest hurt.

On her third day in the infirmary, Demian and Kesi came to visit with a scowling Valek not far behind them.

"Niah!" Kesi shouted, startling another patient.

"What did I say about yelling?" Valek snapped.

"Sorry," she grumbled. And then in a softer voice, "I missed you, Niah."

Kesi bent down to hug her when Valek caught her arm.

"Also, what did I say about leaping on the injured patient?"

"Right," Kesi said. "Her shoulder, I forgot."

"How are you, Niah?" Demian asked. "We begged that cursed hag to let us in, but she refused."

Niah reached for his hand and then lifted her other stiff hand with a wince to hold Kesi's.

"I'm better now that you both are here," she said. "I wish you had come sooner. I've been so bored."

Both of them turned to Valek with an accusatory look.

"Marta only takes orders from him," Kesi said.

"She wasn't ready to hear your loud voices and be jostled with your insensitive limbs," Valek said.

"Spare us, *Commander*," Kesi said. "All you care about is your precious conduit. The only thing that would bother you is if she died without you getting the chance to use her on the field."

"We are her friends, Valek," Demian said, agreeing with Kesi in less cruel words. "We are the only people who care about her here, and we just wanted to make sure she was fine. You could have let us in sooner."

"And what have you done since you walked in besides upset her?" Valek gestured to her downcast eyes.

Niah had been worried Valek would punish Kesi for challenging him and that she'd be too weak to stop it.

But now that their eyes were all on her, she wiped the nervousness from her face and raised her chin.

"I'm fine."

"Don't lie to me," Valek said.

"Maybe she would breathe easier if you left," Kesi suggested. "You are suffocating her."

Valek's jaw clenched, his eyes locked on Niah.

"Is that what you want?" he asked.

Yes.

Once again, Niah found her response struggling to pass her lips. She didn't know what was wrong with her. Why was she trying to spare his feelings?

There were bruised circles under his eyes like he hadn't slept in a while. If Demian and Kesi accosted him every day, it probably meant he hadn't been far from the infirmary.

He hadn't been far from her.

"Maybe you can wait by the door," Niah said.

Kesi's eyes widened, surprised by her response and by Valek's nod. The old Niah would have dismissed him rudely. It was the most cordial interaction they ever had. Niah had meant for him to wait outside the door, but Valek merely stood in front of it, remaining in the room.

"How are you doing?" Kesi asked.

"My shoulder aches, but I'm a lot better," Niah said.

"I don't know what I would do if anything happened to you, Niah," Kesi said. "We were so worried when we heard there were casualties. I can't believe you and Laith were the only survivors."

Niah had seen one of the brothers get shot by an arrow, but nothing else.

"Daria too?" Niah asked.

Kesi nodded.

Niah was sad that Daria died. Even if they had never gotten along. She couldn't help but wonder if Valek was upset by her death. Daria had always been fond of him. And then there was that spring wedding, Daria had mentioned.

"I would never do something so foolish as die when you're stuck here."

"There's my selfless little savior," Kesi teased.

"Thank you both for coming," Niah said. "I feel a lot better seeing your faces."

"Suren asked about you," Demian said. "He wishes he could see you."

"Not a chance," Valek warned from his post. She'd almost forgotten he was still here. "If he comes anywhere near her, I'll cut his throat."

Niah sighed. "Ignore him. He's sulking and jealous that he doesn't have any friends."

Demian snickered.

"You just kissed the boy, not bedded him. Why is he acting like this?" Kesi whispered.

"I can hear you, Novice," Valek barked.

"That was the point, *Commander*," she said.

Niah giggled. She loved it when Kesi poked at the beast, even if she would retreat at the first mention of punishment. She was the greatest friend a girl could ask for.

"Visiting is over," Valek said.

"But we haven't been here for long, it's been ten mi—" Demian began.

"*Now*, Novices," he barked.

"Goodbye," Niah said.

"I shouldn't have provoked him," Kesi said.

"His patience would have run out eventually," she replied. "Don't be upset. I'll be released tomorrow morning."

"We'll be here," Demian said. "Rest easy."

Kesi brushed a kiss on her forehead, and then they were both gone. Niah was glaring at the door when Valek returned.

"I don't like you threatening my friends."

"Then maybe that brat should keep her mouth shut."

"I'm not talking about Kesi. She can handle herself. I meant Suren."

His lips tightened. "I do not care to discuss that opportunist."

"Opportunist?" Niah said, annoyed. "In what manner?"

"Sleep well, Novice," he said coldly.

He opened the door and vanished before she could speak another word.

Niah hated when he got the last word.

It was hours later when the door cracked open again. For a moment, she wondered if Valek had returned. He had left with a bitter look in his eye at the mention of Suren. She could not understand why he even cared about their friendship.

Marta led another injured student into the room. It took her a second to realize it was Suren.

"Suren!"

"Niah, how are you?" he asked.

"Rest," Marta said. "I'll bring some balm for those cuts."

"Shoulder hurts, but it'll heal," she said. "What happened to your face?"

"I wanted to see you," he said. "Winterson has kept the infirmary guarded like a vault. I couldn't come as a visitor, so I became a patient."

"I don't want you hurt on my behalf." Niah frowned. "I'm being released tomorrow. I could have seen you then."

"I wanted to see you for myself."

"How did that happen?" Niah asked, pointing to the purple-black mark on his face.

"I taunted Winterson," Suren said with a shrug. "And he reacted as expected."

Niah frowned. "That was a foolish thing to do."

Suren's green eyes studied her face.

"I'm glad you're safe," he said.

"I'm glad you came."

He reached out for her hand, and Niah let him hold her palm. His touch was strong and assuring. It made her feel less alone.

"I know you will be leaving soon," Suren whispered. "But I would like for us to spend some time together."

Niah released his hand, staring at the ceiling. As much as she wanted to speak with him more, to learn as much about him as she could, it was too dangerous.

She had to focus on the planned attack and remaining beneath Valek's radar. He had reacted so strongly at the mere mention of Suren, she didn't know what he would do if he caught them together. It was Suren's status as an envoy's son that protected him; without it, Valek would have killed him a long time ago. The punch he had landed was nothing but a warning.

"That is a bad idea," she said.

Marta opened the door and began to rub a thick ointment on the cuts on his face, before sending him out.

Suren cast her a long, forlorn look as he walked out the doors.

Niah was escorted back to her dorm the next morning by Demian and Kesi. Valek vanished the moment they arrived, as if he could not get far away from her, and it stung. Even though she should not care an ounce about what Valek did. Or the intricacies of his mind.

"He's behind on correspondence," Demian said, following her gaze to where Valek strode off. "He hasn't left your side since you got hurt."

"He only cares because he presented me like a prize horse before the Chancellor. I don't think it would look too good if his weapon broke so easily."

"I don't think that's the reason," Demian said.

Niah hesitated at the look he gave her. It was obvious that he was implying that she was more than a weapon to Valek, and the idea made her entirely uneasy.

"It's nice to be back in our room," she said, ignoring his words. "I missed my bed. Those cots in the infirmary did more harm than good."

"Okay, Princess," Kesi teased. "Let's get you ready for class."

Demian sat on the chair near her desk and faced the wall to grant her privacy to dress.

"Did you girls find your gowns for the banquet?" Demian asked.

"What banquet?" Niah asked.

Catrin had mentioned it to her because the staff were working hard to prepare for it. But Niah didn't know the purpose behind the affair.

"The winter banquet is a celebratory dinner to acknowledge the achievements of the soldiers who will be passing through. It is awarded for merit and bravery. With the Commander here, the King will likely come to award Valek for his recent victories. The parents of some of the noble children will attend. It's a grand affair."

It must have been a big deal for the King to make a public appearance, considering his supposed illness.

"When is it?"

"In two weeks," he said.

Niah would have assumed the king would be too weak to travel, but perhaps he wanted to attend a public affair to silence any rumors.

This was the moment they had been waiting for. The answers to their prayers.

The King was coming.

And the Sisters would be prepared to strike.

Niah was in the library reading her book when she noticed Catrin wiping down the shelf beside her. Niah shifted aside as Catrin bent close.

"I have a note for you," Catrin said.

Niah frowned. If she'd blinked, she might've missed the sheet Catrin slid between her pages. Niah closed her book and returned to her bedroom. She closed the door and unraveled the letter.

We need to meet two nights from now at the shop you visited. There is a battle brewing, and we require your aid. The King is coming. This changes everything.

Just those four sentences struck her with both fear and hope. She had thought Morgana's target was the Commander, like most of the common folk who supported the rebellion, their issue was with the military, not the monarchy.

The King's death would cause unrest among the civilians, which could aid the Low North in their war efforts. It could also give the Low North a chance to stand on its own while the High North scrambled to regain control. But if the King fell, then the Chancellor would slide into his seat. The man who *truly* ran the continent. It was too great a risk. They had to kill the Chancellor as well.

Valek's father would have to die.

Niah didn't know how she was expected to help them fight with these damned shackles. How could she be the Lightbearer if she could not even summon the light? Her fingers reached towards the bone that belonged to Saint Ylena. Maybe this would help her, and Morgana would tell her how to use it. The mages had never used talismans before. A shiver ran down her back. It felt far too similar to the necromancers and their penchant for bones. But they were not the children of Bersula, they did not disrupt the balance and bathe in chaos.

Sometimes, in the dark, she would think about their teachings, about the existence of conduits, and she'd wonder if even a sliver of their words was true.

Niah burned the paper in the fireplace, watching it crackle before vanishing in the flames.

The time had come to fight, and Niah was prepared to lead the charge.

It was odd to think she had dreaded wielding a blade at one point, but with each week she honed her skills, Niah was ready to face her enemies and to fight for her country and Sisters.

Chapter 28

Niah's shoulder was stiff from her injury. She was given some grace during her physical classes, but she planned to be as close to full-strength within the coming weeks in preparation for her meeting with Morgana.

Just before dinner, Niah headed to the training room on the fifth floor. The space was stark and rigid, with high ceilings and wide windows that let in the fading light of dusk. It was mainly used by the soldiers.

The air smelled faintly of sweat and old leather, mingling with the metallic tang of sharpened blades. It was far better than the run-down training room on the lower levels, which were cramped and dimly lit, its cracked wooden floorboards worn thin by the clumsy boot marks of novices still learning to find their footing. That room was often crowded, filled with the nervous energy and anxious chatter of those desperate to strengthen themselves during the quiet hours of the night.

She didn't expect to find anyone here. There was one thing the soldiers liked more than sparring, and that was food, but of course, Valek Winterson did not eat. He probably feasted on the flesh of his enemies every night if the rumors were to be believed.

His chest was bare, revealing that intricate tattoo of the

snarling wolf that graced his side. His muscles danced beneath his flesh. Lithe and lean like ribbons around a gown.

"This room is occupied," he snapped.

"It is big enough to fit two people."

He turned to face her. His dark hair was plastered to his forehead, face flush pink with exertion.

"*You*," he said with narrowed eyes. "Are you following me?"

"No."

"Are you sure?" Valek asked, lips curling the slightest bit. "I didn't take you for the type to hunt your prey."

Niah rolled her eyes, dropping her heavy bag to the ground. She sat down cross-legged and began to stretch her shoulder. The good one first, and then the healing one. Her muscles were taut, and she flinched. They hadn't spoken much since the infirmary. She assumed he was still upset about Suren. It still baffled her as to why he cared so much.

"You're not my choice of prey," Niah said. "You scowl too much, and your hair..."

Valek lifted a hand as if he were going to touch his hair before he frowned and dropped his arm.

"What's wrong with my hair?"

"I can tell a lot by a man's hairstyle."

"Oh?" He raised a brow. "Enlighten me."

He folded his arms across his chest, muscles straining with the effort. Her eyes struggled to remain on his face. She refused to do anything as foolish as admire his physique. Even if it was a well-toned frame, not too bulky and not too lean. Just right.

"Your hair says that you think that you are the most attractive man alive," she said. "It says that you are arrogant and self-absorbed."

"You've used a lot of words to describe a simple thought."

Valek took several steps forward until he was mere inches away from her. She could smell his scent of mint and midnight mixed with boyish sweat, and more so when he crouched down. Her eyes widened in surprise when he reached for her elbow to help her stretch. He braced his other hand on her waist and began to guide her.

"That you're full of yourself?" Niah asked, trying not to lose her train of thought.

"That *you* think I am the most attractive man alive," he whispered. His breath was warm. "Why did you come here?"

"I wanted to do some light exercises, retrain my muscles," she said, rightfully ignoring his silly accusation. "But I don't need your help."

"No?" He raised a brow.

A small groan escaped her when he began to knead at the muscles in her forearm. With her shoulder weakened, her wrist and elbow had been doing the bulk of the work. His thumb pressed into the knots, slow and deliberate, coaxing them to melt beneath his touch. Valek found every tender spot with unerring precision, and it maddened her how easily he unraveled her.

"You're good at this," she said reluctantly.

"You say that like it's a bad thing."

"Depends on who you practiced on," Niah said.

Valek's mouth curled, but he didn't answer her, leaving her in suspense. Niah couldn't erase the burning jealousy that tore through her at his silence. Her next words were sharp enough to cut.

"Do you miss Daria?" Niah asked deliberately. "You two were close."

"I don't bed my subordinates, if that's what you are hinting at," Valek said. "I've lost many good men and women to this war. It is unfortunate, but a commander never falters."

"How utterly pragmatic of you," Niah said, the words dripping in contempt. "You truly are your father's son."

Valek's hands dropped as if he'd been struck.

"You wouldn't know the first thing about me, Novice," he bit out.

"I know that you keep your guard up, and that it never lowers even the slightest bit. I know that you are cruel, that you wield your rank and power like a sword. I know that you claim to have saved me, but everything you did was for your own selfish goals," Niah snapped.

"You were coddled and protected before the war, but I was always a soldier. I was born with a sword in my hand," Valek said coldly. "I read battle briefs instead of fairytales. I slept in the barrack cots more than I did in my feather bed. I was raising corpses before I had even understood the concept of death. I was never a boy. I was always a Reaper, a soldier, a weapon of war."

"Then lay down your sword," Niah said, approaching him hesitantly.

She had always thought there was a single fate that awaited them. Either he put a blade through her chest, or she did to him, but at this moment, Niah wondered if there was another way and if that answer was *peace*.

"Surrender," she urged.

Valek lowered his head, his hair tickling her forehead. He was so close, closer than he ever had been before. His lashes swept his cheekbones, softly and mesmerizingly.

"I don't know how," he confessed.

"I can teach you," she said.

His hands fell to her waist, firm and unrelenting. He drew her closer to him, as if her presence soothed him.

"You cannot fight darkness with the light," Valek said. "It must be met with kind. You've learned that and accepted it."

Niah *had* accepted it, but she didn't want it to be her truth. She didn't want to defy the rules of death and stain her soul by practicing this magic, but she had no choice. She was a prisoner, but Valek was free. He could make a difference. He could take a stand against injustice.

"I did what I had to do to survive," she said.

"And what do you think *I* am doing if not the same?" Valek asked.

"You are their strongest soldier. Their army does not have a fighting chance without you," she said. "They are losing every day you remain away from the frontlines, but the second you return, the tides will turn in your favor."

"It is not that simple," Valek said.

Last time she had asked him, he had not been ready, but maybe now he would accept her offer.

"It can be," Niah said. "Please, Valek. Stand with me."

Longing struck her—deep and aching—his emotions had spilled into her, weightless and uninvited.

"It is almost impossible to resist you like this," Valek said. His fingers brushed along her cheek, almost affectionately. His next words were soft, a forbidden whisper. "You don't know what you do to me. Even now, when you stand before me with winter in your eyes, I still feel the warmth of your gaze."

Niah opened her mouth, uncertain of what to respond to that, but just as soon as he spoke the words, his mask fell back in place, and she couldn't sense his emotions anymore. It was as if he had built a shield around his heart.

"I cannot be your hero, little saint," he said. "As much as I want to."

"You're making a mistake," Niah warned. "You *will* regret this."

"Perhaps," he said offhandedly, but it was clear he didn't believe it.

He believed himself to be untouchable.

And Niah intended to prove otherwise.

"What are you thinking about?" Kesi asked.

Their bedroom was dark, and Niah faced the ceiling, preparing herself to slip out into the night. Morgana needed to see her and there was immeasurable danger stacked against them. But the risk would be worth the reward. Niah could not erase the cruelty inflicted by her enemies. They had forced her to slay one of her own and for that she would *never* forgive them. Her anger slithered inside her like a starving serpent.

"I might have found a crack in their guard rotations," Niah said. "And Morgana wants to speak to me..."

"You're going to sneak out?" Kesi said, sitting upright. "Take me with you."

"It's too risky." Niah shook her head. "You need to remain here."

"But I can help you," she said. "We are stronger together."

"Morgana intends to land a strike on the King. This will remind them that they are *not* unbreakable," Niah said. "Until then, we have to be careful."

Valek, much like his people, believed that they would never fail. He hadn't said it in words, but that day she had pleaded with him to stand with her he had refused. Because to him they would always be weak and oppressed.

But soon they would prove them wrong.

"I'm worried," Kesi said, chewing her bottom lip. "You were already hurt before, and it's not safe out there."

"We can no longer stand on the sidelines," Niah said. "I must fight for queen and country. For Teren, Caer-Sylisse, and the entirety of the Low North."

"You are right," Kesi said with a deep sigh.

"Make sure nobody knows I left," she said. "I'll try to return before daybreak."

The woods were as quiet as a grave. Each twig that snapped beneath her boots echoed in the air. At a quarter to midnight, there would be a five-minute window between when the guard left to call his replacement and the next guard arrived. Niah had a few minutes to scale the west wall and vanish. She had no horse, and the walk to the village would take her at least a few hours. Niah was relying on Morgana to give her a horse to return or she would have to steal one if she expected to make it back by daybreak.

She hid behind a large, cypress tree and bided her time. A blond-haired man was making his rounds, and just as expected, he turned around, heading back towards the main gate to switch with the other on-duty guard. Niah broke into a run, gripping the old stone and hoisting herself upwards. Her shoulder ached, but she gritted her teeth against the pain and flung herself over the opposite side just as she heard the sound of idle whistling.

The next guard had arrived.

Niah slowly crawled down the other side and let out a breath of relief. She stared off into the dark and headed in the direction of the village.

By the time Niah reached Polina's shop, her feet were numb and sweat drenched her body. Despite the chilly air, she felt hot and damp. The door was locked, and she turned the handle twice. Finally, it was opened by Morgana, who stared at her with shrewd silver eyes. Her gaze had always reminded Niah of a clever fox.

"You look like you fought a bear and won by sheer luck," Morgana said with a wry smile.

"Almost," Niah said, brushing past her to enter the shop. It was too dangerous to stand out here in her Reaper robes. "I walked from the fortress."

Morgana whistled. "Impressive."

"No." Niah collapsed in the nearby armchair. "Stupid. I barely survived."

Morgana vanished through a door and returned with a shirt and water. She placed the jug and cup before her. Niah ignored the cup and tilted back the jug, guzzling down enough water to quench her thirst.

"Thank you," she said, placing the jug down. "I got your note."

"And the trinket from our saint?" Morgana asked, staring at her as if she could see beyond her clothes to the bone that lay on her chest.

Niah lifted it from under her collar, letting the bone sit there.

"I almost died," Niah said. "The voices nearly drowned me."

"The heretics keep the bones of our saints with the other vile people from history. It is their way of punishing the saints, or as they call them, the Sinners," Morgana said. "May I touch it?"

Niah untied the string and handed it to Morgana, who cradled it with a reverent gaze.

"What am I to do with that?" Niah asked.

"You use it to call upon the light," Morgana said. "Even with those shackles on, you are never far from the light. Take that as your comfort, my dear girl."

Morgana handed the bone back to her, and Niah felt the warmth of its touch. Just before she could tuck it under her collar, a spark burned from the forked end of the bone, and it grew into a long, magnificent sword of flame. The burning hilt did not sear her flesh. It was not her magic, nor was it the cursed magic Valek had thrust upon her. This was different. It was ancient and powerful. It was the magic of saints.

"*What is mine is yours*," the Saint whispered in her fluttery voice. It surrounded her in a gentle caress.

The light fizzled, leaving only bone once more.

Morgana smiled in the dark.

"When you call upon it, the light will find you."

"When do you intend to attack?" Niah asked.

"On the night of the banquet. The King shall be there. He is our target."

"How will you enter the fortress?" Niah asked. "I know of a few cracks, but not enough to bring all of you in."

Morgana had about thirty Sisters with her and forty rebel villagers.

"Catrin found a tunnel beneath the old chapel," Morgana

said. "We will travel through the woods and arrive at the Main Hall at a quarter to midnight."

"What about the Chancellor and...and the Commander?"

"I will take care of the Chancellor," Morgana vowed.

She placed her palms on Niah's cheeks.

"*You* will kill the Commander."

A shiver ran through her. The words were said with a striking finality. Niah was surprised that the first thing she felt was vehemence. Some unknown part of her rebelled at the thought of killing Valek Winterson. She knew that was her purpose. Her destiny demanded that she erase him for the good of the lands, but the idea weighed on her as heavily as the shackles that circled her wrists. Even as she nodded her acceptance, Niah wondered how she would keep this heavy promise.

"I understand," Niah whispered.

This had always been how the story ended, and this chapter would close as it had opened—in chaos and bloodshed.

Chapter 29

Dawn arrived with a distressing call, straining between the latticework that concealed their window. It painted the stone floors with hues of pink and butter-yellow light. By the time Niah collapsed on her bed, the weak frame creaking under her weight, it was nearly time to attend her first class. Sweat clung to her forehead, plastering her frosty hair to her skin.

Niah dressed half-heartedly. She had her combat class, and she wasn't looking forward to being in front of Valek so soon. She worried that he'd see the circles under her eyes and assume the worst. She had called upon the light last night. Not her own, but Saint Ylena's, and she was afraid that he would sense it through their bond.

It was odd, but the moment she reached for the light, she felt the magic between her and Valek fade, as if the light had burned it to wisps. That well she pulled from was unbearably dry. It unsettled her to feel the absence of his magic. This was her fault, she should never have risked calling on her gifts.

"He will know that something is amiss," Niah said. "I can't go to his lesson."

"He'll be mad if you skip," Kesi said.

"Better mad than suspicious," Niah said. "Can you tell him I'm sick?"

"You think he will accept it?"

"Maybe?" Niah said, recalling the time he had let her sit out because he thought she had been cramping from her monthly bleeding.

Sometimes, he could be halfway decent.

Kesi vanished, and an hour passed as she rested. Her bedroom door opened, and she blinked at the two Fallen standing in the hallway. Grinning menacingly beside them was Milo.

"The Commander wants to see you," he said.

The Fallen stared at her with their eerie eyes and gray-tinted skin, and before she could react, they grabbed her by the underarm and carried her down the hallway like a misbehaving child.

"Put me down!" she yelled. "Milo, I will kill you!"

"These are the Commander's Fallen." He snickered. "I just agreed to come along to see you punished."

Niah raised her hand to seize their control even if she felt utterly empty, but one grabbed her wrist and the other her legs. Heads turned as she was carried down the hallway. Students whispered, and some snickered in delight. Gone was the little respect and fear she'd gained from proving herself in her class tests.

All they saw now was her being humiliated by Valek.

Again.

A warm flush crawled up her throat. She clenched her teeth so hard it was a wonder they did not snap under the pressure.

The training yard was empty, and they placed her down slowly. Her chest rose and fell with rage, and she was tempted to slash their throats out for the disrespect, but they did not deserve her wrath. It was their master who should be punished for this.

She could hurt Milo, though.

"Leave, Novice," Valek snapped, not glancing their way. "Before she kills you."

Milo's jaw clenched, as if he doubted she could hurt him and was offended that Valek would insinuate such a thing. He vanished before she could do exactly as Valek said.

Valek was shirtless as he swung at the sandbag that hung from a bronze hook. The muscles that corded his back shifted with each move. There was a faint scar that lined his back like someone had used him as target practice. Some of them intersected in silvery knots while others were a pink shade—the color of an unripe peach.

"Do you like what you see?"

Niah recoiled like she'd been slapped. Valek's eyes were black when he turned around. His mouth was quirked in silent amusement.

"How dare you!" she exclaimed. "How dare you parade me before the school with your...with your stupid monsters. And to send Milo along when you know I hate him! You are despicable."

"*Our* monsters," Valek corrected.

Something dark flickered across his eyes, as if he liked the thought that they belonged to them both.

"Do not speak of them as if they are our children!"

"But aren't they?" Valek asked.

"No."

Valek snatched up his discarded shirt and began to wipe the sweat from his abdomen. Niah frowned at his lack of common decency. The shameless scoundrel. It should not have surprised her that he behaved this way, but for some unknown reason, she could not tear her gaze away.

"Didn't know you had such a wandering eye," Valek said. "It almost makes me think you like me."

Niah scoffed. "You wish."

Valek's lips lifted in a sharp smile. He was in an annoyingly good mood; if she cared about him at all, she might have inquired about it, but knowing him, he had probably killed a bunch of pups and was celebrating.

"Didn't Kesi tell you I wasn't feeling well?"

"You forget that I can feel your emotions," Valek said. "You are tired, but beyond that, you are perfectly fine."

"You can't feel everything," Niah said. If he had, he would have known her magic was drained, that she was hiding something, and that she had snuck away last night. "That is a lie."

"I feel enough."

"How come I can't feel you all the time?" Niah asked, annoyed. "Why does it only work one way?"

If he was digging through her feelings, Niah expected to do the same. This bond had felt like a curse before, but maybe she could use it to her benefit. He walked towards her; his steps were slow and relaxed.

"Maybe you should think about me more," Valek teased. "It will help strengthen the bond on your side."

"Are you saying you think about me?"

Valek tucked a strand of her hair behind her ear. She hadn't had the chance to braid it today.

"*Always,*" he said.

Niah swallowed, her insides twisting uncomfortably at the admission. She had expected him to brush her off or to hide his words with humor. But the startling honesty in his voice made her cheeks burn.

Valek tossed his shirt back on the bench.

"Remove your robe," he commanded.

"What, no dinner first?" she asked dryly.

"Never needed a pretense to get what I want," Valek said. "Don't make me repeat myself."

Niah furiously slipped her arms out of her sleeve and draped her robe on a nearby bench.

"Now, what?" Niah folded her arms across her chest.

"Your trousers, next."

Her eyes bugged out and Valek simply smirked.

"It was a joke, Novice," he said.

"Didn't know a stale bread such as yourself had a sense of humor," she said.

"We're going to practice some basic commands," he said, ignoring her. "You can use my Fallen. I will relinquish control once you reach out."

Niah frowned. She didn't have any magic left. Their magic glided naturally between them, but when she had felt the light, it had vanished. She could touch him in pretense and draw from him that way. Magic always flowed between them when they touched. He wouldn't assume it was intentional, but it had to be him who reached for her. Niah had never touched him first before. It might strike his suspicion.

"Any day now, Novice," he said. "I am not getting any younger."

Niah opened her mouth to mock him.

"Mock me, I dare you," Valek warned.

"How did you know I would do that?!" she asked.

He only said a single word. "Predictable."

Niah took a step forward, sealing the space between them and raising her neck higher to look in his eyes. Valek studied her, gaze drifting along her nose, cheekbones and then his gaze slid lower, resting on her mouth. He stared at her for so torturously long, it ached. Her stomach flipped, and her breath quickened.

"Why are you looking at me like that?" Niah whispered.

Valek was barely focused on her words. His eyes were locked so desperately on her lips that it made her tremble.

"You make me lose control," Valek snapped, fingers curling into a fist, as if he were coming to his senses. "I cannot think straight when you're around. There is an ache behind my ribs, and it hurts every time you come too close. In my waking *and* sleeping hours, you haunt me. I am never spared by your cruelty. And the worst of it is that you don't care that I hunger, that I despair, because to you I am nothing but a monster."

Niah felt an odd sensation like her skin was too tight for her bones. It was as if she were bleeding from an invisible cut. She opened her mouth slowly, not certain what to say. Valek cupped his palm over her mouth. His nostrils flared at the gesture. Niah felt the magic flow between them, sliding down her like cold water.

"Just shut up, I don't need you to remind me why this is wrong or that you hate me or that I am undeserving of anyone, least of all you," Valek growled. "I am not a fool. I do not need an eternity with you. I just need a minute."

Niah did not understand what he meant until his palm dropped and the hand that had silenced her slipped behind her nape, yanking her roughly forward. A squeal escaped her as she teetered on her feet, but the frightened sound was quickly swallowed by his lips.

His mouth was soft. For some reason, she had expected it to be firm, unrelenting, just like him. Valek kissed like a man possessed, one hand spanned her jaw, gripping her like she was his to command and the other that had grabbed her neck, slid around to grip her throat. The cool metal of his bone-ring caressed her flesh leaving behind an imprint. Her mind spun, and her stomach tightened.

Niah found herself lost in the brutal kiss. Anger coiled through her, mixed with a shock of lust that confused her. She kissed him back, matching his punishing pace. Her fingers slid between his thick, luscious strands, yanking on the ends.

It didn't feel like kissing.

It felt like war.

They were both fighting for control. Valek's teeth sank painfully into her bottom lip, eliciting a gasp from her. Niah tugged his hair roughly, scraping her nails down his scalp, hoping that it hurt half as much. She could feel his mouth tilt slightly before his tongue slid into her mouth.

Her grip loosened, and she found herself falling softly in his arms, lulled deeper into his intoxicating touch.

Niah let him lead her deep into the surging waters of desire.

 Even though she was betraying everything she fought for, at that moment, she couldn't name a single reason why this was a terrible idea.

"We should stop," Niah said breathlessly when his mouth traced along her throat. "This isn't right."

Valek paused, and she watched as his eyes hardened. She could have sworn something that almost looked like hurt had crossed their expanse.

"As I said, I needed a minute," Valek said coldly. "I reckon I've gotten you out of my system. That will *never* happen again."

Niah's shoulders tightened defensively.

"As if I will ever let it happen again," she said sharply. "That was a mistake."

"Agreed," Valek said.

"Nobody can know about it."

Valek's shoulders tensed. "Hardly anything to brag about."

Pain sliced through her like a blade, and she sucked in a sharp breath.

Valek folded his arms across his chest, staring at her with his hard eyes.

It was silent for one terribly long moment.

"Let us begin our lesson," he said, pretending as if the last five minutes had not occurred. "Seize control of them."

"We should talk abo—"

"I have nothing to say," he said curtly. "Now do as I say, Novice."

Niah's fingers stretched outwards, and she felt the build-up of power as it traveled down her arm and slipped out of her fingers. At last, she seized control of the Fallen. It was like a lock clicking in place.

Valek gave her commands to issue to the Fallen to ensure she maintained control. He told her to make them march, to make them fight each other in hand-to-hand combat, to make them use their weapons.

"Now ask them to attack me," Valek said.

Niah's mouth pulled in a smile.

Finally, something she *wanted* to do.

"It's a wonder your face doesn't hurt from how wide you're smiling."

Valek snatched his sword from the bench, just as the first one came with a blade to his throat. She had given them a single mission.

Kill Valek Winterson.

It was a long shot that they would succeed, but it was fun to watch Valek unknowingly fight for his life. He probably thought they were just sparring and not that she had directed them to kill him. It was what he deserved for kissing her like she was the very air he needed to breathe, only to insult her swiftly after. And that wasn't the *worst* of his crimes.

He was a villain, a monster, a heretic.

A hiss escaped him when one of them grazed his neck. His dark eyes shot up to her, and she delighted in the distraction. He knew exactly what she had done. He knew they were not merely fighting him but were directed to kill him.

"That was not the command I said to use, Novice," he said darkly.

"I altered it to fit the lesson," she said. "No use training your soldiers to fight when they should be killing. That is their one, true purpose."

Valek twisted to clash his blade against the second, ensuring his back wasn't turned to either. He reached for a small dagger from his boot and fought them with both hands. She could feel him attempting to wrestle back control of them, but Niah held on tightly. She gritted her teeth against the cold graze of his magic, slinking against the threads that ran from her to her Fallen like the strings of a puppet.

Only she could see her own magic.

Nobody else could see the shadowy tendrils that spilled from her finger like ink. It was like that for all mages. But sometimes, she wondered if Valek could see *it*. If he had nurtured the bond on his end so tenderly that he had access to far more truths about her than she did him, Niah could not see Valek's magic. But she could feel him. His magic felt deathly and bottomless, like an abyss. And it took everything in her not to shiver from the force of its touch as it sought to sever her hold.

His blade dug into the stomach of one of the Fallen, and Niah frowned, not feeling very confident about her plan. He was an excellent fighter. He was both fleet-footed and swift. Lean muscles corded his torso, veins dancing along his forearms with every brutal slash of his sword. Sweat glistened along his skin like condensation around a metal cup.

Dread filled her when his blade slid into the cavity of the second Fallen, digging through his rotten chest. Sour black blood spilled from the gaping wound as it collapsed, falling atop the other. Valek's face was covered in sweat, and sprays of their onyx blood dotted him like constellations. His blade screeched against the wooden floor as he crossed the space between them.

"You went against my instructions," he hissed.

"I am a novice as you always remind me," Niah said, unrepentantly. "You cannot expect me to be perfect."

"Maybe I would believe your pretty lies if you were capable of being honest," he said. "But you are not."

He stopped mere inches away from her. Niah straightened her back as best she could, but no amount of posturing would close the gap in their height.

He pressed the sharp point of his dagger to her throat, the pointed tip scraping her flesh. At the same time, she nudged her blade between his legs.

"Do you intend to have children someday?" Niah asked, her heart thudding rapidly.

If she moved her head at the slightest angle, he would nick her throat, and she didn't put it past him to give her a warning cut.

"No, I don't," Valek said. "Do you intend to live past today?"

"I will accept death knowing you've been castrated in the process."

"I will happily live my life as a eunuch if it grants me the peace of your death."

"Sounds like the words of a man who has a hard time finding a woman to bed him," she sneered.

"Thinking about my performance in bed, are you?" he asked with a sharp smile. "Did that kiss muddle your mind?"

"As if."

"On the count of three, we both lower our blades," Valek said.

He counted, slowly, steadily—but neither of them moved. Valek's mouth tightened, displeased by the results.

"You lied," she said.

"Because I know exactly how you think," Valek said. "You are a dirty cheat."

"So, we are to stand here all night then?" she asked.

"Let us both take a step back," he said.

Niah could accept that. She cautiously walked backward just as he did the same. Slowly, they both lowered their blades.

Valek left her side and began to clean the rotten blood from his blade. It took her a long moment to realize he was wiping it on the hem of her discarded robe.

"You bastard!" she cried.

"That is the least of what you deserve for costing me two perfectly good soldiers," he said. "I did not intend to kill them."

Once a Fallen died, their second death. Nobody could raise them again, but her. He could have asked her to do it. Niah had that skill, but he must have known her answer. She would do no favors for him.

"You will pay for that," she promised.

"Looking forward to it," Valek said.

Niah could not believe that she had lost herself in that kiss, that she had let it consume her. The way he had looked at her with dark longing made her stomach twist.

It made her realize that the only thing worse than hatred was quiet desperation.

Suren had been summoned back to court. Niah waited at the front gates, prepared for his departure. If Kesi hadn't told her, she would have never known and not saying good-bye to him would have eaten away at her. He was her friend and one of the few people besides Kesi who supported her plans against the enemy.

She would miss him terribly.

"Suren," Niah called.

He was climbing the stairs to his carriage. Niah ran towards him, hair flying behind her. Suren stepped down and caught her, just as she fell into his arms.

"I'm sorry," she whispered.

"I am wanted back at court," Suren said. "That is not your fault."

Niah didn't believe that. It was Valek who had orchestrated this.

"It feels like it is."

"I hate him, but I don't blame him for wanting you," Suren said gently. "You are bewitching."

Her cheeks flushed with his words. There would have been a time when she would have vehemently denied that remark, but now that she had tasted Valek's mouth, she could not refute that statement.

"I wish I could leave with you, and Kesi could come along," Niah said. "I do not belong here."

Suren's eyes glanced upwards, and she followed his gaze. Standing on the stairs was Valek. His eyes were blisteringly cold, mouth tilted in a satisfied smile.

"I hate him," she breathed.

"I know," he said. "Perhaps, if this war ever ends, you will visit me in Masfen?"

"I would like that very much."

Suren took a step back.

"Safe travels," she whispered.

He climbed up his carriage, and Niah watched with a heavy heart as the gates rose and he vanished from sight. A part of her was glad that he would not be here when the battle occurred, but another part of her knew she'd miss him.

Valek was gone by the time she returned to the front doors.

Niah awoke that night in a cold sweat. Something was amiss. Pain struck up her side, and her hand drifted to her skin, but there was nothing there. It took her several long minutes to realize that the ache was not her own. It belonged to Valek.

Niah hesitated for a split second before she grabbed her robe, drawing the heavy fabric over her nightgown. She followed that invisible tether that tied her to him and made her way to the barracks. It was silent at night, and most of the guards kept to the gates, leaving the halls empty. There was a small archway that led up to a crooked set of steps that trailed upwards like an outstretched hand. Sconces held yellow candlelight that reflected obscure patterns on the stone wall that led to a mysterious tower.

Niah didn't bother knocking. They had bypassed formalities the day he had forced these shackles on her. Not to mention that the feeling in her gut was getting worse.

Valek was on his bed, sleeping. For a moment, she had wondered if he'd been hurt, but he looked fine. A small groan escaped him, and Niah approached his bedside. His face was ashen. He wore his uniform, the military coat askew, revealing the fine column of his throat. His bone mask was discarded on the nearby table.

"Winterson?" she called.

His eyes opened. His gaze swam with confusion and then relief.

"Little saint," he whispered.

"What happened?"

"Went after those rebels, killed the one who hurt you," he mumbled. "He cut me with a poisoned blade before he died. A cheap trick if you ask me. Only weak mutts resort to poison."

"Why didn't you go to the infirmary?" Niah asked.

"I didn't know it was poisoned till now. I usually stitch myself up, and handle my own wounds," he muttered. "Can't move."

Sweat dotted his forehead, and his breathing was labored.

Niah bit her lip. She knew a fair bit about poisons and antidotes from her time in the sanatorium, and all those nights spent reading books about medicinal herbs. If she wanted to, she could help him or, at the very least, summon a few guards to carry him to the infirmary. But if she saved Valek his reign of terror would continue. This might be her only chance to get rid of him, how could she let the opportunity pass her by?

Her hesitation must have been clear on her face.

"I understand," he said softly.

"Why did you go by yourself?" Niah asked. "If someone else had been there..."

Niah didn't understand why her stomach was so knotted up. It was one thing to kill someone. It was another to watch them die slowly and painfully. And it was worse that she could feel his pain, that it surrounded her.

"It had to be me," he said. "*I* had to be the one to avenge you."

"But why?"

"From the moment I saw you, I carried a bit of you in my heart, and I am afraid to say that even death cannot displace what I feel for you. You might be the one thing I have ever truly believed in. You are the only noble faith I will ever follow. You are the only altar I will ever kneel before. You are the only prayer I will ever whisper."

"You hate me," Niah whispered, brows furrowing in confusion. "You had a blade to my throat a few days ago. Why are you saying this?"

"You like it when I flirt with you *that* way," Valek said. He swallowed, throat bobbing with the effort. "I don't have much longer, and I would very much appreciate it if you could touch me. I...I don't want to be alone."

Niah reached up to run her fingertips through his hair, slowly and reverently. She traced her finger along his cheek, next was the severe set of his mouth, which parted gently under her touch. His eyes slid shut, and a tremor ran through him.

Guilt tangled around her insides, folding in like a fist. How could she watch him die after his confession? But how could she save a monster?

"The first night I touched you I knew you were special," he said. "It wasn't just because of your power that I spared you. I knew you were special beyond what fate had made you."

"You left a mark on me," Niah said. Her thumb absently stroking her scar.

"I know," he said. "Before we built a mental bond we forged a physical bond. It is a symbol of our connection."

Niah wished she hadn't found him. Maybe then they would have never dug through this rotten web of unsaid words and desire and desperation. It would be foolish to say she liked him. This was attraction—raw and untethered. It could never be anything as pure as love.

"This hurts," she blurted. "I can't watch this. I am not a monster like you."

"It doesn't take much to become one."

His eyes slid closed.

Niah tapped his cheek, and he jolted. For a moment, she had been afraid that he had died.

"Why?" Niah demanded. "Why did you choose to become this way?"

"I had no choice."

"Everyone has a choice."

"Not when you're Valek Winterson," he said.

"Make me understand," Niah said. "*Please.*"

"Anytime you beg me, it weakens me," Valek said. His eyes were bright and feverish. "It *destroys* me."

He had said something similar when they'd spoken the other day in the training room. Maybe there was some truth to his words.

"After my mother died, my father fell apart. I think his soul died with her. Everything he had once been had turned to rot. He became cruel and power-hungry. He focused on politics, barking orders at me, and neglecting Natalia. When he did address her, it was always a scathing comment that made her cry," Valek said. "He was less of a father and more of a nightmare."

Niah felt sympathy strike her, and her fingers fell from his face to clasp his hand. His skin was so cold, it felt like grasping a corpse.

"King Stefan never wanted a war, but my father was always grasping for more. He wanted Teren, because..." He hesitated. "My mother was born there. As part of a peace treaty, she had entered a betrothal with my father. She was the daughter of a valley lord, and my father was the king's brother. It was one of many attempts to end the holy war and for a short time the capital cities of Virelle and Raskovia became siblings who fell to petty squabbles often, but who tolerated each other for their shared blood. Despite the political nature of their nuptials, my father grew to love her."

"Your mother is from Teren?" Niah whispered.

Laith had said he spoke their tongue, that he spoke Virelle. Niah had assumed he had learned it to understand his enemies better, but this shocked her. It shattered everything she thought she knew about him.

"Yes," he said. "When she died, my father could not bear to sit idle. He convinced the king to march against Teren. He thought if he claimed everything that had once belonged to my mother, that it would ease his grief, but it did nothing but feed his hunger for war and bloodshed. It snapped the little progress the nations had made, and they fell to chaos."

Valek smiled wryly.

"It is strange how everyone thought the war escalated with hate, but love was to blame all along," he said. "Love is the greatest curse."

His words cut through her like a blade.

"May I have a lock of your hair?" Valek whispered.

"What for?" Niah asked, confused.

"It is a foolish tradition," he said. "Will you give me this one thing? *Please*, little saint."

Niah slid out her blade and cut a strand long enough for him to fold around his fist. His brows smoothened, and his eyes melted with relief when she slid the white wisp into his palm.

"Bersula, will return you to me," Valek said softly. "In the afterlife, we will find each other."

His eyes closed, and panic bloomed inside her like an unfurling flower. She should have felt thrilled that he had succumbed to his injury, but all she felt was despair. Niah had been certain that this was what she wanted: to see Valek Winterson fall for his sins. But he was just a weapon, he was not the force behind this war. And he had gotten injured *because* of her.

"Winterson." Niah shook his shoulders.

"*I'm sorry*," he said in Virelle. The vowels were soft and lulling on his sharp tongue. It floated through her mind like a lullaby. "*I wanted...I just wanted so badly. Many things, but mainly you.*"

His words lacked clarity, and then he stilled. His body unmoving, lungs frozen in time. Niah stood up and ran down the stairs. She opened the nearby doors until she stumbled upon a bedroom with several cots and snoring soldiers.

"Wake up," Niah yelled.

Several of them roused, alert, weapons at the ready.

"The Commander is injured," she said. "He needs help. Hurry!"

They jumped up in attention and raced past her towards the tower. Niah watched with her heart in her throat as they carried him to the infirmary. It took two men to lift him. One held his wrists and the other his ankles. His face was as pale as the moonlight that streamed through the window.

Niah followed them sullenly into the main building and to the infirmary. Someone must have fetched Marta because she was already there when they arrived alongside one of the Stitchers. She wondered if Valek was dead, and if so, was there enough time to awaken him? There were limits to the gifts of a Stitcher.

Niah stood in the corner, watching as Marta peeled off his shirt. The wound was leaking a black, tar-like substance that dripped onto the clean sheets.

"The poison is Black Hellebore," Niah said softly.

"Are you certain?" Marta asked.

"Activated charcoal will save him," she whispered.

Niah spun on her heels and vanished out the door. The guilt choked her with icy fingers. She hated that she risked his life, but she also hated that she had given him a fighting chance. What kind of person saved the man who had imprisoned her and waged a war against her people?

Niah was disgusted with herself. All those promises of killing Valek Winterson, and when he lay on that bed, minutes away from Death's door, she had spared him.

What would Kesi think of her actions?

It made her weak.

It made her soft.

Kesi was still asleep when she returned to bed, which was a relief, because then she wouldn't hear the sound of Niah weeping herself to sleep or how she cried even harder when she felt the bond awaken with a soft jolt, which meant that he was conscious and healing.

Aden F.M.

Niah couldn't tell if the tears were her mourning her failure or tears of relief.

Chapter 30

For five days, Niah flittered like a ghost across the halls of Silverwood, all to avoid the monstrous boy whose fingers coiled around her heart like a curse. She switched her combat class to the morning and waited in her bedroom every night for Kesi to bring her dinner. She did not enter any shared spaces and skipped the bi-weekly night prayers.

Her bedroom door cracked open, and Niah's smile widened at the sight of Demian and Kesi. Now that she wasn't dining with them, she rarely saw Demian. She had missed his silly jokes and familiar lopsided smile. He carried a silver tray with her dinner and placed it on the desk.

"Demian, I missed you," she said, wrapping her arms around him.

"Me too," he said. "Val's been asking around about you."

Niah flinched at the mention of his name. She hurriedly sat at her desk, distracting herself by slurping up her onion soup. Kesi and Demian didn't know *why* she was avoiding Valek like he had the plague, and she didn't know how to explain what occurred.

There had been mild chatter the day after the poisoning. Word had spun around the halls, and the whispers had grown so distorted that Niah had heard that the poison came from the fangs of a seven-foot-long snake that he wrestled.

"You and Val? What's going on?" Demian asked.

"A shame he survived that poisoning," Kesi said. "Niah is probably just disappointed that he's alive."

Niah stiffened.

"You're right," she said, the lie sour on her tongue. "It angers me that he was spared."

"He wrote you a note," Demian said.

"Burn it."

Demian sighed, placing the letter on her desk.

"I'm serious, burn it or rip it up, I'm not reading it," she said.

"He also said if he doesn't get a response back, he'll be coming to your room."

Kesi groaned. "Just read the damn letter. We don't need him in our space."

"Fine," she snapped.

Niah stood up and scribbled a response on a piece of paper.

"You didn't read his note," Demian said.

"Tell him I did," she said.

Demian snorted, catching a glimpse of her letter. "I don't think '*Leave me alone, or I'll kill you*' was the response he was anticipating."

Niah shrugged. "It's all he's getting."

"You know I'm starting to feel like the child of two separated parents," he said. "Can you not just speak to him instead of passing notes?"

"No," Niah said. "I have vowed to never speak to him again."

"I think you secretly enjoy fighting with him," Demian said. "And he does as well."

"Can we talk about your terrible haircut?" Niah asked, switching the topic. "Who did that to you?"

It was a bit uneven, the ends far too long and the front short.

"Kesi," he mumbled.

"It looks nice!" Kesi said.

"He looks like a little boy who went through his mother's drawers."

"Rude," he muttered.

"Let me fix it," Niah said. "Sit down."

Niah opened her drawer, finding her small shears. She worked on the ends, watching his dark locks flutter to the floor. It took her twenty minutes to fix the end and cut the front so it fell evenly across his forehead.

"Cute as a button," she said, ruffling his hair when she finished.

"Not bad," Demian said, staring at his reflection in her small looking-mirror. "Do you think I should grow a beard? It might make me look rather distinguished?"

"The better question is, *can* you grow a beard?" Kesi teased.

"Maybe," he said a tad defensively. "I haven't tried."

"Good luck." Kesi snickered.

"I should be on my way, can't break curfew," Demian said. "Are you certain you want me to give Valek your letter?"

"Yes."

The door clicked shut, and Kesi stared at her.

"What?" Niah asked.

"What's going on, Niah?" Kesi asked. "You've been on edge all week."

"I'm nervous for the banquet and the attack Morgana is coordinating," Niah said. "We have to be prepared."

"I mean this thing with the Commander," she said. "Why are you riling him up? This could raise his suspicions."

"That is precisely why I am keeping my distance," Niah said. "The less we speak, the better."

Kesi sighed. "He looks for you every time he enters the refectory. He won't let this behavior slide."

"I'm not afraid of him," Niah said.

Kesi left to head to the bathing room, and it wasn't until the door clicked shut that she went to her desk and picked up the note Valek left.

I do not say this often, if ever, but I cannot help saying it to you, I am sorry.

Forgive me.

V. Winterson

Niah crumbled the note into a clean ball and flung it angrily into the fireplace. His empty words wouldn't fix anything. It would not absolve her of her guilt, knowing that she had saved the one man who had ruined countless people's lives. How would Morgana feel if she knew the girl they had hailed as the Lightbearer had saved the life of their enemy? The same villain Morgana had directed her to kill.

There was nothing she could do to change the past, but she could ensure that she kept her wits about her, that she focused on this upcoming attack, and that she lived to make it to the bloody, vicious end.

Niah was walking to class when she saw Valek and Demian speaking under the archway. She eased her steps, keeping to the cover of the students ahead, and remaining close enough to listen. It reminded her of that night when she'd caught them speaking before the night prayer.

"Give her this," Valek said.

Demian groaned.

"Not another damned note," Demian said. "I beg you, cousin, just speak to her. Why did you get a copy of her class schedule if you won't look for her?"

"You are making me sound rather desperate," Valek said. "I draw the line at following her around like a lost pup."

"But you don't draw the line at using me to pass her love letters?" Demian asked.

"You are one to talk," Valek said. "Who fixed your hair? You looked like an idiot yesterday."

"You never said anything yesterday when you saw me," Demian said, folding his arms across his chest. "Did you feel bad for me?"

"No, I just didn't have a good insult; there were too many to pick from," he said. "You looked like you were playing around in Aunt Lilia's drawers and found her shears."

"That's what Niah said!" Demian said. "You are both the worst."

Niah bit her lip to swallow back her laugh.

"Are you smiling?" Demian asked. "You never smile."

"I am not," Valek said gruffly. "Just give her the note."

"This is the last one," he said. "I swear it, Valek. Work out your issues without using me as your messenger."

"Make sure she writes a response longer than a few words with no threats, and I'll consider it," Valek said.

"Children," Demian muttered. "The whole lot of you."

In this case, Niah agreed with him. Valek *was* behaving immaturely.

Niah returned to her bedroom after her classes, slamming the door shut behind her. Kesi sat upright when she entered. Her eyes were red, and she had stuffed something hastily in the cupboard. The air was clinging with a sweet, cloying smell.

"Were you smoking?" Niah demanded. "Smoking is not allowed inside the dorms."

"No," Kesi said innocently.

Niah marched across the room and peeled back Kesi's eyelids, peering at her dilated pupils and lazy smile.

"Where did you get it?" Niah asked.

It was clear from the cloudy air that she had been smoking one of those hallucinatory herbs that were shipped from the south.

"I cannot say," she said with a charming smile. "It's a secret."

Niah gave her a pointed look, slowly folding her arms across her chest. It was the look Kesi called her 'death stare'. It didn't take long for Kesi to crack.

"Valek gave it to me," Kesi blurted. "I told him to leave you alone, and he said if I spoke highly about him to you, then he'd give me some herbs to smoke."

"And you accepted his bribe!"

"Maybe he isn't so bad," Kesi said, falling back onto the bed and gazing at the ceiling. A giggle escaped her. "I think he really likes you, Niah. He wants you to have his babies. I could tell from his eyes. I know when a man hungers! I'm quite smart, you know. Perhaps, too smart."

Niah's cheeks burned. "You're not yourself. Your mind is addled by those toxic fumes you just ingested."

"I mean it. He wants you to be pregnant with his seed!"

Niah tossed her pillow at Kesi's head, resisting the urge to laugh at her dumb words.

"Go to sleep, idiot," she said. "You are not fit to attend class in this state."

"Well, can you tell him I kept my end of the bargain?" Kesi asked eagerly. "It doesn't hurt to accept his offerings. Almost makes this torturous war college bearable."

"No!" Niah said. "We are not letting Valek Winterson win our loyalty with his cheap bribes."

Kesi snickered, pulling her blanket over her head.

This had gone too far.

It was time to confront Valek with another strongly-worded letter.

Niah had responded to his second note as follows:

> *Stop writing me these stupid letters and leave Demian and Kesi alone. I won't respond anymore. This is your last warning!*

That one she'd given Demian an hour ago, and he had returned shortly after with a new response. The paper fluttered wildly on the library table, followed by Demian's deep, withering sigh, before he vanished around the corner.

It wasn't until an hour later that she had another infuriating letter resting on her notebook. From Demian's peeved expression, he was clearly at his wits' end. It was the third letter he had brought her since the day started.

> *Last warning? What will you do to me if I don't stop?*
> *Tell me everything.*

Niah hated herself when she dipped her quill in the bottle of ink and wrote back her response while Demian waited impatiently.

> *I will cut your throat out and string you up naked in the courtyard like you once swore you would do to me.*

Niah promised Demian that this was the last one.

She was deep in her books when the chair across from her scraped forward. Valek sat down, tossing a note her way. Niah hadn't seen him this close in days. Even when she'd overheard him and Demian, she had been at a distance, using the students as a shield to cover her like a veil. His handsome face was clean-shaven, and his eyes were as black as a starless sky.

Niah frowned and opened his letter with great distaste.

I didn't know you wanted to see me naked so bad. I can arrange something if you are interested. My bedroom or yours?

Niah scoffed before turning over the note to scribble her response.

I'd rather tear my own eyes out.

She flung it at Valek, hoping the paper sliced his high cheekbones. Niah began to shuffle her books, prepared to leave, when his hand shot out, grabbing her wrist.

"Liar," he whispered.

Niah just blinked at him, refusing to respond. She was determined not to utter a single word to him. The longer she remained firm in her stance, the less she would find herself corrupted by his promises and his depraved touch, because for some odd reason, Niah wanted to believe there was some good inside him. That behind the bone mask and the uniform and the curt words, there was a man who cared. *Deeply.*

"You know this game tires me, little saint," he said. "Let's play another one."

Valek tugged her wrist hard, and she stumbled backwards, falling onto his lap.

"Winterson." she gasped. "Unhand me."

"Why did you leave me?" Valek asked hoarsely. "You weren't there when I woke up."

Niah's gut twisted at his hollow words. She thought of the days she'd been in the infirmary, how he hadn't left her side. How his eyes had been bruised from the lack of sleep, and his jaw rough with stubble. The thought of him alone, in the dark, made her eyes burn, and Niah had to clear her throat when she next spoke.

"I had no reason to be there," she said. "We are not friends."

"No reason?" he asked quietly, bitterly. "Then why did you save my life?"

Anyone could pass by and see her sitting on the commander's lap. It would spark rumors that she would have difficulty clearing. Niah moved to stand, but his hold was unrelenting. She could have fought harder, but it was best to get this conversation over with, to remind him of the carefully drawn lines between them both. The less they interacted, the more they could fall back into their roles as enemies.

He would always be the villain, and even if he was not born one and was made by his father, it would never change or alter the fact that he was Valek Winterson, Commander of the King's army, the greatest Reaper who lived.

"I don't know," Niah said, frustrated. "Maybe it was a mistake."

"Fix it then," Valek demanded. He plucked out her dagger from her hip, pressed the pointed end to his chest, and wrapped her fingers around the hilt.

"What are you doing?"

"Giving you a second chance," Valek said. His eyes were wild and angry. The blade was digging into his flesh, and the fabric of his shirt darkened with blood that bloomed like an unfurling rose. "Nobody can see us, we're alone, so do it."

Niah swallowed. "You're mad."

"Am I?" he snapped. "Well, you drive me insane. I am losing myself, falling to bits around you, and you look at me like I am *nothing*. Like my heart isn't gnawing on itself, devouring everything in sight to be near you. I am barely functioning, but I am yours, and is that not enough?"

Niah's chest clenched. She tried to draw back the blade, but his hold was unbreakable. She didn't want to sit here and listen to this. She wanted to fill her ears with cotton and forget what it was like to be the source of Valek's misery and desire.

"It can't be," she said softly. "I can't be what you want."

"We have long since passed want. I am helpless against my

need for you. The world has cut me open, but you settle between the chasm of my wound with ease. You heal me, little saint. You understand *me*."

His words fall, soft as a whisper.

In another lifetime, he could have been her savior, she could pretend that his words were sacred and his eyes were promising, but all she saw when she looked at him was a lie with blood-stained hands.

"I have cast aside my morals to practice the magic you forced on me. I will not turn against my country as well," Niah said. She had expected to sound firm, but she just sounded confused. "I will not succumb to you. I will not fall for evil."

His grip had loosened, and she let her hand fall.

"I won't kill you," she said. "You have far more enemies than I do. Someone stronger than me will finish the job."

Morgana would have to do it. Niah could not be the one to kill this beautiful, tortured boy. Her soft, weak heart would not allow it.

"I told you things I've never told anyone before," Valek said. His eyes were dark and piercing. "I bore myself to you that night and now again."

"I asked you to stand by me, and you refused!" Niah reminded him. "I gave you a choice, and you chose wrong."

"How am I to end this war? I am no king, I am a soldier," Valek snapped.

"Then you can fight for the right side."

"I will have my throat cut by any side that I switch to. As you said, I have far too many enemies, many of whom will never forgive me," he said. "Will your Sisters accept a heretic or will they make him bleed for his sins?"

"I can protect you," she said. "I can keep you safe."

"And what of Natalia, my sister, who will keep her safe?" Valek asked. "I am all she has. I will not forsake her."

"They will not punish her if you defect," she said. "Your father is in power; he will protect her."

"Maxim Winterson would feed her to the wolves if he could. He would kill her to spite me or marry her off to the next old bastard who shows a hint of interest," he said.

"We can find a way to protect her," Niah said. "Together."

"It is not that simple," he said. "Power begets power. It was my father's favorite thing to say. You cannot make true change by fighting with wooden swords in treetops. There is a reason why ninety percent of rebellions fail."

"Then nothing has changed," Niah said coldly. "I cannot protect you, and I will not stand by you either."

Valek's eyes were tormented when she climbed off his lap and packed her belongings.

A part of her hoped that he would change his mind, that he would call her back, but there was nothing but silence when she disappeared between the shelves.

Chapter 31

The winter banquet was tonight.

It was one of those rare occasions when they could dress in dinner attire. Excited whispers filled the halls as the novices spoke of the latest styles they'd wear. Niah hadn't thought much about what she planned to wear. She didn't own any dresses. Kesi had befriended a girl and was borrowing her spare dress, but Niah didn't care about looking good. It was hard to worry about such frivolous affairs when so much hinged on the success of their plan.

Catrin had said to remain alert. It was the night the Order would strike.

Niah had been doing her best to calm her nerves. Now that Valek could sense her emotions, she did not wish to raise his suspicions.

"Maybe we should ask the girls if they have a spare dress for you?" Kesi suggested. "Some of them packed entire wardrobes."

Niah shook her head; she would not bring herself to beg for scraps. It didn't matter how she paraded herself tonight. It would suit her better to be dressed practically.

"It's fine," Niah said. "I don't mind wearing my uniform."

Kesi did not seem pleased by that idea. She wanted to make a statement; to show the students they were more than war prisoners.

Niah could admire her intentions even if she did not plan to follow her lead.

Niah returned to her bedroom that evening, prepared to take a short nap before she headed to the Grand Hall for the celebrations. She came to a grinding halt at the sight of an ivory box covered in a blue ribbon. Niah stared at it warily as if the contents of the box would reveal a severed head. She slowly unraveled the ribbon and peeled back the lid to reveal an icy blue dress, the gossamer of the skirt practically spilling out. There were gemstones in all shades of blues—topaz and sapphires, and turquoises, along with beads embroidered in the bodice that looked like they cost a fortune and could likely feed a small army.

Niah pulled out the dress, searching for a card, but came up empty. She frowned, wondering who had sent her the extravagant gift. Maybe it was Demian who had taken pity on her. She hoped Kesi hadn't asked some poor girl for this. Her fingers touched the silky fabric. It was such high-quality that she could not imagine anyone lending this out, and Kesi would have left a note to not damage it or rip out any of the precious gems if it belonged to some other girl.

Niah did not wish to offend her friends by rejecting their offer, so she skipped her nap to sort out her hair. It felt like hours passed while she looped her hair into an intricate updo. The cut of the bodice was low, revealing her breasts, and the skirt flowed around her like water. She stared at her reflection in the mirror, at her silver-blond hair with loose tendrils framing her face and the beautiful gown.

For the first time in many years, Niah felt beautiful. It was like nothing bad had ever touched her, as if she were untainted by war and pain and chaos. But as much as she wanted to pretend and fall into this fairytale, where she was an innocent princess, the shackles around her wrist reminded her otherwise.

A knock sounded on her door just then, drawing her from her thoughts.

Niah felt a spike of panic. She didn't know if she wanted to be perceived by everyone. To feel their eyes soaking her flesh.

"It's Winterson," Valek said.

Niah decided to ignore him, but he sensed her hesitation.

"I'll break down the door," he said. "You have five seconds."

Niah swore under her breath and tore open the door.

"What?" she barked.

Valek blinked, staring at her like she was a foreign creature. His mouth parted slightly. Niah didn't often feel unsettled, but she did just then. So much so that she contemplated hiding behind the door, but she would never give him the satisfaction of knowing that he affected her, that he made her *nervous*.

"You…" He cleared his throat. "You look…it's…."

He paused, looking rather frustrated with himself. Valek muttered something under his breath that sounded suspiciously like 'I've forgotten how to speak'.

"Is there a purpose to this visit?" Niah demanded.

"Do I need a reason to come see my little saint?" Valek asked.

"I am not your trinket, Winterson."

"No," he said. "I dare say you are far more."

Niah shifted, unnerved by his gaze, by the wonder and intrigue that crossed his face. He leaned against the doorframe, looking young and boyish.

A teasing smile danced on his lips.

"Will you save me a dance?" he asked. "I'm sure you have some clever insult you'd like to whisper in my ear, and I would loathe to miss it."

"The dance or my insults?"

"Both."

"A shame," she said. "I only intend to dance with boys that I *like* tonight."

Valek's mouth tightened, reacting to her taunt as she had hoped. A vein ticked painfully in his jaw, and Niah felt a strange thrill at his reaction. One that she would admit only to herself. She turned around when she felt his hand wrap around her throat, yanking her backwards till she collided with his chest.

"You don't have a necklace," he said. His voice was unreadable. "Would you like an accessory?"

Niah felt his mouth on her neck, kissing her. She stiffened. Valek's mouth ran along her pulse, and she felt the biting graze of his teeth sinking into her flesh. She inhaled sharply, feeling his lips quickly soothe the sting.

"What are you doing?" she asked breathlessly.

He ignored her, lavishing her throat with kisses. Occasionally, she would feel the pinching scrape of his teeth before the gentle brush of his mouth.

Valek released her, and she turned to face him, to demand answers.

She had made a vow that she would never kiss him again. Granted, *she* hadn't kissed *him*, but the rules applied to Valek, as well. He couldn't kiss her either.

His eyes gleamed with satisfaction, and before she could chide him, he had turned around and left.

God, she could not stand him and his odd behavior.

The Great Hall was already filled when she arrived—rows of uniformed soldiers were seated shoulder to shoulder, their polished medals glinting beneath the wrought-iron chandeliers. Meanwhile, the students were dressed grandly in a manner befitting the king's court. The girls wore bodices of brocade, heavy with pearls and delicate embroidery, and the boys wore sharp velvet-trimmed coats.

Faculty and high-ranking officers flanked the perimeter, their conversations low and clipped. Niah stood at the top of the grand staircase. She descended slowly; the hem of her gown spilled behind her like crystalline water. She felt the ripple of gazes as the crowd turned towards her.

Banners bearing the crest of different noble families had been hung from the vaulted rafters, and from the center was the black banner with the white wolf. Music played from beyond the archway, a martial, sombre tune.

Kesi and Demian waited for her at the bottom of the stairs. Kesi wore a vibrant crimson gown heavy with pearls that complemented her tan skin, and Demian wore a royal blue overcoat with silver wolves embroidered on the fabric. A token of his ancestry.

"You look lovely," Niah said. "Both of you."

"Us?" Kesi asked. "You look ethereal."

"Like a princess," Demian echoed.

"Thank you," she said.

"How did you get this dress?" Kesi asked. "The beadwork alone would cost a fortune to craft, and that is not including the cost of the gems, which were most likely exported."

"It was just in my room," Niah said. "There was no note."

Niah turned to Demian. "Was it you?"

Demian shook his head. "Sadly, I am not wealthy enough to afford that dress. Have you asked your lover?"

"What lover?" she asked.

If this were about Valek, she would not expect that bastard to give her water if she were stranded in the desert, let alone a dress fit for a queen. Niah frowned. Why did *his* name come to mind the moment Demian said 'lover'? And why did her stomach twist oddly at the thought?

"The one that left that bite on your neck," Demian said with a smirk.

"What bite?" she asked.

"It is rather prominent," Kesi said, studying it with interest. "Perhaps, you should let your hair down."

"What?" Niah asked frantically, touching her neck. "Where?"

Demian picked up a silver chalice, holding it up for her so she could inspect her neck. Niah's fist clenched at the sight of the bruising that marked her flesh.

You don't have a necklace. Would you like an accessory?

He had planned this, and she was going to kill him for it.

Niah felt a spike of rage as Kesi helped her remove the pins that held her hair, so she could let her hair down. She would not give him the satisfaction of seeing his handiwork. He had manipulated her, humiliated her, even. How was she supposed to explain to her friends who this was?

Niah plucked a flute of wine and drank a hearty gulp, feeling the delicious tingling sensation. If she didn't have to be prepared for tonight, she would have downed the entire drink, but she needed her wits about her.

"So, who is the lucky fellow?" Demian asked, leaning against the stone pillar.

"You mean the dead fellow," she said. "Because that is what he is going to be when I get my hands on him."

Demian chuckled, leaving to grab another drink. Kesi was studying her, Niah could tell from the corner of her eye, even if she was not brave enough to face her.

"It's him, isn't it?" Kesi asked. "The Great Reaper."

"No," Niah said, but the word felt hollow.

She hated lying to Kesi, and the confession slipped past her lips before she could control it.

"Yes," she added softly. "It was a mistake."

"I was wondering when you two would put us out of our misery and just bed," Kesi said.

Niah frowned. "You are not upset."

"That you kept it from me, of course, I am. I'm your best friend." Kesi pouted. "But I am not upset that you bedded the

Commander. It was just physical attraction, and you're done with it now, right?"

Niah looked away.

As much as she hated secrets, Kesi could never learn that she had saved his life, that this thing between them consumed her. It was wrong, it was forbidden, yet still she melted under his touch. It was so much more than physical attraction. It had morphed into a beast she could not control, and a small part of her wanted it to devour her whole.

"Morgana will not spare him," Kesi said gently. "Don't forget that."

The orchestra came to a grinding halt as the double doors at the top of the stairs were drawn open and a herald announced the King's arrival.

The King entered, and the room grew silent. His wheat-colored hair rustled in the breeze. His nose was crooked, and a stiff mustache cloaked his thin lips. He was rather big and blocky with little grace about him.

Standing beside Valek, she could not help but see the jarring differences between them. Valek held the kind of dark beauty that could enthrall the most innocent souls. Long, fluttery lashes, full lips that were always locked in a scowl that was a bit too pretty to be taken seriously.

Valek stood to his left, hands folded behind his back, and Headmistress Greymont to the King's right, and then there was Maxim Winterson, aloof and distant in his black attire.

All the people she despised the most were in one place.

A throne had been placed at the front of the room before a long table, and King Stefan made his way across the floor as everyone bowed. His steps were slow and measured.

Demian yanked her hand to pull her down into a bow just as the King turned towards her. He stared at her with curious blue eyes, as if he could read her soul if he only peered hard enough. His thin lips tilted in a smile of acknowledgment.

Niah hunted for signs of an illness. His skin had a strange

pallor, concealed by heavy powders, and his steps were sluggish, but beyond that, you could not witness his frailty. If Niah hadn't heard it from Demian, she might have even doubted the source. Perhaps, the royal physicians had pumped him full of tinctures before this visit.

"This is her, Your Grace," Valek said. "The conduit I have been training. Niah Yarrow. Lord Winterson made her acquaintance during his last visit."

Niah shuddered as the king stared at her with veiled interest. Headmistress Greymont leaned forward to whisper in his ear. Dread filled her as they conspired before her. Niah didn't know how to hide her disgust and hatred, but she would have to mask her emotions if she hoped to convince him of her loyalty. It wouldn't be long now until his blood coated the marble floors, and she was free from this prison.

"Pleased to meet you," the King said. "The girl of light, or should I say the girl of shadows, now? Chancellor Winterson has spoken highly of you."

"The pleasure is mine, Your Grace."

"*Stop looking at him like you are picturing his broken neck,*" Valek spoke in her mind. "*I do not think he shares my penchant for murderous girls.*"

"*Don't talk to me. I'm mad at you.*"

"*You didn't like the gift I left you?*"

"*Marking me like a dog pissing on a tree?*" Niah hissed. "*What is there to like?*"

"*I would like it if you marked me. I'd wear it with pride.*"

"*You do not belong to me, nor I to you.*"

"*Yet...*"

Niah realized she was glaring at Valek and that the King had walked off. Valek passed her, brushing his fingers against her knuckles.

"Please, join us, Niah," the King said. "How do you feel about entering the battlefield and supporting the war efforts?"

If, for some reason, the attack tonight failed and she missed her chance to escape, it would bode well for her to be out there and not stuck in this damned fortress. Maybe she could convince Valek to let Kesi come along, and they could vanish into the night.

"I would be hono—"

"She is unprepared to fight," Valek said curtly. "She has been here for less than three months and has much to learn."

Niah kicked him under the table. She did not plan to remain in this fortress any longer. The walls were suffocating her, and the Commander was sinking beneath her skin like a worm with each passing day.

Valek's hand fell on her thigh, squeezing her flesh in warning.

"The girl should finish her lessons," he continued. "In a few more months, perhaps she will be a weapon worth fearing, but until then, my advice is for her to stay."

"I am ready and willing to serve your cause, my King," Niah said, pinching Valek's forearm under the tablecloth, demanding that he release her. "My instructors can speak to my progress. I've accomplished much in my short ti—"

"Her instructors will confirm, as I have, that she has difficulty bending to authority and is terrible at playing with others," Valek said.

"Sounds like you," King Stefan said, amused. "And yet *you* are permitted to fight."

"Exactly!" Niah said. Her lips lifted in a saccharine smile. "And I am nothing like him, Your Grace. We don't see eye-to-eye, which explains why he is so eager to disparage my good name."

"Of course, you are nothing like me. You are a smart-mouthed novice who doesn't show respect to her superiors," Valek said sharply. "It would take months until she is a disciplined soldier fit to serve, and that is me being optimistic."

He didn't want to give her the chance to escape. It was clear to see from his wild eyes. He knew she was going to leave at the slightest opportunity. He could not control her outside these walls, and he knew it.

"Stop this, you're making me look bad," she hissed, pinching him again, because he was still gripping her thigh.

He caught her wrist before she could pull back her hand, interlacing their fingers and releasing his hold on her leg.

"You could barely slaughter the prisoner from Wryn," Valek said. *"And now you are eager to go out there and kill your people?"*

Niah glared at him. He would not fall for lies. Unlike the king who assumed she had been properly broken in.

Niah tried to tear her hand away, but she couldn't do so without making it look obvious, and she refused to embarrass herself further. So, she resigned herself to holding Valek's hand. His mouth tilted up in victory.

"Hmm," Stefan said. "Interesting. I've never seen you so passionate about pushing a point, Commander Winterson."

"I will not let this war crumble because we put our fate in the hands of a sixteen-year-old novice," Valek said.

"I am eighteen!" Niah said. "And you know that."

"You behave like a sixteen-year-old," Valek said. "You must forgive me for my assumption."

He had surpassed the line of disrespect. He was simply mocking her now for his own amusement. King Stefan didn't look at her with interest anymore a,nd it was all his fault. The king turned to the headmistress as a dance performance unfolded on the floor.

Niah gritted her teeth.

"What is your problem?" she demanded.

"You are my problem," Valek said, taking a slow sip of his wine. "Do you think batting your lashes at the King will make him pick you? He is looking for a soldier, not a bedmate."

"How dare you!" Niah said, digging her nails into his flesh. He didn't wince as expected. The deviant's mouth pulled in a wicked smile.

"If anyone is behaving like a whore, it is you," Niah said. "Your jacket has buttons for a reason; perhaps you should use them. And maybe don't stare at people like you are undressing them in your mind? Oh, and while you're at it, stop licking your lips so much, it makes you look depraved, and don't stare at people beneath your lashes like you wish to be tied to a bedpost and ridden like a horse."

Let's see how he liked it when someone misread his intentions. She had not been flirting with the old king; perhaps she had done a bit of arse kissing, but she could hardly be accused of thrusting her breasts at him.

Valek snorted so loudly that several eyes turned their way before he concealed it with a dramatic cough. He grabbed his wine glass, raising it high to his face to conceal his amusement. Maxim glared at them; eyes narrowed in suspicion. He hadn't made any remarks about their conversation. Simply observed them as if he were solving a complex puzzle.

Niah averted her gaze, remembering his cruelty when they last spoke. She did not wish to make an enemy of him.

"What?" Niah asked, realizing Valek was still looking at her.

"I didn't know you found me so tempting," Valek said, pleased. "It is quite the revelation."

"I was making a point, Winterson." Niah rolled her eyes. "Don't take it personally."

"Too late," he breathed.

His eyes were dark and heady when he looked at her, like the wine had eased him. His tongue ran along the seam of his mouth, doing the exact trick she had warned him about.

Perhaps, there had been a tiny bit of truth to her words. Valek was far too beautiful for his own good. His austere brows and high cheekbones that were flushed from the drink, and his slightly parted mouth deserved to be immortalized in a portrait. He belonged in the parlor room of one of the high families, intermingling with nobles in the finest brocade coat and the ornate rapiers the nobles wore for decor. He did not belong on the battlefield with his hands wet with blood and misery.

"What are you thinking?" Valek asked.

"Nothing," she said quickly. An unwilling flush crawled up her throat. "Just how much I hate you."

"I hate you, too," Valek said softly. His eyes sank to her lips. "I hate you so much it aches."

"Likewise," she said. Her heart thudded at a fast and painful pace. It felt as though the whole room could hear it.

His long fingers stroked her wrist, thumb sliding along the inside of her palm like he was tracing a secret language on her skin. The sound of the guests' chatter faded to a silent buzz as they locked eyes.

"I stay up at night thinking about how much I hate you," Niah said, attempting to fill the silence as if it would ease the feeling of his touch and his tortured stare.

Her words were slippery and awkward. She hoped it would break this spell that wove around them with its invisible threads.

"Me too," Valek said, but his words lacked the same panicked urgency of her own. It was almost as if he liked that he hated her so much. As if it made things interesting. "I think about you so much that there is scarcely any time to do anything else. And I've found myself wanting, no, needing to learn everything there is to know about you." His finger trailed the scar on the inside of her palm—the one he had given her all those years ago. "I want to know why you stand out in the rain when everyone runs for shelter, and why you look down when you smile as if you are undeserving of happiness, and why your eyes shine so brightly as if they were made to torment me. But mainly I want to know if someday you will hate me less than you do today."

The clang of her fork dropping shattered her attention. By the time she numbly ran her fingers on the marble floor and retrieved it, Valek had been pulled into a conversation about the state of the war. Her heart thumped, wildly, painfully. It was harder than usual to erase his words, to ignore the hungry curiosity in his gaze, and to swallow back her own questions about him.

So, she focused on the feast spread before her. There were pickled beets and roasted wild boar, poppy seed rolls with honey and walnuts, sliced into delicate swirls, and fried dough balls filled with rose-hip jam and dusted with powdered sugar.

Valek reached for the salt, and her eyes widened in alarm at the white braided rope around his wrist. Fashioned carelessly around his flesh like a bracelet was the milky lock of hair she had given him the day he had almost died.

Her heart thudded in alarm at the sight.

"What is *that*?" Niah asked hoarsely.

Valek dropped his hand, the fabric of his coat sliding back into place.

"Nothing."

"It isn't *nothing*," she said. Panic laced her tone. "You can't have it. I want it back."

It was meant to be a gift for him before he passed to honor his traditions. Not whatever this was. The thought of her hair around his skin frightened her more than she dared to admit.

"Too late." His eyes narrowed. "It is mine now."

"This is strange," Niah said, unnerved by the sight of this public display. What would Morgana and her Sisters think? "You must take it off. People will assume the worst."

She was the only person here who had hair as white as snow. It was painfully obvious that it belonged to her.

"It is customary in the High North to wear your woman's hair around your wrist," Valek said stiffly. "Nobody will think it odd."

"What?" Niah whispered.

"Look around."

Niah glanced at the Chancellor; there was a dark thread woven around his wrist. He wasn't the only one. Several other men donned the same in varying colors; some were flaxen, others fiery red, and a few raven.

All neatly braided and tied with love and devotion.

"It is not a big deal," Valek grumbled, sensing her alarm.

"Women will know that I am not on the market. I simply do not wish to be hounded at dinner parties. It is a deterrent."

"You can use anyone but me," Niah said. "There is no doubt a handful of girls who will be honored to claim you. Remove it, please."

Niah gave him her sternest look and opened her hand, the one he did not grasp, for him to drop it in.

"I do not want anyone else's hair," Valek said stubbornly. "You can't make me remove it."

"Winters—"

Just when she intended to chide him some more, Maxim Winterson deigned to speak to her.

"Why don't you perform for us, Niah?" Maxim asked. A challenge in his tone. "Show us your power so we may decide if you are ready to serve."

Niah glanced at Valek, waiting for him to refute the idea, but he simply blinked.

"That is an excellent idea," Valek said.

"*I don't want to do this,*" Niah spoke in his mind.

"*Do it for me.*"

"*You say that as though I hold any fondness for you.*"

"*Then do it so my father does not take his anger out on you,*" Valek paused. "*And me.*"

Niah hesitated. She could feel his bitterness and rage, but it wasn't directed at her. Something terrible crossed her mind then.

"*Don't ask me,*" he said softly. "*I don't wish to think of it.*"

Niah swallowed, feeling her anger rise towards his father. He was a cruel man. He had been willing to give his daughter away without a care and had treated Valek like a soldier and not his son. It did not surprise her that his anger erupted in bouts of violence.

Valek hadn't let go of her hand the entire dinner, and their palms were clammy, but he didn't seem to care. It had been almost impossible to cut her meat, but he would slice it for her instead of releasing his hold, as if he feared she would disappear if he let go.

Slowly, reluctantly, his hand dropped, giving her the space she needed to do as she was commanded. Her chair screeched behind her as she stood up. The ballroom floor had been cleared for her, and everyone watched her from their seats.

One last time, Niah would embrace the dark, one last time, before her Sisters came for her.

Chapter 32

The King watched her with limpid eyes.

His fingers quaked when he drew his bejewelled chalice to his mouth. He looked like a frightened lamb, sitting there between Maxim and Valek, whose identical bright, nocturnal eyes were locked on her.

Niah swallowed. Around her were a circle of the Fallen. A servant had placed them around her like pastries assembled on a platter. This act of sacrilege did not belong in the Grand Hall. Not when they had cast away the weight of their robes, and their bones were hidden in places unperceived to the eye. Niah had her own trinket of Saint Ylena tucked in her stockings.

She spread her arms and awakened the Fallen. Niah felt that strange, milky sensation of tethering their souls to her and wrangling them awake. Their limbs twitched as her magic altered them. They were not the same Fallen that the other Reapers controlled. They were vessels of darkness. Grown and distorted in a manner that defied the laws of their magic.

Bitterness coated her tongue. She both hated and accepted this magic that tangled around her heart so miserably. It felt the same as her feelings towards the Commander—wrong and ravaging.

Polite claps sounded around the room among whispers. To them, she was a novelty, a symbol that the High North was strong and unbreakable; after all, they had remade the Lightbearer in their image. Her hands dropped, the corpses falling asleep around her like a circle of poppies. The King's rings clicked as he clapped and laughed jovially, like she was a court jester, and not the most dangerous thing in this room.

Niah wanted to yell at him to remove these shackles. To see her in her true form. To face the Lightbearer.

This was not who she was. She was so much more than a war prisoner.

Her fists curled tight to her side.

They would fear her.

Soon, they would fall before her, begging for mercy.

When Morgana came and Niah used Saint Ylena's bone to craft a sword of light, they would cower beneath their tables, and their rotten blood would pour. Niah had never had a taste for violence, but staring at the men before her, generations of Winterson men who rejoiced in breaking the world, made her want to be a little worse.

Power begets power.

It was what Valek had told her, and perhaps there was some truth to his words. Perhaps, the world could not be saved with flower-threaded hopes and wistful dreams. Perhaps, it could only be repaired with cruel fingers and violent treachery.

"Would you like to dance?"

Valek stood beside her as the servants scurried to clean the mess. A glance at the dais showed Maxim's eyes locked on them. Anger burned across his face, drawing a flush to his skin.

"No."

"Too bad," Valek said.

He tugged her across the marble floor.

"People are watching," she whispered.

"Then we'll dance on the balcony," Valek said in her ear. "Since you're so ashamed of me."

"It is not you," Niah said. "It is everything you represent."

Valek opened the door and glared at the couple who had snuck off to kiss under the moonlight. They rushed past him, hurried apologies on their lips. Niah couldn't help but smile at the blush that stained their cheeks.

"You didn't even have to speak for them to tuck tail and hide."

"It is the perks of being the most feared man in the realm."

The music flowed towards them as he slid the glass door shut. He wrapped an arm around her waist and gently took her hand in his, guiding her into a dance. His movements were graceful, each step reflecting the countless years he had spent in training halls, honing his fighting skills. If she didn't know him any better, she would assume his lithe tread came from lessons with an accomplished ballroom dancer.

"You look beautiful tonight," Valek said. "I didn't think you'd wear the dress."

"Why not?" Niah asked. "It was a gift."

"You hate my gifts."

Niah paused. "It was you."

His brow furrowed. "Who else would it be?"

"I didn't think you cared," she said. "You do not strike me as the type."

Valek's jaw clenched. "I care far more than you think."

Niah was silent, feeling the warmth of his body. For one night, she could pretend, pretend that they weren't enemies, pretend that tonight was not the beginning of the end.

"I have another gift for you," Valek said.

"Will I like this one?" Niah asked.

"I believe so." His hand vanished into his pocket, and when it returned to grip her, she felt metal, sinking its jagged edges into her flesh.

Niah opened her palm to find a small key.

"What is this?"

"Freedom," he whispered.

He tapped the cuffs around her wrist, and Niah's eyes widened in surprise.

"But why?" Niah asked.

"When I took you—"

"Kidnapped," Niah corrected.

"Semantics," he replied.

Niah glowered at him, and he sighed.

"When I *kidnapped* you, I thought I was saving the world," he said. "King Stefan and my father believed that if we killed all the members of the Order, the Corruption would end and the North would stand as one, and for a long time I believed it."

"What changed?"

"*You*," Valek said. "I don't believe any part of you to be corrupt. You are the opposite of all that is unholy. I am so utterly devoted to you, little saint, I can hardly think straight. My soul belongs to you even if you don't want it."

"Valek," she breathed. It was the first time she had called him that. His name tasted like the stars. "Come with me. Fight with me."

Niah knew this key wasn't just for her shackles. It was so much more than that. This was acceptance. He saw what she had seen from the start. There was no hope for them. Not so long as he was a Reaper, and she was the Lightbearer.

So, he was letting her go.

She knew by the devastation in his eyes that he was releasing her not just from this place, but from his life. Niah felt his remorse and anger, and aching need.

Valek Winterson was selfish, and at that moment, all he wanted was her.

He stepped away from her, slowly, reluctantly.

"The King awaits me."

"Don't leave me," she said desperately. "I may forgive you someday, but only if you stand by me."

"I do not deserve your forgiveness," he said. "Monsters can't be loved."

"You are not a monster," she said. "You are mine."

Valek smiled. It was unlike any smile she'd seen before. It was as soft as a poem or a blossoming flower. It was meant to be treasured, and Niah tucked it somewhere deep in her heart.

He turned to leave, and she knew this was the end.

"The keys will work for your friends' shackles," he said, just before the doors sealed shut behind him.

Niah's fingers shook as she stuck the key in the shackles. It had been months since she caressed the light.

"You did it."

The voice wasn't Valek's. It was airy and feminine, but most importantly, it was familiar.

It was Saint Ylena.

It did not drift in her mind. It floated in the wind, like a pair of chiming bells.

"I didn't think I would hear from you again," Niah said.

"You accepted me," she said. *"And I am here for you and your Sisters. I am here to destroy the Reapers."*

Niah didn't know if she could fight the King with the light. There were too many Vykovian swords and shields around, and she was outnumbered. At least with the Fallen, she had an army, but now she was all alone.

"You are never alone," Saint Ylena said. *"I will take care of everything."*

Niah took a step forward, but it was odd because her limbs moved of their own accord. She tried to speak, but her mouth remained firmly shut.

Panic overtook her, and she screamed in her mind, calling out to Valek to return for her. She was so terribly afraid.

"Silence, child," Ylena said. *"I am working."*

Niah watched behind widened eyes as she took out the bone that lay against her flesh and forged a blade of light so bright it rivaled the sun. It wasn't just the gifts of the Saint, but Niah's unleashed power now that the shackles had fallen, that spun into a brilliant sword.

The Saint walked forward using Niah's body as her vessel with a single aim–to unleash destruction.

Chapter 33

Valek

Valek returned to his seat by the King, feeling oddly empty. He had been reaching for that key all night, tracing his thumb along the jagged ends of its teeth. A reminder that he was going to let go of the only person he had ever truly wanted. Someone who did not belong to him by blood, or loyalty, or servitude. A girl who didn't even love him, but whose heart was his most precious possession. It didn't matter if he had trained her all these months for nothing, or that the King would punish him, or that the war would resume with them on opposite sides.

In this moment, all Valek cared about was how he would continue without his little saint. How would he survive the loss of her?

Light shone so brightly it made his eyes ache. Valek turned to the door to find Niah standing there, drenched in divine light. It flowed around her head like a halo and enveloped her body like a shimmering cloth.

And the sword she carried was more magnificent than any she had wielded before.

"Is that your conduit?" King Stefan demanded. "How is this possible?"

Valek had expected her to run with her little friend, to lick her wounds and plot her revenge. Not to wage a battle in the middle of the banquet, in the presence of the king. He would have to capture her again, imprison her, and spoil what little fondness he had forced out of her. She would hate him more than she had before, and for some reason, the thought saddened him.

"*What are you thinking?*" Valek asked in her mind. "*Have you lost your mind?*"

"*The girl is gone,*" a cold voice said. "*You shall all die for your sins.*"

"*Who are you?*" Valek asked. Fists clenched by his side.

That voice did not belong to Niah.

"*I am the Saint of Light.*"

Valek stiffened. He watched as Niah waved her sword in an arc. It didn't even have to touch its target for their skin to char from the heat. The acrid smell of flesh burning scorched the air, intermingled with the choking sound of their screams. The people in the room were mainly soldiers and a few noble families who had come to visit the novices.

"Take the King to the cellars," Valek said to the King's guards, just as his Fallen marched into the banquet.

The guards formed a circle around the King, whose face was red and blotchy with rage. Pouring from the door in a sea of white robes were the Sisters. There had to be at least thirty of them, wielding their swords of light, and behind them, loyal villagers carrying their bows and arrows.

Valek's fist tightened, his Fallen turned to face the insurgents, and the battle began. The Sisters had been wise to shut the door behind them, blocking the only exit out of the hall. None of the other Reapers could call their horde, but they had a few Diviners around. While the Sisters were focused on the Fallen, Niah was cutting a path to the dais with little effort. Her eyes focused on the king, who stood surrounded by his mortal guards.

This would not end well for the Order. Valek didn't know how long they'd been planning this, but it was clear to see there was some thought behind it. They could not outnumber them on the field, so they resorted to an ambush and ensured all the key players were in the same place. Silverwood was less fortified than the palace. So, this was their only chance to launch an attack of this scale.

He could feel several of his Fallen crumble under the searing cut of their light. He was so focused on the battle that he almost missed the shadow that flickered across his vision. He had just enough time to raise his sword before Niah's blade of light came flying towards his throat. Valek noticed that there was a white kernel in the flame hilt. It was impossible to see. It *almost* looked like a bone.

"You almost severed my head," he growled. "Not nice."

"Next time I won't miss," she promised.

Her eyes were vacant of their warmth. The softness he had seen outside had been burned to embers.

"Leave her be," Valek demanded. "Release whatever hold you have on her."

"You do not know what a Lightbearer is, do you, boy?"

"Call me that again, and I'll cut out your tongue," Valek snarled, waving his sword high in the air to evade her attack.

She was a better swordswoman than Niah, and it was a struggle to keep from hurting her. He could not bear to leave a single cut on her. Her blood would never fall at his hands, so long as he lived. He regretted the accidental cut he had given her when they'd been young.

Valek remained on the offense, but her magic was wearing thin on the Vykovian steel. He had never seen anything alter the most endurable metal in the realm. This was no regular mage from the Order. This was a Saint. His mind reeled at the thought that they were real, that one of them was *here*.

He did not believe in the light, but standing before the Lightbearer, her pupils rimmed with a bright yellow glow, Valek wondered if he had underestimated his enemies.

"A Lightbearer is a vessel made to hold a Saint," she said.

"During times of chaos, they are born, until the time comes for them to accept our power."

"The Bone Hall," Valek said. "Your remains are there."

His mind whirled; the gift of Diviners was said to come from the Saints who had been deemed the Sinners after their betrayal. The ability to wield spirits to do your bidding was one of their gifts. The Bone Hall was only intended for Diviners to access; anyone else risked being possessed by an unwilling spirit. He wondered how long this one had been haunting Niah. Regret filled him as he realized that undoing her shackles had damned her. It had given the Saint the power to complete her possession.

"You made it so easy," another voice said.

A woman climbed up the dais from the opposite side, heading towards the King's guard. Her robe was different than the others. It was trimmed in gold threads.

"I am Morgana, Prioress of the Caer-Sylisse monastery," she said. "And Niah's mentor."

"Stand back," Valek said. Not quite sure which one to focus on, the Saint who possessed Niah or the woman whose eyes were eerily clear, as if she foresaw their victory.

"You will regret every pain you caused the Lightbearer," Morgana said. "You will rue the day you were born, Reaper."

Just as she spoke the words, they both lunged. Morgana took down the king's guards, and the Saint returned to fighting with him. Valek's sword was thinning, the light eating away at the metal.

He withdrew his blade at one point, so he did not nick Niah's skin.

"You're afraid to hurt her," the Saint said with a baleful smile. "That works in my favor."

"Winterson!" the King bellowed.

Valek couldn't look at him, and a part of him knew he couldn't save him. His sword was burning to a wisp. His Fallen were being slain, and the door was barricaded against the others he summoned. They were fighting a losing battle. It was time to retreat. His eyes strayed to the balcony, at the velvet-black sky. It was not a difficult jump if he leaped carefully. The worst would be a sprained ankle, but he would survive.

His blade was severed in half, a burning red end staring at him. Valek flung it away and ripped out his dagger. The Saint had that burned within minutes.

Valek retreated backwards. He didn't want to leave without Niah.

"*Niah, fight against it,*" Valek said in her mind. He could sense her there beyond the shackles the Saint wrapped around her mind. "*You are stronger than you know.*"

"*I can't, she's too strong,*" Niah said. Her voice was distant and murky. As if she were speaking to him underwater. "*You must run.*"

"*I can't leave you.*"

"*Go!*"

Valek stared hopelessly at her. Her sword was swung high in an arc, and he ducked beneath it, heading to the balcony. Something coiled around his ankles; it burned through his boots and trousers and yanked him back.

A leash– that damned Saint wrapped a rope of light around him.

"Not so fast, heretic," she hissed.

When Niah called him 'heretic', it was charming and endearing, but when the Saint did it, it made him want to destroy her.

"You will watch," she said.

Morgana had dug a sword into the king's thigh as he was attempting to crawl away. Sweat trickled down his ruddy face, plastering his hair to his forehead. His guards lay around him, dead and sightless.

The Saint walked towards him. Niah's bone-white hair fluttered behind her like a moth's wing. Her beautiful face stared sternly down on him like he was pure filth. How pathetic was it that he wanted Niah's attention on him alone? Her glower and smile, and curses belonged to him. Even now, his chest warmed under her cruel gaze.

"You hunted and killed my daughters," the Saint said, soft as a whisper. "You hung them, and I heard their cries. You called them dissenters. You claimed they infected the realm, but it is you and your corpses who ruined everything. You defy death. You unsettle the balance. You destroy and desecrate and spoil. But that will all end tonight."

"Please, forgive me," Stefan pleaded. Even though the Saint spoke to Valek. "Punish the Reaper. He killed your people."

Valek's eyes widened at how swiftly his monarch turned on him. How long had he enacted the king's will, all in the name of protecting the High North? Of erasing the Corruption. He had done nothing more than what he was instructed to do. He spared children and those who surrendered. He only ever killed the members of the Order.

And where was his damned father? He was nowhere in sight. It did not surprise Valek that he had left him at the Order's mercy. He was no better than the king.

The Saint laughed.

"See how he turns on you," she said. "No loyalty."

In this, they agreed. The King was as selfish as he had always been. He usually had a Royal Stitcher by him to revive him if he died, but his Stitcher was dead with the guards. It was the first time he was facing his imminent demise, and he was frightened. His mouth was parted, eyes blown wide in desperation like a ragged, thirsty dog.

The Saint walked towards Valek while Morgana kept the King pinned to the ground. Valek lay with his back against the wall; that burning leash had dulled its heat, but his flesh was flayed, and it hurt to move his ankle.

She curled her fingers in his hair, yanking his head back. He glared at her, gritting his teeth against the pain.

"Such a beautiful, cruel boy," she whispered. "You are the son of corruption, the sword of despair, the deadness of winter."

Her hand traced along his jaw and then his mouth, cradling his face. He trembled because it was Niah, and he could not resist her touch. His control fractured around her. The beast inside him grew docile at her touch, bending to her will like a knight to his liege. She was a part of him, another scrap of bone protecting the shattered fragments of his heart. Even if her eyes were wrong and magic seeped from her ominously, and a strange otherness painted her like a brush upon a canvas, to him, she was his greatest treasure, his stolen star, his radiant conqueror.

"They say that a hungry demon craves nothing more than the lucid piety of a saint," she said. "And you have always been famished; you have always been deprived."

Valek swallowed. "You know nothing about me."

"You have worn your mask of bones for so long you do not recognize your reflection," the Saint said. "Let me show you."

Her fingertips raised to his temple, and Valek's body grew taut as a flood of memories rushed through him. The Sisters in their white robes hanging from the monastery gates, Reapers descending in a sea of nightfall, smoke choking the lands, and children screaming, buildings crumbling like powder, grime covering the forests like a veil, yellow-eyed mutated animals staring at him with recognition, as if he were their sire.

Then there was a man with blood on his lips and shadows for his hair. A man who resembled him, but not quite.

Her hands fell, and he was in the destroyed ballroom again, breathing heavily.

He did not flinch from his sins.

He was a monster, and monsters did not repent.

The Saint laughed, a sound of madness and chaos.

"You do not care for your crimes," she said.

"I am merely a weapon, and a weapon destroys."

"Yet you believe yourself to be untouchable," she said. Anger sparked in her eyes; it was not the anger of the living, but an immortal rage. It consumed her like wildfire. "You Sons of Riven are as unrepentant as they come."

"Riven?" Valek asked.

"You are a mirror image of him," the Saint said. There was a moment where her gaze was almost nostalgic. "The First Reaper."

Valek was unsettled by her gaze. By the sheer cosmic nature of her sight. He had never been one to believe in fables and myths and faith. Even if he was a Reaper who served Bersula, he had never once bent his knees in prayer. Nor had he lit a candle for the Dark Mother or Riven her Son.

"I am a descendant of Riven?" Valek asked incredulously.

"A Saint cannot lie," she said tightly. "Every word I speak is true."

"Well, apologies if I do not believe you," he said. "I reckon a Saint doesn't torture those that believe in them. Niah is innocent in all of this. She has served you well."

"You do not know how close you trail to Death's door."

"A Reaper does not fear death," Valek said. "It is our domain."

And it was true, even now in the end, all he felt was peace. The Saint would spare Niah. She had never wronged her, and she would live.

He would never see Niah again, but he hoped that in another life she would find him and she would forgive him. He had her hair around his wrist which was often, done by husband and wife, Valek could not resist wearing the claim around his flesh. No other woman would ever approach him, knowing that his heart belonged to another.

Bersula, who favored loyalty above all else, would reward him in the afterlife and bring Niah to him. One day, he would be happy and content. One day, everything wouldn't hurt so much.

"You are not the master of death," the Saint said. "You are Death's slave."

Her fingers returned to his temple, and the vision she showed him was not the past. It was the future. Niah lay on the marble floor during the aftermath of the war. Her dead eyes stared hauntingly at the ceiling. Her limbs sprawled with hopeless abandon above her, beside her, with his eyes writhing in shadows, was Valek, his sword dripping with her blood.

The Saint's hand dropped, and he blinked, rage cutting through him like venom. One of her many tricks. Valek would *never* hurt her. All he had ever done was protect her.

"What was that?" he snarled. "If you hurt her, I will destroy you, I will wage a war unlike any you've seen before. I will raze down fields and burn your shrines and awaken your dead. You will have no mercy. You will have no peace."

She would learn first-hand why they called him the greatest Reaper who lived.

"You value the soul of a single light-touched girl above humanity. You spare her but murder her kin. You do not know what it is to love, Reaper. You only know what it means to possess, to fill your violent hoard, to grasp for a mirror that reflects your innocence and erases your rot."

"If you wish to know a single truth about me, then know this—you will need to call upon divinity itself to contain my wrath if you harm her."

The Saint smiled, as if he had revealed a confession that she ached to hear.

"Shall I tell you a story, little boy?" she whispered.

Her voice trailed along his flesh like the wings of a songbird.

"No," he said. "End this foolish tirade. Release the girl and slay me. I am your enemy. I am the source of your wrath."

"There was once a child born of light and dark. The Lower World and the Upper World were ripe for his taking. He ruled the dead while his mother wept in her river of sorrow. Her great love had left her behind to pursue a world of beauty and gentleness. His face soured at the smell of the dead, and he despised the fickle nature of the spirits, so he did what all men do when they grow bored: he left her behind."

"I do not care for fairytales," Valek said.

But the Saint's eyes were far from him.

"The boy was angry at his father, so he planned to punish

him. He gave the mortals a rare gift; he allowed them to call back souls that had graced the Lower world, and some to revive the dead and others to commune with the spirits to wreak havoc in his father's domain, to bring all that he despised back to him. And in return, his father blessed the mortals to fight against this curse. He sent the Saints after them, and he sent one to the Lower World to call for peace."

Valek blinked. He didn't know what direction this tale was going, but he listened. Not that he had any other choice.

"The son, *Riven*, did not care for peace, only vengeance," she said. "So, the Saint bound him to a deep slumber, never to walk the world again. When the world rots and the people fall to sleep, it means he is close to waking up, and I cannot let the First Reaper rise. You must pay for the violence of your bloodline."

"And Niah, will she be safe?" Valek asked.

It was all he cared about. *Her*. Not Saints and hungry gods and mystic folklore.

"The Lightbearer's soul will burn to ashes when I leave her body. As strong as she is, she was never meant to live; she was never meant to contain a Saint," she said.

Valek's eyes shifted to where Morgana stood, watching them with interest.

"It lies," he whispered. "You would not hurt your fellow sister. Niah is the best of you."

Morgana's mouth fell, and a flickering touch of guilt crossed her eyes.

"I loved Niah as a daughter, and she shall be remembered as a martyr," Morgana said. "The Lightbearer was born to serve, and she has served honorably. It would always end in death, as it began, Reaper. You know better than all the cycle of life."

"You knew this would kill her," Valek growled. "You tricked her."

"I told Niah many times that power sometimes requires sacrifice," Morgana said. "You cannot contain a Saint and live to tell the tale."

"Please," Valek said, facing the Saint. His soul burned with desperation. "Please, release her; she may live if you leave now. Cut out my throat and be done with it."

The Saint tilted her head. "You did not plead for your sins, but you humbled yourself to save her. Do you not see your depravity?"

"Then tear out my heart," he said. "Punish me, but leave her untouched. I forced her to learn my magic. I sought to ruin her. I am the one who deserves to suffer."

"Finally, you speak the truth," she said, eyes glinting in satisfaction. "Now you may die."

"And you will spare her?" Valek asked.

"I will not disrupt the balance for my own selfishness," she said. "The girl will die, but she will live as a martyr. Her name will be remembered when yours falls to ashes."

The Saint raised her sword, high and mighty.

The light was so bright it made him flinch.

It was his end.

And he could do nothing to save himself or Niah.

Chapter 34

Niah watched behind a shadowy curtain as the Saint toyed with Valek. The Saint's anger existed as a palpable force within the confines of her mind. It wasn't enough to torture the king or taunt Valek with his sins, she wanted complete and utter destruction.

Niah watched as Valek's dark, sombre gaze melted into hopelessness. He had fought so hard to protect her, to keep her safe, and it made her frozen heart melt just a little to see how he fell apart at the mention of her loss.

He would die for her.

Niah had never thought he was capable of such a sacrifice, and certainly not for her. Valek had hidden how much he cared for her, but now that their story was coming to an end, he did not fear revealing the truth.

Niah wrestled for control. It was different than when she and Valek would fight to control the Fallen. The Saint was no mortal. It was impossible to gain the upper hand, and each time she was rewarded with an unamused cackle from the Saint.

Saint Ylena did not care for her. She cared for vengeance, but not Niah.

To her, Niah was not a person, but a sword. It didn't matter to her if the light burned her soul to ashes in the end.

It saddened her to know Morgana had known the truth. Morgana had been like a mother to her. Niah had loved and respected her, but she was not Morgana's daughter.

No mother would watch on the sidelines as her daughter died not for peace, but for retribution.

In the distance, her Sisters stood, silent and solemn as they prepared to watch the execution of King Stefan and Valek Winterson, their mortal enemies. All that was missing was Maxim. That rat had probably fled at the first sign of danger.

Niah had imagined that someday she would be standing in white by her Sisters, but she stood on the dais, Saint-possessed, staring into the defeated eyes of the boy she cared about despite her best intentions. She had fought so hard not to fall under his spell, but Valek was no better than an enchanter, and he had lured her into the dark abyss of his heart, placing the wet, miserable organ in her palm. And Niah would protect it. It was the least of what he deserved. Valek was a monster, but she just might be his savior.

His second chance.

Niah would give him something new to believe in.

"You foolish girl," the Saint said, hearing her train of thought. *"A beautiful man will blink his coal-black, soulless eyes at you, and you will forget your purpose like all the foolish, love-starved women before you. You cannot play both sides. You cannot be the king and the thief. You cannot be terror and hope. You shame me. You shame your sisters."*

"They are not my sisters. You are not my Saint. And I am not your martyr."

Niah pushed against the weight that stifled her mind. It was like attempting to move a mountain, impossible and hopeless, but Niah fought with all her might. Blood trickled down her nose and streamed past her eyes, dripping like fallen stars.

A whole other war waged inside her.

The girl versus the Saint.

And Niah hoped she survived.

"You're fighting," Valek said softly.

The Saint could not bring down her sword of light. It remained frozen, her fingers trembling, fighting for the control Niah was wrestling away from her.

"You can do it, Niah," he said. Her name sounded like a prayer on his tongue. Not *novice* or *little saint*, but Niah as if he was not afraid of her anymore. "I believe in you. Only you."

His reassurance strengthened her, and a frustrated scream escaped the Saint.

"*Let me finish this, and I may spare you,*" she said. "*Your soul may still exist if you cease this at once. You need not die. I promise. Give me the boy and the king, and I will give you your body.*"

"Take the king, leave the boy," she said.

"*So, that he may take the king's place?*" the Saint asked. "*Evil breeds evil. They share a surname. They share a bloodline. The Sons of Riven must fall. You cannot cut the tail of a snake and expect the head to wither.*"

"He will change for me," Niah said. "He will be better."

"*You are a fool.*"

"And you have overstayed your welcome."

"He will kill you," she said. "*The prophecy demands it.*"

It felt like her soul was ripping in half, like she was crumbling to ashes, and the world was spinning. For a moment, she wondered if she had died. Her vision blackened, and then it cleared.

Her blade of light vanished, the bone of Ylena that illuminated it dropping from her fingers.

Niah conjured up a new blade of light with her own powers. When she flexed her fingers, it remained in her control; she could swing and cut his head, or she could let it fall.

Relief drowned her like a fisher's net. Her magic felt different, heightened, like the Saint had left behind a scrape of herself. It made sense why a mortal was never made to survive a Saint, because Niah felt rather peculiar. Her magic was chaotic and frayed. There was light consuming her frame. From the corner of her eye, she could see wings of white light, hovering behind her, spanning half the room. Nobody could approach her without suffering burn wounds in the process.

"You shouldn't have done that," Morgana said. Her eyes wide with fear. "You have doomed your sisters."

Her face was cracking like porcelain. Thin lines trailed along her flesh like map work. Horror dawned on her as she realized that Morgana had become the new vessel, and that the Saint's magic was eating away at her.

"You're hurting her," Niah said. "Stop!"

Morgana's mouth pulled in an odd smile before she crumbled into dust, her mortal form unable to withstand the Saint.

"No," Niah cried.

Valek stood upright. He limped towards her, and she felt the light around her fade away. He wrapped an arm around her waist, body folding over her. He hid his face in the crook of her neck, warm breath striking her skin, lips reverently grazing her flesh.

"It's you?" he asked. "My Niah?"

Niah nodded even though she knew he could sense it was her. The shield that had stifled their bond fell away, and he could feel her again just as she could him.

"Good," he said. "Now, let's kill this Saint."

Before Niah could hunt for the Saint, she faced the King. For so long, she had dreamed of this moment. The day when she looked into the eyes of her true enemy, not his soldiers and servants, but the hand that signed the edicts. He had spread misery for so long. His weathered face was veiled in pallor untouched by the sun and bleeding unholiness. Blood trickled from his wounds like a fountain of despair.

"Please," he pleaded. "I will end the war."

"No," Niah whispered. "*I* will end the war."

"Mercy," he said, lips trembling. "Grant me mercy, Saint."

"The Saint is gone," Niah said. "Only I remain, and I will grant you no peace, no reprieve, no forgiveness."

Her hand raised, her blade radiant in the air, before it landed with devastating precision. The arc of her strike was silent. Light cleaved through flesh and sinew, parting muscle like silk. Bone cracked, then gave way with a wet, shattering sound. His head fell cleanly from his shoulders, the severed neck releasing a burst of blood that hissed against the glowing edge of her sword. Silence dawned across the room, faces staring at her with a mixture of awe and horror. There were a few survivors beyond her Sisters, but they did not move or act out. It was as if their feet were frozen to the ground.

The king's limbs folded in on themselves like a puppet whose strings had been cut. His head rolled once, twice—then stilled, face turned upward, dark eyes watching her like a glossy painting.

The light in her blade flickered, then dimmed.

She stood over him, breathless, the weapon in her hand flickering like a dying star.

Valek stared at her with a mix of fear and devotion. His lips parted, but no words came out.

"Where is the Saint?" Niah asked.

"I think she left," he said slowly.

"No, I remain," a familiar voice said. "I will not stop until the Reaper falls. Surrender him to me."

It was Sister Eira. She had been at the monastery in Caer-Sylisse. Just like Morgana, her body began to disintegrate under the Saint's magic. Those dreadful cracks lined her face, and an eerie smile painted her lips. The Sisters gasped as they realized what was happening. They were being punished because Niah had refused to be their scapegoat, their pawn, their cold-blooded killer. Now Saint Ylena would ensure they all died for her choices.

"Leave them alone," Niah said hoarsely. "They are innocent."

"Release the Reaper," she said. "Serve him to me, and only two of your Sisters shall die. Refuse me, and they will all suffer."

"Niah, do as she says," one of the girls said shakily. "*Please.*"

The others chimed in unison.

"I will fight her," Valek said, taking a step forward. "I will protect them."

He was injured, and despite his posturing, he could not win a fight against a Saint.

"No." Niah grabbed his wrist. "Stay by me."

She expected him to refuse, but perhaps he could sense her fear, because he stood by her side. He tucked her close to him, as if he could shield her from the battle.

"Your sister betrays you," the Saint said. "She protects her enemy but watches you all fall."

Sister Eira burst into ashes, her body consumed by the light. Screams surrounded the girls until another spoke.

"How many more of you will die before she makes a decision?" the Saint asked. "Two of you? All of you?"

Niah released Valek and marched down the stairs. Maybe if she killed the body before the Saint switched to a different one, she would have no power. Boots thudded behind her, Valek swift on her heels.

Niah raised her sword, and it clashed against the Saint's. Her vessel was no match for Niah's raw power, and the light cut through her fingers, mutilating her flesh. She screamed in pain, and the eyes that looked at her were not the Saint. It was a wide-eyed, pain-lanced mortal stare.

Niah felt sick to her stomach. The Saint had switched to another vessel before she had hurt the girl. The Sisters had taken a wide berth away from the fight until one stepped in. The new body the Saint had robbed.

Niah had to kill quickly; sparing one girl would ensure the others survived, but it was a sour thought. It was the same choice Morgana had made that Niah had just condemned her for. Niah was no better than her.

"You are no Lightbearer," the Saint snarled. "You are the Reaper's whore."

Niah slid her blade into her chest cavity, watching as she burst into flames. Sweat dripped down her scalp, and for a moment, she wondered if it had worked, if she had caught her in time before another switch.

"You missed again."

Niah stiffened. The voice that spoke was one she knew intimately.

"Kesi?" she whispered.

Niah had hoped Kesi had fled with the people who escaped before the doors were barricaded. She hadn't known she remained. Her stomach roiled painfully. Two of her Sisters were dead, and another was injured, which destroyed her, but seeing Kesi standing there, caught in the Saint's power, made her stomach clench with fear.

The world spun around her.

"Please," Niah pleaded. "Not her."

She couldn't fight Kesi. She could not cause any harm to her. Just like when Valek had risked being captured rather than letting a single drop of her blood stain the ground. It didn't matter if the thing inside her was not her friend. Niah would *never* harm her.

"It is over," the Saint said. "Give him to me."

Niah looked around, but Valek was gone. Her stomach clenched. Where had he gone? The door was still sealed. Her eyes slid towards the balcony. Had he run away? Doubt trickled through her gut, sticking to her like honey.

The Saint laughed. "He tricked you."

Cracks were lining Kesi's face. Within minutes, she would fade to ashes like the others, and no fighting would stop the Saint. Tears fell in thin rivulets from her aching eyes.

Horror dawned on her when the Saint spun around, wrapping her fingers around Demian's throat. He had snuck up behind Kesi to make her faint in the hopes that it would make the Saint seek another. Demian's face was growing blanched, and his eyes popped as he struggled to breathe. Her power was unlike any other mage. It was raw and untameable.

"Take me," Niah said. "I will not resist. Just leave them alone."

"It is too late," she said.

Light spread everywhere, consuming Demian rapidly. Niah ran towards him, but she was too late. The light ate away at his beautiful soul, and his scream was drowned under the weight of his sorrow. Pain cut through her as she crumbled to her feet. It hurt to watch her best friends suffer. This was all her fault.

A dagger cut through Kesi's shoulders and Niah screamed.

Kesi looked at her, eyes burning with ancient wisdom.

"I curse you, Lightbearer," she whispered. "May you never know the gift of true peace."

Blood welled, dripping from the wound, and she crumbled. Her palm opened and something fell to the floor. Valek crouched down and with gloved fingers slid something white and slippery into the vial. Inside the glass was a bone. The same one from the Bone Hall.

"Kesi," she cried, falling to her knees.

Kesi blinked, those terrible cracks had retreated.

"Niah," she said with a wince. "God, that hurts."

Niah hastily cut her hem and pressed it to her wound.

"Leave," Valek said coldly. He was addressing the remaining Sisters. "And never return."

"Kesi, I'm so sorry," she said.

Kesi shook her head and then gritted her teeth when the gesture hurt too much.

"Don't apologize," Kesi said. "You are not to blame."

Valek sank to his knees beside her.

"How is she?" he asked. "Still yapping, so I assume she is fine."

"You stabbed her," Niah accused.

"To save her life," he said. "Did you not see how quickly she fled the girl whose fingers you cut? Pain forces her to seek another, stronger vessel, which is why she chose you to begin with. You are the strongest amongst your kind. It was why she fought me, and Morgana subdued the king. She knew I would never hurt you, and her vessel would remain safe. There were no threats to you."

"What is in the vial?"

"Her bone," he said. "It fell from your palm when you regained control. She used it to control them. The Bone Hall was built to keep the spirits contained. I must return this there for safekeeping."

"Why did she not just possess you?" Niah asked. "You were who she wanted. It doesn't make sense."

"You cannot consume someone who does not believe in your existence," Valek whispered. His fingers brushed aside a strand of her hair. "We have survived the worst. Everything will be okay."

His eyes grew shuttered, and she touched his shoulder.

"What is it?"

"She said I am descended from Riven," Valek said, with a furrow in his brow.

"And that bothers you?" Niah asked.

"There was a story my father told me as a child," Valek said. "He said that each soul that fell at the hands of a Reaper was fed to Riven. He said that one day, Riven would have enough souls to awaken from his slumber and rule the Reapers once more."

"I don't think I like that story," Niah whispered. "You don't believe it, do you?"

"I've always wondered if my father believed it, if this war was his tithe to Riven. It's strange how determined the Saint was to kill the king and me," Valek said. "It seemed bigger than politics and war. It seemed personal, as if our bloodline were cursed."

"You think she targeted you because of your ancestry and not your actions?"

"I don't know what to believe," he said. "I don't know if she said that to unsettle me or if she meant it."

"I don't think we should care for what she said," Niah said. "I mean, she did curse me just now."

The door to the halls was drawn open, but it wasn't the help she anticipated. It was Maxim Winterson. His face was cruel and unyielding.

"Lord Winterson," Valek said. His words were uncertain. Something small and boyish flitted against his eyes, as if he expected his father to comfort him.

But his father's eyes only shifted towards the dais, staring at the king's corpse with victorious eyes. He looked upon the destruction like it were a graveyard of roses. A thing to be admired for its resilience in defying nature by growing on barren soil.

"It is almost done," Maxim said. "The ritual is nearly complete."

Niah's eyes glanced at Valek uncertainly. She had lost all measure of respect for his father for abandoning his son. How could he flee when Valek was in danger? How could he leave his son to fight a Saint? Valek could have been hurt or worse.

"We are so close to fulfilling our purpose," Maxim said. "Come to me, Son."

"What do you speak of?" Valek asked.

"The Saint was threatened by us for a reason," he said. "We are descended from Riven the Great. The First Reaper and we must now answer his call."

"I don't understand," Valek said.

Madness gleamed in Maxim's eyes, and Niah felt a ripple of wariness. Her friend was injured, and many others were dead. They did not have time to listen to this spiel.

"I speak of raising the most powerful Reaper to aid our cause. I speak of awakening Riven," he said. "The war is not done. Not until every mage of Aubrith is dead."

Shivers trailed down her spine, and her eyes widened. Niah braced her fists, feeling the warm glow of light curl into her familiar sword. Her Sisters had not yet left at Valek's command, and it did not matter because Maxim had some silent control over them. He had spirit-bound them to remain where they were.

"You dare threaten my Sisters."

"It is written in the Codex, and Riven swore it on his mother herself, that so long as the Lightbearer lives, his soul will remain trapped," he said. "The Saints are the ones who trapped Riven in an eternal slumber. It is why they were called the Sinners, because they betrayed him. You can free him."

Maxim held out his hand, revealing a patinated blade. The hilt was emblazoned with the familiar sigil that belonged to the royal house of Winterson. The beast with his cruel, brilliant eyes stared at her.

The girl, the saint, the wolf. All of them drawn together by fate.

"Kill the girl, and all will be well."

Valek stared at his father with horror.

"You ask me to harm what is mine?" Valek asked throatily. "How can you ask such a thing of me?"

"Because it was *them*," he hissed. "Her Sisters came into our house in the dark of night and slit your mother's throat."

"That is not true," Valek said. "She died in childbirth."

"That was the tale we spun to hide the fact that our enemies were closer than we thought," he said. "Morgana herself used this very blade to slaughter her. I gave it to your mother many moons ago. Your sister was with her nursemaid, if she had remained with her, she would have been killed as well."

Valek's eyes widened, his fist clenched tight to his side. His eyes traveled towards her, a silent question poised in their depths.

"I do not know what he speaks of," Niah said softly. "If it is true, Morgana did not confide in me."

"Lies," Maxim hissed. "Even now she defends them, she justifies their carnage."

"I know nothing of the sort," Niah said, afraid that Valek would believe him. Pain flittered across his eyes at the remainder of his mother's death. "I swear it!"

"He has promised to return her," Maxim said. "Riven shall return your mother if you destroy the Lightbearer."

"Lord Wi—Father," Valek's voice cracked. "Mother is gone, and nothing we do shall bring her back."

"Riven has her soul in the Lower world. She is in his domain, and he will return her," Maxim said. His words tripped with urgency. "But to do that, we must free him of the curse, we must kill the Lightbearer, and his soul shall be relinquished."

"You have joined the Cult of Riven?" Valek asked. "You called them god-sick fools who would cut out their eye if it meant Riven would awaken."

"I was mistaken. Bersula has retreated from our mortal affairs; it is Riven who rules the Lower world who aches to save us from those who seek our end."

She could see her reflection in the narrowed edge of his blade. Her stark white hair and frightened eyes blinked back at her like a startled crow. Beside her, Valek looked just as hopeless. Something about his father's manic words made him sad.

"I don't want to hurt her," Valek said.

"You have no choice."

The blade spun through the air, a blur of silver catching the dim light as it screamed towards her. Time seemed to stretch, suspended between one breath and the next. She barely had a moment to gasp before he moved, a flash of motion, all instinct and desperation.

Valek lunged in front of her.

A sickening sound followed. The knife buried itself deep into his abdomen with a dull, wet *thunk*. His body jerked, breath hitching as the force of the impact knocked him back into her. For a moment, neither of them spoke.

Her eyes went wide.

"No," she whispered, catching him as he collapsed to his knees.

Heat bloomed beneath her hands, warm and slick—blood. His blood. Pain lanced through her chest like the blade had struck her instead. He had saved her. Without hesitation. Without thought for himself. Valek had come between her and his father.

Rage tore through her like a thunderstorm, and before she knew it, her magic wove into a sword. Light blazing like an inferno into her chosen weapon. She lunged for Maxim, who picked up Valek's discarded sword.

"Look what you've done," he snarled.

"Me?" Niah asked. "You hurt him. You hurt your son."

"I protected him," he said. "You are the one who doomed him. There were many Lightbearers before you. And Riven cursed all of your kind; you will always be tempted by the dark. You could not resist falling for the boy who is the antithesis of everything you believe in."

"Valek is not like you, he is a good person," she said. "He saved my life."

"Only for me to take it."

His blade of Vykovian steel clashed into her sword of light. They circled each other like predators. A slice tore across her elbow where he nicked her, and a sharp gasp escaped her. Maxim's thin lips pulled into a vicious smile.

His footsteps were assured. His swordsmanship was impeccable. She could tell that he had taught Valek.

"You are the monster," Niah said. Sweat dripped down her forehead, and she gritted her teeth against the onslaught of his attacks. His strikes were growing quicker by the moment, as if he had suddenly grown tired of toying with her. "All those innocent people you killed for what? To bring back a dead woman you love?"

"Olena is my world," he snarled. "She did not deserve to die for this war. I swore that night that I would kill every one of your Order. Once I take my rightful place as king, I will destroy everything you have ever treasured."

"You claim to know what love is, but how can you hurt me when Valek will hate you for it?" Niah asked. How could he not see that Valek cared for her, as she did for him?

"He is young and foolish," Maxim said. "And he will outgrow this senseless behavior."

Maxim would die tonight. He would suffer for all the pain he had caused. Her Sisters were not perfect, but they had never killed for selfish reasons. Everything they had done had always been for the good of the world. But there was nothing decent about Maxim Winterson, there never had been.

Her light cut across his abdomen, and the flare of the heat forced him to his knees. His face crumpled with pain, blade clattering on the marble floor.

The blade, forged from her light, thrummed in her hand—alive with power. Across from her, Maxim staggered, one knee on the ground, blood soaking through his side.

Niah stepped forward. Her grip tightened. One strike, and it was over. This was how it would end. In her final victory. She would avenge her parents, her Order, and country.

A hand caught her wrist.

She turned, breath catching in her throat.

"Don't," Valek said. His voice was low, urgent.

He gripped his side, grimacing from the pain.

"It is the only way," Niah whispered. "I cannot let him ruin the balance of the land. Riven *cannot* be awakened. It will be the beginning of the end."

"I won't let you kill him." His dark, stormy eyes held hers, conflicted with emotion. "He is my father."

"He is a monster," Niah said. "He wants me dead, and he has hurt you."

Valek turned her, forcing her to face him.

Her sword dimmed slightly, the light burning to wisps of nothing. Niah did not worry about Maxim behind her. He was wounded, and Valek would not let him touch her.

"You're protecting him?" Niah whispered.

His jaw tightened. "It's not that simple."

"It is," she said coldly. "Either he dies, or more people do. Do you want him to ascend the throne? Do you want him to put a price on my head? This war will never end until he dies. The fate of our realm depends on it."

"He is my father," he repeated, as if that justified his stance.

How could he defend her in one breath and do the same for his father in the next? "He is my family."

They were nothing alike. Maxim Winterson was a cruel villain. He was darkness personified. He had pitted the North against each other in this unending war. He had always been the puppeteer behind the throne. But instead of cutting the head of the viper, Valek was standing there defending it.

Niah ripped her wrist from him.

"I am the Lightbearer," she said. "And I will not falter."

Her sword returned, luminous and blazing like a thousand suns, but when she spun around, Maxim was gone; all that remained was a blotch of blood—the space where his body had been now empty. A small hatch had been lifted from under the dais.

He had escaped.

Niah took a step forward to hunt him down. He was injured and could not go far. It would not be difficult to kill him, but a pair of fingers closed around her neck, thick and heavy.

"I'm sorry, my beautiful, vengeful saint," Valek whispered. "Your fight is over."

And then there was nothing but darkness.

Chapter 35

Her eyes fluttered open, attempting to adjust to the darkness. The low hum of murmured voices and the distant clatter of footsteps filled the infirmary. Her body ached everywhere—muscles bruised, ribs tight, stinging cuts—but it was the ache in her chest that burned the deepest.

Valek had betrayed her.

He did not care that the man he spared wished for her demise. It made her wonder if he had ever truly cared for her. Maybe the Winterson men were more alike than she had thought.

The curtains were sealed around her, granting her the privacy to wade through the tumultuous emotions that ravaged her. Demian was gone, and the pain of the loss cut through her like a blade. Niah had expected that at some point she would be exempt from the grief of losing those closest to her, but this war was determined to destroy her. Tears burned her eyes, and she squeezed her eyes shut. She had failed to save him. The one person who had accepted them from the first day they met. He had always advocated for them and never made them feel small.

Niah did not know where Kesi was or if she had been brought to Marta in time. Fear coiled around her like a tightening noose. She tried to sit up, but a firm hand pressed her back down.

"You shouldn't move yet," a voice said, soft and hesitant.

Niah turned her head slowly, and there he was. The boy who had hurt her. His eyes were dark and unreadable. He looked the same, except for the faint growth of facial hair and the circles beneath his eyes. A bruised, violet-blue that struck out against his porcelain skin. His coat was undone, revealing a layer of thick bandages that wrapped around his abdomen like a belt.

"I—" she began, but he cut her off.

"You hate me," Valek finished. "I know."

"How could you?" she whispered.

"I draw the line at killing my father," he said. "He is grieving and lost. I cannot turn my back on him. He needs help."

"And who will answer for all the destruction he caused?" Niah demanded. "Demian is dead. Is Kesi even safe?"

Her chest tightened at the mention of Demian. It felt like a blade was severing her heart in half at the thought of her friend. Tears prickled her eyes. He had tried to save Kesi and the Saint had killed him for it.

"Your friend rests to your left," Valek said. "And Demian was a tragedy. I will miss him dearly. His bravery shall be commended publicly. He will be remembered as a war hero."

His eyes were sad. Valek hadn't been as close to Demian as Niah was, but he was his family. A Winterson. And in the end, he had died to save them.

Niah scoffed. "Military praise? That is the best you could do."

He reached out, hesitant, like he was afraid she'd push him away.

His fingers grazed her knuckles with open desperation. "I am trying, Niah. I want to fix things."

"It is too late," Niah said, shaking off his touch.

For a long moment, silence stretched between them. Then his gaze dropped, shame flooding his features.

How could he not see that so long as his father breathed, she would never be safe? It wasn't just her life at risk, but everyone close to her. He had doomed her to a life of misery, of always wondering when her enemy would step out of the shadows and drag her to the altar of Riven as a dark offering.

She felt hollow inside. The battle had wrung her dry, and there were no words for her to speak any longer. A tear fell down her cheek, trailing like pearls down her skin.

"Niah," Valek said. His voice was raw and strangled. "Don't cry, my love."

"I risked everything for you," she whispered. "But you let the man who tried to kill me escape."

"He will never hurt you again," Valek promised.

"How can you know that?"

"I am next in line," he said. "The king is deceased, and my father fled. The advisors held a vote, and my father's cowardice cost him the seat. I was voted in a few hours ago."

"You will sit on that throne?" Niah asked. Her voice was thick with accusation. "After *everything?*"

How could he wish to continue his legacy of despair?

"I must fix my mistakes," Valek said. "I have called off the war, and there will be a meeting with the Queen to discuss a peace treaty. The North shall remain separate as always, and the seized territories will be relinquished. You will never be attacked by our soldiers or watch the world burn around you. You will never awaken with fear in your eyes and your heart in your throat. You will never have nightmares with teeth, because I will do everything in my power to pluck out every last creature that haunts you. I will make the world a safer place for you to walk in."

Valek was repenting for all his failures, writing his wrongs one mandate at a time. It was everything she had always wanted to hear, but for some reason, it did not satisfy her.

There was a new ring beside his assortment of jewelry. The king's signet. It sat on his thumb, carrying the ancient weight of power.

"Will you leave me?" Valek asked softly.

Niah could not help but think of the Saint's words.

Evil breeds evil. They share a surname. They share a bloodline. The Sons of Riven must fall.

There was a reason the Saint and Morgana had wanted her dead. It all made sense now. So long as she died at their hands, this curse that contained Riven in the Lower World would remain. But if she died at the hands of Riven's descendants, then whatever binds that contained Riven would snap. Niah knew this truth with certainty. It explained why the Saint never confided in her. She thought that Valek did not know about this, nor the king, and Maxim had disappeared like a weakling, so she hadn't even considered him a threat. But Maxim Winterson knew the entirety of the truth, and so long as she remained here, she would always be in danger.

"Will you *let* me leave?" Niah asked.

"Nothing has changed since our conversation on the balcony," he said. "You are not my prisoner."

Niah's gaze fell, and he lifted her chin with his strong fingers.

"I am incapable of love, but without you I yearn endlessly," he breathed. "Our souls are tangled, and I scarcely know where I end, and you begin. I will not survive the loss of you. Don't make me face the dark; I am ill-prepared for it."

The tears continued to stream down her face.

"We've always known that it would end this way," she said softly. "Divinity conspires against us. Every fragment of our worlds repels the other: our magic, our birthright, our bloodlines. For all my power, I cannot siphon the darkness from your veins, and if I try, it will only consume me."

"So, you will not forgive me?" Valek asked. His eyes darkened with displeasure. "Because I spared my father? For someone with such high morals, I am shocked that you would condone patricide."

His words were sharp and bitter. Valek arose, stepping several paces away from her.

"That is not the only reason," Niah said. "And you know it."

"Then explain it!" Valek demanded. "Explain to me why, when I need you the most, you want to abandon me? Why must everybody leave me? Why will no one stay?"

Niah's mouth opened.

"I do not know what I am doing or how to be king or even how to breathe without you," Valek said. "Whatever festers in me that turns you away, it can only be cured by you. I cannot bury my affection for you."

Valek returned to her side. Wide, dark eyes pleading with her silently. Before she could speak, her words were swallowed by the heaviness of his mouth. Her muscles softened, and her shield collapsed under the taste of his tongue. His fingers slid under her nape, gripping her with need. Every inch of her was drawn to him. Even with the shackles gone and her magic warm in her belly, she could feel the echoes of that old bond, caressing her with its severed fingers.

"*Come back to me,*" Valek whispered in her mind. His smooth, delicate voice lured her into his web of desire. "*Don't be my conduit. Just be mine. Please, be mine.*"

A small, desperate sound escaped her that was quickly swallowed by him. His fingers trailed along her rib, sliding upward to her throat, and locking around her skin, drawing her closer to him.

"Valek," she breathed. It was frightening how easily her troubles faded away at his proximity. How his touch soothed the storm inside her.

"Yes, my love," he answered.

A throat cleared behind the curtain. Valek frowned as his guard spoke beyond the veil.

"An urgent matter has arisen that requires your attention, Your Grace," the guard said.

Your Grace.

It was done then. He was the new King of the High North.

"Can it not wait?" Valek asked.

"I'm afraid not."

Valek tossed her an apologetic look.

"I'll return when I can," he said, fingers brushing her cheekbone. "Rest."

Niah had barely closed her eyes when a knock sounded on the door. Casimir and Eveline entered carrying a bouquet of flowers.

"What are you two doing here?" Niah asked warily.

"We wanted to wish you a speedy recovery," Casimir said.

"Even though you killed the king," Eveline blurted. "Milo says they'll execute you before the week's end. His father is on the king's council."

Casimir elbowed her and Niah's lips lifted wryly.

"You don't hate me?" she asked.

"You were brought as a prisoner. It was foolish to expect you to be loyal." Casimir shrugged.

"And the new king seems keen on you." Eveline waggled her brows. "Imagine he makes you, his queen!"

Niah's eyes widened, and Casimir laughed, placing the flowers by her bedside table.

"She jests," Casimir said. "You becoming queen would begin a civil war. You are not the people's favored."

"I suppose killing the king does that," Niah murmured.

Niah stared at them both, feeling a sense of gratitude. Ever since that challenge, when Casimir had been prepared to kill the prisoners to spare her, she had felt a kinship with her teammates.

It was a friendship born of necessity, but one that she cherished nonetheless.

Niah sat in the infirmary, watching Kesi sleep. The color had returned to her cheeks, and her shoulder had healed nicely. Kesi had joked the other day that they would have matching scars on their shoulder. Niah figured if she was in a good enough mood to make her laugh, then she must be on the mend. And the sooner she recovered, the quicker they could figure out their next steps.

Every time Niah closed her eyes, she saw the death of Morgana and her Sisters playing before her eyes. Sometimes, it was Kesi standing before her skin cracking, mouth gaping and filled with fiery spiders, and other times it was Morgana on her knees, fading to ashes. But most of all her heart ached for Demian, her sweet friend with the bright eyes and the crooked smile. His loss weighed on her heavily.

Most nights, she woke up screaming, with Kesi quietly soothing her. Niah slept in the cot beside her so she couldn't hide her tangled nightmares from her. She couldn't pretend that she was fine, because she was anything but.

The King had been announced dead. Marta gave them updates on what occurred beyond the walls of the infirmary every morning. A stark reminder that the world had not paused after that devastating battle.

"What now?" Kesi whispered, late at night.

"I don't know," Niah answered honestly.

Niah had removed Kesi's cuffs. The key had been placed by her bedside table, most likely by Valek. He had visited, but he never stuck around to resume their conversation, almost as if he were afraid of what she had decided upon in his absence.

"Where shall we go?" Kesi asked. "We can't stay. They blame us for the king's death."

"We will speak when you are feeling better," Niah said.

They should leave, but Niah didn't know what home they had left. Her Sisters, those that remained, were likely scattered and would never forgive her for her actions. The monastery was gone. The High North still stood strong even without the king. And Valek was a puzzle she was afraid to piece together. His betrayal stung, but that kiss had softened her anger. It frightened her how much control he had over her.

There were so many things she did not know. It made her head pound to think of it all, and she closed her eyes, desperate to hunt for a peace she knew she would never find. She was tangled in grief and confusion and despair.

The battle had ended, but she was still in that ballroom, surrounded by the young women in white and standing protectively beside the Reaper who had betrayed her.

A hand roused her with urgency. Niah's eyes shot open, staring into a pair of familiar brown eyes.

"Laith?" Niah asked.

"Hello, Lightbearer," he whispered.

"What are you doing here?"

Niah glanced behind him to see if Valek was there, but the door was sealed behind him. Valek had them moved to Marta's bedroom, which Marta had shared with her apprentice for privacy. It had two thin cots and a bedside table. Kesi had caught a bad fever last night and had to remain longer at the infirmary, and Niah had refused to leave her side. So, they remained stuck here until they could figure out what to do next.

"The Queen of the Low North wishes for you to return home," Laith said. "You are needed in the capital."

Niah blinked in confusion. She rubbed her eyes, the long sleeves of her nightgown, slithering down her wrist with quiet grace. It was odd to see her wrists bare from the shackles.

"How do you know?" Niah asked.

A beat passed before realization dawned on her.

"You are not a traitor," she said. "You are a spy."

Slowly, he nodded, confirming her deepest suspicions. It explained why he had never revealed to Valek that she had snuck off during their hunt. His loyalty had never belonged to the High North. It belonged to Queen Enid.

"I suppose it is a relief to know we are not completely alone," Niah said. "The Queen wishes for us to return?"

Unease spun through her insides like cobwebs. What happened when the Queen learned that she had faltered, that she had let a Reaper live at the cost of her Sisters? She would be branded as a traitor.

"You killed the King," he said. "Every member of the King's Council wants you executed for treason. Valek has been working tirelessly to dissuade them from this path, but I don't know how much longer he can keep them satisfied. The nobles are loyalists; their fealty to the Wintersons runs deep. It won't be long until one of them avenges the dead king by sending an assassin after you. You are not safe here anymore."

"Am I safe at home?" Niah asked. "My Sisters were willing to kill me to further their goals. The Queen will have heard of my failure. It may not be enough that I killed the King, not when Maxim and his son live."

"You are still the Lightbearer," Laith said. "And you killed the King. You are a hero."

Niah was torn with her decision to leave or stay. If the council was itching for her head, how much longer could Valek hold them off? She hadn't seen him in days, not since he'd been drawn away from her side. He had promised peace, but what if her head was the price he needed to pay for it? Could she trust him after he had let that snake, Maxim, slither away to scheme against her?

"This war is not over," Laith said. "The Corruption persists, and our people remain trapped under the Sleeping Fever. Magic is destroying our world, eating away at it like rot. The Queen will not broker peace until we know the cause of this illness. If it is the Reapers at fault, then they will hang for their crimes."

"And what about the Diviners like you?" Niah asked. "Your magic does not follow the path of light. You are a heretic."

"I can put away my bones," he said, fingering the bone

knotted around his throat. His fist tightened around it for one split second before he released it. "I can resist the call of the spirits. If my queen asks it of me. I only used this magic to keep up pretenses."

"You would leave yourself barren of its touch, for her?"

Laith nodded, sharp and firm. "I would do anything for our country, for our queen."

"You are one of the members of her knights, aren't you?" Niah asked.

It was said that the Queen commanded the most loyal men in the realm. Each knight bore the legacy of his forefathers, sworn from father to son across generations. Their oath was not merely spoken but carved into the marrow of their bones.

Niah peeled back the sleeve at his wrist. In black ink was the sigil of the two swans who faced opposite directions, gazing into the distance–the queen's flag. In the capital, their saint of choice was Saint Elirien the Lover. It was said that Saint Elirien loved the glades, and swans followed the path of her footsteps when she lingered there, playing her songs on her lyre.

"Will you come with me, Lightbearer?" Laith asked. His eyes flickered towards Kesi for a long moment. "You and the girl?"

Niah could not refuse a royal order. If the Queen wished her to return home, Niah was bound to answer her call.

A part of her hated being torn away from Valek's side, but she was no help to him anymore. She was not a powerful conduit. She was just a traitor. It would ease his council if she escaped of her own will, rather than him to voice his support of the king-slayer.

"We will," she whispered.

"Get dressed," he said. "I'll wake her up."

Niah glided to the corner. The hem of her nightgown slipped across the floor like ghostly fingers.

The whisper of Laith's voice tumbled towards her.

"Wake up, starling," he said.

"You, fiend," Kesi said sharply. "How dare you come to my

bedroom while I am abed to gawk at me and my bountiful breasts?"

"Bountiful?" Laith snorted. "I've cupped your breasts, and they are no more than a handful."

A cutting sound echoed across the room.

Niah turned around to come between them. She had expected Laith to lose his mind after that heartfelt slap, but he simply ran his tongue along his teeth.

And what did he speak of? Had Kesi and him...? The thought was rather absurd.

"Is that all you've got?" he asked.

"Do not remind me of that terrible kiss, I was drunk at the banquet," Kesi said. "I thought you were someone else."

Niah's brows raised in surprise. They had *kissed*? Kesi hated Laith, she bad-mouthed him any chance she got. Once, she had even ranked the men in the fortress, from least attractive to most, and Laith had been voted number one, and it wasn't in the most attractive category.

"So, drunk you couldn't resist thrusting your hand in my pants and moaning my name?" Laith raised a brow. "So, drunk that you let me slide my tongue in your hungr—"

"Shut up!" Kesi bellowed. She was weak and injured, but still she mustered the strength to toss off her blankets and come stand by Niah. "Burn him, Niah. Burn him to ashes. I am too weak to summon."

"I'm afraid I cannot," Niah said. "Laith is the Queen's knight. He does not serve the High North, and he wishes to take us to the queen's court."

"Lies," Kesi said. "Look at how he attempts to disparage my good name and reputation. He mocks my piety and my strong spiritual nature. He undermines the fact that I am a child of Aubrith, blessed by the light and sworn in its service."

Laith laughed, not a chuckle, but a full-blown, hands-to-his-knees laugh that echoed around the room. He stood upright, brushing a stray tear from his eyes. Niah chuckled, nervously eyeing Kesi in case she called her on her betrayal. It was rather ludicrous that Kesi was painting herself as a pious cleric who served the Order when she dozed through all of Morgana's lectures and cursed like a sailor.

"I have not heard a load of shite like *that* in a very long time," he said. "Even your friend doesn't believe you."

Niah's eyes widened, hands raised in defense. "I was laughing at a thought that crossed my mind. Not Kesi's words."

"Right," Laith said dryly.

"Well, I am not going anywhere with him," Kesi said. "There is nothing knightly about him."

Laith raised his wrist, revealing his markings as a member of the queen's knights.

"You are a desperate admirer who went to a cheap artist." Kesi shrugged. "I refuse to believe *you*, of all people, were knighted. You have to be noble and brave to be a knight. And you are anything but."

"Speak some sense into her," Laith said, staring at Niah. "I refuse to indulge her when she is in her moods."

"This is a bad idea, Niah," Kesi said. "He can't be trusted. He is a traitor. He is no loyal knight come to save us on his white horse."

"My horse is gray-skinned," Laith added.

"Not the point," Kesi said, before her eyes widened. "See! He doesn't even have a white horse. What savior doesn't have a white horse? It is *always* a white horse."

"She is mad," Laith said. "If we take her to court, there are physicians who can give her the proper treatment she needs."

"Kesi, I trust him," Niah said. "He helped me once when he could have reported me. I believe he is on our side."

Kesi folded her arms across her chest, looking oddly vulnerable. Niah rubbed her shoulder. Demian's death had destroyed Kesi, she blamed herself for hurting him, even if the Saint controlled her form, and nightmares ate away at her. They were both haunted by that night.

Niah was asking Kesi to trust her once more. To come with her to court and meet the Queen, who had always been more of a legend than a person.

"I will go anywhere you go," Kesi said, lacing their fingers together. "You are my family."

Niah smiled softly.

"It is time to go home."

Epilogue

His eyes sealed shut, and when he opened them, he stood in the Lower World. The Hall opened like a gash in the earth. A cathedral of stone and bone, ribbed with black iron arches, stood before him. The walls pulsed faintly, as if the spirits that roamed this realm were breathing. High above, a ceiling of jagged black crystal reflected in the marble flooring.

Despair clung to the man, much like it had the night he had lost his heart. Olena Winterson had been the balm of his soul, his torch in the darkness, and those cursed Sisters of the Order had robbed her from him. He had sworn that night to the Dark Mother and her Son that he would erase all those touched by the light from the realm.

Ash clung to his boots. The smell of wet soot and ancient blood thickened the air. Ahead, at the altar of ruin, *he* awaited him, reclined like a corpse on a throne of skulls. Riven possessed no mortal frame or body. He was a wisp of nothing. Darkness molded into the shape of a man. His physical form was locked in an eternal slumber, and with it his power.

"You return," he murmured, eyes like dull coins studying him.

Riven's voice did not echo through the chamber. It lay inside his mind like a flat palm.

"My lord," he whispered, bending on a weak knee.

His defeat weighed heavily on his shoulders. He had promised Riven the soul of the Lightbearer, and he had failed. His son had betrayed him to protect the girl. And now he would be punished for trusting the boy to do right by him. Riven was merciless. He did not tolerate incompetence.

"You failed," Riven said.

His words were a dark caress along his flesh.

The man swallowed, throat bobbing in fear. He had lingered in the Lower World to find Riven, many desperate moons ago. He had not been made to survive a life without his beloved wife. And Riven had answered his miserable call.

"The boy refused," Riven said. "You were so certain he would accept."

Riven had requested that his son strike the finishing blow. He could not fathom why Riven possessed any interest in the boy. Maxim would have accomplished the task himself if the girl had not gouged herself on the Saint's magic.

"He is a love-struck fool," he spat. "He forgets his birthright. He forgets we belong to you, our gracious sire."

"He has taken your crown," Riven drawled. "Your power was claimed by him. How will you keep your promise to destroy them all if you do not sit on the throne?"

"It is temporary," he said. "The boy is too weak to stomach our plans. He will not eradicate the light mages. He will not even kill the Lightbearer."

"No, he is a liability," he hissed. "He must be stopped."

"How?" he asked.

"Do you wish to trade his soul?" Riven asked. "For your beloved wife?"

It was not a question that required thought. He loved Olena far more than the spawn she had left behind as a shallow replacement. The boy was more bearable than the girl. But he would trade them both if it brought Olena home. He was a shell of a man in her absence.

"His soul is yours to claim, my lord," he said.

He thought of his son. He had once been his pride, crafted in his image, cruel and willing to do anything required of him. He had been a good soldier and a better Reaper, but then that wicked girl had sunk her claws into him and turned him against his family. The boy was lost to him now. He was a weak man and would be a weaker king.

"You would give him to the dark?" Riven asked, unsurprised by his answer. "You would sacrifice him to me?"

"Death is inevitable; his soul would always return to you," he said. "It was written in the stars."

"Do you know what I will do with him?"

"I do not wish to know," he said. "I only ask that you return my wife."

"You will have her in a fortnight, as I will have the boy," Riven said. "So, it is spoken, so it is sealed."

A bargain made in the Lower World was bound by the night and ashes. It would endure as unbreakable as a vow. The last time he had come in desperation, he had promised him the Lightbearer in return for his wife.

He had thought Riven would punish him for his failure, but instead, he had asked him for another price.

One that he was all too willing to accept.

When the man arose, Riven was gone.

And the throne before him was empty.

Acknowledgments

I have been working on this book for years. It has lived many lives, shifting genres, and becoming something entirely new more than once. But of all its versions, this one holds my heart.

I am endlessly grateful to the incredible people who helped bring it to life, especially my editor, Emily, whose talent and dedication shaped this story into what it is today, and my cover designer, Wavy Hues.

To my readers, thank you for your constant excitement and your unwavering love for my books. You are the reason I do what I do.

And finally, to my family and friends, thank you for your patience, your encouragement, and your unending support. I could not have done this without you.

 www.ingramcontent.com/pod-product-compliance
Ingram Content Group UK Ltd.
Pitfield, Milton Keynes, MK11 3LW, UK
UKHW042003230426
12048UKWH00009B/513